The Price of Freedom

Tania Park

A Romance Novel

ISBN: 978-0-6455254-5-8 (Paperback)
ISBN: 978-0-6455254-6-5 (E-book)

A catalogue record for this book is available from the National Library of Australia

NATIONAL LIBRARY OF AUSTRALIA

Tania Park Publishing.
For all enquiries contact:
goldpark3@gmail.com

Dedication

This book is dedicated to all those readers who enjoy a little bit of romance in their lives. I want to thank the judges from the Romance Writers of Australia who offered comments when I entered this manuscript in a competition. All advice taken on board.

As with all of my books, I had to include a bit of adventure, tension and action.

Other Titles by Author

The Only Way I Know: 2011 - Biography
Mistaken: 2015 – Crime/mystery/romance
Retribution: 2015 – Crime/mystery
Blind Justice: 2016 – Crime/mystery *Commended 2016 Christina Stead National Literary Awards.*
Road Trip: 2016 – Adventure/mystery
The Swan: 2018 Crime/mystery/romance *Finalist 2020 The Wishing Shelf International Awards.*
Stalked: 2019: Psychological Thriller *Long listed 2020 Davitt Awards.*
Double Cross: 2020 – White collar crime *Long listed 2021 Davitt Awards*
The Chest: 2021 – Mystery/crime
Beloved Intruder: 2022 – Romance *Third place – Romance Writers of Australia – Sapphire Award.*
Workshop Workings: 2023 – Collection of Winning short stories and poems created in writing workshops.
Redemption – 2024 – Crime/mystery
Jilted in Greece – 2024 – Romance/Adventure

One

Sarah re-read the address, glanced up, searched the building front and blew her cheeks with a drop of shoulders. The street numbers along the busy road were higgledy-piggledy but the one she wanted didn't seem to exist.

'Should have come a day earlier,' she muttered to the address on the paper – written in English, when most of the words on the buildings were Arabic. For the past half hour she'd trawled the street, down and back. Not one name looked remotely like the one she needed. Since the nearest number was back to the left, she spun around to retrace her steps. 'Should go inside to get out of this oppressive heat and be sensible – ask,' she said to the shade when she passed under an overhang.

'Hmm, maybe it's this one.' There was no number on the door so she stepped back; took another step and another but pitched sideways when her left foot slipped off the kerb and skewed at an awkward angle. A sharp pain speared through her ankle a split second before she landed on her backside.

At the screech of tyres she scrambled to get back to the pavement but her ankle refused to co-operate. The stench of burnt rubber and tar filled her nostrils.

Whump. The impact on her shoulder jolted her so far forwards, she sprawled on her stomach but managed to get fisted hands under her face to prevent it being shredded on the bitumen. A sharp burn on her knuckles matched the pain in her ankle.

Car doors slammed, foreign words shouted, a figure in white crouched by her side. Long tanned fingers reached out and grasped her hands.

'Are you all right? Are you hurt?' The frantic English was perfect with only a hint of an accent, but the owner was definitely a local, dressed in white robes. 'Tariq,' the deep voice added, 'check her over.'

When another set of arms grasped her shoulders, a wave of *déjà vu* swept over her. 'No, please don't,' stuttered out when familiar panic took hold. Stranger, her brain yelled.

'Tariq has medical training; let him check for injuries.'

'I'm fine.' Sarah forced her body to turn over and windmilled both men's hands away. The wave of panic tore through her innards. Desperate to not have a full-on panic attack in the middle of the street, she scuttled backwards away from the strangers but had to stop at the rumble of speeding tyres and whoosh of hot air from vehicle after vehicle while sped past mere centimetres away.

Breathe, she ordered her lungs. Breathe. Eyes shut, she fought to control each breath but she had to get away from these men. When she scrambled to get upright the pain in her ankle turned into the stab of a serrated knife the moment she put weight on her left foot.

'Please, you are hurt. Let me help you.' The stretched-out hands hovered in front but stopped.

With no contact and face-to-face with danger, she could manage. It took too long but finally she stood balanced on one foot and lifted her eyes to study the man still half-crouched in front of her. He rose to his full height, a good head taller than her. The man was too striking to ignore. Not handsome but more of a magnetic aura. A long fine nose sat beneath large, almost black eyes. The typical day-old beard the majority of the local men wore was immaculate and thick black hair peeked from below a white starched keffiyeh, held in place by a black circlet of rope.

To prevent either man coming closer, Sarah held her hands up in front of her chest. Her heart thumped so hard it was a miracle no-one could hear it. She needed space.

'I will be okay, give me a minute.' But when she took a step backwards and almost passed out with pain, she figured she wasn't okay. No way would her left foot hold any weight. It was impossible to even walk. Brilliant. Could the day get any worse?

The man frowned. 'My car hit you, the thump sent my mind into turmoil. You are unable to walk, you have grazes on your hands yet you say you are all right. Let us get out of this heat so we can sort out what needs to be done.' With an open hand he indicated the still open door of his car, a long white sedan.

A shudder wove its way down her body at the thought of getting into a strange man's car. Won't happen. Not ever.

'No.' She shrank back as far as she could without taking a step.

'No?' he asked but immediately glanced along the shop fronts. 'I understand. You do not know me. You are sensible to have such caution but I swear on Allah's name, I will not harm you.' He swept a hand towards an open door two buildings down; one she had already passed umpteen times. One she should have gone into to ask the question.

3

'How about in there; a café where there are people who will ensure you come to no harm?'

Her thoughts wavered between yes and no but when she considered what a pickle she was in there really was no choice. 'Okay.' She took a step but almost doubled over when the pain speared up her leg. Determined to make the distance on her own, she hopped. Her backpack thumped against her spine, but she didn't care. A laptop could be replaced but not an ankle. Besides, it would be a miracle if it wasn't already damaged from the accident.

White robes swirled, the man hurried ahead and held the glass door open until she was inside. Cool air gave instant relief while the aroma of coffee and fragrant spices sent gastric juices on a frenzy. He indicated the nearest table; tugged a chair free for her to sit. Unable to go any further, she plonked into the wooden seat. A shudder down her spine followed a wince at the screech of legs on tiles. She leant forwards to remove her backpack and hugged it against her stomach. The man sat opposite while the second man drew out an extra chair and sat on a third.

'Put your foot on here.' It surprised her to see him dressed in khaki, like battle fatigues but without dark camouflage patches and more refined. He was a big well-built man, jet-black hair uncovered, a strong but kind face.

'My name is Hakim al Fasir,' said the white-robed man. 'This is my driver, Tariq. And you are?'

'Sarah Anderson.' She peeked over her shoulder to check behind. Since the attack, she couldn't handle not being able to see who came and went through any door.

'Can I ask why you stood so close to the edge of the road? You appeared to be lost.'

'The taxi driver said this was the address I needed but I couldn't find the right number or building name.' She glanced at her watch. 'And now I'm late.'

'Late for what?'

'I was to meet my new employer to sign a contract.' A sigh escaped. 'I'll probably lose the job now.'

'Where is home? You speak English but are not British.'

'Australia – Sydney.' Unnerved at a sound, she shot a glance over her shoulder. Satisfied there was no threat, she turned back to notice a frown on Hakim's brow.

'What number building did you seek? Maybe I can help you find it.'

Sarah was surprised she still had the paper gripped in her hand, albeit now scrunched into an imitation of a tattered relic from an Egyptian tomb. She placed it on the table, tugged the edges apart and ran her hand over the wrinkles to smooth them out.

Hakim scooped the paper up but frowned as he read. 'I know the place. You are to work for Saeed bin Suroor? In what capacity?'

'You know him?'

'I know of him but we have never met.'

'I am to care for his three children for six weeks while he works. His wife left him. I am to teach them to speak English more fluently.'

The silence as the two men glanced at each other, sent her nerves a scary message. Even more scary was the frown and nod.

'How did you learn about the job?'

'On the internet. My university site. Holiday work.'

Hakim's eyebrows rose. 'You study at university?'

'Not any more. I completed my degree two weeks ago.' It was a relief to finally have her thesis done but she would miss university life, well, most parts of it. The thought of the reason she flew halfway around the world to find a job, had her glance over her shoulder again. Every atom in her body stilled at the sight of a man who swept through the

5

door. He wore the local kandourah but it made no difference for she still didn't have a clue what her stalker looked like except rough height and build. Even though the chances of him being here, or to know where she was, were remote to impossible, it didn't ease her fear one iota. He could dress as a local to fit in.

'What field of study?'

Sarah jerked her head back around. 'Science.'

Hakim frowned and stood. 'Would you like to sit here where you can see the door? Tariq will ensure nobody comes near you.'

Embarrassment flamed. Was it so obvious? She must be more careful but she now always sat where she could see everyone who came and went. It was one of the ways she could manage being in public. She stood; hopped to the empty chair. 'Thank you.' Intuition told her she could trust Hakim, which was a miracle for since the attack, she trusted only family.

'What are you so afraid of?' Hakim asked as he reached across the table but kept his hands a few centimetres away, which surprised and pleased her. The man received another Brownie point.

'Men.' It was the only answer she could think of. It was only one man who terrified her but since she didn't know who he was, she kept every other man at bay. There were few men she could trust. Her dad, two brothers and her professor were the only men on her list. A couple of fellow students hovered close but whoever had made her life a misery for the past twelve months knew too much about her to be a complete stranger.

Hakim sat back; his face screwed to indicate he was confused but she didn't care. It was her private business, her pain, her regret, her screwed up life.

'Would you like to join me for some refreshment? Maybe coffee or would you prefer a cold drink?'

Thankful he asked no questions, Sarah nodded. 'Cold would be welcome.' She was thirsty after the long search and hadn't thought to bring water with her. A mistake she wouldn't make again in such a hot country.

'Do you have a preference or would you like to try a local drink?'

'Could you choose a local drink for me?'

Hakim waved a hand in the air. A waiter arrived within seconds as though ready for the order which Hakim gave in Arabic so Sarah had no idea what she was about to experience. Whether she liked it or not, good manners meant she would pretend it was yummy even if it was ghastly but she was so thirsty even ghastly would be welcome.

'Would you let Tariq tend to your ankle now? I have a medical kit in the car. Tariq has the knowledge to see whether the ankle needs medical attention and your hands…' He turned her hands over so fast she didn't realise he had gripped them before he released them again. 'They weep. A little salve will prevent infection which can set in easily in this heat.'

Tariq immediately disappeared outside. In less than a minute he was back and knelt by her side. He grasped her lower leg. Even though she studied every movement, his hand gripped around her leg sent her panic mode onto high alert. Keep calm, she ordered her brain, keep calm. He will not attack you with all these people around. Tariq is not the man.

When long fingers probed inner torn flesh she winced. The pain didn't ease while Tariq gently wiggled her foot from side-to-side, around in a circle and back the other way.

7

She forced her body to relax, accepted the pain and kept her lips sealed. She'd already made a fool of herself.

'Torn but not broken,' Tariq said with a gentle smile. His English was as good as Hakim's but with a stronger accent. 'A support bandage will help. An ice bath would be better and keep it elevated as much as you can. May I remove your sandal?'

The sandal was off before she could answer. She winced at the sight for already her ankle was twice its normal size with a huge indigo bruise. No wonder it hurt so much. How was she supposed to care for three youngsters when it would be almost impossible to even walk? Maybe if she lost the job it would be for the best. But she had to work to fulfill the visa requirements and there was no way she could go home. Not until the police caught the bastard.

The drinks arrived while Tariq wove an elastic bandage up, over and around her ankle in figure eights and clipped the end in place around her calf with a tiny metallic hook. To ignore the pain she concentrated on her drink, surprised at how refreshing it was. 'What's in this?' she asked Hakim.

'Fresh lime juice, soda water, chopped mint and ice cubes. Do you like it?'

'Very much. The lime is tangy but the mint calms the acid. Thank you.'

'You are welcome. Now we need to solve your problem. See the road out there?' With an open hand, he indicated through the large window to his left. There were three lanes of continuous vehicles going each way with an insurmountable concrete barrier between them.

'This is a new major highway, recently opened. It cut off the previous road by dividing it into two, which created a T-junction. Across the other side is the building you require. The tall one with bronze-tinged windows. To get there is a long walk to the nearest overhead crossing followed by a long walk back. With your foot, I doubt you will make the distance. There is another way.'

He eyed her. 'I can take you in my car but only if you trust me enough to know I will not let you come to harm. It is obvious your distrust of men is because a man has not treated you well. Maybe I can alleviate your fear if I tell you I work for the government as the Minister for Art and Cultural Affairs. Tariq is not only my driver but also my bodyguard. There is another bodyguard outside. You will be safe with me.'

His smile didn't alleviate her fear one iota. A government minister? Why did he need bodyguards – two of them? This was supposed to be a safe country. Being a government minister doesn't make him any more trustworthy than any other man - well, maybe a little more. At least she would be able to describe these men. They weren't hidden behind obscene clown masks, latex gloves and disposable coveralls, so maybe she needed to give them a little more trust.

'This man you are to work for, he is one I would not trust.'

Oh, wow, this was all she needed. 'Why not?'

'There are rumours about not such good ethics in his business. To me, rumours begin with a little spark of truth but I am unable to say if the spark dies or flares. Since it was of no concern to me at the time I did no research on the spark.'

'I need to phone him to explain why I missed the appointment.' Sarah searched the pocket of her slacks for her mobile phone, took it out but remembered she hadn't yet bought a local sim card. A long sigh escaped as she searched the ceiling for inspiration. Could things get any worse?

'Maybe you need the number?' Hakim suggested.

9

'I have the number but haven't had time to buy a local sim card. I only flew in last night.'

'If you give me the number I will speak with him to explain your predicament.'

'I'm embarrassed. Already you have done too much for me.'

'It is me who is embarrassed. My car hit you, I need to atone for my actions. Please, the number.'

Sarah pointed to the piece of wrinkled paper still in front of Hakim. She sat back while he punched in numbers and spoke in Arabic. When her shoulder hit the back of the wooden chair, she winced at the sudden pain. No doubt a ginormous bruise had already taken up residence to add to an ankle which belonged to a giant rather than her skinny legs, and grazed knuckles which now needed a new layer of skin. At the sight of her knuckles she wiped the ooze on the front of her striped cotton pants. She noticed Hakim catch Tariq's attention with a nod of his head. His hand wavered at her knuckles. Tariq immediately grasped both of her hands to inspect them. Within seconds he had the medical kit open, took out swabs, a tube of ointment and two large plasters. He opened a small bottle of liquid, poured a glug onto a swab and dabbed it on her wounds. The sting was sharp but eased when he gently rubbed white salve over the top. A long fabric plaster on each hand covered the grazes.

'You have a new appointment in thirty minutes.' Hakim dropped his mobile phone into a hidden pocket in the side of his robe as he stood. 'Let me see how well you can walk.'

Determined to show she was okay, Sarah stood, took a step, but collapsed over the table at the acute pain.

'As I thought. You need crutches. Come. Tariq will drive us to the nearest pharmacy.'

When Hakim hoisted her from the ground and settled her in his arms, panic overwhelmed her for the few seconds it took before he gently lowered her onto a grey leather seat in the rear of what now appeared to be a luxurious limousine, although it wasn't one of those super-long varieties. A hard lump of fear lodged in her throat when Tariq and another similarly dressed swarthy man sat in the front seats. When Hakim eased in next to her, she shrank against the window and gripped one hand against the door catch, ready to open it and jump out at the first sign of an attack. To hit the pavement again and lose another layer of skin was a far better option.

Two

Hakim turned towards his guest. Her fear was obvious, which was a shame. Some unscrupulous man had turned a beautiful woman into a bundle of terror. Short dark-gold hair didn't hide terrified hazel eyes or nose dotted with freckles to match her hair. A long lean body hid under loose cotton clothes. He appreciated the way she abided by the customs of his country to dress with modesty. A lot of tourists didn't care. A watch on her wrist and diamond studs in her ears were the only adornment. Sensible leather sandals wrapped around her feet and she clutched a small leather backpack against her chest as though her life depended on its presence.

Something about her tugged at his gut. It could be guilt told him he needed to see her right after he'd knocked her flat in the street, although the fault was not his. Tariq pulled off a miracle to stop the car in such a short distance when Sarah stumbled onto the road, but defensive driving skills and quick reactions were necessary requirements of his bodyguards.

Before he had a chance to question her further, the car stopped in front of a pharmacy. 'Buy a pair of crutches,' Hakim said in Arabic. Tariq nodded before he eased from the car, while Sarah stiffened and peered around, the fear in her eyes even more intense.

'Miss Anderson, if you prefer to stand outside until Tariq returns, go ahead. I will stay over this side of the seat and Mahmoud will not move a muscle unless he believes I am under threat when he will leap from the car to take down the perpetrator.'

'Okay,' she said after a lengthy pause but she did not relax.

It was a worry how she gripped so tight to the door handle. A woman of few words or maybe fear prevented her from giving much information. Smart woman to be over-cautious.

The boot opened, followed by a soft scrape before the car shook slightly when the boot shut again. Tariq got back into the driver's seat, released the brake and drove off. Five minutes later he drew to a standstill in front of the building Sarah needed. It amused Hakim how quickly she alighted, but after only one step she leant against the car with a long hiss through clenched teeth.

Hakim hurried to the rear and held out one hand. 'Let me assist you to the pathway. Tariq will adjust the crutch handles to suit your body.'

Rosy-pink infused her cheeks but she took his hand in a firm grip and hopped around the car, up onto the footpath where she grabbed a light post for support. Tariq had already loosened a wingnut on a screw. He held one crutch against Sarah's body, wrapped the circular clip around her arm and adjusted the length. For the first time since Hakim had seen Sarah belly-down on the road, she didn't shrink

14

from a man. Maybe now she believed she was safe with them. He guessed it would be difficult to gain her trust.

Backpack on, crutches in place, Sarah spun around to face him, but only caught his eye for a second before her head shifted a tiny way so they were no longer in direct eye contact; the same way she had in the café. Maybe she was shy. It would explain the action.

'Thank you for your help. I need a contact number to return the crutches,' she said to the air at the right of his shoulder.

'For my peace of mind, would you allow me to accompany you while you speak with Saeed?'

'Why?' Startled eyes swung back to his for a second before they shot over his other shoulder.

'Please. You are in my country where I hope you will be safe since we are one of the safest countries in this region. I wish to ensure your terms of employment are satisfactory and you are not taken advantage of.'

Sarah hesitated with her eyes searching the sky and top teeth gnawed the corner of her mouth. 'Okay, thank you.' A wisp of a smile escaped.

The journey inside was slow while Sarah figured out how to use crutches but the trip to the fourth floor in the elevator was rapid.

It amused him the way Saeed shot to his feet when he recognised Hakim but before the man could say a word, Hakim gave instructions in Arabic, for there was no need for Sarah to know what transpired. She didn't need to know who he was.

'I will sit here against the wall.' He pulled out a chair from the side of the large desk where a wary-faced Saeed sank back into his chair on the other side. So, he was right to assume things were not as they should be. It was possible the rumours about this man were true. To be sure, he would instigate an investigation into the man's dealings.

'You have my contract?' Sarah asked before Hakim could make introductions.

A nervous twitch tugged the side of Saeed's mouth. 'Yes, all you need to do is sign at the bottom of each page.' He handed her a thin sheaf of papers and a gold pen. His finger landed on a cross scrawled next to the long blank line at the bottom.

Sarah had to wriggle the papers from under Saeed's finger before she skimmed through the three pages in mere seconds and placed them in neat alignment in front of her. Her shoulders rose high and fell again on an ominous silence.

She stood, balanced on her good leg and turned to Hakim. 'It seems I was brought here under false pretences.'

He straightened, alarmed at her demeanour and the quietness of her voice. 'What do you mean?'

'This contract is not as was agreed over the internet. Paragraphs one, two, three, five and seven are as per our agreement. I have all the emails to confirm what transpired.

'How can you be sure? You barely glanced at it.'

Pinkness bloomed on her cheeks but she handed him the document. 'Read for yourself. Paragraph one states my hours, *five days a week, Sunday to Thursday from 9am to 6pm. Friday and Saturday are free* since it is your weekend when Saeed will be home. Paragraph two gives my *payment rate of twenty Australian dollars per hour deposited into my bank account weekly* which takes into account my board and included meals. *Board is in a separate self-contained unit on the property.* Paragraph three is about the activities I will undertake with the children, *to take them to various places like the market, so they learn to speak fluently in English in as many different situations as possible to increase their vocabulary. Three days out to visit different attractions, two days inside.'*

Hakim scanned as she talked.

'At no time did we discuss, nor did I agree to paragraph four which states I am *to prepare three meals a day, every day, for the family,* which would mean I would begin to cook around seven each day and not get home until eight or nine at night. Every day means no free weekends. Same with paragraph six which indicates I am now *responsible to plan the meals and undertake the weekly shop of food.'*

Hakim glanced at her face where suppressed fury was obvious but he still couldn't figure out how she could relate verbatim, every word written down when she had raced through the pages in mere seconds.

'Paragraph eight eats into my free time even more. I am *responsible to clean the house and family laundering.* Maybe I will arrive before six and not go to bed until midnight but paragraph nine tells me exactly what is expected of me between the hours of midnight and six a.m. when I am to *undertake any other duties a normal wife is bound to undertake.'* She paused, hissed through pursed lips as though she fought hard to contain her fury.

It scared Hakim at the speed with which she spun back around to face Saeed, who appeared to be desperate to do a miraculous magician's vanishing act. Guilt flamed across his cheeks and fear lived in his eyes.

'I may have been raised in a Western country where it is obvious you think women have no scruples but you are wrong. My morals are of the highest standard as are those of my friends, who would never suggest such offensive terms. It is equally obvious you think women are to be treated as slaves and have no value. A good thing about Western culture is how women learn to be independent and stand up for ourselves. I have worked and fended for myself

17

since I was fifteen, financially dependent on no-one. Your biggest mistake is to think I am brainless enough to sign on the bottom and accept this bit of trash without reading the words. I choose who I will share a bed with and it certainly will never be with a man who has no respect for me. I don't do casual sex, I don't tell lies, I am not and never will be some man's slave which is what you have proposed here. No wonder your wife had the good sense to leave you.' She grabbed her backpack and made to leave but forgot both her injury and crutches.

Hakim managed to catch her before she hit the ground. When her body stiffened and hands went in front of her face in protective mode, it didn't take genius status to figure out whatever had happened to cause this fear of the male population, it had been a serious traumatic event.

'I will not harm you. As soon as you are upright I will release you. I promise.' Hakim hoisted her upright. 'You need to sit a moment,' he added when her body began to resemble shelves of goods in an earthquake. Once he had her settled in a chair, he took two steps away and held up his hands to show submission.

Satisfied she wouldn't fall, he turned to Saeed. 'I am appalled to know you would dare treat a guest to our country with such contempt. Your behaviour is unforgiveable.'

The man trembled as much as Sarah, which only emphasised his guilt. 'I am sorry. I thought she understood the terms. My mistake. I apologise and will seek forgiveness from Allah.'

'It is from Miss Anderson you should seek forgiveness. If I were her I would never forgive you. True Arab men never treat women with such disrespect. We honour our women. You shame your heritage and shame Islam.'

'Please, I am sorry but I need Miss Anderson to care for my children. They have been traumatised by the loss of their mother. I promise to abide by the original agreement. I will draw up a new contract right away. Please?'

It was unbelievable he would dare suggest Sarah continue with this charade and no way would Hakim allow her to work for this man. He turned towards her. The tremor had ceased and colour had returned to her cheeks.

'Can I think about this?' she asked, her voice calmer.

'You cannot be serious about working for this man.'

She held up her hands. 'Give me a minute.' Eyes shut, she paused and stilled. 'Can I speak with you in private?' She directed her gaze towards Hakim.

Saeed shot from his seat. 'Please, use my office. I will wait outside.' He was gone in an instant.

Hakim directed Tariq to keep Saeed away from the door before he tugged his chair closer to Sarah but not close enough to alarm her. 'I do not trust him.'

'Nor do I but I need this job. I have a work permit but if I don't fulfill my obligations, I have to leave the country. I have nowhere else to go.'

'You could return home.'

'No, I can't, not until...' She glanced away with her cheeks again a dark shade of pink. A deep frown creased her brow.

'You can trust me, Sarah. Tell me why.'

Her shoulders slumped in resignation. 'For a year, an unknown man constantly stalked me. It ended when he broke into my unit, attacked me and I almost died. Until the mongrel is caught, it's safer here than at home.' Her eyes went on a journey around the room until they settled back on his shoulder. 'I can add a few clauses to ensure Saeed has no contact with me, but I need to check the accommodation before I agree.'

He wanted to demand she say no but he had no right. This was a private arrangement, although he could make life difficult for Saeed if he didn't abide by the conditions. The man knew who he was and since Saeed was not locally born, if he broke the law he would be exiled back to his country of birth, after a prison term. 'What conditions do you want to add?'

'Bring in Saeed.'

'Are you sure?'

'Yes.'

A chastened man returned. As he eased into his chair, he gave the impression of wariness. Hakim leant forward. 'Miss Anderson would like to add some conditions and inspect the accommodation before she agrees.'

Relief spread across Saeed's face. 'What conditions?'

Sarah gripped the arm rests on the chair and straightened in a pose of authority. Saeed wilted under her glare.

'You are never to come anywhere near me. To add to their education, I will teach the children how to research places to visit, plan every outing, work out costs such as fares on public transport, entry fees and meal costs if needed. Each in turn will give you the weekly outline for your approval. You will ensure they have sufficient funds for the day to cover their costs, not mine. I depend on no-one but myself. I wish to have a hundred dirham up-front emergency amount in case of an unforeseen event which results in a change of plan. I will return all unused money to you at the end of the six weeks. The children will retain all receipts for you to verify the amount spent as well as a way the children can learn how to keep to a budget. If the separate accommodation is suitable I wish to install internal locks on every window and change the locks on the doors with all of the keys kept by me. These keys will be returned to you when I leave.'

Saeed straightened. 'There is no need. The premises are secure. My mother lived there before she died.'

Hakim's lips twitched when Sarah laughed - not in a funny way but more of scorn.

'You have already proved I can never trust you. The children will come to my unit when you leave for work. *Never* you. I will have them ready to return to you when you arrive home but you will *never* come to my unit. If you wish to speak to me it will be by phone. I will provide my own meals and eat in my unit or eat out. You will never interfere with my free time and will allow me free access to and from the unit at all times – without question. Those are my terms.'

Hakim had to admire her. Saeed's shoulders sagged before he nodded but he had little choice especially with Hakim present.

'Very well.'

'I will type up the contract as per our original agreement but with these extra terms added. I will email it to you tonight. When will be a suitable time for me to come to sign it?'

'Can you send it to me as well?' Hakim interrupted. 'I will have my lawyer read it to ensure it meets with local legal requirements.' His grin at the irate Saeed, was supercilious. It was evident the man did not appreciate Hakim's intervention. 'The time? How about this time tomorrow?' Hakim glanced at his watch and wanted to groan. Another meeting missed. It was a good job he had a super-efficient second-in-command who was used to standing in for him at the last minute. 'It is almost one. One o'clock tomorrow afternoon.'

Saeed nodded his agreement.

'Oh, and a key for the accommodation, please?' Hakim added.

Saeed fumbled with a bunch of keys from his pocket and wriggled one off the chain. The uncomfortable message in his head yelled how Saeed would have kept this key and very possibly used it.

'Come, Miss Anderson.' Hakim held out his elbow for her to grasp as she stood. It took a few fumbles to get her backpack on and crutches in place.

'I must return to work,' he said, while they descended in the elevator. 'Tariq will drive you to Saeed's place and help you inspect the premises for safety. He will know what to search for, especially secret monitoring devices.'

Sarah hissed through her teeth.

'He will drive you to your hotel and pick you up again at 12.30 tomorrow and will also organise the locks. They will be in place by the time you sign the contract. If I am unable to join you tomorrow, Tariq will stay with you while you are in Saeed's presence to ensure the man abides by the conditions. If my lawyer approves the contract I will have him print off three copies unless you have a printer with you.'

'No, only my laptop. Thank you. You are too kind. I am embarrassed. How can I repay you?'

They stepped out of the elevator. Hakim paused, turned and smiled. 'How about you join me for the evening meal one night soon after you have settled in.' He indicated for her to continue ahead of him. 'In the car, we must exchange email addresses and perhaps phone numbers when you get your sim card.'

Three

The unit was modern, spacious and far enough away from the main house Sarah was certain she would be able to monitor any outside presence. The single bed didn't bother her. It was both comfortable and gave support with the softest ever cotton sheets and two different pillows, one firm, the other perfect. Painted in a fresh pastel green, the unit had an aura of coolness and would be even cooler once she turned on the air conditioner. While she opened cupboard doors and checked out the plush bathroom, Tariq inspected every nook and tiny crack, opened and closed windows. None had secure locks. The knowledge sent a snake down her spine at the thought of what ifs.

'Are you satisfied?' Tariq stood, arms akimbo, in the centre of the lounge area which opened into the small but more than adequate kitchen with a square table and four cushioned chairs. Two single armchairs and a double sofa sat in a semi-circle around a large modern television mounted on a wall. There were also a scary number of knobs on a sound system which looked as though it waited for her to have umpteen spare hours to figure them out.

'Except for the locks, yes.'

'I will arrange the locks.'

'You must give me the bill.'

Tariq smiled. 'If I give you the bill, I will lose my job. The… minister's orders. I do not dare disobey the minister.' He smiled again: so far he always carried a smile. 'He is a good honourable man. You can always trust his word, I promise. With him, you will always be safe. Come, let me get you to your hotel.'

It disconcerted her when Tariq kept the key after he ensured the door was locked. This man she had met mere hours ago had the means to get into her abode. But the locks would be changed, she had to keep in the forefront of her mind. And sometime soon, she had to begin to trust human nature again.

The journey through the ultra-modern city was slow with traffic dense. It gave her a chance to study the surrounds, especially the buildings. All were modern with not one like its neighbour. The architecture on each was unique and pretty darn spectacular. But her mind kept wandering to Tariq's words about his boss. Could she trust Hakim? She wanted to; was desperate to be able to put her faith in individuals again, to convince her mind there were good men in the world. It had only been one man who had destroyed her ability to trust. Hakim invited her to share a meal with him. It would be so awesome to be able to accept and be comfortable seated opposite a man at a table. It would be in a restaurant, with other people around. Surely she would be safe in a restaurant.

'Tariq, may I ask you a question?'

He glanced at her in the rear-vision mirror. 'Certainly.'

'When the minister dines out, does he have bodyguards with him?'

'Always. Not at the same table for privacy but they are nearby.' Sarah caught his grin. 'You will dine with him?'

'He demanded repayment. You are too scared to defy him so what choice do I have?'

Tariq's laugh came from his belly. 'There is always a choice but it is a privilege to dine privately with the minister.'

'He's not married is he?'

'No. If he were, he would not invite you. Honour is strong with the... minister.'

This was the second time Tariq paused before the word minister but she couldn't ask more questions since they had stopped in front of her hotel. It was weird to have the man open the door for her. There was a first time for everything.

'I will be here at 12.30 tomorrow,' Tariq said as he closed the door behind her.

Sarah was always early for an appointment. Well, except when she didn't watch where she placed her feet and made an ignominious tumble in front of a car. Dead on time, the same white limousine pulled to a stop outside her hotel lobby. By the time she grabbed her backpack and settled the crutches in place, Tariq stood next to the already open car door. He handed her a large brown envelope with a significant bulge.

'New keys. All windows have the same lock. There are two keys for the front door and two for the rear laundry door. There is a third spare key for both doors in the glove box of this car. The minister's orders in case there is an emergency. He has no trust of Saeed. We will pick up the minister on the way. He has a free hour.'

Overwhelmed, Sarah struggled to find a response. She wasn't sure she liked the idea someone else had the ability to get into her unit. Wherever they went bamboozled her sense of direction for they turned so many corners and circled umpteen roundabouts before the car drew to a stop in front of the building where Hakim had alighted before Tariq drove her to the unit yesterday. The wait was only seconds before the rear door opened and Hakim folded onto the seat beside her. She assumed this address was his place of work. A quick scan of the building front and she absorbed the building name and number, thankful it was in both English and Arabic. What really alarmed her was the way her body reacted to his presence. Where any other male within cooee of her, sent her nervous system off the charts in panic mode, Hakim turned those same nerves into mush.

'How is your foot?' Hakim half-turned to face her while a second bodyguard folded into the front seat.

'My foot is fine; my ankle is a painful nuisance.'

His eyebrows rose at her correction. Uh, oh, she shouldn't have been so pernickety but she couldn't help the way her weirdly wired brain worked.

'And your shoulder?'

'My shoulder?' Concern turned to surprise. She'd never mentioned her shoulder which was now dark indigo from what she had seen in the mirror after a contortionist act in the bathroom earlier. It had been fun trying to get comfortable in bed when her left ankle demanded no pressure and the opposite shoulder complained if she slept on her right. Flat on her stomach with her foot poked from the covers had been the only solution but she had slept well. Now she was almost human again and not a sleepy sloth with a marshmallow brain in the throes of jetlag.

'It must be bruised.'

'How did...?'

Hakim laughed. 'For my car to jolt at the impact, there must be a bruise and I noticed how you tried to hide your pain whenever you placed your shoulder against both the chair in the office and this car. How bad is it?'

'Better than my ankle.'

He laughed again but immediately turned serious. 'Are you sure you want to go ahead with this work?'

'Yes.'

'You have no reservations?'

'Some.'

'Which are?'

'Will Saeed abide by the contract and stay away from me? But I trust my abilities to defend myself if he doesn't.' After the attack, she'd spent two hours a day, seven days a week for an entire month practising self-defence moves. Never again would a man get the better of her.

'I will speak with him but if at any time he crosses the line please phone me immediately. Do you have a sim card yet?'

'No.'

'Why do you not use your Australian service?'

'The man who attacked me back home, knew my number. I had to disconnect my phone. Until now, I haven't been game to find a new service. One local to this country will ensure he can't contact me.'

'I understand. Tariq will take you to a reputable phone shop when he returns you to your hotel. Please ensure you give him the number. I will email you my private number as well as those of my bodyguards and the times each is on duty. Even if the man you phone is not with me he will forward your message. If at any time you need help, one of my men will come to your aid if I am unable to. My life is busy so I am not always available.'

A warm, fuzzy sensation enveloped her but at the same time shock hit at how life had thrown such curve balls in the few hours she had been in the country. 'Why are you doing this?'

His smile was warm. 'Several reasons. You are a visitor to our country. Already one of our citizens has not done right by you. Already you have had an accident. Our reputation as a safe, friendly country to all people regardless of their religious and cultural beliefs, cannot be compromised by such indiscretions. And I like you.' He reached out and gave her hand a warm grasp. A weird tingle slithered all the way up her arm. Immediately, he released his hold and relaxed back in the corner of his seat, still half-turned towards her. 'I am free tomorrow night for our dinner date if you are up to it.'

Oh, wow, to go or not? So soon? Tariq said there would be bodyguards but how safe would she be? It was all down to her trust level which had been non-existent until now but she had to start to trust again sometime. Time, she needed time to think. 'Can I see how this meeting goes before I answer?'

'Certainly and here we are.'

The crutches were a nuisance, for everyone had to wait while she stumbled. When she managed to get upright she had to manoeuvre arms through straps to set her backpack in place. Tariq opened doors for her, men stood back to let her crump past. It was a torment to get to the door of Saeed's office but no-where near as scary as when she hobbled into the room.

Alarm bells clanged when the man rose at the same time she sat. She should run, not agree to this job. But what choice did she have? Even though she had a good amount of money in her bank account, she needed to earn while she searched for the next job as far away from home as possible

– until the police caught the man who had almost ended her life.

Before she could change her mind, she signed the three copies of the contract Hakim's lawyer had okayed in a flurry of emails last night. While Saeed signed, Hakim sounded serious as he spoke in Arabic, which sent a sheepish air to Saeed's face before he nodded vehemently. A tense silence ensued while Hakim handed out copies, one to Saeed, one to her and the third into a folder which he handed to Tariq.

'Can you start tomorrow?' Saeed asked when Sarah managed to get to her feet again.

Oh, sure, she thought. Gammy ankle and bruised shoulder made for an over-abundance of energy and agility to entertain three youngsters. 'Yes, I will move in sometime today.' How to manage it, she would figure out later but it would be before Saeed arrived home. No way did she want to arrive when the man was home. She could defend herself but a useless ankle was a *what if* her trainer had never considered while she learnt and mastered all the various defensive moves. And now she also needed to buy basic supplies this afternoon. Oh, and for sure, she knew where the nearest supermarket was. Somehow she would find out. That's what mobile phones were for and if taxi drivers were like the ones back home – they knew everything. It would be an interesting few hours.

Back in Hakim's car, Sarah released a long sigh, closed her eyes and rested her head back against the seat. Now she was committed. Six weeks with nerves on tenterhooks, which wasn't any different to the way she had spent the last year but at least here, she knew the identity of her adversary and was better prepared after the intense course of self-defence.

Four

Hakim studied Sarah seated across the table. Ever since they had arrived she shot glances at every person who entered. Each man and woman was examined from the head down, men in particular. The women received only a cursory glance. Aware of her intense fear, he sat her where she could see the door, but they were in the middle of the room, against a curved head-high wall which gave them privacy – the best table in the restaurant. They would have been better hidden away at the back, but such a position would create a speculation neither of them needed.

'Sarah.'

Her head shot up. 'Yes?'

He indicated to his left where his two men sat at the next table. 'Ali and Ahmed will not allow anyone to come near us. Nor will our server. I chose this restaurant because it is a place where privacy of the diners is of utmost importance. A place where people can discuss confidential business deals; important guests can be entertained over a quiet meal. I can guarantee no-one will approach us. Please relax.'

Her eyes dropped. 'Sorry.'

'There is no need to apologise for being afraid. What would you like to eat - traditional dishes or more western?'

'Traditional, but I'm not familiar with most of these names.' She swept her hand down the menu she had studied between each examination of the diners who came and went.

'Would you like me to select a few dishes we can share?'

A tiny smile escaped. 'That would be nice, thank you.'

He called the waiter over, ordered six different dishes and offered Sarah a choice of drinks including wine.

She frowned. 'I thought Muslims didn't drink alcohol.'

'I do not, but this does not mean I will prevent you from having what you prefer. Many of my overseas visitors prefer wine or beer.'

'No alcohol for me. The mint and lime drink I had was delicious. Maybe a similar drink.'

Orders given; he relaxed back into his seat. 'How was your first day with the children?'

Sarah's eyes skittered up. 'It was a good day.'

'Did you go out?'

'No, we needed to get to know each other while we made plans.'

Both amused and concerned about such short answers, Hakim figured he would try more open-ended questions. 'Describe the children for me so I can get a picture of them.'

Her eyes shot back to him. Honey coloured, he decided, to match her incredible gold hair which was neither ginger nor brown.

'Aliya is six. Pretty with huge dark but sad eyes. Her English is not good. Laylah is seven. Not so pretty. Chattier. Rashid is nine. Takes after his father. A bit bossy. Thinks he can speak for the girls. There is something about them which concerns me. Haunted is the word I would use.'

'Like you.'

Sarah's eyes finally caught his in a curious stare. 'What do you mean?'

'Haunted is how I would describe you. There are a few more words - afraid, cautious, shy, charming, considerate and beautiful.'

Her eyes popped with her head skewed to one side and her mouth agape. At least now he had her full attention.

'If I asked if I was correct, I believe you would say no because I think you are one who downplays your attributes. I get the impression you lack self-confidence, yet you stood up to Saeed bin Suroor. This tells me you have inner strength and will not allow people to walk over you. Am I right?'

'Yes.' When her cheeks turned pink, she dropped her head.

It was unfortunate for him their food arrived but with the relief on Sarah's face, he figured the interruption was timely from her point of view. He wondered how long it would take for her to not be afraid in his company. Sarah was a pleasant change. Usually the women he dined with were overkeen to gain and keep his attention. Most gushed with over-pretentiousness, agreed with every word he said, forced laughter or prattled on about what they thought would impress him. It rarely did but Sarah was anything but the type of woman he had ever been with before.

Delight rumbled through him while Sarah picked a tiny morsel of each dish after he explained the ingredients. She placed each morsel on her tongue, let it react with her taste buds before she either grimaced or smiled. Those she liked; she heaped spoonsful onto her plate. It appeared she was one who was attentive to food, savoured the flavours and did not simply shovel it in to fill a void and despite how lean she was, she had a healthy appetite. So far, everything about her pleased him to a level no other woman had ever been able to achieve.

It intrigued him the timid way she tilted her head when asked a question but eye contact wasn't direct as though she was too afraid to go the last centimetre for a full-on eye-to-eye connection. He wondered if it was fear or plain shyness but was keen to find out.

When Sarah placed her knife and fork together and pushed the plate in front of her to indicate she had finished, he followed suit and sat back in his chair. 'What area of science did you study?' The question must have been unexpected for she jerked her head up.

'Dirt.'

'Excuse me?' It was not what he expected.

'I studied soil.'

'Why soil?'

'It interests me.'

'I need you to explain why you find soil an interesting field to study.'

'Without soil we would find it difficult to live. Plants need soil to gain nourishment to grow. No soil - no plants - no food - no animals. We wouldn't be able to exist. Soil contains basic metals which we extract to create building products and various tools. We bake soil to make bricks. No soil - no building products - no homes or shelter unless we go back to live in caves. Soil is as important as water for life to exist on our planet. I analyse soil from different areas; study each grain, find what elements are in abundance or are missing. It's amazing what different particles you can find in ten grams of soil.'

The animation on her face was a joy. It was obvious Sarah was passionate about her chosen subject. Would she be this passionate in bed? He shook his head at the thought. So inappropriate. To get his mind away from such carnal thoughts he returned to the topic of science.

'Do you intend to study further, maybe get a master's degree?'

Her face screwed in puzzlement. 'I... I hope to further my research and work in the field.' She glanced at the floor, bent and retrieved the crutches. Flustered, she stood. 'Excuse me, I need to find the bathroom.'

She searched the room, set the crutches in place and scuttled away. Hakim wondered what had happened as he watched her weave between tables to the rear. She seemed to have been spooked but he couldn't figure out why even after thinking back to his last question. It had been perfectly logical but maybe her arrival here had put off the possibility of further study. Maybe the uncertainty of when she could return home meant she wasn't able to enrol or there could be a lack of funds and she needed to work for an income. Thoughts still churned when he noticed her return at a more sedate pace.

With each step the shiny dark green fabric of her long skirt swayed from side-to-side. The top fitted snugly around lean hips and shimmered at each movement but it didn't outline her shape in an overt sexual nature. The loose, long-sleeved top had swirls in different shades of green and a similar sheen as though woven with silk. It hid her body shape in a discreet manner to suit the cultural standards of his country but at the same time, her outfit invited a man to find out what was underneath. First, he was a normal red-blooded man. Sarah was tall and lean, with an elegant neck; the one area she exposed. Even out for an evening meal, she wore no visible make-up or extra jewellery. The more time he spent with her, the more he liked and the more he wanted to see her again but she was only here for six weeks to work. Pity.

'Sorry,' Sarah settled back into her seat and placed the crutches on the floor.

'Are you all right?'

'Yes, of course.'

'Would you like dessert or maybe coffee?'

'No, thank you. I couldn't eat another bite and coffee at night keeps me awake. I enjoyed these eastern dishes. Thank you.'

'Which was your favourite?'

'The green beans.'

'Not the stew? Although many westerners prefer not to eat goat.'

'Goat is not much different to lamb. A little earthier but I found the spices too intense.'

'Maybe you are not used to such spicy food?'

'No, but I intend to try as many eastern dishes as I can while I am here, which is why I asked you to describe the dishes for me. Those I like I can order again.'

'And those you did not enjoy you will not order again.'

'Maybe.' A half-grin slipped out.

'Come then, I will return you home so you can get enough sleep to face three active children tomorrow.' Hakim stood, retrieved the crutches and held them out. 'Will you have indoor activities tomorrow?'

Sarah settled her arms in the crutches. 'No, we will go to the museum.' She turned and clomped towards the door.

Hakim raced to catch up. 'Surely your ankle is not yet ready for such a journey.'

'My suggestion. I will find a seat to rest my foot while the children study the exhibits. They can come to me to explain in English what they find.'

Ali had the door open for them by the time Hakim had paid the bill. Ten minutes later they pulled into the drive and parked by the side of Sarah's unit. When Sarah rushed to alight, Hakim placed a hand on her arm.

'I will see you to the door.'

'That's not necessary.'

'It is always necessary for a man to ensure his guest reaches their door safely. Ahmed will check to ensure there is no-one near your unit.'

Sarah's audible hiss was his only response as Ahmed hurried from the front passenger seat and vanished into the darkness. Ensuring there was a visible space between them, he walked beside her but stood back while she found her key and opened the door.

Ahmed came from behind. 'Saeed peers through the second window on the right,' he said in Arabic.

It was as Hakim had thought. To ensure there could be no suggestion of inappropriate behaviour, he took another step away from Sarah, towards the main house. 'I will say goodnight. Thank you for sharing your evening with me. I will phone tomorrow night. I have already warned Saeed to expect me to call in unannounced at various times to check on you.'

Sarah turned as she stepped inside. 'I'm sure there is no need.'

'I do not trust a man who spies on you through his window as he is right now. I will protect you. Tariq gave me your phone number and I have emailed all of my contact numbers as well as those of my men. Please log them into your phone so you are able to contact me at a moment's notice if the need arises. But it is not the only reason I will visit. I wish to see you again for you intrigue me. Goodnight.' He made a slight bow, turned and walked to his car, unable to supress his grin at the surprise on the delightful Sarah's face.

Five

E very part of her ached: her head, body, shoulder and ankle, which thrummed a constant message it wanted to be elevated. She eyed the white blisters on her palms where she had constantly gripped the crutch handles. It had been a huge mistake to take the children out today, with the chairs she had envisioned, non-existent. The only place she was able to settle her backside was on a parapet wall out in the full sun, which in the Middle East seemed to burn twice as hot as back home even though it was supposed to be early winter here.

Too tired to cook, even after a long cold shower, Sarah hacked off a lump of goat's cheese, sliced a red apple, filled a large tumbler with iced tea, added half a dozen ice cubes and sank onto the sofa with her legs stretched out. Sore muscles twitched as they settled into the welcome cushion. Now she had been game to remove the bandage, she could see the bruise under the anklebone. Tomorrow they will stay in her unit to plan the next three weeks of outside activities. She reached across to the coffee table, tugged her laptop closer to log onto sites to find interesting spots in the city and surrounds.

On the list of public holidays, she noticed the school winter holidays didn't begin for two weeks and ended on 5th January, so why was she needed for six weeks? Surely the children should be at school before and after those dates. After further scrutiny, she discovered both New Year's Eve and New Year's Day were public holidays and she already knew Christmas wasn't an Islamic celebration but it didn't prevent her from having her own private feast while on face time with family and friends.

With the thought of family, she logged onto her emails and spent the next half-hour reading and typing but left out the not so positive bits. No-one needed to know about the accident nor the contract kerfuffle. If they didn't ask specific questions she didn't have to answer. Sometimes it was convenient the way her brain worked.

When her phone began to play its catchy tune, she sighed. She so didn't want Saeed to spoil the night. Every muscle in her body groaned when she struggled upright and hopped to retrieve her mobile. She pressed the green button and leant against the kitchen bench. 'Hello.'

'Sarah?'

Every organ in her body shivered in delight at Hakim's voice. 'Yes.'

'Are you at home?'

'Yes.'

'May I call in for a minute or two?'

'Certainly.'

'When I knock come out into the open.'

'Why?'

'It would be improper for me to enter your home alone.'

'You have two bodyguards so you wouldn't be alone.'

'To maintain your honour, I cannot enter your home without a female chaperone in attendance, usually a member of your family but since you have no family, we must meet out in the open.'

'Okay.' Sarah rolled her eyes, grinned and hung up. These customs were difficult to understand but if she wanted to last the six weeks, she would abide. What was she supposed to do if she made an awful social gaffe? She shuddered at the thought. The never touch in public rule, she already knew. Her mind sifted through the rules she had read about. Take shoes off at the entrance, don't point at another person, right hand to eat with because your left hand is unclean but she used a knife and fork – well, she hadn't tonight and had picked off small knobs of cheese with her left hand. Way to go, Sarah. Right hand to shake hands and present gifts – like that would ever happen. The hardest for her was how eye contact was important when, for her it was downright scary. All her life her parents and older brothers had taught her to catch a person's eyes so she focussed on the top of their ear.

Three raps at the door. 'Coming.' She scrabbled and hopped to pick up the crutches. When she opened the door, Hakim stood halfway to the side fence with Ali two metres to his left, between house and Hakim. The second man wasn't within sight but he would be there, she was certain.

'Please turn on the outside light.' Hakim indicated the overhead light set in the portico ceiling.

Sarah hated being the centre of attention but did as asked. When the light highlighted her, she winced but immediately straightened and turned on a brave face.

'Come to the edge of the porch.'

She crumped forward but was surprised when Hakim closed the gap with no more than a metre between them.

'How was your day?'

41

'Good but I'm a bit tired.'

'Any problems with Saeed?'

'No.'

'He abides by the contract?'

'So far, yes.'

'Tomorrow night I am to attend a performance at the opera house. Various stars from around the world will present popular arias and duets from famous operas. As the Minister for Arts, I am the patron and must attend. Would you like to come with me? I should ask if you enjoy classical music.'

A shudder of pleasure wove its way down her body. Why didn't she fear this man the way she did all others? Why did the thought of going out with him not give her the heebie-jeebies? 'I enjoy all forms of music. What dress code is expected?'

'Opening night is a formal occasion. The ladies wear their jewels and a formal gown. Is this a problem?'

'No, I have one.' But only because her mother insisted, dragged her to the shops and coerced her into trying on long gowns and purchase one. Thank you, Mum.

'Would you care to join me?'

'Thank you, yes. What time?'

'The curtain rises at 8pm. I will be here at 7.15.' He turned towards Ahmed, who appeared from the dark and mumbled in Arabic. Hakim turned towards the house. 'As I suspected, Saeed watches us. Go inside and lock your door before I leave.' Hakim's voice had softened to a whisper. 'Do you need your ankle re-strapped?'

Stunned he had noticed, Sarah straightened. 'No.'

'Then I bid you goodnight and a peaceful sleep.'

Sarah turned too fast and almost tripped. It took a second to find her balance. A hiss from Hakim as he stepped forward. 'I'm fine.' She waved him away.

He laughed as she closed the door and turned the key. A smile hovered around her mouth while she undressed, donned a short cotton nightie and settled in bed with her ankle raised on a pillow to ease the ache. She liked this man and even better, he didn't scare the bejesus out of her.

The very instant the clock clicked onto 7.15 there was a single knock on the door. An unbidden grin broke out. Sarah turned the key and opened the door wide enough to ease through. The grin turned into a gasp. Hakim had gone for western dress - a tuxedo. He was striking in robes but in a black tuxedo with a snowy white shirt, bow tie and ebony studs, he was cover material for a men's fashion magazine. Already, she had figured out he had a body many men would be envious of but now she could make out exactly how broad his shoulders were and how his body tapered down to slim hips and long, long legs.

'Turn around.' He twirled his fingers in the air.

Now with only one crutch because two were a nuisance, Sarah slowly turned. Her stomach roiled.

'Beautiful, no, not the right word. Exquisite is far better.' He stepped to one side to reveal an older woman with the traditional black abaya over her clothes. 'This is Mariam, my housekeeper, who will be your chaperone for the night.'

The older, but not aged woman stepped forward with her right hand held out. Sarah grasped it on a word of welcome but discomfort settled in her gut at the glare she received.

'I appreciate you coming, thank you,' Sarah smiled. When Mariam didn't respond, Sarah wondered whether the lady spoke English but had no opportunity to ask because Hakim whisked them into the car, where the extra person meant she was thigh-to-thigh with him. For the entire fifteen-minute journey, tingles of warmth ran up and down her leg. When she edged her thigh away a fraction, the contact didn't ease. What surprised her the most was how much she didn't mind, which was a miracle.

She dared a peek to find his eyes on her. His smile turned her innards into a storm.

'Your gown suits you but where are your jewels?' His open hand indicated her neck.

An unbidden gasp escaped as she flung her hands to her neck. 'I can't tolerate anything around my neck.' She screwed her eyes shut. Why, oh, why did she mention it?

A frown formed across his brow. 'Can I ask why not?'

'No.' To avoid any more questions she turned to Mariam but the car drew to a halt in front of a glass building which reminded her of an enormous passenger liner. In an instant, both bodyguards leapt from the front and opened the rear doors. Hakim got out and had her crutch held out.

Her nerves shot to full alert when a path seemed to automatically clear for them while they walked inside to a vast reception area. They didn't stop until they were in a lift, which soared up at a rapid rate. She had barely managed to settle into a comfortable stance when the lift door opened to a carpeted passage. Ali led the way to a door, which he opened and they all trooped inside. It was a shock to find they were in a huge box jutting out from the side wall to overlook the main auditorium. Hakim ushered her to a seat slap-bang in the middle where everybody in the entire theatre could gawk at her.

'Sit here a while. I need to meet with the VIPs,' Hakim said before he vanished.

Sarah plonked onto the cushioned seat and studied the theatre. It was magnificent with plush, red upholstered seats and polished wood balustrades. The walls were a web of wood while the ceiling replicated the wooden skeleton of a boat. Now, she understood why the outside appeared boat-like; an ancient dhow, she figured. It made sense. Their own box had four rows of four seats. Mariam settled to the left of Sarah.

A black and white river of patrons flowed in. Most men wore white robes and head pieces while their partners were covered in black. Westerners wore long gowns or dinner suits, the only colour from the gowns of the western women and glitter from abundant jewels. Even though patrons whispered, the noise level increased as seats filled. When hundreds of eyes turned her way, Sarah shrank down, placed her elbows on the armrests and hid her head in her hands. If she had known she would be the centre of attention, she wouldn't have come.

Somewhere outside, bells dinged. A flood of patrons hurried in and filled the seats while orchestra players picked up instruments. A single oboe played a long note, joined by various other instruments as each tuned to the lead note. The conductor strode in to applause. He turned to the audience, waved his arms around and up. The audience stood, turned towards the box where Sarah sat. Mortified and with her heart thumping, she wondered what this was all about. Hakim came to stand by her. He nodded his head and sat. The audience turned away and retook their seats.

'What was that about?' Sarah said through the side of her mouth, her heart still replicating the kettle drums down below. What if he was here and recognised her?

'I am... the patron.'

The way he paused set off her internal alarm bells. 'A patron is so important? You could have warned me.'

'Sarah, you need not be afraid. To have a guest with me is normal. With Mariam as your chaperone, there will be no gossip.'

'Gossip doesn't concern me.'

'Then what does concern you?'

45

Unsure how to answer she closed her eyes to figure out what to say without disclosing her private turmoil. 'All these people gawping at me.'

'It was me they acknowledged, not you.'

His statement didn't ease her fear, in fact, it was kind of an insult. His inference that she wasn't worthy of other's attention, rankled in a way she couldn't understand.

When the music began, Sarah hunkered in her seat, only lifting her head far enough to see the activity on stage where two men and two women stood in a group, obviously singers since they were dressed in the best formal finery. She wasn't able to sit back and relax until well into the third song when she was so enamoured by the piece, her tense nerves relaxed.

Six

It had been foolish to forget about the formality of the audience greeting but Hakim prayed his explanation was sufficient. He did not reveal the truth, nor did he lie. He eyed Sarah, relieved she was now absorbed in the music. It was a delight to have her next to him. Why there was this need to be with her, he could not explain but there was a sharp pang of longing lodged inside: in his bones, his blood, in every atom.

Even in the darkness, her gold hair glinted like jewels which should sparkle around her neck. If she belonged to him, he would ensure her jewels were of the best quality. Not too gaudy. Sarah needed simple and elegant.

He smiled when she leant forwards to rest her forearms on the balustrade and at her sigh of pleasure. This duet from The Pearl Fishers was one of his favourites and seemed to have captured Sarah with its perfection. Perfect like Sarah. Still, he could not work out what it was about her that had him intrigued. Beautiful, yes, in a natural way. Still she wore no make-up despite the formality of the occasion but she was one who did not require artificial enhancement. It could be her unusual hair, like dark spun honey. There was no pretence about her: no put-on airs or vain behaviour to seek attention. It was quite the opposite. Sarah did her best to ensure no-one noticed her.

Her dress was simple in design but elegant. It flowed from her shoulders with long sleeves that ended above fine-boned wrists. Again her neck was exposed. He studied the smooth white skin between chin and shoulders. Elegant like a white swan but sprinkled with gold flecks. Why would she have a hang-up about her neck? There was a strong temptation to run his fingers down the milky smoothness but years of brainwashing about physical contact in public kept his hands anchored in his lap.

When the piece ended, Sarah's smile was wide and applause was enthusiastic. Delight shone from her eyes. She turned suddenly, caught him watching her. Her eyes widened for a second before lids closed over the amber irises to bring back her shyness in a mere second.

'It seems you enjoy the music,' Hakim said to give a reason for staring.

'Yes, very much.'

'The last piece is one of my favourites.'

A coy smile turned up the corners of her mouth. 'Mine too.'

'What about the first piece?'

'Not so much. Sopranos don't do it for me. I prefer deeper voices.'

Hakim laughed. 'I am sure our visiting soprano would not like to hear your words.'

'But it is the truth. I never tell lies.' She turned back at the introduction to the next piece.

For the rest of the session, Hakim found it difficult to keep his eyes from Sarah while thoughts of the interval supper he had to attend, took hold. The people would address him by his title. In English - a risk he wasn't prepared to take. The very second the curtains began to close, he stood, took Ali aside and gave instructions in Arabic.

He turned back to Sarah. 'I have social duties to attend in the interval. Ali will take you ladies to supper.' Before he turned away he noticed the flash of alarm in Sarah's eyes and the slight grin on Mariam's face. With only one man to guard him, he walked beside Ahmed as he rushed to be in place before the patrons on the VIP list entered the separate roped off area of the supper room.

Supper was a trial. High-ranked guests spouted what they thought he wanted to hear. He hated this pretence for he was certain most would never speak this way in their normal social situations and he would much prefer normal everyday chat. He glanced over the other side of the room in search for the golden-haired angel in a long, deep-blue dress. Her beauty made her stand out as did the way she shrank against the wall as though she wished she were anywhere else but there, as did he. Mariam shielded Sarah from male contact which was a pity for Sarah gave an aura of loneliness, nor would she be used to these restrictive customs. Alone, it would have been acceptable for her to speak with other westerners.

It pleased him to see Ali move closer to speak with Sarah. Her ready smile at Ali twisted Hakim's heart. This woman needed to smile all the time, not live with the fear she carried. Never before had he been so glad when the bells began their call to return to the theatre. He placed his still full plate and half-empty glass on the counter, nodded to Ahmed, sped across the room, and tagged on behind Mariam as Ali led the ladies back to their seats. A grin escaped at the thought of him behind other members of his

49

group. Unheard of and might create talk but right now he did not care.

'Did you enjoy your supper?' he asked when Sarah sat. Her stifled scream as she jerked around, surprised him. 'Sorry, I did not mean to frighten you.'

Her fear was evident in the way her chest heaved and eyes widened before they closed on a hiss. She settled one hand on her chest as though to calm her heart. Why did a simple question alarm her with such ease?

The second half of the show excelled, although he absorbed little since he preferred to watch Sarah who sighed, smiled and clapped with enthusiasm. It flooded his heart with warmth.

On the journey home Mariam managed to sit in the middle. Amused at her tactics, he said little until they reached Sarah's unit where he sent both bodyguards to scout the property. Sarah alighted from the car before he had a chance to move around to her side. With the usual one metre distance between them, he walked beside her to the edge of her small veranda. Ali arrived at the same time.

'Saeed is against the wall behind the unit,' said Ali in English.

Sarah whirled around with her key held high. 'I need to get inside.' She spun back, jammed the key in the lock, twisted and shoved the door open.

'A minute, Sarah. Let Ali check the inside.'

Sarah slumped against the door frame. The naked fear in her eyes alarmed him.

'Mariam,' Hakim called as he retrieved the key. 'We will all go inside,' he added when Mariam joined them. He indicated towards Sarah. 'Take care of Sarah, she has had a fright.'

It pleased him when Mariam grasped Sarah's shoulders and assisted her inside. Ali followed and immediately began to examine the windows, rooms and corners.

'No breaches.' Ali shook his head.

'Find Saeed, I need to have a word,' said Hakim before he turned to Mariam. 'See what you can do to get Sarah settled and ensure the drapes cover all windows. We will wait outside.' He turned, strode outside, glad Ahmed had Saeed held by the arm.

'Over there.' He indicated Saeed's portico.

'Explain,' he said to Saeed.

'I checked the garden as I do every night before bed. We have had intruders before. I have three children to protect.'

Hakim sighed with his eyes searching the heavens for an adequate response. He did not believe the man but there was little he could do. 'It is your property but maybe it would be better if you stay away from the unit. Miss Anderson has good reason to be afraid. She is to phone me if she has even the slightest thought she is in danger. I pray she has no need.'

'You have my word, Sir.' Saeed sounded humble but it could well be an act. It was rare for Hakim to regard a person as oily but it fitted this man and the oil was not clean and pure but full of sludge.

'Very well. Have a good night.' He watched Saeed scuttle inside. 'Have Shahir make random covert searches of the grounds every couple of hours,' he said to Ali as he strode back to the unit, knocked and waited for Mariam.

'How is Sarah?'

'I'm fine.' Sarah appeared behind Mariam's shoulder. 'Thank you for the brilliant performance. It's been over a year since I've been able to enjoy the theatre.'

51

A year? Had she had no social life for over a year? There had to be more to her story. 'You are welcome but please phone if you think Saeed acts in a suspicious manner.'

'I will. Good night and thank you, Mariam, for your kindness.'

Back in the car, Hakim sighed at Mariam's crossed arms. 'You may speak your mind, Mariam.'

'She is not for you.'

Hakim laughed. 'I take a woman who I almost killed, to a pleasant night out as a way to atone for my sins and you think I am about to marry her? Out of interest, why is Sarah not for me?'

'She is not one of us.'

'I presume you mean she is neither Arab nor Muslim.'

'Yes.'

'You sound racist, which disappoints me but so far, since I turned twenty, my parents have introduced me to dozens of Arab Muslim women who might make a suitable wife. I have found not one who suits me. Sarah is here for mere weeks. If I choose to show her places of interest in our city to make up for the injury I caused her, you, my dear Mariam, will have no say but I would appreciate it if you showed her the kindness and generosity of heart you give to all people. And do not forget, my grandmother was not of our religion nor Arab but the marriage to my grandfather could not have been better.'

'You like her.' Mariam's glare was fierce but cute. Few people would dare speak to him the way Mariam does but she had been a part of his life since as long back as he could remember. A nursemaid before she turned eighteen, she had cared for him and his brothers for much of their childhood.

'Yes, very much. Sarah is different from any woman I have ever met, which is a pleasant change. But this does not mean I am about to marry her.'

Seven

With her head against the car seat, lulled by the swish of tyres as they raced over the bitumen, visions of her first two weeks flickered through Sarah's mind. The children were sweet. Maybe not Rashid who dominated the girls, a trait he would have learnt from his father whom she didn't like one little bit. Saeed was downright creepy. Number two on her list of least liked men in the world but so far he had done nothing inappropriate if you didn't count the leery stares on the odd occasion she had caught sight of him.

The opera had been brilliant. She couldn't help the grin at the thought of Hakim. Never before had she taken to anyone as much or as quick as she had to this man. She really, really liked him - a lot.

Childless on Friday due to the Holy day, she dedicated the morning to household chores and managed to stock up on a week's supply of food via a taxi both ways because crutches and bags of food didn't equate. She caught up on emails and managed to elevate and massage her ankle before she searched the internet for a library. Library found she had to figure out the easiest way to get there via public transport. It was a relief to discover the nearest bus-stop was only a five-minute walk from the unit. A visit ensured the library had adequate resources for her to continue her research and was open until ten at night.

Then there was Saturday. Such an amazing slow boat trip along the coast. The lunch in a restaurant had been pure gourmet while she and Hakim debated what she perceived to be old-fashioned rules, set in a time before modern inventions. The best part of the day? Hakim held her hand while they sat in the cabin and even dared a kiss in her palm. The look in his eyes and warm smile when his soft lips lingered on her skin had sent her innards into turmoil. Even more so when he wrapped her fingers around the kiss.

His men were noticeable by their absence even though they were aboard. The two new bodyguards, his weekend crew, Hakim said, didn't seem to be as friendly as the others she had met. In fact, Hafiz radiated an aura that he didn't like her one little bit since all he did was scowl at her.

The next week had been full despite no dates with Hakim but he managed to phone each day and visited briefly at various times on four nights. And now she was in a limousine, on the way to meet Hakim – destination unknown. A surprise, he had said.

'Miss Anderson, we have arrived.'

Sarah jerked upright, peered through the windows to discover they were parked on the edge of the river. When the rear door opened, she squealed and shrank against the opposite door. Terrified, she scrabbled for the handle so she could get out.

'Sarah.'

The air whooshed from her lungs at Hakim's voice.

'Still you are so afraid. My men will never let you come to harm.' His head appeared, followed by his right hand held out. 'Come.'

Sarah grasped the hand because she was desperate for the security while her heart ceased its attempt to thump out of her chest and the spurt of adrenalin evened out to less than full-on panic mode.

'No crutch?' Hakim smiled.

'No, I can manage without it.' It still hurt but now she could take even steps without the stab of a lance up her leg. Massages had helped, along with the elastic heel-sock she purchased after a conversation with a pharmacist in the local mall. It gave more support than she had expected but was hot to wear.

'Why are we here?' She studied the area. Family groups wandered along the river promenade or gathered to unpack picnics at tables and benches set in a vast grassed area. About two dozen wooden dhows, bedecked in bright lights and banners, were lined up along the bank, each with a gangplank connecting them to land. Even though darkness had settled it was still warm, although a slight breeze had begun to chase away the heat of the day. The soft wind brought with it an aroma of moist dankness.

'Walk beside me.'

Sarah fell into step next to Hakim. She peered around him to find the bodyguards and frowned when she noticed Hafiz but glad Ali was the other.

'No chaperone tonight?' asked Sarah.

Hakim laughed. 'There will be, which frustrates me more than it does you.'

Stunned, Sarah stopped. 'What do you mean?'

He came to a standstill about three metres ahead, turned and came back. 'What do you think it means, sweet Sarah?'

Heat blossomed up her neck. She searched for the right words. 'Umm... oh... maybe...'

'Yes to the maybe.' He spun back around and strode to a dhow where two people greeted him with bows, smiles and wild hand gestures.

When Sarah caught up, a young woman dressed in Arabian Nights' costume led Sarah up the gangplank. Tiny brass bells tied around the teenager's ankle tinkled at each step. Above the scent of river brine, a strong aroma of cooked spices greeted her while the young lady ushered her to a wooden bench-seat behind a table covered in a bright cotton cloth. Three small brass lanterns with lit candles cast flickers of light over the table. She had seen these tourist dhows on the internet and knew they would dine while they sailed along the river and out into the bay. Hakim sat on the other end of her bench so they could see where they were headed while his two bodyguards sat at a forward table on the opposite side of the boat to give them privacy.

It was a surprise when the gangplank lifted for Sarah figured other guests would be needed to fill all the tables. 'We are to dine alone?'

'Of course. People can hire a dhow for private parties.'

'May I watch them cast off?'

'Certainly, you are free to roam, speak to the owners, ask questions. There is a bathroom below deck to the right for the ladies. I might warn you it is not the classiest of bathrooms but adequate.'

'Classy doesn't impress me.' She wriggled from the bench, rose and limped to the edge to watch one of the three men cast off two ropes, toss them aboard then agilely leap across the already small chasm. Even though it was a dhow with sails set, an engine thrummed underfoot, and sent up a waft of diesel. Her limp and the rock of the boat made it a bit unsteady to reach the stern where a second man moved a large wooden tiller from side-to-side as the boat drifted from the dock and settled into a steady stream of other such tourist boats floating down one side of the river. While she made her way along the other side, the aroma of food strengthened until she found the source. A solid structure with bain-maries filled with stainless steel dishes of food, had been uncovered. The colours were amazing as was the aroma but no way could four people eat the amount of food. An older woman, dressed like the younger, stirred the dishes with large ladles.

Hakim joined her. 'Would you like me to explain the ingredients or are you now more familiar with our dishes?'

Sarah peered; sure she knew four. The ever-present lamb/goat stew with couscous. Kebabs gave off a yummy aroma, next to a dish of hummus with vegetable crudites and a bright salad with tomatoes, cucumbers, onion, mint and parsley. She would give a miss to a dish of different seafoods and one of chickpeas, her least favourite eastern food although she didn't mind them mushed up into hummus. 'I think I can make them all out.' She picked up a spoon and scooped two tiny spiced roasted potatoes onto the plate Hakim held out for her.

While they ate, Hakim described the places and buildings as the dhow floated by. The food was delicious, although the goat/lamb stew was again too spicy but she had seconds of her favourite, the tomato salad, a dish she could eat every meal. The commercial variety of sugary drinks were a disappointment, so she settled for unsweetened iced tea.

The younger woman cleared their dishes and returned with a tray laden with a variety of eastern pastries. Saliva pooled at the site of the baklava and what she called honey balls because she couldn't pronounce the real name.

57

'*Katayef.*' Hakim indicated deep fried pancakes folded over. 'There are nuts inside.' His hand moved over. '*Bamiyeh, ghoriba, lgeimat* and you will recognise *baklava.*'

The older woman settled two small plates and a new set of cutlery in front of them. With the small fork, Sarah chose two different pastries she had never eaten before, along with a honey ball and placed them on her plate.

'Your Highness,' the woman said.

Stunned, Sarah eyed Hakim. He caught her glance with a frown across his brow. 'Your Highness?' Mortified, she rose and limped to the stern where she leant over the rail to catch her breath. Sweet mercy, who is this man?

'Sarah,' came from beside her.

'Who are you?' She twisted her head towards Hakim.

'Hakim al Fasir, fourth son of Sheikh Iqbal bin Suhail al Fasir.'

She spun around. 'The ruler of this country?'

'Yes.'

'You lied to me.'

'No, never.'

'But you never mentioned you were, what - a prince?'

'Yes, I am a prince.'

'Why didn't you tell me?'

Hakim settled on the rail with one leg stretched out to keep his balance. 'For these past two weeks, I have enjoyed, beyond measure, the way you treat me as an ordinary man. I have had genuine conversations without you guarding your words or saying what you *think* I want to hear. We even debated points, which most people would never dare do simply because I was born with a title. It is such a joy to have everyday conversations which lack in my life unless I am with my family. Unless you are in my position, you could never understand how incredible it is to be treated the same way you would treat your friends. At first I did not reveal my title because I thought it unnecessary when the meeting would be so brief. Circumstances mean we still meet.'

'Saeed knows who you are?'

'Yes.'

'Which is why he obeyed you.'

'Most likely but surely, now you know me, it should not make a difference. How much I like the person you are, does not change.'

'It makes a huge difference.'

'Why?'

A scoff escaped as Sarah lifted her head to face Hakim. 'You are royalty while I am a foreign commoner.'

'This does not matter to me.'

'It matters to me.'

'Why?'

'To me, all people are equal. I detest the class system where groups of people think they are above others, denigrate those with less opportunity or wealth. Take off our layer of skin and we are all built the same. We all have 206 bones, one heart, two lungs, two kidneys, two legs and arms, a stomach, the same muscle structure, the same alimentary, nervous and circulatory systems. I don't differentiate between races. Yes, some of us have paler skin than others the same way we have different coloured hair and eyes but we are all humans. I accept everyone for who they are as humans and believe we all should but now I will be expected to kowtow to you because of a title.'

'No, please, never do I want that.' He twisted towards her with a definite plea in his eyes. 'Maybe you could practise your beliefs and accept me for who I am as a human. I am just a man who had no choice in parentage. I was born the son of a ruler which means I have certain

59

obligations to my people and my country, which, believe me, is more of a hindrance than you can imagine. I will never have the same freedom you enjoy. I must lead by example, to ensure I never cross the line of our customs and beliefs. In many situations I am unable to say what I would like to say. I had little choice in what career I must follow for it would always be one of leadership. I envy you with your study in science for it is a subject I excelled at and loved during my school years. Many times I detest who I am. You have given me immense joy, allowing me to be a simple man without all the pretence, airs and propriety I usually must endure. You intrigue me, challenge me and are never afraid to argue a point with me, which makes far more intense and detailed conversation than I am used to. Right now I would like to take you in my arms, hold you close and seek the pleasure of your mouth, but I cannot. To do so would land me in a prison cell. I am not above the law but must obey it and be seen to do so.'

Stunned at his honesty, Sarah couldn't draw her eyes away from his face, amazed at the squishy sensation flooding through her innards. 'I... I don't... you want to kiss me?'

'Very much.'

'Oh, I think I might like that.' When the heat rushed up inside her cheeks, she turned away to hide what must be neon redness. 'I don't know what to say but yes, I can accept you for who you are as a human but don't have a clue how I am supposed to be.'

'Be yourself, the amazing woman I met two weeks ago.' He placed one finger on her chin, turned her face towards him and smiled. 'There is no need to be embarrassed because a man finds you desirable.'

'Easy for you to say.' Mortified, she closed her eyes, blew out her cheeks and took a few seconds to force sanity to a body which was in free-fall. 'What am I supposed to call you?' she managed to get out as she opened her eyes and stared at his chest.

'Hakim. It is how I introduced myself. It would give me immense pleasure if you would still use my name without any title. I can even order you to do so but it would not please me. You have given me a wonderful two weeks of a normalcy I have never been able to enjoy before, even while at university in England. There are only another four weeks before you must leave: four weeks I wish to spend with you while I enjoy a few hours of being a normal man, if you could find it in your heart to give me the time.'

Overwhelmed, Sarah buried her face in her hands desperate to sort out confused thoughts.

'Why don't we return to our seats so we can enjoy these sweet treats while you think through my request?'

Confused, Sarah shot him a forced smile. 'Okay.' She turned and went back to the table where she sank back into her seat, lifted the fork and crashed it through the cake-like sweet with a semolina appearance. In one swift move she tore away a corner with a hand determined to replicate an earthquake. Life here sure was full of surprises. Could she do this? Why not? She was an ordinary woman with ordinary needs, wants, desires and likes even though her brain didn't work the ordinary way. She certainly liked Hakim - better than any other guy she had dated. Dated? Were they dating? But since homesickness had already taken hold, she sure needed a friend in this country where she virtually knew no-one else and it was only for another four weeks. But he was a prince, for goodness sake, a real live prince. Sarah Anderson didn't do royalty. If her family found out she had befriended a prince, they would roll on the ground with raucous laughter.

While she chewed, she snuck a peek at him, only to find his eyes centred on her. His worried frown tugged her heart strings tight.

Fear of their hosts thinking the food wasn't good enough if she didn't finish, she forced the honey ball down her throat and shoved the plate to one side. When she noticed Hakim had left a small portion on his plate, she scrolled through her grey matter to search all the data to see whether it was good manners to leave a morsel on her plate as it was with some customs. Unsure, she watched Hakim move his plate aside then sit back while he still eyed her. The small morsel stared right back at her.

'Have you reached a decision?' he asked.

Even though she jerked her eyes up, the glob of pastry still stabbed a message. 'Yes.'

He went rigid. 'Am I to enjoy your company for the next four weeks or will you send me back to the stuffy, mundane, lonely life I must endure because of my parentage?'

'Being royal sounds downright awful so how could I not agree to give you a change for a month?'

His grin was wide as his eyes lit up. 'Thank you.'

Sarah pointed to his plate but quickly flicked her other fingers out when she recalled it was rude to point. 'I think I have done the wrong thing. Am I supposed to leave a small amount on my plate the way one does in the Chinese culture?'

Hakim frowned before a belly laugh rumbled from deep down. 'Only necessary when there is a hard piece of something indigestible wedged in the pastry, although if dining in a private home, a small morsel left on the side indicates you are finished eating. If you continue to clean your plate, your host will continue to serve you.'

Eight

Desperate for contact, Hakim dialled Sarah's number. This five-minute break was about the only spare time he would have until after ten tonight.

'Hello.'

His heart twitched at her voice. 'Sarah, sorry to interrupt your work but I have no time to see you today. My schedule is overfull. What are you and the children up to today?'

'Cooking, or rather we girls are. Rashid has refused since, to him, it's the women's role to cook for the men.'

Hakim laughed at Sarah's imitation of Rashid. 'What have you cooked?'

'We made Aussie-style sandwiches for lunch and are now baking orange cupcakes with spiced syrup topping. Flour, orange zest and eggshells are scattered everywhere but at least we got a laugh from Aliya.'

'Is there a problem with Aliya?'

'She had a melt-down. Hang on, I need privacy.'

There were footsteps, a mumble of voices, a door opened followed by more footsteps.

'Hakim, something about these children doesn't make sense.'

'What do you mean?'

'When I asked if they cooked with their mother, Aliya became inconsolable. I took her into my bedroom to lie down. What she revealed is downright scary. Her mother disappeared over-night. She read each a story, kissed them goodnight but had vanished when the children woke next morning. All her mother's belongings are still in the house, even her handbag and money purse. Who would leave behind their basic credentials if they were to run away?'

'You think she may have come to harm?'

'Maybe, yes, especially since... umm... in the garden, behind the main house, is a slab of new concrete which doesn't seem to have any purpose. Darn it, I may be letting my imagination run riot here but there is one more thing.'

'Spit it out, Sarah,' Hakim demanded after a long pause. He didn't like the pictures in his mind.

'Aliyah is covered in fresh bruises.'

'You think she has been beaten?'

'They are not the kind you get from a mere fall. When I gave her a cuddle she whimpered and shrank into a ball. She let me see her back but wouldn't say what happened. I don't know what to do. No child deserves to be beaten. In my country it is against the law.'

'There is little you can do. Please, do not confront Saeed. Let me think about it. In the meantime, let me speak with Rashid so I can set him right about the need for men to know how to cook.'

'You can cook?'

He laughed. 'Well enough to not starve. I will say goodbye as I have a meeting to get to but will phone again when I can. Please, Sarah, do not speak with Saeed about your concerns. Promise me.'

64

'Okay, I promise but I'm worried about this.'

'So am I. I will have Tariq investigate. Now, Rashid.'

'Okay, bye.'

While he spoke with Rashid about his own culinary skills from university and army days where he would have starved if he had not fended for himself, the only picture in his mind was a lump of concrete. Even before he hung up, he had his computer open to search for street views on the internet. After homing on to the property, he enlarged the square of concrete set in the middle of a larger rectangle of brown sand not far from a narrow stretch of artificial lawn.

'Tariq, what do you think this is for?'

Together they studied the images.

'Could be a base for a shed,' Tariq murmured.

'Small shed and there is already a large shed in the grounds.'

'Why are you interested in this? Is this not the home of Saeed?'

'Yes.'

'I need another clue, my friend.'

'Do you think Sarah is a smart woman?'

'Smarter than most, although she tries to hide her intelligence. Why and what has Sarah got to do with a shed pad?' Tariq placed his hand over the image to gain Hakim's full attention.

Hakim straightened, made eye contact with his best friend and the one man he trusted above all others. 'She is concerned about the children.'

'I still do not see a connection.'

'I need you to find out exactly when this concrete was laid and by whom. If Sarah's theory is correct, it was laid the day after Saeed's wife disappeared.'

Tariq reeled backwards. His eyes flared and mouth opened and closed again on silence. 'She thinks there is a body beneath the concrete?' he finally managed to get out.

'It would explain the missing mother.' A knock interrupted him. 'Come.' The door opened to reveal his trusted and over-worked personal assistant.

'Sir, your guest has arrived.'

'Give me a minute.' When the door closed again Hakim continued. 'I am concerned about Sarah's safety. If what she says is true and Saeed finds out about her suspicions, she is in danger.' He repeated all Sarah had told him.

'I believe Sarah means more to you than you have let on.'

'After my final prayers last night, the reason for Sarah's presence in our country was revealed to me. Allah sent her for he knows she is the right woman for me.'

'You want to marry her?' Tariq's shock turned to a grin. 'About time my friend but she is not Muslim.'

'Which has an easy solution. The Christian and Muslim teachings are not so different. Conversion for a woman is not difficult nor uncommon.'

'What will your family think if you marry a westerner?'

'My grandmother was Spanish. This will not be of concern especially since there is little chance I will ever be leader, thank goodness.' He laughed. 'They will be delighted I have finally found a wife.'

'True but what does Sarah think of this?'

'Ah, I think it may take more than the time we have left for Sarah to develop sufficient trust in me to agree. I am certain she has little trust of men after a traumatic event. Surely you must think the same.'

'Always she peeks over her shoulder, startles at sudden approaches and sits or stands with her back to the wall so she can see everyone around her. Her eyes show her fear.'

66

'Yes. Now I must go. I will be busy for the rest of the day. See what you can find out about Saeed, his wife and any dealings he has had in the past month or so. Mahmoud can stay guard since I will be in this building all day.' Already late, Hakim strode to the door but turned back before he tugged the door open. 'Organise for Shahir to covertly guard Sarah tonight.'

'All night?'

'Yes until his shift ends. By then it will be light.'

Nine

Twelve men bickered around the oval table. Normally Hakim would step in to demand only one speak at a time, to guide them to a consensus but his own mind refused to concentrate on the new legislation. Visions of Sarah and a concrete slab kept invading. Yesterday's continual round of meetings had run overtime which made him late for the formal dinner shared with fellow Ministers. Exhaustion had set in by the time he drove home. Even so, he had driven past Sarah's unit, in hope she was still awake but a chat with Shahir at the corner, confirmed Sarah had turned her lights off an hour earlier. He would never disturb her sleep.

Shahir recounted in detail the heated exchange shouted through Sarah's closed door. Saeed was not happy Sarah had spent private time with his youngest child and demanded to know every word of the conversation. The only logical reason to make such a demand was a guilty conscience. But it seemed Sarah was clever in her answers, saying only what was needed to placate the man.

'Your Highness!'

Hakim spun around at the shout. Tariq hurried into the meeting, which he would never do unless it was of vital importance.

'Tariq?'

'Sir, my apologies but it is urgent.' As he hurried down the room, Hakim's heart rate increased to a gallop. Tariq held out his mobile phone. 'You must read this.'

Hakim took the phone, cast his eyes down and read.

Pls help me. Where is Hakim? S.

R U OK? Tariq had asked.

No.

RU you hurt?

Yes.

Where RU?

In my room.

With his heart like a thousand drums, Hakim glanced at Tariq. 'Get the car.' He turned to twelve sets of eyes. 'Gentlemen, an emergency has arisen. I must go. Take over,' he added to his second-in-command. He ran with one hand shoved in the pocket of his robe in search of his own mobile phone which he always switched off in such meetings. Sarah must have tried to message him. It wasn't until he sat in the car he was able to flick to the message from Sarah.

H. Pls help me. S - said the first message. A second followed a minute later, then a third and fourth. None gave him even a hint as to what was wrong. His mind pictured ghastly images of an injured Sarah. Even though Tariq ignored speed restrictions it seemed way too slow.

Tariq careened around the final corner, yanked the wheel left, spun into the driveway, jammed his foot on the brake pedal when they were met by Saeed's car on the way out. The man's face turned to shock as the two cars neared each other. Tariq managed to yank the wheels around and spin into a broadside to block the driveway entrance.

Hakim shoved the door open and ran. 'Where is Sarah?' He yanked the other man's door open.

Saeed straightened with his face in a sneer. 'Gone.'

'Excuse me?'

'She quit this morning. Said she was flying home. Had a taxi here and left. If you will excuse me, your Highness, I have to get my children to my sister.'

Hakim peered further into the car where three pale faces stared at him from between an inordinate amount of belongings packed around them. All three gave the impression they were in shock while every bag and toy shouted at him.

'Out,' he ordered Saeed, leant in and grabbed the neck of the other man's kandourah. He didn't care how much he hurt the man while he dragged him out and shoved him against the side of the car.

'Mahmoud take care of the children. Tariq get Sarah's spare key,' he ordered before he spun around to Saeed. 'You dare lie to me.' The punch to the man's gut was not light. He folded to the ground like a concertina, where Hakim planted a foot in the small of his back so he had no chance to get up.

When Tariq held out the key, Hakim took it. 'Deal with this coward who dares lie to me.' Hakim turned away and sprinted to Sarah's door, jammed in the key, tugged on the handle only to find the room empty except for a trail of blood across the tiles. Adrenalin spurted at the same rate his breath gushed out.

'Sarah,' he yelled when he managed to suck in enough air to formulate words.

A faint whimper answered. He followed the sound to find Sarah crouched behind the bathroom door, a kitchen

71

knife in each hand, ready to attack. Wild eyes stared between streaks of blood down her face while waves of tremors followed each other down her body. He knelt on the floor, reached out slowly.

'Sarah.'

A whimper squeaked out. She tightened her grip on the knives and tensioned as though ready to attack.

'Sarah, drop the knives. Tariq has Saeed and Mahmoud has the children. You are safe now.' He reached out, placed his hand on her tense arm and ignored the shiver which raced down her body. Still she did not relax.

'Sarah, it is Hakim.' He managed to place his hands over her wrists and ease the knives from white knuckles. Unable to find words, he stared, too afraid to speak in case Sarah still didn't realise who he was.

He held up his hand to prevent Mahmoud coming closer. 'Call an ambulance and police then wait outside.'

He turned back to Sarah who began to blink. 'Sarah?'

'Hakim?'

He plonked onto the floor opposite her, wrapped his arms around bent knees to show he meant no harm. 'Do you trust me?'

'Y… y… yes.'

He held out one hand, palm up. 'Your answer sends joy to my heart. Take my hand.' He thought it would take a while but her hand shot out and gripped hard, followed by the rest of her body as she launched herself at him and sent him flat on his back. It took a few seconds to untangle limbs but finally he sat on the floor leant up against the wall with Sarah in his lap. She clung like a limpet: a trembling limpet with fingers gripped into his shoulders. Her unbridled fear terrified him.

'First, are you all right?'

72

'Mostly,' she mumbled against his chest. The tension from her fingers eased a fraction.

'Mostly does not tell me enough. Where are you hurt?'

'Only my head.'

'Which is covered in blood. This does not ease my worry. Let me check.' With a hand each side of her face, he eased her away to find the source of the blood. There was a large gash above her temple with the skin already indigo and swollen. He knew he would not like the cause. 'Please tell me exactly what happened.'

'He tricked me.' She peeked up at him but her eyes skittered sideways. 'The swish of tyres indicated the car had left. The children knocked a minute later. I opened the door but it wasn't the children. Saeed swung a hard object at me, caught me on the side of the head, shoved me inside, yelled and screamed obscenities. He was... was... said it was his right to enjoy the same favours I give you since he brought me here.'

Hakim closed his eyes on a groan. It was difficult to swallow down the block of wood lodged in his throat. No words would be adequate. He had failed to keep her safe. 'He will pay for his crime. I am sorry, sweet Sarah, for not giving you the protection I promised.'

Sarah eased back a little. 'You have...' Sirens sounded.

'Much as I enjoy holding you in my arms, I must set you on your feet for we are about to be invaded by police officers and paramedics.' He dared a kiss on her bloodied brow. Her eyes rounded in surprise. 'I have ached to kiss you since the day we met but would prefer your sweet mouth. Sadly, now is not the time.'

At the sound of footsteps, Sarah struggled upright but swayed. He held out his hands to steady her until she leant against the wall but still her body wavered. 'Sit here.' With one arm around her shoulders he settled her on the lid of the commode. Ready to catch her, he took his time to step far enough away for it to be acceptable. Sometimes he detested their customs although with Sarah injured, it would not be inappropriate to hold her upright.

While paramedics examined Sarah and treated her injuries, Hakim joined the furore outside.

'She accosted me, begged for sex,' Saeed repeated over and over while he struggled to free himself from Tariq's hold.

The accusation was so ridiculous Hakim laughed. 'I doubt Sarah would plead for sex with three young children present. Maybe you can explain the injury to her head.'

'She hit it on the door when I fought her off.'

Hakim laughed again and made of show of sauntering towards the door. 'Since her head is covered in blood, there would be blood on the door or maybe the frame.' He made an issue of inspecting both items which were clear of any red bloody stain.

'I cleaned it off.'

'Your contract states you are never to come to her door, yet you admit you did. Surely you realise forensic tests will find minute traces of blood if they are there. What the officers will find is the trail of blood through Sarah's unit to the bathroom where I found her crouched on the floor, too terrified to move. She would not be in such a state if she were the instigator. She would have fled. Yet it was you who was in the process of fleeing. The officers will also search for the fabric you say you used to clean the woodwork and the hard object you hit her with to cause the injury. While they do their search I might suggest they dig up the concrete pad in the back garden. Take the man away.' A grin broke out at Saeed's sudden pallor. Hakim turned, anxious to see Sarah.

She was still undergoing treatment in the bathroom but now there was a large swab over her wound with strips of tape to hold it in place. Most of the blood had been washed away.

'Please tell me the extent of Sarah's injuries?' he asked the man knelt on the floor, who was packing up his medical kit.

'Stitches are needed, an x-ray to the head to check for fractures or internal bleeding. Possible concussion.'

'It's against the law in my country for medico's to reveal any medical condition to anyone other than direct family. I'm okay.' Sarah sent a fierce glare towards Hakim.

He grinned back. 'As it is here. My apologies but I will accept the opinion of a trained doctor after a thorough examination at the best hospital in the city as to whether *okay* is his diagnosis.' He issued orders in Arabic to ensure Sarah was given a private room in his name before he turned back to face her. 'While you undergo treatment I will organise care for the children and speak with the police officers about your concerns with the concrete. Then, I will come to the hospital for the medical report.' He smiled at Sarah, nodded to the paramedics and left, taking a huge gulp of air to re-inflate lungs which had forgotten how to work properly. Guilt was strong for not keeping Sarah safe but anger at Saeed overwhelmed him. Give him five minutes alone with the man. He would tear Saeed apart and bury the pieces in a remote area of the desert or maybe leave them for the falcons to shred.

Ten

E very item in her room had been read and committed to memory. Now her overactive brain was in the process of driving her nuts. The English news channel was on its umpteenth repeat of headlines, none of them cheerful.

With Saeed in prison and the children in the care of a relative, Sarah hadn't yet figured what to do, workwise. No way could she stay in the unit since it was a crime scene, Hakim said when he called in last night. While she searched for another job it was possible to return to the hotel she had first stayed in but it would eat into her savings. A week would be fine but longer could be a problem. To return home would be a last resort since the police in Sydney hadn't yet tracked down the man who wanted her dead. Without hesitation, Mum and Dad would send her as much money as she needed but she would never ask.

At the knock on the door, she swung her head around but grimaced at the pain from the sudden movement. 'Come in.' A smile broke out at the sight of Hakim.

'How are you today?'

'Much better, thank you but I need to get out of here.'

'Why?'

'I'm about to go crazy sitting idle.'

'You will sit idle whether you are in here or not. The crack on your head was nasty along with the many bruises you failed to tell me about.'

'How did…'

He indicated the\r treatment card tucked into a metal tray at the foot of the bed. 'The doctor insists on a few days rest but has given permission for your rest to be elsewhere.' He held out a small bag. 'Mariam packed a change of clothes but the hospital gown is…' he cocked his head and smiled. 'Enticing.'

Sarah glanced down, tugged at the thin cotton, dragged the sheet up over her outlined breasts and ignored Hakim's smile while desperate to not blush.

'I will give you five minutes to dress.' He turned and left.

Frustrating man, Sarah thought, as she threw the covers back. But he was also gorgeous, likeable, kind and gentle. It was a struggle to get upright, especially when she had to grab the side of the bed until the dizziness subsided before she was able to shuffle across the room to the en suite. Dressed, she bent over to do up the sandal straps and had to swallow down the wave of nausea but breakfast managed to stay down. Hakim knocked and entered. Too bad if she was still in the process of dressing which had been difficult with her head like a kettle drum at the slightest movement. The painkiller she had refused to take with breakfast hadn't yet dissolved in her stomach - one minute not long enough for it to have taken effect.

Unease crept across her shoulders at the way Hakim studied her.

'You are too pale. Maybe you should stay another twenty-four hours.'

'No, I'm fine.' To prove it, she stood, passed Hakim, stalked through the doorway and kept on past both bodyguards spaced out along the empty corridor. It was fortunate the car was parked right outside the automatic glass doors of the reception area. Had she paused, she would have folded to the ground.

Hakim eased onto the seat next to her after her less than elegant crawl into the car while she ordered her stomach to not heave.

'Your pallor has changed from pale to green. Sit back, relax, close your eyes. If you are unwell, let me know, preferably before you throw up.' His hand patted hers before long fingers wove through in a tight grip which went some way to settle her innards. This man could annoy her with his high-handedness but one brief touch, or a simple glance, her body went all mushy. When her head was clearer she'd figure out why.

Sarah tried all three of his suggestions but had to open her eyes when her sense of balance became skewed. 'Where are we going?' she asked when neither the street nor buildings outside appeared familiar.

'To my home.'

Her head shot around towards him. 'Excuse me?' The insides of her head yo-yoed at the sudden movement.

'You cannot live in the unit. It is not possible to gain access to any part of the property since your guess was correct about the concrete. Under the watchful eye of police officers, Mariam packed all of your possessions.'

'Saeed murdered his wife?' Sarah had to cough to clear the squeak from her voice while her mind went on a rampage. Would she have joined the body under the concrete if she hadn't taken those classes in self-defence? Horrified, she tugged her hand free, swept both hands up to her face and buried it in shock.

'It is more than likely but not yet proven. An autopsy will be done today.' Hakim retrieved her right hand, wrapped his fingers around it. 'I regret I did not insist you not take the job but there was little I could do. It was a private matter. I had no right to interfere but now my guilt for the attack on you, is unforgivable.'

'The only person guilty is the perpetrator. I knew the man couldn't be trusted, had serious doubts about the job but I had to fulfill the conditions of my visa and really, had no-where else to go at short notice.'

'Which is why my home is the best place to stay until we can sort what to do next. You need time to recuperate.'

'A hotel will be fine.'

'My home gives you better protection.'

'With Saeed in jail, I won't need protection.'

'You wish to argue with me?'

'Yes.'

The shout of laughter echoed through the car. 'Very well, we will argue but only after we reach home and your pallor returns to a healthy colour. In the meantime relax for I have phone calls to make.'

It was impossible to relax with Hakim's deep voice and the rhythm of husky Arabic words. When the car slowed and turned into a large circular concrete driveway, Sarah stared at the two-storey mansion seated behind lush greenery at the centre of the drive-way arch.

'What do you think of my home?'

'It's huge but not as big as I thought it would be. I figured royalty lived in massive palaces.'

'My parents live in the palace with my oldest brother and his family. I have my own rooms there but prefer a more modest home.'

When the car drew to a halt, both bodyguards alighted and opened both rear doors at the same time. She eased out and rose slowly so her head didn't spin.

It was a surprise when Hakim grasped her elbow. 'Before we go inside. If Saeed attacked you inside the unit, how did you manage to lock him out?'

She sighed and paused. How to answer? 'No matter how big and strong a man is, he has one vulnerable spot. After the… after what happened in Sydney I took lessons in how to escape various holds and to attack that one spot.' She tugged free and mounted the steps.

Polished marble tiles paved the long covered veranda and huge entry-hall which led into a vast formal room. It was like a show room, with every item so perfect she figured no-one would dare sit in one of the four double sofas in case they left a crease or dip.

Hakim drew her to a halt. 'I will take heed of your words. This is the main room, where I entertain guests. The passage to the left has two bedrooms for unmarried men only. You cannot go there. The central passage leads to my private rooms, also out of bounds. Through the arch to the side you can see the dining room where I eat my meals. I have breakfast at seven. Rarely am I home for lunch but eat at one if I am. My evening meal is at seven if I am home which is only two or three nights a week. The kitchen is beyond the dining room. Also a laundry.' Hakim dropped her elbow and indicated with his hand towards a third passage. 'This leads to the unmarried women's rooms. Upstairs contains a suite of rooms for a married couple or family but is rarely used. In fact it is rare for any of the rooms, apart from mine, to be used. Come, I will show you where you are to stay before I must go for I have many meetings to attend.'

This time he took her hand and led her to the end of the third passage where he opened an ornate door painted in a soft gold with darker trim. 'You are to stay in this room.' An open hand indicated for her to precede him.

'I am to stay in here?' Troubled by the implication, Sarah stepped in, overawed by the elegance of the huge bedroom with a section at one side filled with a sofa and large flat screen television. A small bar fridge sat nestled under a long bench on which sat the implements and ingredients for hot beverages. It was more like a luxury hotel suite.

'Yes.'

'What if I need a bathroom?'

'Behind the blue door is an en suite with all you will need.'

With her mind like a maelstrom, Sarah limped across the room to a set of French doors which led to a courtyard. 'Am I permitted to go out there?'

'Of course. There is a pool behind the gate to the right. You are free to use the pool at any time.'

When Sarah turned to study the room, she noticed her suitcase on the end of the bed. She unzipped it, lifted the lid to find only her clothes neatly folded inside. 'Not all of my possessions are here.'

Hakim stood beside her. 'I will send Mariam. Tell her what is missing. I must go. I cannot be late for government meetings. I will not be home until late tonight and will be gone early tomorrow. Try to rest. The doctor will call in sometime in the morning to check your wound.'

Sarah stared after him. What happened to the man who was kindness personified but was now so terse? And why did she have to stay in this room? Was she to be hidden away? Could it be inappropriate for her to live here when they were both unmarried? Miffed, she unlocked the French doors and stepped outside. A waft of hot air singed her lungs. The small courtyard was private to the two bedrooms. Bougainvillea covered walls enclosed the entire area apart from a wooden slatted gate which she presumed lead to the pool. A group of five mature palms shaded a small square of lawn surrounded on all sides by a slabbed pathway. Modern outdoor chairs and tables sat evenly spaced along the veranda of the bedrooms with two wooden benches set amongst the palms. It was plain but pretty.

'Miss Anderson.'

Sarah spun around. Mariam stood in the open doorway, her mouth a stern, thin line.

'The Prince asked me to find some missing items. If you could tell me what they are I will find them for you.'

'Six oranges, six apples, one pomegranate, a large bag of mixed salad greens, a kilo of tomatoes, half a kilo of cheddar cheese, a tub of yoghurt, one box of muesli, three boxes of crackers, a jar of pickles, a bag each of roasted almonds and pistachio nuts, one kilo of dates, two Lebanese cucumbers, a box of tea bags, a jar of instant coffee and a litre of milk.'

Mariam's eyes popped wide and her jaw dropped. 'The food, I put in the kitchen.'

'Why? It's my food. I will need it here or am I supposed to starve while a prisoner?'

Mariam frowned before her lips thinned. 'I will fetch the food.'

'Thank you, I appreciate it.' But I'm as upset as you, she wanted to add. Miffed, she returned to the room and took out the first pile of clothes to find a brief home for them.

Eleven

A mixture of satisfaction and indignation stirred. Hakim shoved the front door open: glad to be home but disgruntled at the continual round of work and royal duties he'd had to endure over the past thirty-six hours with only time for five hours in his bed. At last he would get a chance to spend time with Sarah but only because he cancelled yet another meal with associates. He must find a way to lessen the load of his crazy full schedule.

Puzzled at the silence, he strode towards his room, tugged off his keffiyeh, tossed the fabric into the laundry basket, added his kandourah and stepped into the shower stall under a full blast of warm water. He sighed in pleasure, lathered soap over his body to rid it of the day's heat and grime and rinsed off under chilly water. Even though he shivered at the sudden cold, he also appreciated it.

Dressed in white linen slacks and a loose cotton shirt he hurried to the dining room, eager to share a meal with Sarah. At the door he stopped mid-stride to see the table set for only one and the room empty.

'Mariam,' he called, with a glance at the gold watch on his wrist. It was barely after seven so where was everyone?

'Food is ready.' Mariam bustled in with two hot dishes. The rich spiced steam enticed his juices to flow.

'Where is Sarah?'

'In her room.'

'Why is she not here? Please will you fetch her?'

With a deep a frown, Mariam placed the two dishes in front of his plate, turned and hurried across the room. While she was gone, he paced, paused at the window, stared out at the garden but took no notice of the objects outside.

'Sir, Sarah says she must stay in her room.'

'Excuse me? Why?'

'Your orders.'

'My what? Has Sarah not come out at all?'

'No. She walks in the courtyard for thirty minutes, swims laps for thirty minutes, retires to her room for an hour. Over and over she repeats all day.'

'Has she not come out to eat?'

'No, sir.'

'At all since she arrived?'

'No, sir.'

'You did take meals to her.'

'No, sir. She had food from her unit.'

'Set another place next to mine.' He stalked along the passage and pounded on Sarah's door. It took too long to open. He was about to turn the polished brass handle when it twisted. Sarah stood there. Even with a black eye and stitched gash her beauty stood out, as did the wariness, as if she was afraid.

'Why have you not come out for your meals?'

'You said I was to stay in this room.' Her arms folded in a defiant stance but a glaze of moisture swept across her eyes.

'I did not mean you could never come out.'

'I asked to check. You said I was to stay in here but gave permission for me to go into the courtyard and pool area. I obeyed your orders.'

'Sarah, I did not mean…' he swept a hand down his face. 'What I meant was… this is your room while you are here, where you can have privacy, to bathe and sleep. You are free to use the rest of the house as if it were your own home.'

'Why do you say words you don't mean?' When she turned her head away Hakim was certain she was close to tears.

'Surely you understood what I meant.'

'I understand what you *said*. I am not stupid but already you confuse me again. Now you say I'm free to use the rest of the house but yesterday I was not permitted to enter either of the other passageways.'

Frustrated, Hakim grasped Sarah by her shoulders and drew her closer. 'Never would I think you to be stupid. You are one of the smartest women I have ever met. And you are right, I have given you mixed messages for, since you are unmarried, you cannot enter the other two passages but apart from those the rest of my house is available to you. Now, I cancelled dinner with associates tonight because I wanted to spend the evening with you. Will you please join me for our meal?' When he tipped her face up, the sadness in her eyes sent his heart into a tumble-turn. He dared a kiss on her brow, grasped her hand and tugged gently until she followed.

Even though Sarah ate little, her company eased the tension he had lived with for the past few days but he was concerned about her silence and lack of appetite. 'Surely you need to eat more.'

'No.'

Irritation simmered at her answer. He set his cutlery aside. Another track might break her prim, pointed responses. 'Did the doctor come?' In an attempt to appear nonchalant, he lifted his glass of water, took a sip.

'Yes.'

'What did he say?'

'My wound has begun to heal well. There is no need for him to see me again until the stitches are removed six days from today.' With her eyes downcast and hands in her lap, she appeared demure and scared.

'Do you think you should get the wound wet with all your swimming?' Hakim grinned when Sarah turned her head towards the kitchen. It was obvious she understood where the information came from. He took another sip.

'Your spy misinforms you for the wound doesn't get wet.'

He choked on the water. 'My spy?' he spluttered after he managed to force the water down his throat.

'She watches me through the window when I exercise in the yard or swim – breaststroke. It's obvious she relates to you what she sees. A spy.'

'Maybe she is concerned about you.'

'No. Mariam doesn't approve of me or my presence.'

'What makes you think Mariam disapproves?'

'There is a well-used adage in my country, *actions speak louder than words*. Her angry face and folded arms tell me far more than her non-existent words.'

Unsure what to say, Hakim indicated the plates of food. 'Would you like more or maybe a sweet?'

'No thank you.' She actually cracked a smile, which sent a shaft of warmth through him.

'How about we retire to the sitting room?'

Surprise lit up her face. 'You have a sitting room?'

'Of course.' He stood, pulled back her chair and grinned at her stunned face. 'Come.' He held out his hand and was delighted when she slipped her warm fingers into it and curled them around his. A small step but it was definite progress.

She stalled in the archway. 'You call this a sitting room?'

Hakim turned to face her. 'Yes, what would you call it?'

She shrugged as her eyes journeyed around the room. 'A display of precious artifacts like in some famous historical museum where one can look but don't dare touch any item.'

'Nothing in here is precious to me so pick up, put down, sit on or move all of it.' Still with her hand in his, he continued into the room, paused at a sofa. As he sat, he tugged her to sit next to him but she resisted. Her glance held uncertainty. 'You do not wish to sit next to me?'

She bit her lower lip. The tiny action managed to stir his body to attention. 'What about the rules?'

'What rules?' Intrigued, he waited for her answer.

'No physical contact.'

Hakim tried to stifle his laugh without success. 'This is my home where I can do as I please. About the only place there are no restrictions but if you prefer to keep your distance,' he swept one arm around the room. 'Take your pick.' There was a tightness in his chest while she eyed each seat in turn. Now he regretted he had given her the choice but he had to remember her fear which surely had intensified with Saeed's attack. The tightness in his chest snapped away when Sarah finally settled on the end of his sofa although she would fall off the end if she were any further away.

With rigid back, Sarah's hands folded in her lap with her eyes staring at the blank television screen.

'Sarah.'

Her head turned. 'Yes.'

'You trusted me enough to crawl into my lap when I found you in the bathroom, you seem happy to hold my hand yet now you appear to not trust me at all. I understand your mistrust of men because of unpleasantness they have meted out to you but I will never go beyond what you permit. Yes, I would like us to become closer but only at a rate you can manage. I will not pressure you. If you do not wish to further our relationship, please tell me and I promise to back off but I would be disappointed.'

'You want more?' Her eyes swung to catch his before they shifted a fraction but the tension in her body seemed to relax a little.

'Very much. I am certain I mentioned how much you intrigue me.' A scoff escaped as he rested back into the soft cushions. 'I doubt you would believe the number of meetings and functions I have cut short, re-scheduled or cancelled since the day we met so I could spend a few minutes with you. You have also caused me to forget my words in meetings because visions of you appear, which take my mind away from important matters. You caused my heart to forget how to beat when I read your messages on Tariq's phone.' He reached out, took her hand and wriggled closer. 'My parents have introduced me to many suitable women since I turned twenty and not one has affected me the way you do so yes, I very much want more.'

'Oh… um… I was unsure. I don't know what to say.' Her grip tightened as she squirmed and ended up a tiny bit closer with her body brushed against his.

'Let us discuss your feelings?'

Her eyes shot to his. 'My feelings?'

'Are you afraid of me as you are with other men? Be honest.'

'I am always honest. The answer is no.'

'Your answer pleases me. Do you trust me?'

'Yes, which is why I am here in your home. With any other man, I would never have even got into his car.'

Hakim's heart swelled to a level he thought was impossible to endure. 'Thank you. I will not betray your trust. Would you like me to show you more of our city?'

'You are too busy.'

'Is there any place in particular you would like to see or experience?'

'Number one on my list is the desert.'

Surprised, Hakim turned towards her and managed to edge even closer. 'The desert? Why?'

'I love Australia's remote areas: the outback, we call it. I love the silence, the solitude, the stark beauty, the colours. Here, I would like to collect soil samples, examine them under a microscope, see what the desert is made up from. Do you like to be out in the desert?'

Hakim laughed. 'I am an Arab. The desert is in my blood. Let me see what I can arrange.'

Sarah's face twisted into a frown. 'You are a busy man. I don't want to interfere with your life. Guilt already eats at me for the time you have given me.'

'Sarah, I have a schedule that scares even me but it is one I filled with appointments because work and functions fill the hours of a lonely man. I have already given my personal assistant the task to free up time over the next few weeks while you are here.' He dared to wrap his arm around her shoulders, waited to see her reaction with a held breath but smiled when she relaxed against him. One more step.

'Are there any places in the city you would like to see?'

'Surprise me.' When she turned her head towards him her mouth was mere centimetres from his. Every atom in his body spun around on its axis.

'I am about to kiss you unless you draw away this very instant,' he murmured and dropped his head. She did not

91

move so he swept his mouth over hers. Male hormones went on a rampage in an instant. One sweep was nowhere near enough. He cupped her face with both hands, deepened the kiss, swallowed her sigh. The slow burn which had smouldered since the day they met, flared into an inferno. Logic told him this was a bad idea with such differences in their culture. But surely, with this natural and strong arc of attraction between them, it could not be wrong.

Her body twisted further towards him, both hands swept up his chest. His blood boiled in an instant. When she gripped his shoulders and opened her sweet mouth in invitation, he had no power to ignore her. Her mouth was soft, hot and wet. The spices of their meal latched onto his tongue. The pressure of her soft breasts against his hard chest tortured him. He shifted, skated his hand down her spine and drew her closer still.

Sarah pulled away a fraction on a gasp to take in some air. He caught her wide eyes. They glowed, the amber a deeper hue. Her mouth was slick and swollen from his kiss. Her eyes dropped to his mouth a split second before she leant forwards and brushed his mouth in the sweetest of kisses. It was not enough. He wanted more but at the moment she was out of bounds, although he would do all in his power to develop a closer relationship – much closer. It took what was left of his willpower to release her and draw back. Surprise filled her eyes before her lids hid them.

'One of us has to leave,' he whispered through a throat which found it difficult to work.

'Why?' Her head was low.

A wry laugh escaped. 'You need to ask why? Surely you are not so naïve. I may be a prince but I am also a normal red-blooded man whose body turns to fire when he is kissed with such delectable passion. I must leave now or there is every chance we will end up naked on this sofa, locked together and I am sure we will both regret it.' He stood on shaky legs he doubted would hold him upright. He managed to take three steps towards his private quarters.

'You would regret making love with me?'

He stopped dead, tunnelled a hand through his hair. 'Never.'

'Then why did you say so? No, don't answer for I know I am not good enough for you.'

He turned slowly, stunned at the sadness in her voice. 'You are perfect for me but we barely know each other.' Not sure what to say he shook his head in an effort to bring clarity. 'I would like nothing better than to take you to my bed but am not prepared to make the mistake of taking you too soon, for you to discover this obvious attraction between us is only a mere flirtation, although to me it is no flirtation. I have never had such a strong connection with a woman before but I have no wish to hurt you if either of us discover this is not right. Too much pain has already been served to you by men who had no respect for you. We both need time: time to spend together, to learn about each other, to see how far we want to take this relationship.'

There was a long silence before Sarah moved. 'Okay, what you say makes sense. I agree.' Her smile was timid as she stood, turned and strode towards her room. 'But I like the bit about perfect,' she added over her shoulder before she vanished.

Twelve

Mortified, Sarah buried her head in her hands with her back slumped against the back of the door. Every fragment of her DNA trembled from shock and disbelief. Did she really say those words? Never before had she been so daring. And to kiss him. Sweet mercy.

Already she had figured it was dangerous to have such intense connection to this man: a connection she couldn't explain - but it was there. He was a prince, for goodness sake, but there was no way she could deny the attraction between them; almost as though they were magnets – the north and south – positive and negative – with the iron filings aligned in synchronicity.

There had been kisses with guys before but none had ever scrambled her brain the way Hakim's did. Not only her brain: all of her innards had turned into scrambled eggs. And for the first time ever, the thought of a hot and close-up physical relationship didn't give her the heebie-jeebies.

Unable to stay upright, she slithered to the ground, swept arms around bent knees, her mind stuck on one thought. She wanted Hakim – man to woman, naked and joined. Wonderment followed disbelief. Could she be in love with the man? Was it possible after such a brief time? Yet why did she instinctively trust this one man when she trusted no other, not even his security guards whom Hakim depended on for his life.

In a daze, she managed to stand, stumble to the bathroom, carry out basic toiletries, drag on pyjama shorts and tug the top over her head. Stretched out under the sheet, she figured she would never be able to sleep with her mind on repeat of the scene on the sofa and the sensation of his kiss: over and over and over.

At a loud splash she bolted upright, glanced around. A muffled groan followed. The pool. Someone had fallen in the pool. It took mere seconds to get the glass door open and race to the gate. Soft splashes eased her panic. Whoever it was must be swimming but maybe the sounds are of a struggle? She grappled with the gate, managed to stumble through but came to a standstill at the sight of a naked man pounding through the water. Mesmerised, she watched muscled limbs swim lap after lap as though the devil chased on his heels.

'Go to bed.' Hakim had stilled and stood chest deep at the end nearest her.

'Why?'

He groaned, lifted his eyes and stared. 'So I can get out without offending you.'

It was impossible to stifle a grin. 'I fail to see how I would be offended. You are a beautiful man.'

'Women are beautiful – not men.' He waded a little closer to the edge, revealed another few inches of his magnificent body but it also put the area below his waist out of sight.

'Rodin's sculptures and the statue of David are considered to be masterpieces of beauty.' She dared step closer but paused when he held up one hand. 'David represents a man with broad shoulders and a chest outlined with the muscle structure of a very fit man. It tapers down to a well-honed abdomen and long, powerful legs. The beauty is in the structure of the man. If Rodin or Michelangelo were around now, I think they might choose you as their model.' Embarrassed to the nth degree, she spun around. 'Good night, sleep well.'

There was a string of mumbled words and a few splashes while she stumbled to the gate. She managed to escape through but her arm was grabbed. The moment she was spun back around, her mouth was covered in a hot, wet kiss. A zing of adrenalin shot through her veins and zapped her body as though electricity. His lips were hot beneath the wash of water which still dripped from his skin. He held her face steady, his big hands against her cheeks, long fingers threaded through her hair. His lips moved over hers, his tongue ran across the seam of her mouth. She opened her lips on a gasp. He took advantage and the sensual friction of tongue against tongue sent a sharp pang of raw need through her before it settled in her core.

It was a shock when he jerked back, released her and rubbed a hand down his own face. 'I have never forced myself on a woman but you make it almost impossible to resist the temptation. Please, Sarah, go to bed.' His husky voice was more of a plea than an order. He turned and walked away so fast his feet pounded on the tiles.

She stared after him, noticed he had managed to wrap a towel around his waist. He scooped up the pile of discarded clothes and disappeared around the corner. Still in a daze,

Sarah stumbled back to the bedroom, where she changed her saturated top. In bed she was certain sleep was not about to happen.

It was a surprise when her eyes opened to a shaft of light square in her face. When she twisted sideways, she realised she hadn't drawn the blinds across the French doors. This early was the only time the fierce sun managed to penetrate into the room for clever design meant most rooms in the house were protected from direct rays. A necessity in this forever hot climate.

Even though lethargy lingered, Sarah rose and took the shower she missed last night, determined to not think about the kisses or her forward behaviour. She needed to concentrate on some inane subject – certainly not last night's events. After she pulled on an outfit for the day she opened her laptop, logged on to the emails where she was able to concentrate on those from her family. Long answers about what she had seen and done minus the bits like stitches - and attacks - and how she now lived with a prince - filled an hour. Do not mention the kisses, she ordered her brain, which seemed to want to force the sensation to the forefront. First, they would never believe her after a lifetime of her denigration of the class system and she'd never been complimentary about royalty. If only they knew but they never would because they would never think to ask, which meant she would never have to tell them.

At a loud knock, she dropped the lid, crossed the room to open the door. Every cell in her body stood to attention at the sight of Hakim, dressed in a kandourah.

'Why are you not at breakfast?'

'Huh?'

'Breakfast is at seven.'

Confused, Sarah could only stare at his chest until her brain caught up. 'For you, yes. I know. You told me.' Where was the man from last night? Today he seemed so terse, the exact opposite to the man who kissed her with such passion.

'So, why are you not at the table?'

'I wasn't invited.'

'Invited? I gave you the times of all the meals.'

'You gave me the times when *you* ate.'

'I gave the times so you would know when meals are served.' A hand brushed down his face. 'Why do you take comments so literally?'

'Because it's the way my brain works. Not once did you mention I was to eat at those times. Nor did you say I was welcome to join you at your meals. My parents drummed into me at an early age to never eat at someone else's place unless I receive an invitation. When you utter words you don't mean it confuses me.' Not sure what to say or do she turned back into the room, one hand on the door, ready to shut it in his face. The moisture of tears rushed across her eyes but to let them fall she needed privacy. When the door didn't move, she turned back. A frown had settled across his face. A foot was wedged against the door.

'Do you honestly think I would invite you to stay in my home and not allow you to eat? The invitation is a tacit one but to ensure you understand, I invite you to dine at the times I gave. Whenever you are here. Not when you are somewhere else.' He shook his head. 'Now even I am confused but to make it clear, even if I am not here and you are, you are invited to eat at those times. Allah, please give me strength,' he added in an undertone as he grasped her hand and tugged. 'Come, our food is getting cold.'

Sarah had no choice but to follow but had to hide the grin she had no hope of supressing. Now she understood but why couldn't he have explained more clearly to start with? Even though there was too much food for a mere two people, what she ate was yummy. A plate of hummus had sliced vegetables splayed around the edge. There was a dish of mashed beans with delicate spices. Not the harsh spices she had encountered with goat stew. Flatbread, olives, sliced tomatoes and hard-boiled eggs were washed down with hot scented tea.

Conversation was stilted. She wasn't sure why, but Hakim asked no questions which meant she had no reason to answer and it wasn't a strength of hers to begin a conversation. If she wanted to know something, she asked. If the other person didn't ask, they didn't want to know so she kept her lips sealed. It was just the way she was.

'I apologise for my behaviour last night.' The sudden outburst brought her back to awareness.

'Why?'

'I should not have kissed you.'

'You're sorry you kissed me?' A sharp spear stabbed into her heart.

'Yes.'

The barbs twisted. Sarah popped a tomato wedge into her mouth to prevent a comment. A few simple words shouldn't cause pain but they did.

'You have no response?' He raised his eyebrows.

'No,' Sarah wrapped the word around the tomato, chewed, swallowed.

A hand grasped hers. Hakim's warm fingers folded around her fist. 'It is our Holy day today.'

'I know.' She tugged her hand free, set the empty plate aside and dropped her hands into her lap.

'I will attend the mosque this morning.'

'Okay, I have a few chores I need to get done.' She rose and left, head down because for some stupid reason embarrassment simmered. This brusqueness was a concern. Was he embarrassed about last night? Had she kissed the wrong way? No-one had ever complained before about the way she kissed. Why else could he be sorry it happened?

Once in her room, she hand-washed the clothes from the previous day, hung them on the backs of the chairs on the veranda outside. In this weather, they didn't need sun to dry, the outside heat was more than enough. It took less than ten minutes to have both the bathroom and bedroom spotless for she was pernickety about tidiness. She knew she was obsessive and compulsive in some of her habits but there were benefits. Her place was never messy, her clothes always clean and she knew where every item was. But it also meant she now had to fill another day of boredom.

An itch developed to get her hands on books so she went on-line to find the nearest public transport to get her to the library she had found a few days previous.

An intense sense of relief settled over her while she strode to the corner, turned and found the bus shelter – air-conditioned if you don't mind. Freedom. A grin broke out when she settled into the rear bus seat and it remained the entire journey to the spot where she needed to alight and hurried through an air-conditioned walkway to the light rail station. It felt so darn good to be able to spend the day in a library – her favourite place to be. When she finally stood in front of the enormous glass doors, every cell in her body seemed to shiver in anticipation.

She stepped inside, glanced around and smiled. Happy, she roamed the aisles in a search for the geology section where she pulled out book after book to read the covers, replaced those written in Arabic. She was a homely person in her ideal homely atmosphere. Not like Hakim's pristine home where one didn't dare leave a footprint or touch an item.

Selection made, she found a desk facing the front door and settled down with her back against the wall where she could see everyone enter and no-one could sneak up on her. She took out a notebook, three pencils and an eraser. For the next thirty minutes she delved into the geological features of the Arabian peninsula until her mobile phone buzzed with a message. Frustrated with the interruption, she ignored it until it buzzed again. She didn't need or want an interruption but the thought came it might be a message from family so she pressed the green button and read.

Where are you? H.

In the library. She typed back.

What are you doing there?

Library. Guess.

You are not permitted there.

'Huh?' hissed out as she stood, glanced around to see at least fifty other patrons from various countries. Could this library be for locals only? But there were several Asians, as many who appeared to be from the Indian/Pakistani region if she took into account their dress. Half the people wore the local kandourah and abaya but there were also a number of Caucasians. To make sure, she made her way to the central desk.

'Can I help you?' asked a young man with a crocheted skull cap.

'A friend of mine said I was not permitted in here but there are many others of my race here. I need to make sure. Am I able to use this library?'

'Of course, it is a public library but you cannot take out books unless you live here and have a membership card. Many tourists use the free wi-fi. Many come to read. Many students use our facilities.'

'Oh, thank you. So it's all right if I use your books to research material?'

'Of course. Any books you use go on this trolley for us to return to the shelves.' He indicated a large double-decker trolley to the left.

'Am I able to use my own laptop? Is there a special password to log on?'

The man scribbled on a piece of scrap paper and skimmed it across the desk towards her. 'Use this password. You can plug in your computer to keep it charged. There are points in the wall behind each desk.'

'And I can stay as long as I like?'

'From eight in the morning until ten at night.'

'Oh, wow, thank you.'

As she returned to her desk, she glanced back at her phone to see another message had come through.

Where are you? I cannot see you.

Now she was confused. She searched the area but no-one who looked even remotely like Hakim was within sight. *At the desk nearest the librarian station, ground floor, opposite the main door,* she typed as she sat.

Which library?

Public library.

What are you doing there?

Library. Books. Guess.

Sarah, which public library? We have three in this city. I thought you were in my library.

'Hakim has a library?' she mumbled under her breath as she returned to the librarian and asked him to type in the name of the library since she didn't have a clue. All it said on the outside was Public Library. Mind you there was some Arabic as well. Miffed, she returned to her pile of books and settled down to learn all she could about the geological features and rock types of the part of the world where she was to live for a few more weeks. But there was no way she could settle or concentrate on research with constant thoughts of Hakim and his library in her mind. Why hadn't he shown her his library? Ah, she wasn't permitted in his library so it must be in his private wing. Well, tough, she would spend all her days until she found another job, in this library where she was welcome fourteen hours every day.

Always alert for the approach of strangers, she noticed the sudden silence when Hakim entered through the door. For a brief moment everyone straightened and stared while Hakim stilled with his eyes honed onto her. Heads dropped in succinct deference as he stalked past, but he ignored every bowed head since his dark eyes were fixed on her. Hafiz followed while the other bodyguard waited outside the door. Her innards stood to attention at the grim line of Hakim's mouth.

Still he stared when he stopped in front of her before he reached down, dragged out the opposite seat and dropped into it.

'Why did you choose the public library furthest from my home?'

'I didn't know there were any others. This is close to Saeed's place.'

His lips thinned before he rifled through her pile of books and lifted one to read the cover. 'The Geological Features of the Arabian Peninsula?' he read aloud with his head cocked to one side in query.

Sarah snatched it back. 'You have a problem with my choice of book?'

'No, of course not. I am curious. I figured you would favour some silly romance novel.'

Sarah wasn't sure if his words were an insult: it felt like an insult. 'Have you ever read a romance novel?'

'No and have no desire to read such rubbish.'

'If you have never read one, what gives you the right to class all romances as silly and full of rubbish?'

He grinned. 'Have you ever read one?'

'Yes, and crime, and mystery, and horror, and almost every other genre but I'm not so keen on fantasy or sci-fi.'

The long pause while he read the titles of the other books, sent her nerves into a quiver. He lifted his head. 'Why did you not tell someone where you were going?'

As she folded her arms over her chest, Sarah sat back. It was difficult to figure out if his question was pointed or if he was only curious. 'I wasn't aware I needed to tell anyone. I am an independent adult of legal age who has spent many hours in libraries since I began school. I have never had to ask permission before and I don't recall a list of terms on what I can or cannot do or am I now a prisoner who must spend twenty-four hours a day in your home, going stir crazy with nothing to do? If so, I will find an hotel where I can maintain my independence.' She stood, gathered together her personal bits and pieces and shoved them into her backpack. Arms through the straps, she bundled up the books and carried them over to the trolley where she placed them with the care books deserved.

'Sarah.'

She ignored him and strode to the door but came to a halt when Hafiz stood in front of her, arms akimbo, obvious he wouldn't let her out. She turned to Hakim who stood only half a metre behind. 'Really? I am a prisoner?'

Hakim flicked a hand towards Hafiz. 'No, of course not but I wish to speak with you and would prefer a little privacy.'

It was only then she noticed they had a considerable audience, some with mobile phones held high. As she dropped her head, her breath wheezed out. She sure didn't need her photo to go out to the world. She turned back around to find Hafiz had gone but the other bodyguard stood at ease outside the door. With her head low, she hurried to the top of the steps.

By the time she reached the bottom, his car sat there, rear doors open, a guard at each. Those guys sure moved fast was her only thought as she scampered in for she now knew the windows were tinted in such a way, people couldn't see in but passengers could see out. Still miffed, she crunched her body against the door. Front seats filled, doors snicked shut, the car moved away, Hakim reached over, grasped her hand, gave it a little tug.

'I am sorry if you think you are a prisoner. It certainly is not my intention. You are free to do as you wish, spend the day at the shops or in the library, sightsee, or any other activity. I only ask you let someone know where you are so I can keep you safe and let Mariam know if you will or won't be in for a meal. I had intended a trip into the desert today.'

Her heart managed a little skip. 'The desert?' She caught Hakim's eye. 'You didn't say this morning.'

'No, my mistake but now it is too late for it will be far too hot. Instead, there is an attraction I think you might enjoy in the city tonight. Will you join me for a meal at a restaurant?'

A shiver of pleasure ran up her arm from where Hakim held her hand. 'Thank you, yes. How dressy?'

'Not formal. What you wear now will be fine but we need to be seated before six. Now, since we will not be covered in sand today, if you wish to continue your study of our geological features, I can send a car to pick you up in time for you to shower and change but if you wish to return home, we will. Your choice.'

Her ire vanished in an instant with pleasure in its place. It wasn't Hakim's fault he didn't understand how her brain worked. It had taken her family years to understand and for her to figure out everyone else didn't think the way she did. And how could she stay angry at a man who she liked so much; a man who... gosh, a man with whom she wanted the whole enchilada. 'Since I am to miss all the sand, I would like to read about your desert but I can go home on public transport.'

'How about I have a car here at four? Not this car but a more discreet vehicle. Hafiz will drive so keep an eye out for him.'

Hakim must have caught the frown she tried to hide because he sat forward with a raised eyebrow. 'You do not like Hafiz?'

'I don't think he likes me. His body language tells me he doesn't approve of my presence.'

'His job is to protect me. Maybe he believes I need protection from you.' He squeezed her hand. 'He would not be wrong.' Their eyes caught. His held a whole lot of meaning, which sent her heart on a tumble-turn followed by a flood of heat through her veins. 'Now go, I will see you soon after four and enjoy the rest of your day.'

Sarah glanced outside to discover the car had returned to the library. Confusion reigned as she strode inside. Hakim sent out so many mixed messages. Last night he kissed her as though his life depended on the connection, earlier it seemed he was sorry he did it. And then he goes and says he needs protection from her.

Thirteen

akim led the way to a table at the edge of the balcony, the best seat for what they were about to see, but now he thought Sarah might be uncomfortable with so many patrons behind her. When he spotted Tariq already seated, he turned to Sarah. 'Since we are in public and have the issue of propriety, I asked Tariq and his wife to join us. Tariq is my best friend. His wife is expecting their first child. Aisha is a lovely woman; one whose company I think you might enjoy.'

After a round of introductions, he pulled out a seat for Sarah. 'This chair is the best to see but if you prefer to face the patrons, let me know. Tonight, Shahir and Mohammad will be seated at the table behind us and will not let anyone come near.' He indicated their table before turning back to Sarah.

'What is to see apart from a lake?'

'Ah, a little surprise. So which chair would you prefer?'

'If you say this seat is the best, I trust your word and I trust your men.' The gentle smile and her words as she settled into the cane chair, gave Hakim hope. Sarah trusted him. A huge step this time but after his behaviour last night he had doubted he would ever gain her trust. He sat opposite her, as far away as he could safely get without sitting at another table. At least opposite, he could not be tempted to drag her into his lap and devour her mouth. Well, he was tempted but could not act. Next to Tariq was much safer. He glanced at his friend who raised his eyebrows and grinned.

The waiter had handed out menus and taken drink orders when the first bars of music came over the loudspeakers. Hakim kept his eyes on Sarah's face when she lifted it with surprise shooting through her eyes. Her mouth opened at the same time the fountain sprang to life and began to dance to an aria sung by Dame Kiri Te Kanawa. The hairs on his arms stood to attention at the sheer haunting beauty of voice, lights and co-ordinated water spouts. Even though he had seen this before, this piece always had such an effect on him but this time he had the added bonus of seeing Sarah equally moved if he correctly read the awe on her face.

Ten minutes later, the music stopped, the water stilled, coloured lights faded but Sarah's face still held awe.

'That was amazing,' she whispered as though to speak louder would dispel the magic.

'Every hour, on the hour, there is another piece, the last at ten. Did you enjoy the experience?'

'It was stunning, so beautiful, like magic. Thank you.' It worried him when she hung her head to sweep tears away with the back of her hand as though tears were an embarrassment. To him, they showed how tender her heart was, how easily intrinsic beauty moved her, all assets of a woman he was enamoured with - assets which managed to twitch his heart.

After the server had taken their orders, Hakim led the conversation to break into Sarah's apparent shyness with Aisha and Tariq. He now recognised her hesitancy with people she did not know, much the same way she was with him when they first met. He was not sure if it was because of her fear of strangers or if shyness was a natural trait but he was keen to find out. After the food was served they all tucked into their individual dishes although he was not happy with what Sarah had ordered: a plate of salad with flat bread on the side.

'You did not want a more substantial dish?' he dared ask. Her glare told him of his error.

'I knew what would be on the plate,' she whispered.

'I apologise. I did not think to explain the ingredients for you. You can order more if you wish.'

'I'm fine. This way I can enjoy a sweet dish.'

But fine was not how he would describe her. Her eyes sent a dagger towards him before pink suffused her neck and cheeks when she dropped her head to hide the heightened colour. So, she did not like being singled out in front of others. He must remember, and to explain ingredients. Such a complicated woman in one sense but so unsophisticated and straightforward in another. Always a challenge, which he liked, and so different to the wishy-washy women who went overboard to maintain his interest, usually for the status he could give them, along with the trappings of his wealth. So far, Sarah had asked nothing of him except to come to her aid when she feared for her life. Independence was her middle name: which he could never deprive her of but it could be a problem if the relationship went the way he now knew he wanted. Sarah would never be able to live the sheltered life of most Muslim women -

111

sheltered because Arab men were fiercely protective of their family.

His introspection vanished at the start of next piece of music. Sarah dropped her cutlery, lifted her head to reveal a radiant smile as she watched the lights turn the dancing water spouts into bright colours. This more modern piece didn't appeal to him as much but Sarah seemed to be absorbed. His heart swelled to impossible proportions as he watched her enjoyment. It was almost at the end of the piece when he realised why this woman had such an effect on him.

He loved her. Another section of his mind asked how this was feasible. They had known each other for only a few weeks. It was crazy to think it was possible to know he loved her but the knowledge was undeniable. For the first time in his life he had figured out what the sensation of love meant, how it felt. Overwhelmed with emotion, he had to hide his own eyes when moisture created a haze. He leant towards Tariq. 'I now understand your passion for Aisha,' he said in Arabic.

Tariq grinned. 'You are in love with her. Could be a problem.'

'All problems have a solution. I will find the solution for Sarah is mine. Allah sent her to me for a reason.'

'Good luck.' Tariq turned to his wife in response to her nudge.

Hakim glanced up to see Sarah with a raised eyebrow. 'Sorry, I should not speak in Arabic when you are around. My apologies.'

'No need to apologise. Your private conversation is none of my business.'

'It is still not appropriate. Finish your meal so we can search the menu for some sweet delicacy.'

Determined Sarah would experience all the shows, he slowed the rate of orders, took Sarah and Aisha for a walk around the man-made lake, leaving Tariq to keep their tables. He managed to keep the conversation flowing, to include details of Aisha's life so the women became more familiar with each other for Sarah will need female friends. He sent Shahir for the car before the final show so it would be at the nearest entrance as soon as the lights dimmed and music ceased. While they headed towards the car, he ensured the two ladies walked ahead to keep speculation at bay.

Once in the car, he grasped Sarah's hand and tugged her close enough he was able to slip his arm around her shoulders. It was a step further than he had gone before but Sarah stiffened.

'You don't wish me to touch you?' he asked.

'I'm confused.' With her head hung low it was difficult to make out her words. He hooked the fingers of one hand under her chin to draw her face around.

'Confused about what?'

'Last night… your kiss… it was like it was important. But this morning…' Her eyes lifted, caught his. Hers held sadness.

'Go on.'

'You were sorry you kissed me. You acted aloof, cold and now…'

'And now?'

'You put your arm around me as if… I'm confused.'

It was so rare for her eyes to hold his but they hadn't moved. He smiled as he nudged her a little closer. 'Our kiss last night was so amazing I almost lost control. I didn't want it to stop, wanted more, wanted all the things I swore we were not ready for. Sleep eluded me afterwards until I concluded I had to step back for the same reasons. If I was

113

aloof this morning it was because I had to force myself to not kiss you again, to maintain a respectful distance. Never have I had such an attraction to a woman: a deep, strong attraction I cannot explain. Tonight I kept my eyes on you when you were enthralled in the music. No longer can I deny to myself, or to you, how strong this attraction is.

'Oh.' Her eyes dropped at the same time she tugged her chin free.

It was a shock when she relaxed into his side which sent all his heated blood southwards in an instant. He dropped a kiss on her head, smiled at her soft sigh and the way her tension eased. He wanted to say more but was afraid words would break the connection. Sarah said actions spoke to her better than words, well, he would give her actions since he found it almost impossible to keep his hands off her.

When he pressed his thigh against hers, his heart thundered when she increased the pressure even more. He caressed the top of her arm. Another sigh escaped her lips so he dared to lift his hand higher to stroke the softness of her cheek. Her head dropped onto his shoulder, nuzzled into his neck which sent his hormones on a frenzy and his body rock-hard. He hadn't thought to set the privacy partition into place but to do so now would be blatant and stupid. It was a good thing for he doubted they would arrive home with all their clothes in place if he did have privacy. When the need to make love to Sarah overwhelmed him, he placed his lips against her ear.

'Have you dated men before?' Such a stupid question, he realised when the words were out. She was not a child and a woman with such beauty would appeal to all men.

Her body tensed. Her head twisted. 'Of course. I'm almost twenty-three not thirteen.' Her head dropped.

It was as he expected and a relief to know she was not inexperienced. Western women nowadays didn't have the same sexual restrictions as those from his country. 'Then you know what I want?' he whispered.

Sarah lifted her head and smiled. 'Yes.'

Their eyes held but again for only a second. 'What do you want?' he asked.

There was a pause – she swallowed. 'You.'

It took a monumental effort to not haul her into his lap. Instead, he gripped her tighter, reached over with his other hand and ran it up her thigh. 'Be sure, sweet Sarah. I will never betray your trust, will never force you to do anything for which you are not ready. The decision is yours. How far we take this is for you to decide but you only have about two minutes to think before we reach home.'

Two minutes can be torturous, he thought when the car finally came to a standstill in front of the entry. When Sarah wriggled, he released her to see her entire body tremble before she managed to straighten with a distance between them. Both rear doors opened at the same time. They emerged on opposite sides. His body thrummed when they came closer and walked side-by-side to the front door which the night guard opened. As they stepped inside, he was glad he had given Mariam the afternoon and night off to visit with her son and his family.

They would be alone.

Door shut, he reached out, grasped Sarah by her shoulders and slowly turned her around. His mouth dried at the hunger in her eyes. Speaking was beyond him. Instead he lifted one hand and brushed a few stray tendrils of gold from her face. Her soft skin torched his fingers. His hands roamed, down her cheeks, her chin, dropped to her shoulders, down her arms until he reached her fingers, which he gripped.

'Your decision,' he managed to croak through a throat which felt as swollen as more manly parts of his body.

Fourteen

The decision should have been hard but wasn't. All her life Sarah had vowed to only give herself to a man she knew for sure, she loved. This man. How and why it happened, she didn't have a clue. Despite all her views on class and status, she loved this man. He might have a privileged title, one he had never used to his advantage with her, but Hakim was still just a man: the one man who had managed to leap into her heart, for she had been drawn to him on sight. Pure logic told her it only took mere seconds to meet the person you fall in love with even though it might take longer for the realisation to hit.

Naked hunger simmered in his eyes; a lustful challenge she had no hope of denying when his fingertips explored her arms and shoulders and found erogenous zones she never knew existed. None of the men she had dated before had ever come close to creating the havoc this man managed. It had to be because her affection for any of those guys was only friendship. But this man? Oh, wow.

Even though she knew he waited for her consent it was hard to concentrate when his soft, warm palms skated under the long sleeves and up the skin of her arms. Her mind turned into mush as a trail of goose bumps followed the trace of his fingers. As though magnetised, she leant into him; her hands crept to his chest. He hissed when her fingers explored the solid dips and mounds of his muscular torso. Even through the soft cotton of his kandourah and the white T-shirt he wore underneath, her fingers were sensitised sparks of electricity.

Sarah reached up, flicked the keffiyeh from his head. 'I choose you,' she said, delighted with the rumble of his groan.

It took less than a second before Hakim had her airborne. Held tight against his considerable chest, he carried her into the forbidden zone, past closed doors, along a wide passage, into a vast room with a huge bed in the centre. The bed he laid her on was covered in burgundy with more soft pillows at the head than were in her entire house back home. The only light was from a gibbous moon streaming through the uncovered wall of windows through which she could make out tall palms in a courtyard. The tinkle of water sounded as though it came from a fountain but she had no interest in searching it out.

Her only interest was the man who stood tall at the foot of the bed. His eyes swept up her body and left a warm sensation in their wake. He stripped off his robes, dropped them to the floor. The white undershirt followed. Hakim Al Fasir was one gorgeous hunk of a man with well-defined muscles, lean hips clad in only silk shorts the colour of his skin, and long, long legs.

'So many times I have envisioned you here on my bed. I dream about it every night but never imagined it could come true.' He reached forward, grasped the waist of her long skirt and tugged it down. The soft fabric sent a ripple of awareness as it skimmed her skin. He stood, gasped in a breath and stared with a sparkle in his eyes. 'So beautiful,' wheezed out in such a way, it was not a simple compliment but came from his heart.

The bed dipped. He leant over her and settled his weight on his elbows. His kiss was gentle, warm as though seeking permission. She gave it, opened her mouth but was immediately assailed by intense heat and passion when he deepened the kiss. It said so much. She was lost and returned his kisses with equal passion. Her heart hammered in time with his, her limbs turned boneless as he tunnelled his hands through her hair and twisted his head to make the fit of their mouths even better.

Sometime, somehow, her top and bra disappeared to leave her exposed to his steady gaze. She always thought she would be embarrassed by such scrutiny with her nakedness exposed to a man for the first time, but she wasn't, she felt empowered.

'You were made for me,' he rasped against her mouth. His hand cupped one breast before strong fingers circled the nipple. A shaft of deep need shot to her core. 'Allah made you for me, I know this now.'

There was no part of her body he didn't caress or kiss, which turned her mindless with need, until a fierce tension screamed through her and sent her frantic with a hunger she had never experienced before.

'I want - you,' she managed to pant out. She grabbed his head and tugged it down in a hot kiss, 'but I...'

'No more words,' he ordered before his mouth plastered against hers to prevent the escape of another sound. He rose and surged into her.

Even though she tried to hide it, a yelp escaped at the sudden sharp sear of pain.

He stopped dead, speared cold eyes through her. 'You were untouched,' he rasped. 'Why did you not tell me?' Anger laced his words.

Fear shot through her. 'I tried…'

'You did not try hard enough.' As though he had been electrocuted, he withdrew and stood.

'You ordered me to not speak, clamped your mouth over mine.' Too stunned to move, she could only stare.

'You told me you had been with other men.' One hand speared through his hair as he glared down at her.

'Never. You asked if I had dated. I told the truth. There is a stark difference between dating and sleeping with a man which you did *not* ask me.'

'Mere semantics. You bring me great shame,' he growled as he wheeled around, snatched up his kandourah and raced from the room as though the devil was on his tail.

Stunned, she shot up as unbidden tears flooded and fell. 'Ashamed?' she squeaked. 'He's ashamed of me because I've never slept with a guy before?' Disbelief, with a strong dose of humiliation, flooded her innards. Mortified, she crawled off the bed, gave up the search for her clothes and fled as she dragged on her top, the only item she could find. Full pelt she ran to her own room, slammed the door, turned the key and stood under a hot shower to drown a deluge of tears, deep humiliation and stark pain of rejection. So many times she had been rejected by school mates because her brain worked different to theirs. So many times guys rejected her because she was smarter than them. And now? Who had ever been rejected because they had never been intimate with a guy before?

When she woke, Sarah couldn't recall if she turned off the shower, pulled on pyjamas or climbed into bed, but she must have. One peek in the bathroom mirror proved she looked as wretched as she felt. Swollen eyes told a story as did the bird's nest of hair which she obviously hadn't dried before she went to bed. Unusual soreness twinged in intimate parts every time she moved but it was nowhere near as painful as the region where her heart had once stood.

Glad it was past eight with Hakim already gone, she staggered to the dining room in search of food to fill the hollow in her stomach, although she figured the painful vacuum wasn't caused by hunger. She stopped dead when Hakim dropped a newspaper and caught her eye.

'We need to talk,' he said.

'No thanks, your actions last night told me all I need to know.' Sarah turned to leave; a new wash of tears blurred her vision while a serrated knife tore her innards to shreds.

He grasped her arm, spun her around. 'We are to be married in three days.'

Dumbfounded, Sarah could only stare at the man. 'What did you say?' She swept the moisture from her eyes with a clenched fist and dropped her head, too embarrassed to let him see. When she tried to wriggle free his grip only tightened.

'We must marry.'

'Why?' she asked his chest.

'We did not take precautions. My fault since my brain lost all reason with need for you but now there is a chance you are with child. A royal baby can never be born out of wedlock.'

A spurt of anger gave her strength to tear out of his hold and straighten with her arms folded. 'No way. Not possible. You never... you know. You were too angry, too ashamed of me, too mean...' She spun around when tears returned.

'I was shocked, not angry.'

'Angry, yelled,' she shot back.

'I took from you your most precious gift: your innocence, when it was not mine to take. This is another reason we must marry.'

Fired up with humiliation, Sarah spun around again. 'It was *my* gift to give to the man of my choice. I chose *you* but you threw it back in my face, humiliated me, rejected me.' She managed to get halfway down the passage before he caught her again.

'Sarah, please, let us talk?'

'About what?' she mumbled into the cotton of his chest when he tugged her into his arms.

'Our future together gives us much to talk about.' His chin rested on her head.

'There is no future together.' She struggled to get free, to no avail.

'There must be.' Hakim shuffled her towards the mausoleum of a sitting room, tugged her into a sofa but didn't release her.

'I was drawn to you the moment we met. I have no idea why but you are the only woman I have ever considered as a life partner, the only woman who has managed to touch my heart. Why this strong connection between us happened so quickly I have no answer? Last night proved we both have the same deep affection for each other. You cannot deny you wanted me as much as I wanted you. It was your choice; your decision and I am certain you are not one who would make such a decision if you thought it was not right for you. I can never apologise enough for how the night ended but when I realised you were untouched it was an enormous shock. In our culture, to take a woman's innocence when she is not your wife, is serious. I was overwhelmed, reacted in the worst way and will forever be deeply sorry. But I cannot undo what was done, despite how much I wish I could.'

Most of what he said was true and logical. She did love him, did want him, had made the decision to sleep with him but whether she could forgive him for the hurt he inflicted - she needed time to consider. She didn't know what to do, what to say. This was all so new to her. 'Okay, you can talk.'

A wry scoff came from him. 'I can talk, but to find the right words is impossible. I can apologise over and over but am sure it will take more than mere words for you to believe me. You said once how actions tell you more than words but what actions can I show? Kiss you? The way I want to kiss you? I doubt your anger has dissipated enough for you to accept my kisses. I can take you back to my bed to show you the way I should have last night, but I doubt you are in the space to accept me. After I admitted my stupidity to Allah in my prayer room last night, I came back to you but you were gone and did not answer my knocks to your door, which left me unable to sleep because of my worry. So, how can I show you?'

He chucked one hand under her chin to lift her face up but she kept her eyes shut, unable to face him. Light kisses brushed both eyes and her mouth. Desperate need wove through her innards but equally as desperate, she didn't want him to touch her. Was it normal to be so darn confused?

'So many thoughts went through my mind while I begged for sleep,' he continued as one hand brushed down her cheek. 'I dismissed most. Marriage is really the only solution and I do want to marry you.'

'You do?' Sarah managed to get out when the first twinge of hope shifted something inside her.

'Yes, but I wondered why I had these thoughts so soon after we met and concluded we needed time to learn more about each other, to be sure what I felt was true and not some flight of fancy. Last night as I watched you enthralled by the fountain, it hit me that what I felt for you was so much deeper and stronger than I have ever felt for anyone before. And there is the chance you carry my child.'

'Hardly. We did not... um... complete...'

'You are a scientist. Surely there is no need for me to explain the mechanics of a man's sexual processes. There is always fluid leakage before actual...'

'I know,' Sarah squeaked, embarrassed. She shouldn't be embarrassed; she'd understood every detail since she read a rather explicit book when she was eight, after which she gave her entire family a blow-by-blow description, which embarrassed the lot of them, especially her two brothers who were going through puberty at the time. Beetroot red was a more than apt description for the colour of their faces. Proficient in reading by the age of four had always been an advantage but right now it felt kind of embarrassing.

A suppressed snort told her Hakim tried to stifle his laughter. 'Therefore, you also know there is a chance of pregnancy. The chance may be small and would depend on your cycle.'

'Oh, for heaven's sake,' Sarah said under her breath. 'Why don't you ask outright? Right slap, bang in the middle if you really need to know.'

'Not the answer I hoped for but yes, I need to know, which makes it even more imperative we marry soon. As I said, there can never be a royal baby born out of wedlock nor with any hint of conception before the wedding date.'

'Oh, fabulous,' Sarah groaned. 'Give me a minute, I need to think.' This time Hakim didn't hold her down when she stood and paced to the front door and back while she tried to align brain cells to make sense of all he'd said.

Usually plain logic was the only way her brain worked but today it defied her.

She paused when a thought came. 'What if marriage doesn't work and we hate each other?'

Hakim smiled. 'Unlikely given my desire for you but we need to give it a chance. If, after a time, we believe marriage is not for us, I can promise to release you.'

'What if there is a baby, I could never give up my child?'

'A royal child will always be a royal child. There can be no other way but we are both reasonable, responsible adults. I would never deny a mother her child, especially when the child is young. I am not a man mired in the old-fashioned ways of our country where the child would stay with the father's family regardless. A child's needs are the most important and children need both parents even if they no longer live together.

'I need more time to think.'

He lifted her face, bent over and swept his mouth across her lips in a gentle kiss. 'I will go ahead with the plans but for propriety's sake will move to my rooms in the palace until we make our vows. Mariam will instruct you on what an Islamic ceremony entails. If you have any questions, ask. If you decide not to marry, decide soon, preferably within the next twenty-four hours but I pray you will agree. I realise you need more time to know me, to learn to maybe love me.'

'But…'

He pressed one finger against her mouth. 'I asked Mariam to keep breakfast for you. Go and eat but before you do…' Hakim drew her into his arms and kissed her, long and hard. His mouth did wonders to turn her insides into molten heat. As quickly as he had kissed her, he released her and walked away, down the forbidden passage to his rooms.

Sarah sat at the table, managed to eat but not enjoy, her mind on a non-stop repeat. There was only one reason she would ever marry a man – because she loved him and was sure he loved her. In this case, by his actions and some of his words, she thought there was hope but wasn't sure, especially about how fond he was of her. But she sure knew the depth of passion he invoked in her.

Fifteen

'No, I won't wear it.' Sarah grabbed the silk hijab from the top of her head and tossed it onto the bed.

'You must.' Mariam insisted while she flung the fine silk fabric back over Sarah's head and wound the long tails around her neck.

A flashback rocketed through Sarah's brain. Panic surged. She shuddered, ripped the fabric off and scrunched it into a ball. A wave of tremors began to take hold. She turned away to take a few moments to regain her equilibrium.

'You cannot enter a holy place with the hair not covered.'

'I understand your custom but this not only covers the hair it strangles the throat, cuts off the air supply…' Sarah wheezed to gain some oxygen in depleted lungs. The memory surged again. The fear, the terror, the sensation of constriction around her throat, the inability to breathe, the blackness when she passed out.

To get rid of the flashback, she paused, shook her head and thought. 'Okay, I have a solution.' She grabbed the fabric, found her pair of nail scissors and made a small nick. With a hand on each end, she tore the fabric apart. Another nick, another rip, Sarah had a much smaller square of fabric.

In the bathroom, she pinned it to her hair, tucked in every thick strand and used bobby pins to fix the dreaded fabric in place but at least it no longer suffocated her. A final glance told her she looked ridiculous. Below neck level looked heaps better. The heavily embroidered silk gown was gorgeous and fitted perfectly, but it was not her choice – she didn't get a say.

Back in the bedroom, she spun around to make a point. 'Happy? No hair on show.'

Mariam's horrified face told a story. The prince will not be happy.'

'The prince has two choices. Either he accepts me the way I am or there will be no wedding. Which do you think he will choose?' Sarah didn't wait for an answer but stormed from the room, reached the front door in seconds.

Outside, Tariq, dressed in richly embroidered robes, stood by the open car door, reading the screen of his phone. Sarah wasn't happy about the smirk Tariq wasn't able to hide when he glanced at her but who cared? She didn't. This was only a marriage of convenience until there was no sign of a baby. It would never be a proper marriage.

The drive to the ceremony was short but in the few minutes her stomach managed to tie itself in knots as doubts took precedence. There was only one reason she was about to marry a man she met only a few weeks ago. She loved him. This certainty had her type in the word, okay, at the twenty-four hour mark. Two words came back – thank you. This morning Mariam coached her on Arabic words Sarah was to listen for and what her responses were to be, again in Arabic. It was lucky she had a phenomenal capacity to remember or she would be embarrassed.

The knots tightened when she realised they had entered the gates to the palace. Nausea rose up her gullet at the same speed she buried her face in her hands. This was so not what she had expected and why did Mariam call this a holy place? Ah, there had to be a private mosque.

The car drew to a halt at the base of wide marble steps with perfectly trimmed potted bushes perched on each end. The rear door opened. Panic shot through her so fast, she shrank back against the opposite door but must have made some noise for Tariq spun his head around.

'You are safe, Sarah,' he said.

'I can't…' stuttered from her mouth as her hands instinctively covered her head to protect her throat. 'You don't understand.' She grappled for the door latch but couldn't find it in her panic.

'Wait there.' Tariq shot from the car, muttered in Arabic, the volume changing as he raced around the car. 'It's okay, he has gone.'

The words from the familiar voice penetrated her panic. She opened her eyes, dropped her hands from her face at the sight of a man she trusted.

'Come.' He held out his right hand, palm up. 'I will walk you inside.'

It was difficult to scramble out in the tight underskirt. Bridal elegant she wasn't by the time she stood on the paved drive to straighten the gauzy silk of the dress.

'Put your hand in my elbow.' Tariq poked his bent elbow out. 'Why are you so afraid of strangers?' he asked as they mounted the steps.

'I can't talk about it.'

'Cannot or too afraid?' They paused at the top while massive doors opened.

'If I talk, I re-live and panic attacks slam into me.'

'It was not long ago, was it?'

'No.'

'Which is why you are in my country.'

Sarah couldn't answer for all words vanished at the opulence of the gigantic entry hall with a soaring ornate ceiling. This was why she wasn't a fan of royalty or upper classes with ridiculous wealth. Why should an elite group of people have so much wealth when the normal everyday people work hard but struggle to survive? It wasn't fair. So why was she about to marry into this obscene show of wealth? 'I can't do this,' she whispered to herself.

'Pardon?' Tariq asked as he continued across the highly polished marble tiles with his elbow jammed against his side to prevent her from wriggling her hand free.

'This is obscene. All this money on show when people like you get a pittance to put your life on the line to protect the owners. I can't be a part of this.'

'Why do you think Hakim built his own home? Why do you think he donates his entire annual wage from his ministerial work to a charity for children: one he set up? This is not Hakim. This palace was built by the people for the ruler in his grandfather's time. The present Sheikh lives in a small, less opulent wing. This section is for show and ceremonial activities. And I would give my life for Hakim, as he would for me. We have been like brothers since we were toddlers. Plus, I do not work for a pittance. Hakim pays his men very well.'

'He gives his wage away?'

'As a silent donation. Few people know and he will not be happy I have told you. So please forget my slip.'

'Not likely. The knowledge gives me more confidence. You said he was a good man.' They passed through a huge arch, into an even more opulent room where a small group of people stood in a semi-circle at the far end.

'The best. I hope that now he has you; he will take more time for himself. He needs to.' Tariq released her hand and moved away. She stood alone like a marooned sailor on an island with only sand and a sole palm tree.

A lead cannon ball sank to the pit of her stomach when she studied the ten people who stared at her. The men wore ceremonial robes while the women were dressed in western finery. No hijabs or black shrouds. The cannon ball exploded. Even though she recognised the Sheikh and his wife from photographs, she had never met any of these people except for Tariq and the one who now came towards her. With a serious frown on his brow Hakim didn't give the impression of being happy.

'What is this?' He flicked a hand to her head.

'Mariam insisted I hide my hair.'

'What happened to the rest of the hijab?'

'In the bin.'

He stifled a grin. 'Why?' came out as an awkward squawk.

'She wrapped it around my neck. I couldn't...'

Hakim's face changed in an instant to one of concern. 'I understand. Take this off.' He reached up, removed a pin, shoved it in the deep side pocket of the most luxurious kandourah Sarah had ever seen. The rich colours, embroidered amongst gold thread, matched her dress. Pin followed pin before the shredded fabric vanished into the same pocket.

131

'It is a crime to hide such glorious hair. To cover it is not necessary when there are family only. His smile chased away the frown. 'You are beautiful. There has been an ache in my heart for the three days I was unable to see you. Come, we have paperwork to sign. It is usually done before the day but we did not have the time. Little about today is a traditional marriage ceremony but will be legal.'

It was a surprise when he took her hand but it sure settled a few frazzled nerves while they walked across the room to a marble-topped table with curlicue brass legs on which sat a couple of documents.

Hakim indicated a piece of decorated paper. 'This is the *nikahnama* or marriage document. It contains a set of terms and conditions we both must respect and obey. It also gives you the right to divorce me.' He eyed her with one quirked eyebrow, turned back to the papers and read out the conditions which were generous to her but also basic to any marriage. 'Is there anything you would like to change?'

Surprised he had given her an option Sarah shook her head. 'No.'

'Also, you need to fill in your personal details on this document.' He handed her the document to read, along with a gold pen. After she added her details, Hakim instructed her to sign both papers before he did the same. Tariq and the Sheikh signed at the bottoms as witnesses.

'Tariq is standing in for your father. Legally, he is now your guardian in this country which means I must be wary of him if I fail to treat you with the respect you deserve. You are free to relate any of my transgressions to him for which he will probably demand severe retribution.' The smile between the two men showed their tight relationship. 'I would trust no other man for the role,' Hakim added.

'Now for the ceremony.' He took her hand, led her to an elderly man dressed in white robes and a crocheted skull cap. They stood before him hand-in-hand. On an angle to their side, Tariq read verses in Arabic from an open Qur'an after which the Sheikh said words Sarah recognised from the drilling she had received. The proposal and acceptance, Mariam had explained. Sarah stumbled over the pronunciation but a squeeze of her hand by Hakim told her she passed muster. There must be a reason they couldn't use English but she hadn't thought to ask. When the imam said more words, she recognised both of their names but for the rest, she didn't have a clue. When Hakim began to place a ring on her right hand, she stopped him.

'We use the left hand because it is closer to the heart. Please?' she added when Hakim stalled.

He made a silent plea to the imam. When the other man nodded, Hakim eased the jewel encrusted ring on her left hand, lifted it to his mouth and pressed a kiss to it. 'Maybe it will be better this way,' he murmured as the imam held their hands together while he spouted more words in Arabic.

There was a short silence. 'We are now legally husband and wife. Which means,' Hakim smiled, 'I am free to do this.' He drew her close, dropped his head and settled his mouth over hers. What should have been a brief peck turned hot and steamy, which sent a deluge of hormones through her veins and her innards into mush. A clearing of a throat broke them apart.

'Welcome to my family.' The Sheikh took her right hand in a tight grip. 'My son tells me you are very special. You must be to have captured his heart when no other woman had the ability.'

Captured his heart. Did he love her? 'Your Highness,' Sarah mumbled because his words overwhelmed her and she didn't have a clue what she was supposed to say to the king of a country. Was she supposed to curtsy, or bow, or nod her head or what? When the Sheikh released her hand she became swamped by perfume when his wife's arms wrapped around Sarah's shoulders and tugged her close.

'I am so delighted to see my last son married.'

Sarah wasn't sure what the statement meant so she smiled and gave a slight nod of her head. 'Your Highness.'

Greetings from Hakim's brothers were more reserved with no hugs or kisses, only words but at least they were more friendly than the severe frowns she received from the three wives whose faces showed not a skerrick of welcome or friendship. One woman was pointed in a glare at Sarah's hair.

A feast followed in a dining room. She and Hakim sat next to each other at one end of a long table with his parents at the other. Two brothers with their wives sat down one side while the other couple plus Tariq and the imam sat opposite with Tariq closest to her. Since she was the worst conversationist to ever exist, Sarah said little. She answered Hakim and Tariq in monosyllables when they fielded a couple of questions in her direction. All the men were verbose, trying to outdo each other with jest and good humour while the three wives spoke only in Arabic amongst themselves with pointed glances towards Sarah. Hakim's mother said little but her facial expressions were explicit; obviously displeased. With such a long table it was impossible for Sarah to speak with Hakim's parents. They probably didn't approve of Hakim marrying an Aussie commoner, but they shouldn't worry for she figured the marriage would be short-lived when there was no child. It was the only reason Hakim demanded this speedy wedding. When there was no pregnancy in less than two weeks, the marriage would be over for there would be no need. Something deep inside her twisted and tightened at the thought.

It was a relief when the server cleared the table and Hakim took her hand to help her stand.

'Time to take my beautiful wife home.' He smiled, nodded to each side of the table and wrapped one arm around her waist.

She sure needed his support for the goodbyes were as awkward as the dinner-table conversation, especially since she hadn't been introduced to any of them and knew no names. She did her best to be effusive and genuine with her thanks. His parents' smiles seemed kind and sincere; his brothers a little more guarded but the other women speared hostile glowers at her.

It was a relief to get into the car where Hakim tugged her close. 'Are you okay, you were quiet all night?'

'Since no-one asked me any questions there was no need for me to answer.'

One eyebrow rose. 'I do not understand. You were free to speak to everyone.'

'Who, apart from you and Tariq? I answered the few questions from you. Your parents were too far away for me to speak with, you men spent most of the night joking amongst yourselves and your brother's wives spoke amongst themselves in Arabic.'

'I am sorry. I did not realise.'

A twist of pain stabbed. Their wedding feast and her brand new husband couldn't centre his attention on his wife. But she should remember this was not a normal marriage but one of short-term convenience in the almost impossible chance she was pregnant. Less than two weeks of happy families and the marriage would be over. And besides, her visa would run out soon and she would have to leave the country.

The pain deepened when Hakim drew away. 'A part of the marriage rituals is the *mehr*.' He took a paper from his pocket and held it out. 'It is an amount of money given to the bride by the groom's family.' He opened out a cheque with an obscene amount written on it.

Horrified, Sarah stared at the number with way too many zeros. 'No way. I cannot accept this.'

'It is tradition.'

'Tradition to *buy* a woman?' Sarah grabbed the cheque and tore it in half. 'A man will never buy me. It reeks of being treated as a whore. Payment for services rendered.'

'No, the *mehr* is to give the bride financial independence from her family, to ensure she is financially secure even if the husband dies or they part through divorce where the money stays with the wife. The amount depends on the wealth of the husband to ensure her life is of equal standing if they are forced apart.'

'I *am* financially independent from my family. I have worked since I was fifteen, sometimes at two jobs to pay my way through university. I am quite capable of earning my own money. I have more than I need. If you die, I work. If we divorce, I work.' And soon she would have to find another job.

'The *mehr* is a legal requirement of the marriage contract.'

'Not where I come from.'

'But you now live here.' He thrust his fingers through his hair. 'You are a complex woman. I appreciate your views on money but you are my wife. There is no need for you to work. What is mine, is now yours but this is not the time to argue.' He shoved the torn paper back into his pocket and swung his arm around her shoulders. 'Now is the time for us to learn more about each other.' He smiled. 'Although I have discovered a great deal in the past few minutes. My beautiful wife cannot be bought and I have the impression the independence you have, is fierce to the extent there might be a few battles on the horizon for I don't wish my wife to work. There is no need.'

'Why do you work? I can't imagine there is a financial need given the wealth on display in the palace.'

'I enjoy working for my people, to make this country better, to make life for my people more secure.'

'What would you do if you didn't work?'

'I would go insane. I could never live the life of idolatry.'

'Which is the same for me. My brain is always on fast speed. It needs to be occupied all the time or it drives me nuts, which is why I spend so much time in a library, to read, absorb knowledge. I enjoy my work, have always earned more than enough to cover my needs. Are you about to deny me my pleasure?'

'No, of course not but now I understand. We will figure out all these details. If you wish to continue your study, I will not prevent you but I will provide for you. You are now my princess.'

'Please don't,' she groaned. 'Don't ever use that title. I am Sarah: plain, simple Sarah.'

Hakim drew her face around, swept his mouth across her lips in a cursory kiss, lifted his face a few inches and smiled. 'There is nothing plain about you. You are beautiful, and not only in your physical beauty. You have a beautiful soul. And nor are you simple. You must be the most complex, beguiling and intriguing woman I have ever met. Never change.'

He settled his mouth back over hers, his lips hot and gentle. A shaft of desperate need rocketed to her core until her brain sent a definite message: this is not a real marriage. She had no right to want more. Relief surged when the kiss was cut short as the car came to a standstill in front of his home.

Sixteen

'Where are you going?' Hakim called after her as Sarah raced down the passage, desperate to escape, to hide away, to fight this... she couldn't think of the right words.

'To my room,' she said over her shoulder.

'Why?' His footsteps followed.

'To get out of this dress, to shower and get some sleep. It's been a long day.' Desperate to find some clarity to a confused brain, she turned the door handle, shoved the door open and stalled. The room didn't seem right.

'I had Mariam move your possessions to my rooms,' said a quiet voice in her ear. The warm breath tickled her senses into over-drive while her insides jammed.

'Why?'

Hakim brushed up against her back. 'We are husband and wife. As in your country, we share a bed.'

Too scared to face him, Sarah straightened. This wasn't what she thought would happen. There had been no mention of this being a proper marriage. A gulp of air wedged itself in her throat. She coughed to shift it. 'This was not part of the agreement.'

He turned her around, gripped her chin and eased her face upwards. 'Marriage was the agreement. Marriage entails two people who live together, sleep together. What did you not understand?'

'You said we were to marry in case there was a child and to assuage your guilt for tearing my hymen apart.'

He reeled back, shock on his face. 'Crude words are unbecoming of you.'

'Crude? To call a part of the body by its true name is crude? Face, hands, shin must also be crude. It is not shameful to use proper medical terminology for body parts.'

'My apologies but this was never intended as a marriage of convenience, surely you understood. The vows we made tonight and to which you agreed, were the vows of a true union between a husband and wife.'

'Vows in Arabic – words not explained to me.' Disbelief, confusion and a shot of anger caused her to twist away. Why hadn't he explained? If they share a bed it will be impossible to repair her heart when they parted in two weeks. She strode along the passage, determined to remove every skerrick of her possessions from his room. 'Did you really imagine I would again put myself through the utter humiliation you inflicted on me when you rejected me with such haste? Ashamed of me, you said.' She ran so he wouldn't see the wash of tears she fought to control.

'Sarah!'

She reached his room, strode to the wall of wardrobes and yanked open door after door. Racks and shelves were filled with his clothes and footwear. The last door was a shock, even to her. Four items hung on hangers: her formal gown, two evening skirts and a pair of long silky evening pants. One narrow shelf had her seven everyday cotton slacks, neatly folded on top of each other. Another had an equal number of long cotton skirts and the third pile sat higher with ten loose tops and four dressy tops for more formal occasions. Six sets of underwear were in a lower drawer next to two sets of nightwear, seven pairs of white socks, her workout gear and a bathing suit. On the floor, her shoes marched in a neat line as though a ruler had been placed along the heels. Rubber flip-flops, everyday sandals, flat evening shoes, gym shoes and dressier flat sandals. Her only other pair, elegant, heeled sandals were still on her feet. Compared to Hakim's vast wardrobe, hers appeared paltry but she had more than she needed. There was no sign of her food. Maybe now she was married, she would be given meals.

'This is all you have? Surely there must be more.' Hakim stood beside her.

Miffed at his derogatory assessment, she stood tall. 'You can only wear one set of clothes at a time. I don't need more. Every garment has the same tone so I can mix and match. Ten tops with fourteen bottoms gives me hundreds of different combinations so I only wear the same outfit a couple of times a year but now the system is all mucked up. Mariam had no right to handle my clothes.' Sarah reached in, took out the first pile and dropped them on Hakim's bed. When she turned back for the next pile, he grasped her hands.

'What are you doing?'

'Taking my clothes back to my room.' She squealed when he hoisted her from the ground and dumped her on the other side of the bed.

'Not going to happen.' He dropped over her with his weight supported on bent arms, hands either side of her head. 'Tonight, you will get your wish. I will never force myself on you. The union of a man and woman must always be consensual. I understand your fear so we will not consummate this marriage tonight but you *will* sleep in my bed. There is an en suite through the door to your right. Have your shower, or soak in a tub. I will be in the office next door with an overflowing pile of important paperwork to wade through. I will keep the door open so don't think you will be able to sneak away. There will be a guard with strict instructions posted at the end of my passage. The glass doors to the courtyard are alarmed for my safety in case of evil intent. I never thought the alarm would be used to keep someone inside. Get the sleep you need for in the morning we will talk to resolve any apprehension you have. Goodnight, my lovely wife.' He dropped his head and sealed his mouth over hers. A deep groan came from his chest when the kiss became heated.

It was impossible to fight the need as the kiss melted her resolve, dissipated her anger. Why wasn't she able to resist him when he kissed her like this? She wanted to change her mind but an insidious message broke through. He rejected you; has never mentioned he loves you.

She was about to fight him off when the air above her cleared and his weight lifted. He walked away without a glance back. A mixture of joy and disappointment accompanied her into a bathroom which belittled the word *large*. It was humungous with understated luxury. Here, as in his bedroom, Sarah could see what Tariq meant by the obscene luxury of the palace wasn't what Hakim was about. Not one item was over the top even though it was obvious the best quality had been used. The hardware was made of brushed stainless steel, not gold-plated. The style was minimalist, not crudely dripping as a showpiece of wealth.

After a quick shower, Sarah had to drape her dress over the back of a chair for there were no spare hangers in her wardrobe and no way would she wade through Hakim's clothes. It smacked of an intimacy they didn't have despite a little niggle telling her it was what she wanted. Dismissing the thought, she crawled into the edge of the huge bed, tossed six pillows to the other side and snuggled under a cool cotton sheet which must have a thread count in the thousands, it was so soft. She tugged up a single cotton blanket. Even with the air-conditioned atmosphere, it was too warm for the quilt.

Sarah froze. The warmth along her back could only be Hakim and the arm around her waist definitely belonged to him.

'Good morning, beautiful. I was beginning to wonder if you were ever going to waken before I had to leave for a meeting.'

'You lied to me,' she managed to get out through a tight throat.

'What did I say that was untrue?'

'You promised you wouldn't touch me.'

Hakim laughed. 'You are usually the one who is particular about what is said. I did not use those words. I said we would not consummate our marriage last night. I kept my word but I never said I would not sleep in my own bed, which is far more pleasant with you in it. You slept well. I did not but received a great deal of pleasure watching you. Come,' he rolled from his side of the bed, walked around to stand in front of her with his right hand held out. 'There is something I wish to show you.'

With a quiver of apprehension, Sarah put her hand in his and followed him into a small, unfurnished room with a line of dark marble inlaid into the grey tiles. A small multi-coloured mat sat unfurled in the centre.

'This is my private prayer room.'

'I shouldn't be here.'

'Why not?'

'I'm not of your faith.'

'It matters not. Muslims accept everyone who enters the mosques, so I see no difference. Kneel there.' Hakim placed his bare foot on a spot on the line in front of the prayer mat. Above his foot he wore only long silk pyjama pants which rode precariously low on his hips. His broad chest, flat stomach and arrow of dark hairs were delicious. It was difficult to drag her eyes away and impossible to deny the rush of lust sweeping through her. On a gulp she managed to force her eyes away as she knelt back on her heels.

'I will go through my morning prayers so you understand since I doubt you have been inside a prayer room or mosque before. I will swap to English at the relevant part. It matters not what language we use as long as our prayers are sincere and come from our heart. He knelt, open hands held out at an angle, palms up. His voice was melodious as he chanted and tapped his head to the floor in a series of prayers Sarah knew about from her studies.

'Dear Allah,' he said in English all of a sudden and sat back on his heels. 'Once again I thank you for bringing Sarah to me. You knew she was the one woman who could touch my heart.'

Sarah's eyes popped open while a shiver wound its way down her body. What did he mean?

'Now I need your guidance, beloved Allah.' Hakim's eyes were fixed on the wall opposite. 'I need you to show me the way to Sarah's heart, to convince her my intent was never to hurt her, which I foolishly did when I did not realise you sent me a woman so pure of body and heart, she was left untouched for me. Even when I first saw her at my feet in the road, you sent me an instant jolt to tell me this

144

woman was special. The attraction was instant and grew at such a rapid rate it was hard to understand until a week ago, when I knew with certainty you had sent Sarah to me to become my life partner, to bear my children, to stand by my side.'

Sarah's heart and lungs had forgotten how to work when his eyes turned to her.

'My sorrow for the way I behaved, will be a thorn in my heart forever. I cannot undo my mistake. I cannot take away your pain and distrust. All I can do is make a plea from my heart to give me the chance to show you how pleasurable the union of a man and a woman can and should be. If I had known of your innocence I would have ensured to take much more care to eliminate the pain. I would not have reeled away in shock. I would not have left you alone for even a second. *Habibti*, I know you have the same passion for me as I have for you, for you are not one to make the decision you did four nights ago without certainty in your heart. For you to be a virgin at twenty-three tells me this, especially when you had dated men before but had not let them take your innocence.'

Still on his knees, Hakim shuffled forward, grasped her hands in his. 'Your words about giving your most precious gift to me, have burrowed their way into my heart and give me hope you might forgive me: give me hope we can start again.'

Sarah's heart managed to twist itself into a tight knot even though it had also melted into a puddle. 'Hakim, there are twenty-four hours in a day so technically it is still our wedding day. Take me back to bed.'

His eyes flared as he leant forwards and took her mouth in a kiss unlike any other. Gentle, yet full of passion, she leant into it, the pleasure so intense she couldn't move. It was a shock when he leant back on a sigh and rested on his heels with his eyes towards the ceiling.

'It seems Allah has thought of a way to punish me even more.' His head dropped. 'I postponed a meeting scheduled for last night to make room for our wedding. The meeting is to finalise details for a fund-raising event for a group of about fifty disadvantaged and orphaned children; to purchase the necessities their parents can't afford for their school activities.' His eyes opened but the pain in them replicated her sense of loss. 'Because of the urgency of the decision, I rescheduled the meeting for this morning. I have about fifteen minutes before I must leave. Fifteen minutes is no-where near enough time to make love to you the way you deserve. If I could, I would tell them I can't attend but the final decision rests with me.' His head dropped to his chest. 'I am sorry, sweet Sarah. I am unable to come back after the meeting for our parliament is in an extraordinary session and I must spend the day listening to ministers argue points and cast my vote when all I want is to spend my day with you.'

He stood, reached out to help her up. His arm went around her waist. He led her back to the bedroom.

'Tonight, my beauty. Tonight I will show you exactly what you mean to me.' He turned towards the bathroom. 'Oh, before I forget, the imam will arrive at nine to speak with you.'

'Why?'

'To begin your lessons.'

'What lessons?'

'To teach you the Qur'an.'

'Why?'

'To convert to Islam.'

'Convert means change from one set of ideals to another. What am I to change from?'

'Christian, of course.'

'Of course.' She couldn't help the scoff of derision. 'I'll see your imam. Enjoy your day.' Still in pyjamas Sarah made her way to the dining room as though she didn't have a care in the world whereas anger simmered at his arrogance. Karma in this instance would bite him back.

But it seemed she was the one to receive the surprise. Like every other day, there was no breakfast to eat and she had no idea what had happened to her cache of food. It hadn't been in the cupboard allotted to her. It was now obvious – if Hakim wasn't home for a meal – there was no meal.

Seventeen

A nxiety thrummed. Hakim knocked on the door of the imam's house. They exchanged greetings with smiles and reverence to each other.

'My boy, your choice of wife was a good one.'

'My boy?' Hakim raised his eyes.

'To me, you will always be the young boy so fervent in his learning of the Qur'an. The boy who always stumbled in the same places, unlike your wife. There is nothing I can teach her.'

Hakim reeled back. 'What do you mean?'

'Young Sarah knows the words of the Qur'an better than you.'

'Excuse me?'

'I tested her with over fifty quotations. Not only did she know the next verses, word perfect, but she knew the number of the verse and which Surah each came from. She even corrected me when I missed a phrase or word.'

'But Sarah does not speak or understand Arabic.'

'No, but she knows the official English version.'

'Are you certain?'

'Absolutely, she also has an unbelievable depth of knowledge about the teachings of most of the major religions of the world; will tell you how many of the familiar stories, like Noah and the Ark, are common to many faiths. But you were wrong when you told me she is a Christian. She is not.'

Stunned, Hakim's brain cells ceased to function. He stilled with his eyes on the wizened man in front of him. 'Why did Sarah not tell me this?'

The imam laughed. 'This is for you to discuss with your wife, not me, but her answer to me was simple and not in the least complimentary to you, my boy. You do realise how intelligent young Sarah is?'

'To earn a degree in science requires an above average level of intelligence, yes, I know.' Hakim wasn't sure he liked the way the man grinned as he shook his head.

'Ah, I now understand better what Sarah meant. In my prayers tonight I will ask Allah to guide you for you need guidance. Go in peace, your Highness.'

When the man walked to the door and held it open, Hakim followed. 'I don't understand what you mean,' he said as he passed through and twisted towards the man.

The imam smiled. 'This, I know but it is not me you need to learn from, it is the delightful young woman you married. Do you love her?'

'Yes, very much. Sarah is the only woman who has been able to take a hold of my heart.'

'Then why did she tell me her wedding day was one of the saddest days of her life? She needs your love and you

150

need to speak with her. Now I must prepare for the evening prayers.' He raced down the passage towards the mosque.

Hakim stared after the elderly man, trying to figure out if he was in the here and now or if he had been transferred to some alternate world. The saddest day of her life? Even though he should stay for prayers, he hurried to his car, anxious to get home where he would make sense of the past few minutes. It was now obvious he had much to learn about the woman he married.

The drive seemed to take twice as long as normal yet there was little traffic and no hold-ups at traffic lights. He had the door open before Ali brought the car to a standstill.

'Sarah,' he called as he hurried through the house, poked his head into every room. The resultant silence sent a clamour of alarm bells as did the lack of human presence until he made his way to the kitchen. His breath blew out to see Mariam stirring a pot on the stove.

'Is Sarah home?'

Mariam squealed, spun around and flicked droplets of sauce around the room. 'Sir, you scared me.'

'Sorry, I cannot find Sarah.'

'She rang to say she was held up, to eat without her.'

'Where is she?'

'She did not say but will be home within the hour.'

'Are you able to hold the meal for an hour, or will it spoil?'

'I can turn it off.'

'I would appreciate it, thank you.'

He turned away, took out his mobile phone, searched for Sarah's number and typed in a message. *Where are you?* The wait for an answer was torment until a ping indicated a return message.

In a bus.

His sucked-in breath echoed at the simplistic but honest response.

Where?

On the rear seat.

He muttered in Arabic at the inadequate answer which was too darn logical but did not tell what he wanted to know. He made a circle of the sitting room to calm his mind and think before he dared type another word.

Where is the bus?

On the road.

His eyes searched the ceiling for inspiration.

Mariam said you are on your way home but where have you been? There was no way she could misconstrue this message.

The doctor.

His heart thundered in response to a surge of adrenalin.

Why did you need a doctor?

Home soon. Ten mins.

The next few messages received no answer, which managed to send his worry levels to such a high, he stalked along the driveway to the gate. When he noticed Ali and Ahmed hover nearby, he sent both along the road to walk with Sarah despite not having a clue from which direction she would come. And why was she even on a bus? He had a fleet of cars at her disposal.

Ten minutes felt like five hours before he spied Ahmed walk beside her. As soon as she reached him, he dismissed the men, grasped Sarah's hand and brought her to a standstill. 'My heart thunders with worry. Why did you need a doctor?'

Her left hand lifted and brushed against her temple. 'The stitches should have come out yesterday but I wasn't allowed to leave the house. If they stay in too long the skin grows over the sutures which creates problems when they have to be dug out from under the healing skin.'

'The doctor would have come to the home.'

There was an ominous hiss. 'I knew this - how?' Sarah tugged her hand free with a speared glare in his direction. 'Did you mention it? Did you even remember the day I was supposed to visit the hospital?'

Hakim had to lengthen his stride to catch up. 'You are right, I am sorry. Our wedding took over my mind. But why did this take all day?'

Sarah came to a sudden halt, straightened her spine, turned so slow Hakim knew to the depths of his soul what he had just said was wrong but had not a clue as to why.

'It didn't. First I had to spend three hours with your imam, who was very nice, kind and smart. Next, I searched for the library you told me was closer to your home. Since I had no idea where the hospital was, or even the name of the hospital, I wasn't able to see the doctor who treated me so I had to find a medical centre where they would treat a non-resident who wasn't on their books and didn't have fee assistance from the government. I never believed it would be so difficult in a country like this to get a few stitches taken out. To make my day even better, I had to figure out how to get home from an unfamiliar area. It took a train and two buses.' She spun around and stalked.

'There is no need to use public transport. I have a garage full of cars and a driver always ready to take you anywhere you want.'

Her head shot around. The glare stilled him. 'Again, I know this – how? Even though my brain works funny it can't read minds.'

This time her walk was at the rate of a camel in full canter. She reached the still open front door before Hakim was able to catch up. He wasn't sure he wanted to for it was obvious Sarah was again angry with him despite the way she always kept her voice soft. But he had no choice. There were still matters to discuss, to straighten out.

When it took a moment for Sarah to remove her sandals, Hakim was able to grasp her by the arms. 'Mariam held off dinner until your arrival. Let us eat in peace, then we need to discuss this as husband and wife. I have no desire for disharmony or argument.' He dared to lean forward, settle his mouth over hers until he sensed her tension had eased a bit. This was one area where they connected, mouth-to-mouth.

It amused him how meek Sarah was while she ate. Nods of deference came whenever he spoke. Replies came in a soft voice but with few words. After a while, her compliance to his request for a peaceful meal began to grate. He preferred the fiery version of Sarah, not this subservience. In the end, he pushed his unfinished plate of food to the side.

'Come to the sitting room and sit with me.' He stood, reached for her hand and was relieved when she took it but it irked when she tagged behind as though she was about to be led to her room for time-out as punishment. She sat next to him, perched on the edge of the sofa with her hands held together in her lap. It took him a few seconds to search for the right words.

'Why did you not tell me you knew the words to the Qur'an?'

'You didn't ask me.'

Now he understood the imam's words – her answer was simple. A wry snort escaped. And it did reflect on him.

'Why can you not tell me these important details?'

'If you were interested, you would ask. I would answer.'

Her simple logic annoyed him as much as the way her hands gripped together so he took one and carried it to his own lap where he held it tight enough she couldn't wriggle it free. 'If you are not Christian, what faith do you follow?'

'None.'

Shock caused him to tighten his grip. 'Why not?'

'I don't believe there is a God. I deal in provable facts. To follow a religion would, to me, live a permanent lie and I never tell lies. It is dishonest to pretend a belief. But I do believe we should follow the morals taught in all religions and they all prescribe the same ethics: don't commit murder, don't steal, don't commit adultery, love your friends, family and neighbours, always show respect and kindness. I practise good morals and ethics but you don't have to follow a particular faith to live a good honest life. I also respect the right of every person to have their beliefs but in return I expect others to respect my beliefs.'

Stunned, Hakim focussed on Sarah's face. It was the most she had said in one outburst since they had met but now her head hung low as though she waited for him to retaliate. Afraid - she was afraid and he could say the wrong thing - again.

'Thank you. Your explanation makes sense. The imam said you have studied the scriptures of many of the major religions. You speak from knowledge, which I admire. Few would have such an understanding. Few realise the similarities between Christianity, Judaism and Islam because they are blinded by insular thoughts...'

'More like they are brain washed from birth,' Sarah interrupted. 'I was baptised a Catholic but after all the scandal about the rampant sexual, physical and emotional abuse meted out by so many members of the clergy, including our own parish priest who now resides in prison, I realised what they *said*, meant zilch since what they *did* was appalling. I lost faith by the time I was ten. So I worked my way through other religious scriptures to give me perspective. Even your Islam is tainted by extremists who take only certain words and put their own interpretation to them, and don't give a damn about the atrocities they commit. Yet if you take the Qur'an as a whole, it has a very gentle code of ethics, even though some are outdated and don't take account of modern scientific facts.'

'Yes, I agree, but many, like me, love their religion. They love the grounding it gives them, the faith. For many, their belief gives them strength. I am not sure how my family will accept your beliefs but as you said, we all have the right to our personal beliefs and I will always respect your right.'

'You will?' Her head twisted around, caught his eye but immediately her eyes shifted to the left. He lifted one arm to tug her against him.

'Yes, the same way I will respect your need to learn, to keep busy with intellectual pursuits instead of wasting your days with endless shopping and socialising as my sisters-in-law prefer. It does not alter my affection for you. There is another item I need you to explain.' He was not surprised when her body stiffened. 'Tell me why our wedding was one of the saddest days of your life.'

Sarah drew away, wriggled along the sofa until she was jammed against the arm rest. 'Most young girls fantasise about their wedding day. In western countries their dream is for their dad to walk them down the aisle, to have a sister and/or best friends stand by them as bridesmaids, their brothers to take important roles and to have special mother-daughter shopping trips to search for the best-ever dress, plan the music, the invitations, the food at the reception along with every other minor detail. To have close friends and family members to celebrate the day.' She squished even closer to the arm rest.

It scared him.

'I had none of those. I had a service in a language I didn't understand in front of complete strangers, who I wasn't even introduced to. I was told what to say and when to say it but didn't have a clue what the words meant. I had no choice about place, food, words and there was no music.' She stood. 'I didn't even get to choose my own wedding gown.' She jerked around and ran. 'Excuse me but I need a shower.'

With a stab of pain to his heart, Hakim followed. Regret churned his innards. How had he got it so wrong? When he reached the bedroom, Sarah's clothes were piled on a chair. Water already gushed behind the door. When he stepped into the bathroom, a hand wrapped around his heart and squeezed the blood from it at the sight of Sarah crouched on the shower floor, shaking with tears while the water pounded into her back to stifle the sound.

He tore off his clothes, opened the screen, sat on the floor and pulled Sarah into his lap with her head held against his shoulder.

'*Habibti*, it breaks my heart to know you hide your tears and pain from me. I am sorry. There is much I need to learn to be the husband you deserve. I wish you had told me of your dreams but realise I did not give you the chance. There are no words I can say to ease your pain. For some reason you find it hard to tell me these important facts. If your tears give you relief, let them fall. Each one will penetrate my heart, making it ache.'

Some innate hunch told him she forced her tears at bay for she immediately fisted them away. He cupped her face in his hands, used his thumbs to wipe under her eyes but shower water replaced the tears. With her face held up to his, he kissed both eyes, the new scar, her nose then settled his mouth over hers, drawing a shudder from her before she sank into him. Without breaking the connection between

157

them, he drew her upright and wrapped his arms around her slick body. It was a struggle to fill the soft cloth washer with soap with his arms around her. Starting at the top of her back, he gently circled the washer down her spine, over her buttocks, up the sides before he dared step back a fraction to repeat the process on her front, starting with her taut abdomen.

'You are exquisite.' He ran the washer down her arms. 'Milk-white skin, so soft - so smooth.'

'Covered in ugly freckles.'

The way she said the words told him Sarah thought the freckles were a blemish. 'Allah decided you were so precious he sprinkled you with specks of gold dust because he knew I would want to explore and kiss every speck.' He used the tip of his tongue to highlight each mark before pressing his lips to the spot. He started on one shoulder, across her clavicles to the other. There were not so many, far fewer than he expected given the colour of her hair. 'Not enough, turn around.'

When she hesitated, he turned her, held her at the waist and kissed a line of golden specks across her shoulders. A smile escaped at her sigh and relaxation of tense muscles. 'Tonight is for you,' he whispered against her ear before he sucked on the lobe and enjoyed the huff of breath when she blew it out. 'Close your eyes, relax and enjoy the sensations. Let me show you how good it can be between a man and woman but remember you can tell me to stop at any time. I promise I will.' Even if it killed him to pull away at the critical moment. But it was crucial he suffer the agony if he was to earn her trust.

Eighteen

A quiver followed the line of butterfly kisses down her spine. The sensation arrowed into her feminine centre which seemed to bloom out in heat - as though she had been set alight from the inside. The rasp of stubble sent the nerves in her skin rippling into awareness. Hakim's hands spread around her hips, drew her closer until her body moulded into his in a perfect fit. When the scent of soap increased, she realised he was lathering his hands. They slithered across her stomach, upwards over her rib cage, cupped her breasts. Her heart missed a beat then raced to catch up at the same time her breath caught in her throat as a shaft of need shot to her core. Her head rolled back into his shoulder. At the continual repetition, she lost all control. He murmured in her ear, soft words in Arabic. She didn't care what it meant for the sensual tone rippled through her, sent her emotional pain away to be replaced by blatant need.

His hands created havoc until it increased to a crescendo. Even though she had never experienced this apart from the night of disaster, she knew about it: had read about it in both the technical and romantic sense but never believed there could be such an intensity of sensation. Heat tingled across her skin, her lungs stalled and a desperate ache of need overtook her. She cried out his name when her body soared into a cataclysm of sensation. He spun her around and held her tight with his warm lips kissing her so sweetly she wanted to cry as she sailed back to earth.

Within seconds she was wrapped in a large towel, patted dry and flown through the air in Hakim's arms. He spread her out on the bed, stretched alongside her and tugged her into his arms. Not only was she boneless but her voice and mind had vanished. She managed to get her eyes open to catch his gaze which held such intense emotion.

'Words defy me.' He caught her hand and held it against his chest.

The coarse roughness refired her nerves so she ran her fingers through the ebony sprinkle of hair. When air hissed through his teeth, she couldn't hold back a grin. 'I want to touch you,' she managed to get out from a throat blocked with intense emotion.

'Anywhere,' he said before his mouth caught hers in another long kiss. She wriggled her hand free, ran her fingers down his side, explored all the dips and ridges until she reached his smooth but taut backside, which she tugged closer only because there was an innate need to be much closer.

When he shifted, a deep sense of disappointment shafted into her until he wedged one leg between her thighs and moved over her, both hands a cradle around her head.

'There are no adequate words in my language, nor yours to describe how I feel right at this moment. My heart is so full it needs to burst from my chest.'

This time his kiss plundered her soul until a new wave of sensation overwhelmed her and the urgent need for relief surged back. He positioned himself over her, gently pressed for entry, took his time, his tongue mating with hers in a frenzy. His body mirrored his tongue, drew them both faster and harder to a pinnacle until she crashed over in an unbelievable sensation she would never be able to describe.

When he dropped to her side, his harsh breaths mirrored her own. She burrowed into his chest, desperate to maintain contact. Never before had she felt the need to be so close to a person. One hand went on a journey of exploration to learn about all the ridges, planes and hollows. At every soft moan and quiet hiss she figured those spots were more sensitive.

She rose a fraction, leant on one elbow. 'The latest of those silly romances I read, got it right.' She dropped a kiss on his mouth, now game to take more control.

A laugh rumbled from his chest. 'Got what right?'

'How it would feel.'

'I am curious. How did it feel?'

'Maybe you should read the book for an adequate description but pretty darn amazing.'

He cupped her head in his big hands, brushed a kiss against her brow but his eyes, when he sank back onto the pillow, were serious.

'I will always regret our first night but maybe I should read your book for I cannot find the words to describe how pretty darn amazing tonight has been for me. Never have I felt such a closeness to a person, in every way, not only physical but also in my head, my heart and my soul.'

Stunned at the way he voiced her thoughts, Sarah dropped her head back into the crook of his shoulder and couldn't believe how much she enjoyed the moistness of perspiration, the musty scent of their lovemaking, the soft rises and falls of his chest, the warm hands on her bare skin as they ran slow circles on her hip and belly. She closed her eyes, intent on making the most of this glorious sensation until a little niggle told her once was not enough but how did you say such a thing? This was all so new. What would he think if she made a move? Would he think her to be a hussy? Was that even a word in his language? Nipples: her nipples were a skyrocket of sensation. His would be the same.

With a surge of power, Sarah let her open hand drift up his belly. The rasp of his chest hair sent a ripple of fire to her nerve endings while her hand continued upwards until she reached the small nub, amazed when it hardened under her caress.

She circled her palm.

He tensed on a hiss.

When a small grin escaped, she repeated the process on the other side, this time delighted at the low rumble from his chest. 'Do you like that?'

'This much.' He grabbed her hand and carried it lower to where his hardening length straightened and grew under her fingers.

A mixture of embarrassment and wonder swirled as she ran two fingers up and down. Even though she had read widely and had sound knowledge of the mechanics, this was the first time she had touched a man this intimately. There was a vast difference between knowledge and the actual act. Action was much better, she decided when he squirmed and pulled away.

'Enough,' he growled in her ear and flipped her onto her back and positioned himself over her. 'You have wicked hands, sweet Sarah.' His mouth covered hers in a searing kiss before his tongue began to mate with hers again, matching hers in fervour. His own fingers were far more wicked than hers. They took little time to bring her to the edge of another cataclysm of intense need until she screamed out his name in a star-studded explosion.

When her eyes opened it was to the silver of dawn through the palm leaves outside the uncovered window and a warm length wrapped around her back. Inside, it felt strange and for a moment she couldn't figure out what it was. But after running through a list of words, she landed on calm. Her brain was calm, at peace, which was so unusual for it always seemed to race at a super speed. A sigh escaped. An arm tightened around her waist.

'Good morning, beautiful,' Hakim mumbled in her ear.

'Morning.'

'Unfortunately, after one of the best nights of my life, I have to drag myself out of this bed to spend the day listening to fellow ministers argue. I would much prefer to stay right here with you in my arms. What have you got planned for the day?'

'The library.'

Hakim pulled himself up to sit at her side. 'Why don't you go shopping? Buy some new clothes.'

'You don't like my clothes?'

'I never said that; you are always beautiful but there are so few.'

The tranquillity in her brain vanished. 'I don't need more clothes and to spend a day at the shops is not enjoyable to me.' She shot from the bed, grabbed the towel still on the floor from last night and wrapped it around her body.

'I thought all women loved to spend hours at the shops.' Hakim wore wariness in his eyes as he stood, leant forwards and took her mouth in a bone-melting kiss.

'Not all.' Sarah scurried away to search for a clean set of clothes. Clothes in hand, she scampered to the shower, not sure why tension invaded her body all of a sudden. Inadequacy came to her as an answer. He must think her clothes were not good enough. Why else would he suggest she buy more? But her clothes were comfortable, the cotton suitable for this climate and were of decent quality. Anxious to escape this rush of self-doubt, her shower was quick as was dressing and running a comb through her hair. Hakim still searched his vast wardrobe for fresh robes when Sarah returned to the bedroom. He stopped her at the passage door.

'This is for you.' He held out a credit card. 'I will organise for the bank to have one issued with your name but until then use this one. The PIN number is taped to the back. There is no limit on what you can spend.'

Sarah shoved his hand away. 'I don't need or want your money.'

He frowned as he dropped the card in her bra. 'You are my wife. I don't understand this desperation of yours to refuse my financial support but for now I will respect your wishes until we have time to discuss it. If you are uncomfortable to use my card, keep it in case of an emergency. At least let me have peace of mind that my wife will not be caught in a dangerous situation where lack of funds is an issue. By the way, you are covered on my health insurance.' He pecked her on the mouth, winked and sashayed to the en suite.

Sarah had to check her watch when she reached the dining room for there were no indications of breakfast about to be served. Only five minutes to seven but there were no cutlery, plates or food. With a niggle of worry for Mariam's health, she returned to the bedroom, tapped on the bathroom door and poked her head in at Hakim's answer. 'Are you having breakfast here?'

'No, I have to discuss the items with my staff before meeting with the ministers. We have a snack while we talk.'

'Does Mariam know?'

'Yes, she has my schedule. I won't be able to make it home for the meal tonight.'

'Thank you,' was all she could think of to say when a shaft of disappointment speared through her innards. At least another fourteen hours of acute loneliness.

Sarah wasn't an idiot. Her stupid brain had already reached a conclusion but in the vaguest of hopes she was wrong, she returned to the dining room to find it as empty as the kitchen. No Hakim therefore no breakfast for the unwanted interloper. So much for stupid thoughts about the change in the meal situation once they were married. Fine – she could handle this – she was tough. Message received.

She fetched her backpack filled with the essentials for a day in the library and left, running the trek to the gate to work off the urge to cry. She turned onto the pavement, strode to the corner and turned right where she ran full pelt to the bus stop to use up excess energy and rid herself of a new level of unwanted angst.

Once on the bus, she counted off positives to force negativity away. At the stop before the library, she decided to continue on to the city where she found a cute little café where she pigged out on fried tomatoes, eggs, hand-made hash browns with two slices of toast and a large mug of white coffee. It was a shock to discover how many hotels had planned full-on Christmas dinners since Muslims didn't celebrate the day but with so many expats here it shouldn't have been such a surprise. It took two hours to find a fake tree in a plastic pot and some shiny strands to hang over the branches, all from a flea-market in the old town where the prices were cheap enough to suit her strict budget.

Happy with her purchases, a smile hovered on the journey home while she recalled family fun on past Christmas Days. Her joy managed to turn into sadness when she realised tomorrow would be the first ever Christmas without family. To inject her own private little piece of tradition into the Muslim home, she set up the tiny green tree on the table by the pool so it wouldn't offend anyone. Pleasure hummed the next half-hour while she dangled little strips of silver, red and gold over individual branches, tweaked up the ends so the strands didn't slither off and tied a number of strands into tiny bows. There was still no sign of Mariam or lunch at one, not that she was hungry after the substantial breakfast but she figured she needed to make a trip to the nearby general store to replenish her food stock. With no bar fridge in the bedroom, she would have to stash non-perishables in with her clothes where there sure was plenty of room.

By dinner time, hunger pangs gnawed. The only reason she hovered outside the dining room at the designated time was to confirm her unwanted status. While she trekked to the bus stop sadness sank deep but she wondered how Mariam thought she could get away with her tactics. Hakim was bound to find out.

While relishing a dish of yummy traditional food, she figured Hakim would be horrified at the tiny eatery which catered for the less fortunate. But the atmosphere hummed with quiet chatter and laughter, which gave her a sense of belonging, especially with the friendly greetings diners and staff bestowed on her as though she was a regular. She wasn't the only foreigner, with couples from several different races at nearby tables but she was the only sole diner, which etched at her innards.

It annoyed her when her phone pinged while she scraped together the final remnants of sauce soaked rice, which was too delicious to waste. She glanced at the screen.

Where are you?

In a café. She typed back after a few seconds to think.

Why?

I was hungry, she typed back.

Why did you not eat at home?

Well this is a loaded question; one she wasn't sure how to answer.

Did you eat at home?

No.

Why not?

I had an engagement booked.

So, ok for you to eat out but not ok for me. About to leave.
She switched her phone off, paid the tiny bill with a substantial tip and ambled to the bus stop with her mind in a turmoil.

Nineteen

The second the key rattled in the lock Hakim switched off the TV and stood with eyes honed on the front door. It always twisted his heart when fear lived in Sarah's eyes. Tonight was no different but her stance hinted at determination. The very second she turned from the door, he swept one arm around her, drew her close and kissed her.

'I have wanted to kiss you all day,' he said before taking her mouth again while he ran one hand down her spine to her cute butt so he could tug her closer. Only when one of her hands looped around his neck was he sure he could talk.

'I cut dinner short tonight because I was anxious to come home to you.' Still with her held against him, he led her to the sofa. 'The house has an empty aura when you are not here.'

'If I had known what time you were to arrive home, I would have been here.'

'My mistake. Please forgive me.' He smiled at her upturned face which held a curious expression. He dropped another kiss on her brow, ran his hand down her arm, tugged her even closer. 'You fill my thoughts all day, even when I am supposed to concentrate on what others say.'

This time she drew away with curiosity in her eyes.

'Why did you not tell Mariam you would be out for the evening meal?' Even though he expected it, the way her tension returned in an instant sent him on alert. When she tried to pull away, he tightened his hold and kissed her again.

She avoided his mouth by dropping her chin to her chest. 'Impossible to tell her when she's not here.'

'Not here? She was still here when I arrived home. Please explain what you mean.'

Her shoulders rose high then fell on a huff as she lifted her head. 'This morning I asked if you were having breakfast at home because there was no food, plates or cutlery in the dining room, no Mariam in the kitchen. Same at one and at seven. I was hungry so I caught the bus to a café where I enjoyed a lovely traditional meal with locals who accepted me into their little group and went overboard to make me welcome.' Sarah turned and headed along the passage with a rigid back.

He chased after her, turned her around and wrapped her in his arms. 'Mariam said you were not here for any of the meals she prepared.'

Sarah stiffened even more. 'I detest dishonesty.'

'Mariam would not lie to me.'

Sarah's fierce glare said a lot. 'Which makes me the liar. Thank you for your support and your trust. Excuse me but I need a shower.' She tore from his arms and ran.

By the time he reached the bedroom, the shower ran - behind a locked door. He rested his brow against the wood, unsure what to believe. Surely Mariam would not lie, surely she would not treat Sarah with disrespect. Sarah must be mistaken. But how was it possible? As he straightened, his fingers grubbed through his hair in frustration. He so wanted to spend quality time with Sarah but with little free time at the moment it was difficult to fit in time with her. Since it was useless to attempt to talk through the barrier of a solid door, he keyed in the code to disarm the security system to the outside, rolled a glass door to one side and stepped out onto the covered patio. He turned a lounge sideways so he could see when Sarah emerged, settled down with legs outstretched and thought about the woman he loved but who was still an enigma to him.

Sometimes she came across as super-confident but other times there was a certain naïveté about her. Sometimes her words and actions confused him yet she was plain-spoken: to the point with simple logic. Nobody could ever accuse her of being a chatterbox. In fact she was the opposite – often painfully opposite with simple one word answers. Reserved was a good way to describe her until someone maligned her when she became fiery in defence. There was a sadness about her but even when she seemed down, she always rallied fast. Her refusal to accept his financial support was a worry. Maybe an incident in the past made this such an issue but it was difficult to get her to talk about the past for she never opened up.

A shadow caught his eye. He glanced up to see Sarah step into the room with only a towel caught against her chest. His pulse quickened. When she glanced around the room, he caught the paleness of her face but there was a redness around her eyes. His heart twisted at the thought she still didn't trust him with her tears. It twisted even more when he noticed her shoulders slump when she eyed his side of the bed. Was she disappointed he wasn't there? Hope soared but still he watched. The towel dropped to reveal the pale sheen of her skin. She was perfect in every way: long-limbed, curvaceous in all the right places and so beautiful. When she turned, he studied the perfect globes of her breasts, and dark gold thatch hiding her precious jewels. Everything about his manhood rumbled to life and stood to attention.

She must have noticed him for her eyes narrowed in challenge but she couldn't hide the trace of a smile as her lips parted. Dear, Allah, please let her be glad I am here, he thought. Eager to be with her, he stood and returned to the room.

'You are the most beautiful woman I have ever met.'

It amused him how she grabbed a nightgown and flung it over her head to hide the blush on her cheeks until her head emerged with eyes downcast while she tugged the cotton down to hide her assets. This was the unsure Sarah, the one who lacked self-confidence. He reached her, held out his hand. 'Come outside to enjoy the freshness of this beautiful night.'

'I thought the doors were alarmed.' Her voice was as unsure as the woman, but she followed without resistance.

'This one is but it does not mean we cannot go outside.' He indicated a panel. 'The code is the same as my pin number but with a zero in front and another at the end. You can come out here any time you like but make sure you reset the alarm although no-one has ever attempted to climb the wall to get in. It is purely an extra level of security needed when you are born with a royal title. Another of the things I dislike about being who I am.'

He led her to the lounge, tugged her down next to him. After raising the back, he settled against it and twisted Sarah around until she sat between his legs, leant against his chest. A sigh of pure contentment escaped, especially when the warmth from her body seeped through the fine fabric of her nightgown and his loose top. He wrapped his arms around her. 'What did you research in the library today?'

'I didn't go.'

Determined to keep this conversation neutral, he fought to not move. 'What did you do instead?'

'Went into the city for a couple of hours, came home for lunch but since there was none I went to the local general store.'

He so didn't want to discuss missed meals but really could not avoid it. 'Mariam has gone to her unit for the night but I will speak with her in the morning to clear up any misunderstanding.'

The stiffening of her body said so much.

'Relax. All day I think of the time I can come home to be with you, to hold you in my arms, to delight in your company, to...' He kissed her ear and smiled at the quiver across her shoulders.

'Please don't put your hands on my neck?'

He stilled at the plea in her voice. 'Can you tell me why?'

Her body stiffened even more before she eased back against him. 'It's... I can't talk about it.'

'It would help me understand but for now I can only speculate it is the reason you are so afraid of men in general and I presume it was recent and why you came to my country. Am I right?'

'Yes.'

'Thank you. Maybe when you learn to trust me more, you will find the words to give me the full story. But for now, show me where you are comfortable for me to touch. How about here?' He brushed his fingers against the top of her shoulder.

'Anywhere below, just not my neck but anywhere else.'

A smile escaped. 'Anywhere? How about here?' His hand dropped to her lap and swept across her hips before he bunched up the nightgown and probed those golden curls he adored. Sarah squirmed, causing him to harden even more.

'Maybe we would be more comfortable in bed,' she murmured at the same time she pressed her backside against his groin, sending his hormones on a rampage. Vixen knew what she was doing to him.

'We would be but for now we will remain right here while I explore your delightful body.'

Her body quivered against his, he prayed it was with pleasure as he showed her what he meant by exploring every inch he could reach without moving her until the orgasm took a hold of her. Only then did he move them to the bed where his meek wife became a tigress. He adored this Sarah.

With her head rested on Hakim's sweat-moistened shoulder, she breathed him in, terrified for her heart because if this marriage went pear-shaped, her heart would be in tatters and she doubted she would ever be able to drag the pieces together to heal. All day, she had missed him, even when less than favourable thoughts invaded her stupid brain. But it wasn't Hakim who had treated her with disrespect. He never did. Always he was gentle, his caresses soft but sure, his kisses bone-melting. His consideration for her pleasure, even denying his own, blew her mind. How many men were so generous? But he was like a magnet: one she had no hope of resisting.

It was scary to know she loved this man when he didn't love her the same. How could he? This marriage was only because of a miniscule chance she had conceived although no precautions had been taken these past two nights but with less than a week before she was due, the chances of falling pregnant were even less. What will happen when she confirms there is no child? Will this be one of the shortest marriages on record? If it was, she would never regret it, but it would be for the best for she would never fit into the type of life Hakim led. Should have thought of it before she turned up at the palace for the ceremony, she thought and flipped over.

'Where are going?' Hakim murmured in her ear.

'Nowhere.'

His arm reached around her waist, tugged her into the curve of his big body so was spooned against her back. 'Sleep well, my beauty.'

The soft kiss he planted on the tip of her shoulder ended with a long sigh; she hoped it was one of pleasure. Maybe if there were more nights like tonight he might want to stay married. It was up to her to prove she was worthy. But how?

The very second Sarah opened her eyes, she knew she was alone, which left a heavy sensation of loss in her gut. Light streamed through the window in a definite message it was later than normal. She shot upright, swung her legs to the floor and hurried to the bathroom for a quick shower. It wasn't until she pulled a top over her head she remembered it was Christmas Day. Already her extended family would be in the throes of their traditional sea-food barbecue. She scoffed at the thought they wouldn't have to accommodate her allergy to shellfish. No special foil-wrapped package of turkey or chicken grilled to one side to avoid shellfish contamination.

Eager to make the promised face-time call, she hurried, but carried her laptop out to the pool area to give her a few minutes to find the courage to face up to breakfast alone. If there was any breakfast. Her feet stumbled to a halt in front of the table which should hold her little tree. Like in Oliver

175

Twist, the table was bare. A quick scan of the area revealed a tiny piece of tinsel stuck to the side of the mat in front of the door to the kitchen. It wasn't a shaft of anger which lanced through her but more one of pain. What was so offensive about a tiny green tree and pieces of shiny metallic strips? It wasn't as if she had planted it in the middle of the sitting room and it wasn't even a pine tree. Nobody but her came out here. It didn't take genius status to know who had taken it. Gut instinct told her Hakim wouldn't be so mean. There was only one other person here, well, apart from the groundsman she had discovered on one of her journeys along the driveway. He lived in a separate cottage behind the garage, maintained the grounds and was about the only friendly member of staff, apart from Tariq, she had met so far.

Doing an about turn, she stalked inside, through the dining room and straight into the kitchen where Mariam stood at the sink. Mariam spun around, frowned and opened her mouth.

'Where is my tree?'

'What tree?' Even with the gorgeous pale brown skin of a native, Mariam couldn't hide the blush of dishonesty nor the quick glance towards the garbage bin.

Sarah beat her to the bin, lifted the lid and gasped at the mangled ruins of her tree - now twisted and squashed. The metallic strips were mushed in with slop.

'Why?' Sarah lifted the tree out and began to straighten the branches.

'Heresy,' Mariam spat.

'Excuse me? Heresy is an opinion opposed to a religion. I don't oppose your religion - have never said a word against it. And how does a tiny tree oppose a religion. You have trees in the garden here.'

'We are Muslims. You cannot go against our beliefs.' It stunned Sarah how Mariam shouted.

'A tree has no religious significance. For goodness sakes, there is a huge Christmas tree in the centre of the city, put there by your Muslim leaders. Why don't you go and tear that one down?'

'What is this about?'

She jumped at Hakim's voice. Silence ensued while he turned his questioning glance to both women in turn. She didn't have a clue what to say. She fought her own battles and wasn't about to land Mariam in the manure pit, especially when she already didn't like Sarah.

'Mariam?' Hakim asked with one raised eyebrow.

Mariam kept her mouth shut and turned back to the sink.

'Sarah?' Hakim crept closer, took the tree from her hands. 'What is this?' He held it up.

Sarah straightened her spine. 'It's mine but Mariam stole it, destroyed it.'

'Stole? A bit harsh do you not think?' When Hakim's hands moved to his hips the branches poked through the gaps in his fingers.

Sarah copied his stance. 'If I went into your study, took a gold pen from the desk and threw it in the bin after I'd stomped on it to destroy it, I would be stealing from you, wouldn't I?'

'Yes, but there is a vast difference between a valuable gold pen and a cheap plastic tree.'

It was stupid but a wash of tears spread across her eyes. 'An item doesn't have to be worth a lot of money for it to be precious to a person. Nothing I own will ever have the value of any item you own but the things I do own are precious to me.' She snatched the tree from Hakim's fingers and held it against her chest. 'All I wanted was a tiny bit of Christmas cheer since I'm not with my family and friends for the first time ever.' When the tears began to leak, she ran.

Back in the pool area, she fought to untwist the gnarled branches while daring any tears to fall. It was a silly little tree, for goodness sake. Footsteps padded across the concrete. She ignored them, set the tree in the middle of the table, sat and opened her laptop.

'I am sorry.' Hakim stood in front of her. 'Muslims don't celebrate Christmas.' He pulled out a chair. 'To us it is a normal day of work but I have no objection for you to carry out your traditions. I have spoken with Mariam.' He reached across and took her hands in his. 'I have no desire for you to be unhappy. We had such a fabulous night. Please, let us not have disharmony to spoil the day. I know it is a special day for you and guess you may be a little homesick. I wish I could stay home for you but I have a busy schedule today.' He stood, rounded the table and drew her up into his arms.

It wasn't hard to relax against his chest. If only she could stay right there. It was one place she felt secure and at ease.

'Come, let us eat breakfast together,' he added with a smile meant to ease her angst.

'Why are you even here at this time? You're usually gone by now. I thought you had left.'

'Today is a normal office day. When we sit in parliament all ministers have Thursday to deal with office matters. Today I have the pleasure of not starting my day until ten, which means I get to enjoy your company over breakfast. But before we go inside…'

His kiss curled her toes and set her innards on fire. If only she could resist him.

Twenty

A fter another fantastic night of exquisite pleasure, Sarah's heart twisted when she waved Hakim goodbye. Her hopes of spending a day with him were dashed when he announced he had royal functions to attend for most of the day and into the night. First he would attend the mosque for Holy day prayers. It wasn't this hour she was miffed about, for she already accepted his Friday would include the traditional prayer session, just as he did his best to pause five times a day for prayer. It was the rest of the work-free day she had been keen to spend with him. Instead, she forced an aura of positivity and returned to the bedroom to collect her backpack and laptop. Might as well spend the day in the library.

While in the bus she visualised yesterday's session on Facetime. Even though she loved to chitchat with her family, she had to force a smile when the entire time her heart had hurt because she wasn't home. Yesterday was the first time homesickness had brought her to her knees. Mum, Dad, Pete, Danny and Samantha had each spent five minutes talking to her while they opened the presents she had left for them. Even though she was super glad of the substantial sum of money they had banded together to deposit into her account as their gift to her, the disappointment of not even one gift to open had been like a serrated knife sawing through her heart. It shouldn't have hurt for she wasn't big on receiving gifts. They had never been as important to her as the day with family – until yesterday.

To make up for her heartache she had gone into the city to enjoy a full-on Christmas lunch amongst ex-pats in a hotel. Big mistake. She'd sat at a table for one, chased the food around the plate simply because the loneliness etched away her appetite. It was ridiculous how one could be incredibly lonely in a room full of happy, chatty people. The only really fabulous part of the day had been when Hakim came home in time to share the evening meal with her and afterwards. A grin broke out. How many times had he brought her to a climax during the night of exquisite lovemaking? The entire night had been about him giving her the most amazing pleasure.

She mounted the steps to the library to find less patrons than normal. She figured most locals would be at prayer which made it easy to find a seat facing the door. One day she might get over her fear and be comfortable to sit anywhere, she thought as she settled down, plugged in her laptop.

It frustrated her when visions of the night interfered with the words she was supposed to type, especially when the number *six* ended up as *sex* and *lived* managed to type itself in as *loved*. When she figured nourishment might feed her brain, she re-packed her gear and headed to the coffee shop tucked to one side of the ground floor. After she'd plonked her gear on a table set against the glass wall, she ordered coffee and a salad filled wrap. Food in hand, she returned to the table and settled back to watch the overhead television set to a low volume.

She bit into the wrap and chewed, enjoyed the freshness while watching the local news on an English speaking channel. Her jaw jammed when she recognised a group of people in a new bulletin. Sure she had made a mistake; she rose to move closer to the screen hung high on the wall. Nope, not a mistake. There was her husband next to not only his parents, but his brothers, their wives and all of their offspring. She tuned out noises in the room to make out the commentary, which managed to bring back the serrated knife to tear away at her innards. The family was celebrating the anniversary of the present Sheikh's rule. There was to be a public meet and greet with special displays of dancing and activities followed by a private family celebratory feast at the palace. A family affair: one she hadn't been invited to. If she hadn't understood the message before, she sure did now.

Every cell in her body froze. She didn't know how long she stood there but when her brain managed to function again, the news bulletin was over and a new programme had begun. Like a robot, she flung her bag onto her back, picked up the cardboard mug of coffee and remains of the wrap she could no longer stomach. She tossed the food into the bin as she walked through the doorway, without a clue about what to do. Concentrating on research wasn't about to happen, nor would she return to an empty house where she didn't belong and wasn't welcome.

The agony of homesickness returned with a vengeance while she roamed. She took little notice of where she went, nor did she care. When the thought came she was supposed to let Mariam know she would not be home for a meal, she phoned to give her apologies even though it was pointless with Hakim not home.

The sun had gone to bed before she hailed a taxi for there was little choice but to return to Hakim's house. Never one to carry a lot of cash, she hadn't brought enough to book into a hotel and she sure wouldn't use Hakim's credit card. She really should carry her Cashcard but it would only tempt her to use more than the strict weekly budget she took out in cash every Monday. Until she found a new job, she needed to take care with her budget.

She had the taxi stop at the corner for she was certain they would question her destination if she said she wanted to enter the high and mighty Prince Hakim's property. With her recent spate of bad luck, the driver could call the police on his radio, in Arabic so Sarah didn't know what was said.

A sense of dread accompanied her along the circular driveway. She shoved her key into the keyhole, twisted and pushed only to find the door yanked open.

'Where have you been?' Hakim sounded angry.

'Out, where have you been?' She stalked inside and kept on, taking arms out of straps as she went. With anger vibes shooting into her back, she knew Hakim was behind her.

'Why did you not answer your phone?' Hakim asked.

'I rang Mariam.'

'Turn around and face me,' he ordered.

Oh, oh, he was more than angry. She turned but kept her eyes glued to the floor.

'I have been worried about you. You did not tell Mariam where you were.' At least his tone was more conciliatory.

'Not true. I told her I would be in the library.'

'But you were not there.'

Her eyes shot up. 'How do you know?'

'I sent Shahir to pick you up. The librarian informed him you left early in the afternoon.'

Miffed, Sarah rolled her eyes. 'So now you're checking up on me?' But a thought shot into her brain. Shahir was a night guard, so it hadn't been so long ago Hakim had sent him. When Hakim came closer she shook free from his arms.

'What is wrong?' His hands dropped to the side. 'I was not checking up on you. I was concerned because you were so late so asked Shahir to pick you up so you would be safe. Mariam tells me you were out for the evening meal.'

'As per your orders, I informed her well before.' Sarah plonked onto the bed. The mattress dipped; Hakim settled next to her.

'Can I ask where you were?'

'I'm not sure. I walked.'

'Why?'

'I wasn't able to concentrate on the books.'

'Why did you not come home?'

'A bit hard when my home is in Sydney.' She squirmed at the loud hiss beside her.

'I am unsure what to think about your answer. I would appreciate it if you could explain why you do not consider this as your home.'

She blew out her cheeks. 'A home is a place where you are comfortable: a place you can cuddle up in the corner of a sofa with a mug of hot chocolate. It's where you can leave a book overturned and it will still be there when you go back to read another chapter. A home is a place you are welcome, where people don't judge you but accept you for who you are. It's not a mausoleum where you don't dare leave a crease on the sofa or have a plastic tree on an outside table. It's not a place where half of it is forbidden to you, where you are unwelcome. A home doesn't have regulated mealtimes served only to the owner. A home is where you are part of a family who love you as you love them. In Sydney I have a home.'

Hakim dropped to his knees in front of her. 'But you have no family.'

Sarah's shook her head in disbelief. 'Really?' She turned head away, wondering if he would follow up on her answer.

Instead, he took her hand, gripped it tight. 'It appears we have a few issues to discuss. Let me see if I can remember them and deal with them one at a time. You have always been welcome in my home. I have never judged you and adore the person you are. So why do you think you are being judged?' He gripped her chin to turn her face towards him.

'You might accept me but are never here. Your normal hours at home are from ten at night to seven in the morning, most of which is spent asleep.'

'Not last night, my sweet. There was little sleep last night.'

With her head still caught in his fingers, she couldn't hide the heat on her face, which also rushed inside and sent hormones on a deluge through her veins before the entire amount centred in her core. His lingering kiss made her determination to not melt into a puddle of need almost impossible but at a picture of the television item she wriggled free.

Hakim eyed her with his head skewed to one side. 'You did not really answer my question. If it is not me who judges you, who does? Mariam?'

Uncomfortable, she twisted her head to one side. 'Tariq is the only one who has no issue with my presence. And maybe Ali. He is always kind.'

'You have issues with Mariam?'

'No, she has issues with me.'

'What issues?'

'I wish I knew. Maybe you should ask her.'

'I will but now let us deal with another item. Are you not comfortable living here?'

'I can live anywhere and make it comfortable but apart from this room, there is nowhere I can relax. I can't spread out my papers and books to work. There is no cuddly seat to curl up in…'

'There are enough lounges and chairs in the sitting room for twenty people to cuddle in,' Hakim interrupted.

Sarah whipped her head around. 'You might get away with it.'

'What does that mean?'

'You are an intelligent man.'

'As you are intelligent when you give half answers but do not reveal all. From what little you have said to date, I have the impression Mariam is giving you a hard time. Am I correct?'

Sarah lifted her shoulders. 'I don't wish to answer.'

The snort from Hakim sounded like a half laugh. 'Because you insist you never lie but are not one to be negative about people, I presume. I admire your loyalty to someone who, I fear, does not give you the same level of consideration. I will speak with her.'

'I can fight my own battles.'

Hakim laughed. 'Of that, I have no doubt but this is not a battle of your making. It is Mariam who needs to treat you with the respect you are due. You are my princess, the woman I have chosen as my partner. If she cannot treat you as such, she will be replaced.'

Horrified, Sarah shot from the bed. 'You can't fire her.'

Hakim stood, wheeled her against his body. 'I can since it is my home and my money pays the wages.'

'It is only my presence which has caused this friction,' she mumbled against Hakim's chest. 'I cannot be responsible for a loyal employee to lose their position.'

His hands swept down her spine to cradle around her backside and draw her even closer. 'It is early days. We will

185

sort this problem. Now, there are countless tables in this house. We will find a suitable spot for you to work. Even in my study. You can cuddle up on any chair, leave your romance book open but be careful I don't read the page you leave it at to find out how the author describes *darn good.*' He dropped a kiss on her head. 'I don't care how many plastic trees you put on display and you have free rein to make any changes you like to turn this mausoleum into a home. An interior designer was employed to decorate it but the décor has never bothered me since I spend so little time here. Now you are my wife, there are no sections out of bounds to you but if we do have unmarried men as guests, I beg you to not enter the passage to their rooms, purely for the sake of propriety and good manners. I do not understand the bit about mealtimes but presume it is another of Mariam's ploys.' He drew away, held her hands at arms-length while he eyed her. 'It is late, you appear to be tired so maybe we should retire to bed.'

'I need a shower.' Sarah ducked under his hands and turned towards the bathroom.

'Better still.' Hakim laughed at her squeal when he lifted her into his arms and carried her through the doorway. The seduction began before he lifted the top over her head. By the time they were both naked, she squirmed with need.

Twenty-One

'**B**reakfast can wait a minute.'
At the sound of Sarah's soft voice, Hakim paused at the kitchen door and leant against the wall. He wondered if Mariam realised how the quieter Sarah's voice got, the madder she was. He now understood, to his detriment.

'You are not allowed in here.'

Hakim jerked upright at Mariam's terse words. No wonder Sarah hinted that half the house was out of bounds. He settled back against the wall in the hope he would hear what Sarah found difficult to reveal.

'Hakim said I am permitted to go anywhere in this house.'

'This is my kitchen.' Mariam's tone had not eased.

'Oh, I'm sure Hakim said this house belonged to him but maybe I am wrong. If so, please forgive me but I wish to know why you are so mean to me. Why do you lie to Hakim to discredit me?'

'I not lie.'

'Really? Then it must be Hakim who lied. You told him I didn't appear for any of the meals you prepared on Wednesday yet I was in the dining room on time and still there ten minutes later but there were no meals. Last night you told him I didn't turn up for the evening meal, yet you didn't mention I had rung to let you know I was unable to get home. What have I done to offend you?'

'You trick Hakim to marry you for his money. You gold-digger.'

'Yes, I dig in the soil for samples to study under the electron microscope and x-ray diffraction machine. On occasion I find gold particles but I don't specifically dig for it.'

Hakim had to stifle a laugh at Sarah's pernickety answer.

'You came here to throw yourself at a rich man to use his money.'

'You really think I threw myself in front of a car to gain the attention of a complete stranger? You're crazy. I had only been here twelve hours, had no idea who Hakim was when I fell in the road while I searched for the address of my employer. I didn't even know he was a prince until two weeks later.'

'You lie.'

Hakim stepped into the kitchen. 'Everything Sarah says is true.'

Both women squealed as they spun around. Mariam paled with shock while Sarah hung her head.

'I now understand why Sarah is so unhappy in my home. You disappoint me, Mariam. You treat my wife with disrespect and yet Sarah supported you last night when I threatened to let you go. Sarah insisted you remain as my housekeeper. As for Sarah being a gold-digger, she refused to accept the *mehr* I gave her and to date has not spent one dirham on my credit card. For some reason she insists she will only use her own money.'

Not prepared to give the stunned woman a chance to say a word, he hovered over Mariam and enjoyed the way she cringed. 'I could not understand a comment Sarah made about meals only for the owner. You had specific instructions to cater for all her needs. But now I know you refuse her entry to *my* kitchen.'

He moved his glance to Sarah whose head had risen with eyes wide. 'You will tell me exactly how many meals Mariam prepared for you when I was not here.'

Sarah choked as she shook her head. 'I can't.'

He turned back to Mariam. 'See how Sarah defends you? One of you will tell me the truth.'

The silence was heavy.

'From your silence I must assume the answer is not one meal. Mariam, I *will* release you from your duties if you do one more thing,' he lifted a finger and shook it front of Mariam's face, 'to make Sarah unwelcome. She is my wife. You will show her the same respect you show me. If you disrespect Sarah, you disrespect Allah for it is Allah who sent Sarah to me. Now we will enjoy our breakfast.' He turned, stalked through the doorway but caught Sarah's whispered apology to Mariam. How she could apologise was beyond him but it confirmed his belief that his wife was one of the most gentle, caring and kind people he had ever met.

The tension in the air was thick while Mariam placed dishes of food in front of him. Sarah crept to her seat where she sat with head bowed and hands in her lap. He waited until Mariam returned to the kitchen before he dared speak again, praying he could keep his anger at bay. Sarah certainly did not deserve his anger. Somehow he would find a way to bridge the chasm between the two women.

'Eat, sweet Sarah.' He watched as she served a small spoonful of spiced mashed beans and spread it on a piece of flatbread. 'I presume I still do not know every detail.' Her glance caught his eyes before it shifted a fraction. If only she knew the rush of red to her cheeks told the truth. 'And I presume you will not be the one who tells me.'

'No.'

'Your loyalty is to be commended but is not deserved. I am shocked by Mariam's behaviour.'

'She wishes to protect you from the wiles of a complete stranger from the other side of the world. I understand when we married with such haste. There was barely time for her to get to know me.'

'What did you eat the first few days before we married?' He knew the question was loaded so was not surprised by Sarah's slight hiss but somehow he would learn the truth.

'I had the supplies from the unit.' She shoved a piece of rolled up flatbread in her mouth, probably to not answer any more questions.

'And since then?' Hakim stilled with his fork in the air while he studied Sarah's facial expressions. They said so much more than her words.

She swallowed her food and paused. 'I got by.'

Hakim laughed. 'An answer which tells me little in one sense but says a lot. You are very clever with your words when you are desperate to not criticise someone who deserves to be criticised.'

'I don't like to denigrate anyone.'

Hakim reached over to brush his hand down her face. 'One of the many attributes I like about you. What have you got planned for today?'

When he caught her eye he swore he spied hurt in the depths before she dropped her head. 'Please tell me what troubles you.'

'I am not troubled,' she said to the plate but scooped up the last of her bread and popped it into her mouth. She chewed and took utmost care to place her cutlery on the plate as though she had eaten sufficient when she had eaten so little.

'Sarah,' he said louder to catch her attention.

She stilled, lifted her head a fraction but wouldn't catch his eye.

'It is obvious you are not happy with my question. Neither of us will leave this table until you eat enough to sustain you until lunch and you tell me what concerns you.'

'You have appointments today?'

'Sorry, yes, I am required to open a new section of highway today. One of the joys of being a member of the royal family. My brothers and I share the load with my father when a request is made for royal presence.'

'I understand.'

'But you are not happy. Let me see your face for I never enjoy speaking to the top of your head.' It shocked him to see her eyes awash with tears. 'Sarah, please tell me what troubles you?'

'I hoped we could spend the day together.'

Hakim dropped his head into his hands. 'I also wish we could but my timetable was filled with appointments long before we met. Most are impossible to cancel. It is the schedule of an unmarried man who filled the hours with work and community events to allay a deep loneliness. Many time slots are annual events, like yesterday. Despite my assistant trying to re-arrange my schedule to give me more time with you, many events cannot be changed. Today is one of them. I will be home by five so we can enjoy the night together. After we have finished our meal I will show you my schedule. Now please eat or I will worry all day that you might faint through lack of food.'

It was a relief when Sarah piled sliced tomatoes and a hard-boiled egg on top of a spoonful of hummus on her plate. Within minutes it had all gone, confirming his suspicions about her lack of sufficient food. A thought came to him. 'Did you have a meal last night?' She certainly had nothing after she arrived home and they expended an awful lot of energy both in the shower and his bed. Her silence gave him the answer.

'Why did you not say?'

'You didn't ask so it wasn't important.'

'To me it is vital. I will not be pleased if I discover you miss any more meals. Now come, I will show you my schedule so you better understand my time constraints.' With her hand wrapped in his, he led her to his office, but paused when she gasped at the doorway.

'Oh, wow, you have so many books.'

He glanced around, took note of the three walls of shelves filled with books: books he rarely noticed any more. He supposed it would appear to be a lot to someone who had never been in here. 'You are welcome to read them all.'

'Are they in Arabic or English?'

'Half in each. I was raised bi-lingual since English is virtually an international language. Many have both titles next to each other. Fiction on these two walls.' He swept an open hand to indicate the walls he meant. 'Non-fiction over there.'

'I can read them, are you sure?' For once her eyes held his, hers with more animation than he had seen before. At last, something to give her joy.

'Of course. This room is yours to enjoy but not my computer as there are many private government programmes and messages which cannot be revealed.'

'I understand but would never use another person's computer in any case the same as I would hate for anyone to use mine. I have too much research material I can't afford to lose. I trust your computer is password protected.'

'Of course. Come, sit here.' He held out a chair before taking out a file of papers and opened it at this week's schedule. It was too full, with little free time for a married man, especially one so newly married. No wonder Sarah was desperate for time together. This was no way to build a relationship. Sarah lifted the page, scanned it for a few seconds, turned the page, repeated the process until she had seen an entire six months of blocked in spaces. Nausea churned in his stomach as he grasped her hand.

'My assistant still must work to free up more time and shorten the time spent at each function. It is not an easy task. I have given instructions to halve times I spend at functions where possible. It will take time, especially to change functions which come up soon. Later functions are easier to find replacements for and I have made instructions to not accept any future requests. Choose one of the free nights for us to have a special meal out. You choose the venue and I promise to keep the date free, barring an urgent event of importance.'

He watched Sarah study the sheets until she finally filled in a night six weeks from now. Why not one sooner, he thought but decided not to say anything since he had given her the option. 'And the venue?'

'Why not the place we went to where you said we would have privacy. I will make the booking for eight.'

'An excellent choice. I will see what other date nights we can wangle in the meantime.' He filled in the time and restaurant name.

Twenty Two

It wasn't often a book didn't hold her interest but today not a word did. Sarah placed the bookmark between the pages and set the book on the side table. She curled her legs under her body and snuggled back into the soft leather. Nausea had worsened by the hour, along with the cramp. The only plus was the knowledge she wasn't pregnant. Would this be the end of the marriage?

After four days of relative calm with a tenuous friendship now developed with Mariam, life had been more pleasant. She had reached an agreement with Mariam to fix her own breakfast and lunch if Hakim wasn't home with the upside she got to eat toast and fresh fruit in the mornings with basic salad sandwiches or chopped fresh vegetables for lunch.

Now she knew Hakim's schedule, she accepted time alone would be a major component of her life for several months. A grin broke out. A picture centred in her mind of the job application she had emailed earlier. It wasn't much of a job; a few weeks lecturing at a local university while a lecturer was on sick leave but it was right up her alley - teaching chemistry to first year students. Her Sydney professor's recommendation should help. He confirmed she had tutored science students for several years, which should be an asset. Plus she lived here. With the position for only four or five weeks it might swing the job her way. Few would seek such a short term position, certainly not people from overseas. She didn't care. Work was work which was better than hours spent each day in a library. If she was successful and proved herself, it could lead to a more permanent position in the future. Sarah crossed the fingers of her right hand and closed her eyes in an attempt to relax. It often worked to ease the severity of the dreaded dysmenorrhea on the first day of her cycle.

'Sarah, are you not ready?'

She jolted at the voice. 'Uh, what... Hakim?' She straightened too quickly and winced at the stab in her tummy.

'Why are you not ready?' Hakim crouched in front of her.

'Ready for what?'

'We are dining out tonight.'

Please no, not tonight. 'You never said.' She pictured his schedule. He was supposed to be at a planned meal.

'Did Mariam not tell you?'

'You gave Mariam the day off because of the public holiday.'

Hakim brushed a hand down his face. 'Sorry, I thought she would have told you. The family always get together on New Year's Eve to give thanks for the year we have had and welcome the new year in.'

'And you want me to go?'

'Of course. You are family.'

Sarah really wanted to point out how, since the wedding, he had been on several *family* functions which hadn't included her but it would only create more angst. Nor did she need to dine out and be sociable when her stomach was about to explode. 'I'm not in the space to socialise tonight, nor am I hungry.'

'You are expected. Tonight is also to welcome you into the family. Come.' Hakim rose with an outstretched hand. Only then did she realise he must have been home for a while since his hair was damp and he wore fresh casual slacks and a white cotton shirt with the top two buttons open.

'Give me ten minutes.' She rose, stretched and regretted the movement when a wave of nausea brought out a band of sweat across her brow. Tonight would be an ordeal but she could hide away in a corner to feign sleep if the nausea became too bad. She had survived worse when the dysmenorrhea had been so severe she needed medical intervention. Nowadays she had learnt how to handle it but going out wasn't one of the coping mechanisms. Sleep was.

The shower took as long as sucking a peppermint. It often helped settle the stomach. Since Hakim wore casual clothes, she dragged on a long dark-blue cotton skirt with a pretty, paler top with an embroidered sweet-heart neckline and sleeves gathered lightly at the wrist.

Another peppermint the moment the car engine turned over managed to settle her stomach for the short journey to a house she had never seen before. It didn't take long to figure out it belonged to the second oldest brother, Karim, who was much like Hakim in appearance but stockier in build.

Her heart managed a couple of tumble-turns when Karim led them inside where a line of three women confronted her.

'You will remember, my wife, Faria.' Karim indicated a pretty-faced woman.

Sarah only remembered the haughty nose but now she could put a name to the face, which didn't seem any friendlier tonight.

'Khalid's wife, Aziza and Pari, Rafal's wife.' Karim indicated each with an open hand.

'I'm glad we get another chance to meet,' Sarah said with a smile at each; one they didn't return. The barefaced glares sent a definite message – tonight would not be pleasant but it wouldn't be because of what Sarah said or did. She was glad of Hakim's arm around her waist while they walked through a vast room dripping with gaudy wealth, into an even larger dining room which must seat fifty people. It seemed Karim, or his wife, was keen to display their wealth. More like the wife, Sarah thought after she noticed the obscene amount of jewellery the woman wore around her neck, along both arms and dangling from her ears.

Drinks were handed around. The men stood in a group and spoke amongst themselves while the three wives stood shoulder to shoulder and spoke in undertones in Arabic. Sarah stood alone between the two groups with a forced smile on her lips. Everyone turned at footsteps near the arched doorway. The Sheikh and his wife stood there. There was a brief silence before cheerful greetings and smiles resembled her own family get-togethers. Her nerves settled at the noise. It was possible this meal wouldn't be as bad as she thought.

The head waiter gave instructions in Arabic. Seats were pulled out and everyone settled into their designated chair, Sarah next to Hakim on one side at the end.

'Are you okay?' Hakim asked in a whisper.

'Just dandy.'

A trio of waiters prevented any more words when they brought dishes from the kitchen. A thick soup was ladled into bowls. She swallowed down bile at the stench of seafood. Now she was in trouble. While the Sheikh said a prayer, Sarah eyed a prawn tail surrounded by lumps of fish and the pink flesh of crab. Her stomach curdled. This was her worst nightmare.

Prayer finished; everyone lifted their spoons in unison. 'I can't eat this,' she whispered to Hakim from the side of her mouth.

'You must. It is the height of rudeness to not eat what your hosts have prepared for you.'

'You don't understand.'

'Eat. You cannot offend the host.'

Even though her stomach tightened and roiled, she lifted the spoon, dipped it into the spicy chowder-type sauce, lifted a tiny amount to her lips, sipped and swallowed. Her stomach sampled and rebelled. Acid rose up - she managed to swallow it down. She wiped the cold sweat from her brow, certain this would not end well. 'Where is the bathroom?' She nudged Hakim.

'Eat.' He nudged her back.

It was a fight to keep the contents of her stomach down so she stood. 'I'm going to be sick, where is the damn bathroom?' She turned and ran towards the doors from where the waiters had come, hoping it was the kitchen.

With her hand over her mouth, she wove around massive benches to reach a pair of sinks on the other side of the room. She retched and swallowed but made it in time to bend over the sink before her stomach rebelled, three times before it was safe enough to lift her head. Every centimetre of her skin had gone clammy, her stomach hurt like blazes and her knees were so weak she folded to the kitchen floor with her head buried in her hands.

'Sarah, are you okay?' Hakim squatted in front of her.
She couldn't help a scoff. 'No.'

'What happened?'

'I threw up.'

'This I know but why?'

'Because my stomach didn't like what was in it.'

'Why did you not mention you were unwell?' He held out his hand to help her up.

'Why didn't you… never mind.' Ignoring his hand, she struggled up to clean out the sink. Her stomach tightened but she managed to turn the tap on full and swished water around the bowl. After ten years of painful periods, she was used to this but also after ten years, she knew the signs. Tonight she had to find a corner to sit – close to a bathroom.

'Leave that.' It was a different soft, sweet voice.

Sarah twisted her head to see a young face peer from a white tucked-in hijab.

'I will clean it for you. You need to rest.' The smile was gentle and the most genuine smile Sarah had received since she'd arrived in this country.

'Thank you.'

'Come, you are to go home,' Hakim said from behind as he took her hand.

It was the worst thing to happen for the motion of the car always made the nausea worse. 'No, please, let me sit quietly to settle my stomach.'

'I have already called Hafiz to have the car at the door.'

Sarah struggled to pull away but Hakim lifted her into his arms and carried her through the dining room where eight pairs of eyes followed, along with mutters which Sarah bet weren't complimentary. Hakim placed her on the back seat of the car and pushed her inside. When the door closed, she expected him to get in the other side but the car

200

moved off. She turned to see his back returning to the house. How could he just leave her?

Years of experience told her what would happen next so she wound down the window and stuck her head in the opening.

The journey home, despite not being long, was a nightmare. Every hundred metres or so, she had to yell for Hafiz to stop the car so she could get out and throw up in the gutter, even when there was not a skerrick of food left to eject. Back home, she could call her G.P. for an injection to stop the nausea but here she didn't even have a G.P. Once home, she staggered inside, raced to the bathroom where she sank to the floor with her arms around the porcelain bowl, wishing she was dead, she felt so ghastly.

'Sarah, wake up.'

'Go away' She shoved at the hand on her arm.

'You cannot sleep on the bathroom floor,' the voice continued.

'Why not?'

There was no answer. Instead Hakim lifted her from the ground, carried her into the bedroom and placed her on the mattress. He unbuckled the sandals she hadn't dared take off at the door, dropped them to the floor, the thuds echoing from the tiles. Finally awake enough to register what was going on, she opened her eyes to peer at the bedside clock. After one. It had taken him five hours to come home.

'The bathroom floor is not the place for someone in your condition.' Hakim drew the covers over her.

'My condition?' Sarah choked on the words. She shoved the covers away and struggled upright. 'Exactly what condition are you referring to?'

'You are with child.' While he undressed on the other side of the bed, Hakim had a pleased grin on his face.

'What makes you think I'm pregnant?'

'My mother, my sisters-in-law, they all say the same. The vomiting at the sight of food.'

'So your mother and sisters-in-law know my body better than I do?'

'Of course not but they all had the same signs, the same morning sickness. We will arrange for a doctor's appointment tomorrow.' Hakim bundled up his clothes, tossed them into the hamper.

'I will not see any doctor. As for morning sickness, even though I have never experienced it I do know it rarely begins before the six week mark of a pregnancy. Since we haven't known each other for six weeks, this child must belong to some other man.' With an unusual rage, she stood, arms akimbo. 'But since I was a virgin three weeks ago, we must have an immaculate conception as cited in the religious scriptures.'

Half bent while getting into bed, Hakim paused. 'You are not with child?'

'No.'

He eased into the bed. 'Then why were you so ill?'

'What the hell do you care?'

He appeared to be stunned as he sat against the headboard. 'Of course I care.'

'Really? If you had thrown up with such violence, there is no way I would have tossed you into a car to fend for yourself then leave you alone for five freaking hours before I bothered to check to see if you were still actually alive. I would have called a doctor to make sure you hadn't been poisoned or had some fatal infection.'

Hakim leapt from the bed. 'You need a doctor?'

'Not now. Five hours ago a doctor would have been appreciated.'

'I do not understand why you would need a doctor five hours ago but not now.' He reached her, took her hands but she shook him off. 'Why did you not ask Hafiz to take you to a doctor?'

'You really are a piece of work. I was so ill I could barely manage to ask Hafiz to stop the car umpteen times so I could throw up. Take her home, you said – he obeyed your orders.'

'He never said you were ill on the way home.'

Sarah couldn't help rolling her eyes. 'Unbelievable,' she muttered under her breath as she climbed back into bed.

Hakim sat on the edge. 'I will call a doctor to find out why you were ill.'

'I know why.'

'Then please explain.'

'I suffer from dysmenorrhea which is severe cramps and nausea at the onset of the monthly cycle. Sometimes it is not so bad but sometimes it can be severe, like tonight.'

Hakim stood. 'So you are untouchable for a few days?' He headed for the door. 'I will leave you to sleep alone and will sleep elsewhere.'

Her mouth gaped at his back. He strode through the doorway without another word or a look in her direction but she had no energy to chase after him. Arguing wouldn't make an iota of difference so she crawled back into bed and curled up in the foetal position; the most comfortable position to ride out the pain but nothing would ease the ache in the region of her heart. Already, he didn't want her because she wasn't pregnant. Tomorrow he will ask for a divorce.

Twenty Three

Worried about Sarah's health, Hakim created an excuse to leave the event before luncheon was served. Why he even agreed to attend such a trivial celebration on New Year's Day said a lot about his desperation to fill the hours pre-Sarah. Not a single minute of the activity had he absorbed since Sarah's angry face had centred in his mind all morning. While he dressed he had watched her sleep. She had been too pale to waken. She needed the sleep more than he needed to resolve last night's dispute but he owed her an apology for he had been so overjoyed at the thought she was with child he hadn't even thought she might be in need of medical care. Now he needed to beg her forgiveness.

When he spied Mariam mopping the entry floor, he paused. 'How is Sarah? Is she out of bed yet?' The screwed face of bewilderment sent a rock to the pit of his stomach.

'Miss Sarah left in a taxi less than an hour ago.'

'Left? Where did she go?'

Mariam dumped the wet mop into the bucket. 'She did not say but mentioned you would know where to find her if you wanted to.'

'Excuse me?'

'She carried a bag. I think with clothes.'

'Clothes? But why?' A niggle of unease sent a message to his brain. He scrabbled in the pocket of his robe for his mobile phone, punched in Sarah's number, held the phone to his ear and raised his eyes heavenward at the message her phone was either switched off or out of range. It would never be out of range in this city but being switched off was more than possible. A second call summoned his car along with two men.

Once seated in the car, logic told him hotels would be high on the list on where to look. 'How many hotels in this city,' he asked Abdullah, one of his fill-in guards when the regular men had days off.

'Sir, I don't know for sure but over five hundred, why?'

'We need to search them all until we find Sarah.'

He grimaced when he noticed the two men glance at each other. 'Yes, I was at fault and am a fool. Drive. Muhammad search your phone for hotel names starting with the last half of the alphabet. Ring each one, ask for the presence of Sarah Anderson. I will take the first half.'

Five hours later, a wodge of fear had lodged firmly in his stomach. Certain they had either phoned or appeared in person at every hotel, Hakim began the list again but paused when an idea surged. He speed-dialled Tariq. 'My friend,' he said when Tariq answered.

'Hakim, you have a problem?'

'Why do you think I have a problem?'

'When you phone on my day off, you have a problem.'

'All I need is a name. Which hotel did Sarah stay in when she arrived here?' He grimaced at the ominous pause.

'What did you do, my friend?'

Hakim winced. Tariq knew him too well. To call each other friend meant they spoke as best friends, not employer/employee nor prince and bodyguard.

'Why do you think I did anything?'

Tariq's laugh was more of a scoff. 'For the gentle-hearted but strong-willed Sarah to have fled to an hotel, the pain you caused is severe.'

'Hotel name.'

'Not without a confession.'

'Okay, my fault. A mistake I will never repeat.'

'Ah, but will the delightful Sarah forgive you enough to give you a chance? Poor woman loves a man who has little clue about what a wife needs in marriage.'

'You think she loves me?'

'She has not told you?' Tariq laughed. 'You have not told her how much you love her, have you? Oh, this is so good. Since I am her guardian do you want me to talk to her?'

'All I need is the hotel name. I can make my own apologies.'

'For once I wish I did not have the day off. This I would love to see.'

'Name or job?' Hakim was desperate.

'Threat does not work, my friend for every week the crown prince offers me work as the head of his security.'

'Do not even think I will allow you to work for my brother. All I need is the name.'

Another laugh from Tariq. 'Try the old city, opposite the museum and mosque.'

'The old city? Why would she go there? Never mind.' Embarrassed, Hakim hung up and gave directions.

Thirty long minutes later, he stepped from the car with a glance to the local mosque, one he had visited on innumerable occasions. Concern niggled about the poorer area with the textile souk so close and the spice souk nearby. His questions to the receptionist were met with caution, which he appreciated in one sense but he finally managed to illicit enough information to tell him Sarah Al Fasir was at this moment supposed to be in the American Grill, one of the hotel restaurants. It pleased him to know Sarah used his surname but at the same time her own name would be safer for her and he would not have wasted five fruitless hours in search of a ghost. Of course none of the hotels had a Sarah Anderson registered, even this one when he first phoned.

His stomach muscles were tense by the time he managed to reach the archway to a small eatery. His held breath gushed out at the sight of Sarah's gold hair. The next breath stalled at her frown when she spied him.

'What are you doing here?' The moment the words were out, he knew they were a bad choice but common sense had taken a leave of absence.

'Eating.' She tapped a fork on the edge of a plate piled high with a burger, salad and fries.

'I meant, why this hotel?'

'It's quaint with its Arabian nights decor, clean, comfortable and affordable to underlings like me.'

He dared not sit too close but pulled out a chair opposite. 'In a not so safe area.'

Sarah shrugged. 'I'm safer and more welcome here than in your area. Everyone has been kind and helpful. No-one has treated me as though I have the plague.'

A groan rumbled from his mouth. When he spotted a glass of wine in front of Sarah he lifted it and tipped the contents into a vase of flowers. 'We do not drink alcohol.'

With tight lips, Sarah snatched the glass from his hand. '*You* don't drink alcohol. I don't have the same restrictions. I choose not to most of the time, but if presented with a glass of champagne to drink a toast, I will imbibe.'

'I need to apologise...' He glanced around the room, half-filled with diners. 'Can we go somewhere a little more private?'

Sarah cocked her head. 'No.'

'No?' So few people dared say no to him it was a novelty but Sarah had no hesitation in speaking her mind.

'No. My food has just arrived. I'm hungry. This is the first meal I have been able to stomach since...'

'Last night. I will join you. We will eat before we talk.' He flicked a hand in the air to attract a waiter. After ordering the same as Sarah and a glass of iced tea, he asked Sarah what she would like to drink.

Her smile to the waiter was over-sweet. 'The juice of a lemon in half a glass of water with a teaspoon of grated ginger and a teaspoon of baking soda stirred in as it is served.'

Words defied him at the request. Hakim locked his eyes on Sarah's face but the waiter had no qualms at the weird request, giving her a smile and nod before he left. It annoyed him when Sarah took a large bite of her burger and rolled her eyes in pleasure. Darn woman knew how to annoy him and also knew there was little he could or would do. Tossing her over his shoulder and carting her to the car was high on the list of what he wanted to do. Kissing her senseless was a close second. The third was what got him into this mess to start with so he forced from his mind the picture of a naked Sarah in his bed.

The waiter served the drinks before he dropped a teaspoon of white powder in Sarah's glass and stirred. She grinned while it fizzed up to the top. 'You owe the man a decent tip,' she said before she took a sip at the foaming liquid. 'He had to go to the kitchen to find the ingredients. Twice now,' she added and made a show of tapping the side of the glass to show him the liquid was the same as the glass he emptied out.

'Why did you not tell me?'

'You didn't ask before you jumped to a baseless conclusion. A bad habit of yours.' Sarah stuffed a few chips in her mouth and chewed, the movement erotic when a vision of what else she could do with those lips stirred his manhood into action.

His cheeks heated with guilt. How she managed to unsettle him when he had, had a lifetime of training to not react to comments, was hard to understand but there was a lot about Sarah he still did not have a handle on. It was a relief when his food arrived. To avoid any more blunders, he hoed into a meal he rarely ate because it was messy and unbecoming of a prince to indulge in when in public but tonight he did not care, especially when the flavours were so good. Hopefully, none of the guests present knew who he was, although there was a good chance the staff chatted behind the scenes. Rumour would be rife so he needed to be careful to not give credence to supposition. Getting close to her could not happen despite his desperation to drag her into his arms.

When he finished first, he fiddled with his empty glass while Sarah took her time, deliberately, he bet to himself. When she finally pushed her plate to one side, he was ready to explode with frustration. The fuse hissed when he noticed her bare left hand. 'Where is your ring?'

'On the bathroom bench.'

'Why?'

'I figured you wanted it back.'

'Excuse me? Why would I want it back?'

'Since you only insisted on this marriage in case I was pregnant and you walked out on me the very moment you learned I wasn't, logic told me the next step was divorce.'

His mouth opened but no words would form. 'Allah, please guide me,' he managed to rasp out through a constricted throat. The constriction went south and threatened to eject his meal when he noticed Sarah fighting back tears.

'You are so wrong, *habibti*. You have no idea how hard it is right now to not reach across this table and haul you into my arms. But I cannot and this is not the place to discuss this. Are you ready to come home?'

'I have a room booked.'

He searched the walls for inspiration. 'Please, Sarah, would you allow me to join you in your room so I can beg your forgiveness in privacy?'

Without a word, she stood and sauntered through the doorway. He had to scramble after her. As he passed Muhammad, he gave orders to pay the bill, including her room. When they reached the room, he held up his hand for Abdullah to stand guard at the end of the passage. It would create an uproar if anyone spied him anywhere near a woman's room in a hotel, despite said woman being his wife, a situation he wasn't prepared to make public yet so Sarah could have the freedom she was used to.

The very second he clicked the door shut, Sarah swung around to face him. Both ferocity and sadness lived in her eyes.

'I am sorry for every crime I committed last night,' he said. 'I was so overjoyed at the thought of a child it did not register your illness could be for another reason. And I certainly have no wish for a divorce.'

With her head cocked to one side, Sarah seemed to think about his words. 'When you sent me home on my own, it hurt, a lot. It indicated you didn't care about my welfare. It showed a meal with your family was far more important than ensuring I wasn't about to succumb to some dastardly illness. When you called me untouchable and walked out on me, a giant pad of steel wool scoured out my innards. Then I remembered why you married me and figured since there was no child, the marriage was over. Logic told me you didn't want me any longer.'

Even though he was stunned, Hakim's heart twisted at the brush of tears caught on the end of her lashes and the utter pain in her voice. 'Sarah, no. I left because you needed to sleep undisturbed by me. You were unwell. I know I used the poorest choice of words but all I meant was that we would not be able to make love for a few days.' He swept his hands through his hair. 'Dear, Allah, I have made such a mess of this,' he muttered to himself while he searched for the right words to say.

'Never do I want to cause you pain but it seems I am a master of failure in this respect. This morning while I dressed, I watched you sleep. I was desperate to waken you to clear the air but your cheeks were too pale with dark bruises under your eyes. This told me your sleep had been as scanty as mine and your illness had taken its toll. Sleep is the greatest of healers and you needed to heal so I left you to sleep and gave Mariam orders to not disturb you. I was so concerned about your welfare I left the function early so I could return home. I have searched for you since. Your phone is off. I could not find you: maybe Allah's punishment for me for I have been overcome with worry and regret.'

'I left a note to explain where I was and my phone is flat. I forgot to bring a charger.'

'I found no note. I am sorry, so sorry and this is how untouchable you are.' Sure she would resist if given a chance, he swept his arms around her, drew her in tight and kissed her, long and hard until her tension dissolved and she kissed him in return. This was one area they always connected like Yin and Yang. There was never any disharmony when they physically joined like this. How he wished he could spend more time together. His dislike for his royal connections intensified.

When he managed to draw apart, blood thundered through his veins. It took a moment to catch his breath. 'We either go home or I stay here with you so I can hold you in my arms. Without you, I cannot sleep.' It worried him when Sarah wriggled from his hold. It sent his heartrate even higher while he watched her back disappear into the bathroom. The tightness in his chest eased when she returned carrying her toiletries. She dropped them into a small overnight bag he recognised as one of his. She glanced around the room, zipped up the bag and stood in front of him.

'Ready?' she asked as though nothing had happened.

'More than ready.' No way would he utter another word.

At home, he found a large note taped in the middle of the bathroom mirror and her wedding band on the bench underneath. Impossible to miss. He read the words which detailed exactly where she would be and why. He tore the page from the mirror, screwed it tight and tossed it into the garbage bin, angry with himself while humbled by Sarah's honesty. He had to be the biggest fool ever to exist.

He snatched up the ring, returned to Sarah who had already changed into night clothes and sat on the edge of the bed. He knelt in front of her, grasped her left hand, slipped the ring where it belonged and planted a kiss on it.

'I married you because you are the only woman for me, the only woman who has ever touched my heart. I married you because I could never bear to lose you. *Never* do I want a divorce.' He swept the three tears from her cheeks, settled his mouth over hers and crawled onto the bed next to her where he wrapped her in his arms, glad he did not prescribe to the days of separation when a woman bled as was written in the Qur'an.

Twenty Four

Disbelief simmered, along with an excited shimmer of nerves. Sarah searched for the science building at the British University set in the International Academic Centre. The message last night for her to come for a final interview meant a restless night. Now she was sleep deprived. Another yawn escaped before she could study the façade of the building to which she had been directed, glad to see the British University logo on the outside. This time she made sure she had precise directions to ensure there was no accident to disrupt the start of a new job. Although, she grinned, last time she had met Hakim. For the past five days he had done his best to atone for his poor choice of words. She wasn't sure how he managed it but he'd cut short a few engagements to spend quality time with her, but still it wasn't enough. Loneliness had become the major feature of her life. Maybe this job would help alleviate the soul-destroying emptiness she lived with most days. With an open hand she shoved the glass doors open and stepped inside.

Two hours later she stepped out through the same doorway, overjoyed but worried. The job was hers on one condition. Since she was married to a local she needed Hakim's permission to work. Ridiculous in this day and age but no signature, no job. She wriggled into a taxi, eased back with a sigh and recalled his words about supporting her need to work.

Once home she had a pile of work to do, to figure out lesson plans for the subjects she was required to teach for the next four weeks, maybe five, but the thought of Hakim's agreement kept centred in her brain.

Dinnertime loomed with Hakim due fifteen minutes before to give him time to shower after a day in the office. While packing up her gear she thought of one way to make him amenable. The moment car tyres crunched on the drive, she scooted to the bedroom to lay back on the bed as though she'd had a nap, which was ridiculous for she never napped during the day unless illness made it essential.

Hakim walked in, smiled, bent over her and took her mouth in a delicious kiss.

'Give me five minutes.' He straightened, whipped off his Keffiyeh followed by the white Kandourah, both limp after the day's work. He tossed them into the cane laundry basket. The second he went into the bathroom, Sarah stood, tugged off her own clothes, stepped into the shower recess behind him and snaked her arms around his already wet body. Both hands crept upwards, rubbed against his chest. He grabbed her hands and swung her around.

'You are ready for me?' he growled.

She didn't have to ask what he meant. 'I've waited for you all day,' was all she managed to get out before his mouth clamped over hers, hands gripped her backside and lifted her to straddle his waist with her back pressed against the marble wall.

'All day I have thought of this, hopeful and even prayed. Never can I get enough of you,' he whispered in her ear. A bevy of kisses swept over her face, skipped her neck and crept lower, turning her into an instant bucket of desperate need.

Their coupling was fast, hard and hot, exactly what she needed after five days of abstinence. Hakim was the most generous of lovers, always ensuring her pleasure before his own. And, oh, wow, didn't he know how to pleasure her?

The only way she could describe dinner was hot, with sexy innuendos slipped into the conversation and steamy gazes sent in her direction. Each glance caused her body to ache with need. By the time the plates were empty, every cell inside her was aroused in desperation.

'Come.' He held out his hand and rose.

She took it. He wrapped his fingers around her hand and tugged her against his solid length. His arm swept her hard against him so she knew how aroused he was. But she needed his signature so drew away a fraction.

'Do you have any objection to me taking a few classes at university? Two days a week. Tuesday and Thursday,' she gabbled out as he tugged her along the passage.

'Which university?' A hot suck on her ear lobe sent her need into a frenzy.

'British Uni.'

'Go for it.'

'I need your signature.' She yanked him to a halt.

'Why?' A peck landed on her nose.

'I am married to a local.'

Hakim drew back. 'I do not understand.'

'Being married to a local means I need my husband's permission to work at the university which is ridiculous for if I was unmarried or married to a foreigner, I don't need permission.'

'You told them who you were married to?'

'No, why?'

'For your own safety it is better our marriage be kept from the public.'

She jerked out of his arms. 'Why?'

Hakim rubbed both hands through his hair. 'You are not used to our ways. For you to have the freedom to attend such places as the university alone, without a family member as chaperone, it is better you are regarded as an unmarried tourist.'

Miffed, she stood in front of him. 'Chaperone? Really? This is the 21st century.'

'Surely you understand our ways. Arab men are protective of their women. It is even more important for members of the royal family to be protected. There is always a risk some crank might take a pot-shot at royalty. My brothers' wives cannot go out alone. They must be in a group of women or have a male relative with them at all times, or in their case, a bodyguard.'

'Yet your wife can go out alone.' Anger rose but now clarity fought its way through the confusion in her brain. Now she knew why she was excluded from all family public events.

'Only because I have kept our marriage quiet. This way you are not a target of the media or unsavoury people who would like to harm members of the family. You are used to your independence and would be stifled by such restrictions.'

She turned into Hakim's office. 'Instead I am to lead a life of utter loneliness.' She picked up the form and a pen, flattened the paper on Hakim's desk and pointed to the blank line at the bottom. 'I need you to sign here for your permission. At least if I work at the university, I might have a chance to actually talk to someone other than you in the sparse hours you are home.' It was a relief Hakim signed without reading. He hadn't even asked what she was teaching so obviously wasn't interested. The thought caused her innards to hitch and tighten. She folded the paper and shoved it into the plastic file to keep company with the other papers she would need tomorrow. A deep wodge of sorrow managed to settle in her gut.

'You have many people to talk to,' Hakim held out the pen.

'Really? Who?' She snatched the pen and crossed her arms.

'Me.'

'One person, between the hours of 10 p.m. and 6 a.m. most of which you are asleep.'

'Mariam, your friends.'

'Mariam, yes, now she actually talks to me and all of my friends live in Sydney.'

'Surely you have friends here. You can have coffee dates with my brother's wives.'

Sarah couldn't help the snort of derision. 'You are kidding, aren't you?'

'No, why?'

'They don't like me.' She cocked her head. At his silence she turned and headed for the bedroom. Deep hurt replaced the sorrow and chased away sexual need.

His footfalls followed. One hand grasped her upper arm. 'Surely you have friends at the library.'

'No.' She shook his hand off.

'No-one?' The other hand went to her shoulder and drew her around.

'No-one. You spend all day talking to workmates, your men, members of the public, your assistant. You have non-stop social engagements, have family functions where you talk to everyone. Me? I live in a vacuum of nothingness.'

She spun around, grabbed her nightclothes and locked herself in the bathroom where she fought back tears. Here she could drown her pain under the spray of hot water. Never had so many tears threatened, more in the past few weeks than her entire life.

After she'd dried off and tugged a nightie over her head, she hesitated, certain Hakim would be on the other side of the door but unless she planned to spend the night in the bathroom she had to open the darn door. She turned the key, flicked the doorknob and yanked the door open. He sat on the side of their bed. Doing her best to ignore him, she sidled around to reach the covers, tugged them back, wriggled into the bed and turned her back on him. The entire situation was ridiculous since it was nowhere near bedtime and a huge surge of adrenalin meant there was no way she would be able to sleep.

'Why do you not tell me about these situations which upset you?' Hakim's hot breath brushed against her ear.

'I just did.'

'After you let your thoughts simmer and brew into anger. You must tell me as soon as they happen so I know what distresses you and we can discuss them to sort out solutions. I am sorry. I had no idea you felt this way.' He nipped at her earlobe then licked the spot. An instant shaft of need shot to her core. Darn man knew how to stir her libido into a frenzy.

'I will work out ways for you to join me at some of my functions, maybe introduce you to people who may become closer friends.' His mouth kissed its way down her arm before he sucked her fingers into his mouth. 'In the meantime, let me see if I can turn your pain into pleasure.' He tugged the covers down, twisted her over and set her body on fire.

Twenty Five

'Hello, you must be Sarah.'

Sarah paused with one foot on the ground and glanced up to study the young woman dressed in a hijab draped over a plain evening gown in navy blue. The only parts of the woman visible were her pretty face and long hands; one held out in greeting.

'Yes.' Sarah stepped from the car, smoothed down the creases in her evening slacks then grasped the proffered hand in a brief handshake.

'I am Rana. His Highness asked me to explain about the events for tonight. He is with the crown Prince. I am one of the team leaders for the younger children.'

Confused, Sarah walked beside the woman into a large reception area filled with a noisy crowd of well-dressed locals and expats. To give an indication of the wealth present, jewellery glittered under an abundance of recessed lights. All she knew was that they were to attend a charity fundraiser for disadvantaged children but she thought Hakim would be the one to meet her after her arrival in a silver 4WD driven by the groundsman. At least her sparkly top fitted in but it didn't take long to figure she would be the only woman with no jewels hung from ears, throats and hands. Even Rana wore a row of bracelets on both arms as well as a drop pendant over the fabric of her hijab. The large red stone was no doubt a true ruby.

'Tonight there is a silent auction.' Rana led Sarah into a huge ballroom with three massive chandeliers lined up across the ceiling. Tables nestled together around the walls, displayed a vast array of different objects high-lighted by LED lights.

'Generous people and businesses donate goods. Our guests pencil in bids on those items over the next two hours. The highest bidder buys the item.'

They stood at the first table. A pad and two pencils lay in front of a large modernistic painting of the beach.

'Everyone is given a number. They write their number next to the bid so no-one knows who has made each offer.' Rana indicated the sole number written on the page. The amount was measly given the size of the painting. 'We must get you a number.' Rana slipped her arm through Sarah's elbow and drew her around.

'Oh, no.' Sarah brought the other woman to a standstill. 'There is no way I could compete with these people and besides, I don't need any of these items.' She swept a hand around the room.

'But everyone must bid. It is why they are here – to raise funds for the children.'

Unsure what to do, Sarah decided discretion meant she would get a number but left alone, no-one would know she didn't bid. It took fifteen minutes before she had number in hand but with Rana stuck like a limpet at her side, they paused at each item to study it as they strolled around the tables. Sarah gulped at the obvious value of most. No way could she afford any of these. And what would she do with them?

'Which ones do you like?' Rana asked.

'I have no need for most of these items. What would I do with a huge sculpture?' She waved her hand up a down a modern monstrosity cast in bronze.

'But surely you might like some jewellery?' Rana ran her fingers over a diamond necklace, set in gold: twenty-four carats by the rich colour.

Sarah laughed to hide an unbidden wince. 'No way, I never wear anything around my neck.'

'But it would be so pretty on you.'

'What would be the point of having it if I never wore it?'

'A pashmina?' Rana fingered the finely spun wool in shades of grey and soft blues.

'In this heat? It's never cold enough in this country.'

'But it would be great when you travel.'

It would, and it was gorgeous but Sarah shuffled to the next item. The bracelet was pretty with inlaid sparkles and the only item she would consider wearing but already there were two bids, both well over her annual income. 'Why is this so expensive?'

Rana read from the little card. 'White gold with diamonds and sapphires, from Tiffany. Do you like it?'

'Yes, but I could never afford it.'

For the next thirty minutes, Rana discussed each item as though Sarah had to make a bid but after she'd snuck a peak at bids already written down, she knew they were all out of her reach. It would be an insult to write down an amount she could afford. Every now and again she searched the room for Hakim and began to wonder if he was actually present. The only indication he was here had been what her limpet had said earlier.

'I was told there would be refreshments,' Sarah finally said in an effort to get away.

'Oh, yes, sorry. Through the door at the end. I will come with you.'

Sarah paused. 'I really appreciate the time you have spent with me but I need the bathroom before I eat.' Since she had already spied the sign earlier, she hurried away, glad she was at last alone. Even though she had used the visit as an excuse to escape, she made use of the facilities then took her time to amble through the ballroom. To avoid individuals in the crush she kept her back to the wall. Even here, where she was certain no-one was about to pounce on her, instinct and a deep-seated fear, insisted she keep an eye on every individual. It was a relief to find few people in the large anteroom set up with refreshments. She bypassed the cold drinks, found a counter where hot drinks were made to order by impressively dressed servers. She dawdled over her selection of haute cuisine finger-foods, enough to fill a stomach on the verge of grumbling with hunger pangs. With both hands full, she found a spot against a wall in a corner, the empty chair a relief for sore feet.

While she tasted and enjoyed each morsel, thoughts of the past couple of days wove through her mind. The first day in front of students had been a challenge but also a joy to actually interact with students with fun repartee. Today had been hectic. It took some time to ensure the preparation for tomorrow's classes was perfect but she'd managed three hours research at the library before rushing home to dress for tonight, the first real foray into public life with her husband: her non-existent husband.

She searched the room and stilled. Hakim stood in a group of men. The very second she caught his eye, he turned away. The simple action shouldn't have hurt but the shaft of an arrow speared through her. The arrowhead twisted in her stomach when the men dispersed and Hakim moved on to another group without so much as a glance or smile in her direction. When a woman reached out and placed her hand on Hakim's arm and they smiled at each other, the arrow shredded her heart. She turned away.

By the time she placed the remains of her snack on the end of a table and returned to the main ballroom, she had worked out what Hakim meant when he told her he would figure out a way to include her in some of his social events. She was far from stupid but it didn't require a high IQ to conclude her attendance at such functions would be as lonely as if she wasn't present. He had ordered poor Rana to keep her company. And who was the woman who had no qualms about touching him in public?

Miffed, she returned to the auction items and put ridiculous bids she would never be able to pay, on each one, but double-checked they were at least one dirham below the highest and to make the bid appear genuine, she squeezed in her number above the highest bidder. It scared her to write several zeroes after a digit but it filled the time until a gong struck several times. There was instant silence but the rumble of voices began again while the people crowded down one end of the room where a long dais had been set up. To ensure no-one would notice her, she hid at the rear of the crowd with her back to the wall.

'Why do you hide back here?'

Sarah stifled a squeal at the brush against her shoulder the same time a man spoke. She wrenched her shoulder away and glanced up to see Hakim's oldest brother. 'Oh, Your Highness, you scared me.'

'Please forgive me. In private you may call me by my name. You are family but why are you not with your husband?'

225

Good question. 'If I answered, I would be lying and I do not tell lies so maybe the question would be better asked of Hakim.'

'You have not been by his side at all tonight.'

'No.' Awkward. 'I believe he has been busy.'

'It is a wife's role to support her husband.'

With her cheeks instantly ablaze from the inside, Sarah made a show of searching for Khalid's wife. 'Yet, Aziza is not with you.'

'No, our daughter is unwell. Aziza was needed at home.'

'I'm sorry, I trust it is not serious.'

'No, a head cold I think. I must leave you.' As quickly as he had arrived, Khalid was gone, striding towards the dais where Hakim stood behind the microphone. Sarah recognised four security guards near the two royals. Tonight they wore evening wear to appear as normal patrons but few present wouldn't realise who they were.

A woman made an announcement, followed by a lengthy commentary about the charity. It became obvious she was one of the administrators for she gabbled on so long restless feet scuffled, which only ceased when she announced the auction lots were about to be handed out. One by one, Khalid was handed each item with the corresponding card handed to Hakim who called out the numbers. The successful bidder went forward to collect their item before going to a discreet table at one side where they made their payment, hidden by a carved bi-fold panel. Sarah couldn't see the logic since the person had been named and bids had been written on cards for all to see.

The list was endless. Bored, Sarah switched off but did a double take when a clear voice called her number. Horrified, she shot a glance at Hakim who smiled and held up the white-gold bracelet she had admired. She shook her head and waved her hands from side-to-side, certain she had kept her bid lower than the highest.

'Miss Anderson,' Hakim called with the bracelet held in the air.

Every darn person in the room honed their eyes on her. Mortified, she walked to the guillotine. Hakim handed her the bracelet. 'There has to be a mistake,' she whispered. 'I didn't have the highest bid. I can't afford this.'

'Please take it. I will explain in the car. You can't make a scene.'

'Make a scene? The highest bidder will be the one who makes a scene.'

'I was the highest bidder and have already paid. Now please, take it.' To make sure she did, he clipped it around her wrist but immediately turned away to read out the next item.

Dismissed, Sarah held her head high all the way back to her hidey spot at the back of the room where she stood behind the tallest nearby man. When the last numbers were about to be called, she snuck outside to find a taxi to take her home. It was ridiculous to be so conscious of being out of place as though she had landed on a remote planet amongst creatures who had no resemblance to a human when her wish to attend social functions had been granted. But she hadn't envisioned she would be an outcast in a room full of over four hundred people.

Her freedom was short-lived. Hafiz approached. 'The Prince asks for you to wait in the car.' He crowded her around a corner to the car parked in the shadows.

The long wait gave her over-active mind an opportunity to conclude it had been deliberate to usher her to the car when no-one else was around. The bet she made to herself came to fruition when Hafiz got in, the engine hummed to life, the car crawled around the corner to the front steps and

Hakim slunk in within seconds so no-one knew there was a woman inside. Every organ inside her shrivelled into desiccated coconut.

She huddled against the door and closed her eyes to feign sleep but the moment the car pulled onto the road, Hakim eased along the seat and drew her against his shoulder.

'Did you enjoy the night?' He dropped a kiss onto her head.

She couldn't lie but to tell the truth was beyond awkward. 'It was different.' She undid the bracelet and dropped it in Hakim's lap. 'This belongs to you.'

'No, I bought it for you.' He scooped it up and grasped her hand.

'Why?' She tugged her hand away, tucked it under her backside.

'It is the one item you took a fancy to. I always buy one of the items as my donation to the charity. If it is jewellery I give it to my mother or sisters-in-law but now I have a wife I can have the pleasure of buying for. Do you like it?'

'Yes, but I have no need of such expensive jewellery and how do you know… never mind, I've figured it out. Rana was ordered to stay with me the entire night.'

'Not ordered, no. I asked if she would show you around, to keep you company. I thought you would enjoy a young female to chat with, maybe find friendship. Yes, I asked if she would let me know which items you liked because I wanted to give you a gift. Since I was to buy an item I wanted it to be one you would enjoy. You do not have to need something to simply enjoy it. Now, my beautiful wife,' he tugged her hand free, 'let me put this where it belongs.' He clipped the bracelet around her right wrist. 'It suits you. Elegant but not over the top. I understand why it appealed to you. You are not one for flashy jewels but suit more refined jewellery, like you. Elegant beauty and tonight you are beyond beautiful but I would prefer you not wear this outfit in public.'

Sarah drew back. 'Why not?'

'The pants show off your figure too much.'

'Hardly, they are loose and not clingy.'

'Elegant, like you but they attract too many eyes from other men.'

'Tough.'

'Excuse me?'

'Tough. They can stare all they like. It doesn't mean they will ever get to touch.'

'Arab men prefer other men to not even glance at their wives.'

'But since they all regard me as an unmarried woman, as you demand, they have the right to feast their eyes as much as they want. I will buy tight pants next time. Ones that cling to my backside and are tight around the crotch.'

'I will cut such clothes into a thousand pieces.' He wrapped his arms tight around her, drew her close, nuzzled her head into his shoulder, growled then kissed her, long and searching, which managed to melt her innards into a puddle of wanton need within seconds.

Twenty Six

This time Sarah was in the same car as Hakim so maybe, after three days where they'd spent a tad more time together, he wouldn't palm her off. The car slowed in front of a different theatre to the one they had been to before. Not so modern but more traditional.

Hakim leant towards her. 'Stay in the car. Hafiz will park around the back then walk you to your seat.'

'Huh, why?' But Sarah knew why and it stung so bad, she turned her head away and squeezed eyelids together in case they leaked. Nothing had changed. So much for a night of togetherness.

The very instant the car drew to a halt, Hakim and Mahmoud alighted. Doors closed - Hafiz eased his foot on the accelerator. They circled from the theatre entry, back the way they had come and turned into a gate where a security officer lifted the barrier so Hafiz could drive in. It was obvious this had been pre-planned or the car was recognised.

Too hurt to speak, Sarah didn't wait for Hafiz to open the door but scrambled out, brushed the creases from her long skirt and headed for a door with a small neon light over the top with Arabic writing. Back entrance for the nobody. She was inside before Hafiz caught up and eased ahead of her.

'This way.'

She followed along a passage, through two doorways, up a winding staircase for two floors, through another doorway opened from the inside only by a long bar. They came out to a carpeted passage, which they followed until they came to a door. Hafiz opened it to reveal a private box. Three rows of three seats.

'You are to sit there.' Hafiz pointed to the far rear corner seat.

'Why?'

'So you are not seen by any of the patrons. You are not to speak for there will be patrons in boxes either side.'

Miffed, Sarah sat where the view to the stage was barely enough. Thoughts stewed and stewed some more while the rustle of theatregoers increased. It took a great deal of soul-searching to calm self-inflicted anger. Eyes closed, long deep breaths and a whispered a mantra of positive words until instruments began to tune and warning bells dinged. Hakim entered, frowned at her and sat in the middle front seat with Hafiz and Mahmoud on either side of him. Absolutely brilliant. The limited view became non-existent apart from a strip on the right side of the stage. And it was a ballet they were here to see.

It wasn't until halfway through the first act, Hakim half-turned. 'Are you enjoying the show?'

'The music is brilliant but…'

Hafiz eyed her and shook his head with one finger over his lips.

Sarah shrugged, leant back with closed her eyes. Since she knew the music of Giselle well, she opened her eyes at the end of the scene and could actually see the curtains slide shut.

Hakim stood. 'Stay here. I will bring you a tray of refreshment.'

Hafiz smirked while Mahmoud wore a puzzled frown. Tough that she needed to visit the loo. Oops, she wasn't to use such uncouth language. 'The ladies' lounge,' she muttered. By the time the bells dinged to bring everyone back to their seats, her legs were crossed in desperation. She stood next to the door, waited until it opened then shoved her way past Hakim.

'Sarah, where are you going?'

'To empty an overfull bladder before it bursts.' She turned away.

Hakim grasped her elbow. 'Why didn't you go during intermission?'

She stared in disbelief. 'Because *you,*' she stabbed a finger into his chest, 'ordered me to stay here.'

'I did not mean you couldn't visit the ladies' lounge.'

'You have a habit of saying things then later telling me you didn't mean what you said. It appears I can't trust any of your words. Just like you said you would bring me back a tray of refreshment.' She made a show of searching his hands and those of his men. 'Or didn't you mean those words either.'

'I ordered a tray to be brought here.'

Sarah quirked up an eyebrow. 'Why don't I believe you?'

'I'm sorry, I'll send Mahmoud to get another.'

'Don't bother. I'll find my own. At least I can trust myself.' Desperate to escape, she fled in search of a loo.

'Loo, loo, loo,' she dared mutter while powerwalking along the corridor.

At last, a sign with a woman next to Arabic words. With a splat on the door, she pushed the door open.

'No, closed,' said a voice in broken English.

'Excuse me?'

'Closed for cleaning.' A woman dressed in a pale blue uniform and a hijab tucked into the top, stood in front of Sarah. She held out a bucket of cleaning implements.

'I'm desperate.'

'Not here.'

Fed up with life, Sarah lifted her skirt, bundled it into a roll and pretended to lower her knickers. 'Then I'll have to pee on the floor right here. Bigger mess for you to clean.'

The poor woman's eyes boggled before she stood aside and waved Sarah inside.

Hands washed and dried, Sarah went in search of some sort of bar or eating place only to find all exit doors from the passage closed. When she figured the double doors had to be the main ones to get out, she lifted the bar to unlock it and eased through the opening onto a wide landing. Steps led down to the next landing then divided into two curves to the lower floor but she caught sight of a bar to the left. This had to be where food and drinks were served to the upper level. Three servers were stacking glasses, plates and cups. Sarah approached but was ignored.

'Excuse me, am I able to get a drink and something to eat?'

'Sorry, we are closed.'

Just dandy. She pointed to bottles of water. 'What about water.'

'Sorry.'

'Why not?'

'The till is shut. Money has been collected. No more sales.'

Even though she wanted to argue, Sarah turned away, strode to the double door and gripped the knob with a tug. It didn't budge. Frustrated to the nth degree she banged her forehead on the wood three times, turned and sat on the top step. There was only one thing she could do so she took out her mobile phone and messaged not only Hakim, for of course, his phone would be turned off, but also Hafiz.

Can't get in. On top step outside the double door.

Five minutes later she sent the message again but added – *Please come and get me.*

Every five minutes she sent another message until it became obvious neither man was about to arrive. It was also obvious Hakim hadn't missed her presence – or didn't care she hadn't returned.

After forty-five minutes she sent a final message – *Thanks for caring,* descended the steps all the way to the bottom and kept going – through the main doors and onto the pavement. A slow spin around revealed a restaurant one way and a hotel the other. Hotel meant a bar with pub food. It was difficult to describe the turmoil in her gut while she walked. Deep disappointment came to the fore, along with a sort of dull pain around the heart region. Tears hovered but she fought them back for they were useless and unwelcome.

At the door, hesitancy had her pause. Maybe she should just find a taxi and go home. But she hadn't eaten since breakfast because Hakim had said they would dine at the theatre. A stomach growl had her open the door.

Inside was a surprise. It was a classy hotel with subdued elegance. To one side was a nice looking eatery next to a bar. She headed towards it, crept inside and hovered against a wall to scan the area. The last thing she needed tonight was to meet up with some scary character.

An undertone of voices rumbled over soft background music of the pleasant variety. No harsh, noisy rock or punk. Usual scents of alcohol and brewed coffee dominated less distinctive food smells. For the number of people it was relatively quiet. Most were in groups with a few couples. None, apart from her, were solo. A sense of loneliness rose and stabbed but she stepped towards the bar.

At the sound of a definite Aussie twang, she paused and eyed three men. The loneliness turned into sheer, desperate homesickness. Not giving a damn about rudeness or propriety, she turned to the trio. 'Are you all Aussies?'

'Hey, yes and it sounds like you are too,' said the nearest man. 'Come and join us.'

Her step quickened, along with her heart. 'You have no idea how good it is to hear your voices.'

Pure joy filled her innards while she shared plates of food and a bottle of wine with three fellow Sydneysiders. Laughter came from all four until her phone pinged. Uh, oh. She took it out, read the message from Hakim.

Where are you?

What do you care? She wrote back after a long pause.

Her phone rang. 'Excuse me a minute,' she said to the guys and stepped away before pressing the green button.

'Sarah, where are you. I've been worried.'

'If you were worried, why didn't you answer my messages? It's been…' she glanced at her watch and was shocked to see how late it was. The show must have been over ages ago.

'You know I turn my phone off at such functions. When you didn't return after fifteen minutes I sent Hafiz to search the theatre. You weren't anywhere.'

'Then you'd better retrain him to look properly. I was where I messaged both you and him. I waited three quarters of an hour on the top step before hunger pangs drove me to find somewhere I could get food. It's now been two hours. Two hours before you bother sending me a message.'

'Sarah, where are you?'

'Within walking distance of the theatre enjoying the best conversation I've had since I left Sydney.' She hung up, turned off the phone. Let him search. An idea struck. She took a photo of the three guys and sent it to Hakim with a message. *Meet my new friends.* To rub it in, she rejoined the new friends and stood as close to them as was inappropriate.

She was laughing at an anecdote when the sensation of eyes bored into her back. She turned to see the two bodyguards stalking towards them with intent in their eyes.

'Excuse me a minute,' she said to the men and headed towards Hakim.

'Call the Rottweilers off before they do something you will regret.'

'I beg your pardon.' Shock lit up his eyes.

'Call them off.'

'Sarah.' He paused. 'I don't understand.' But she noticed he flicked a hand towards Hafiz and Mahmoud. He came closer, 'What is this all about? Who are these men?'

Sarah blew out a long breath. 'You say the desert lives in the blood of all Arabs.'

'Yes, it is inborn.'

'Well something lives in the blood of all true blue Aussies. It's called mateship. Mateship is giving a shoulder to rest on when the chips are down. Not in a physical sense.'

'I do not understand.'

'You don't have serious bushfires or floods in your country but it is common back home. A mate can be a complete stranger who turns up and pitches in to help clean up the mess after a flood or offers you a bed when your house has been razed by a fire. They donate money, clothes, household goods or time and assistance in times of need. They give you a shoulder to lean on. These three men are from Sydney. They're here for some conference about the latest electronic gizmo. Tonight they shared their meal and a bottle of wine with me. They brought me up to date with news from back home. They gave me something to laugh about with their funny personal anecdotes when I had nothing in my life to laugh about.'

Hakim hissed in a breath at her insult but she ignored it.

'Just hearing their Aussie voices reduced the level of my intense homesickness. They were mates when my own husband shoved me in a dark corner where I couldn't see the stage and didn't care enough about me to immediately message me to find out why I hadn't returned.'

'And don't give my any hogwash excuses,' she added at Hakim's open mouth. 'Now, if you will excuse me, I need to thank these three amazing mates for their kindness and mateship in a true Aussie way, which you won't like but tough, live with it.'

'Sarah…'

She ignored him and went back to the men where she gave each a firm hug and smile as she thanked them. Hakim will be furious but she didn't much care. When she turned back to Hakim, he passed her, shook the hands of the three men.

'Thank you for taking care of Sarah for me,' she overheard him say.

'You could have been arrested for inappropriate touching,' he muttered in her ear while they walked outside towards the car which was parked next to the kerb. He opened the door for her. 'Get in.'

She waited until he got in the other side. 'And no doubt it would delight you to know I was in a prison cell, out of your life.'

Hakim stabbed the button to close the privacy shield and waited for it to seal them in a cocoon. He sat back with a hand over his eyes for a good minute. 'I have no idea where you get these ridiculous notions from. Tonight has been a nightmare for me. To start with, I don't understand why you insisted on sitting where you sat yet you blame me for you not being able to see the stage.'

'Your orders.'

'Excuse me? When did I order you to sit in the corner?'

'Hafiz told me I had to sit there, to not move and not talk so patrons didn't see or hear me.'

'He told me you insisted you sit there for the same reasons.'

'It was a ballet where one needs to see the entire stage. Do you honestly think I would sit where three huge men blocked all view of the stage at a ballet? Hafiz insisted I had to sit there.'

'He would never lie to me.'

Sarah scoffed. 'Of course not. The sun shines out of their backsides in your view. And he did not come looking for me. He knew where I was.'

'How could he know?'

'Did you ever read the messages I sent to you?'

'Yes, after the show.'

'I sent the same messages to his phone at the same time I sent them to you.'

'Maybe his phone was turned off as well or he would have said.'

Sarah shook her head in disbelief. 'Of course. Your men can do no wrong. But little old Sarah? She is always wrong, always lies, always imagines things. Well thank you for your faith and trust.'

Overcome with emotion, she huddled into the corner of the seat with hands gripped together in her lap.

'Such a nightmare.' Hakim wrested one of her hands free and wrapped his fingers around it. 'I am sorry for any misunderstanding. I did send Hafiz to search for you.'

'But not you. I am not important enough for you to come.'

'Not true. If I was to stand and leave in the middle of a show, what message does it send to the performers and the audience? That I find the show not to my liking? It shows rudeness and disrespect.'

'You didn't even bother to message me to ask where I was.'

'My phone is always off at such functions for the same reasons. You know this. Which is why I sent Hafiz to find you.'

'Yet even though he knew where I was, he didn't come to me.'

'I am sure he did not receive your messages. None of my men would lie to me.'

Just like Mariam would never lie to you, yet she did, Sarah wanted to say but thought better of it. But to the depths of her soul, she knew Hafiz needed watching.

'Forget it. I don't wish to argue for despite the first half the evening being one of the worst I've ever spent the second half was the best I've had since I arrived. Three friendly Aussies who had no hesitation in accepting me into their little social for who I am. Now just let me be so I can conjure more positive thoughts.' She turned away and stared out of the window for the rest of the journey home.

Twenty Seven

Joy simmered when they entered the hotel foyer side-by-side. For once she hadn't been dropped off around some dim corner to keep her hidden. They had alighted from the same car in front of the building.

'Excuse me a moment, I have matters to discuss,' Hakim said a split second before he left her alone in the middle of the foyer with Ali and Ahmed trailing after their boss.

Disappointment swept the joy away in an instant. Unsure what to do she searched the room for somewhere to wait. Since the night was a formal dinner with presentations afterwards, she wore her only evening gown. Tonight she didn't stand out especially since she now had a jewelled bracelet to wear; one she hadn't yet taken off and deep down was chuffed Hakim had given it to her. It was gorgeous and matched well with her jewelled wedding band.

When she spotted a large noticeboard with the seating arrangement, she ambled over, studied the plan, found Hakim was to sit at the head table but her name wasn't next to his. A trident stabbed in her heart. So much for a night spent together. It took a long scan of the chart to find her name – on the very last table, in the far corner, between two unmarried women. The three names in English had the word *Miss* in front of their name. There were a couple of other names written in Arabic. Fabulous, so this was another attempt to find her female friends.

'Hello.'

Her pulse rate instantly pounded. She spun around so fast, her hand thumped into the stranger's stomach. 'Sorry, you scared me.' The swarthy man wore sandy robes with a white and red checked keffiyeh. So not a local, she knew.

'My apologies, you stand her alone. I also am alone. Maybe we can get to know each other.'

'I don't think so. Please excuse me.' With her nerves imitating taut piano wires stretched to their fullest, Sarah turned away, searched for Hakim, his men or somewhere to hide. When none of the men were anywhere in sight, she figured it was time to search for her table in the function room as a way to escape a scary stranger. Relief surged to find a number of guests had the same idea – enough to ensure her safety. It didn't take long to find the place-card with her name scrolled in gold. She dropped her evening bag beside it. All she needed now was the security of close proximity to Hakim or even the bodyguards. It was stupid to become so anxious because a strange man had snuck up on her but visions of her attack had taken unwelcome residence in the forefront of her brain and didn't want to go away. There had been flashbacks before – too many times, along with panic attacks. The last thing she needed right now was a suffocating panic attack. P.T.S.D. she had been told she suffered from. It was a difficult diagnosis to accept for she thought herself to be a strong independent woman but after she'd read umpteen reports on what post-traumatic stress meant, she realised the diagnosis was correct.

When she lifted her eyes a wave of tremors raced down her spine. The man stood across the room; his eyes planted on her. Desperate to escape, she went the other way, wove through the tables, shot through the doorway, turned right and mingled in the crowd with constant peeks over her shoulder. When she spied Hakim, she headed for him but paused mid-stride when he shook his head and held up one hand in the stop position.

A quick peek behind.

The stranger watched her.

Nausea rose, along with a band of perspiration across her brow. Not giving a damn what Hakim wanted, she made a beeline for him until Ali barred her way with both hands held up.

'You cannot interrupt the prince.'

'I'm afraid.'

'We are at a private function with many invited people. No harm will come to you here but you cannot come any closer to the prince when he has important discussions.'

'Fine, I will stand over there.' With an open hand, she indicated a spot against the wall, a good five metres from Hakim. Head high, nerves ready to snap, she stalked to the spot and plastered her back against the wall. No way would the unpleasant stranger sneak up on her again.

Five minutes later, soft gongs sounded, voices stopped and a stream of bodies began to move towards the function room. With her heart still at full gallop on the verge of panic, Sarah didn't move – couldn't move.

'We need to find our seats.' She spun around at Hakim's voice, mad at herself she hadn't noticed him move towards her but she had been so intent on searching for the stranger.

'I don't feel safe.'

'Guests are vetted whenever royalty attend such functions. There were none who sent out alarms. You will sit with young women around your own age. They work for this company.'

He turned to Ali. 'Ali, please show Sarah to her seat?'

Glad Hakim had listened to her concerns, she walked beside Ali, as close to him as she dared – probably too close but she didn't give a damn about local conventions. Her tension eased a tad when she spied a couple of women to the left of her chair.

Ali pulled her chair out, waited for her to sit and pushed it back in. 'Are you okay now?'

'Thank you, yes.' She turned to the two young ladies, smiled and introduced herself. Both wore modest western gowns with hijabs. When the chair on her right moved, she turned to greet the newcomer.

Her heart stalled. The same man smiled, nodded and sat. A quick glance at the name on the place-card told her he had swapped the previous one for his own, even though it also was written in Arabic. Her heart kick-started at a gallop. Only someone with evil intent would be so sneaky.

'How much does the prince pay you?'

'Excuse me?'

'How much does he pay you?'

'Pay me? For what?'

'To sleep with him.'

'You... How dare you?' Eyes closed, she fought for sanity and turned back to the ladies.

'You arrived with the prince,' hissed into her ear. 'You scuttled back to him. His guard showed you to the seat. He is an unmarried man. You an unmarried woman. There is only one reason a westerner would be in such a situation.'

'You're sick,' she spat and turned her head back to him but leant away as far as she dared without falling. 'You assume a great deal. None of which is true. Your insinuation is way off the mark.'

'I will pay you five hundred.'

'For what?'

'To spend twenty-four hours with me.'

'Sick is not a good enough word to describe you.' Sarah turned back towards the women who seemed absorbed in the conversation, their eyes wide and mouths formed in huge circles.

Waiters interrupted them, placed dishes of spiced prawns on a bed of couscous in front of each person. Her stomach rebelled at the fishy stench. Did everyone in this country serve fish? Maybe it's regarded as a delicacy but she sure didn't. Plates of flat bread came next. While the others forked prawns into their mouths or wrapped them in torn pieces of bread, she nibbled on flat bread.

A hand crept onto her thigh.

The bread shot down her throat.

'Get your hand off.' She jabbed the man in his ribs and grinned when couscous spilled into his lap.

Arabic words hissed back. She bet they weren't polite. Desperate to settle tense nerves, she shoved another small piece of bread into her mouth.

The hand bit into her thigh. She yanked her leg away, turned her back on the jerk.

'Is he not your husband?' The woman next to her whispered in heavily accented English.

'Definitely not.'

'Why is he at our table?'

'I have no idea – don't know who he is.'

The woman wavered her fork in the man's direction and spoke in Arabic. The man thumped the table with an angry retort that Sarah couldn't understand.

'He says he is your escort but you have a disagreement with him.'

'No way. He lies. I don't even know his name.' Sarah edged her chair closer to the woman while she racked her brain on what to do. Phone, she thought and immediately eased her mobile from her handbag, turned it on and thought about who to send it to. Hakim usually turned his phone off at public functions so she searched for Ahmed's number, typed in a message. *I need to change tables.* Ahmed stood further from Hakim than Ali, who was always the closest. To see if Ahmed received the message she had to twist her head. He took out his phone.

The hand gripped her thigh again.

Her phone pinged. She glanced down at the screen the same time she jerked her leg away.

Will speak with the prince. Ahmed moved towards Hakim who glanced at her and shook his head with a frown of displeasure while he spoke to Ahmed.

She was less impressed with his response. *No danger in a room full of people. Deal with it.*

Fine. Annoyed, she pretended to dip the flatbread in the dish but only nibbled on the bread, still half-turned towards the women. When the scumbag reached over and grasped the very top of her thigh with a deliberate nudge against her genital area she picked up her plate and tipped the contents into the cretin's lap.

'It is against the teachings of the Qur'an to touch a woman who is not your wife. I don't appreciate being sexually assaulted.' She thought she'd whispered but it must have been louder than she intended for there was instant silence in the room. Too scared to glance around, she snatched up her purse, shoved the chair back and strode from the room, through the reception area, out the front doorway. She was about to phone for a taxi when Ahmed raced through the entrance.

'Princess, the prince wishes to speak with you.'

'The prince has refused to speak to me since we got here. He can go take a flying leap and don't ever call me princess. My name is Sarah.'

'Miss Sarah, you must come back.'

'Not going to happen. The prince refused to help me when I asked because I was so scared, so I will go home.' She pointed to a taxi dispersing two passengers and ran with her hand flapping in the air to catch the driver's attention. Ahmed still stood on the pavement when the taxi drove past him but she was too damn hurt to care. Hakim sure didn't care about her.

When Hakim arrived home she was wide awake, her brain not giving a smidgin of relief with reruns of the night. Even worse were the reruns of the night she was attacked which insisted on flashing through in bright technicolour.

'Do you want to explain your behaviour tonight?' Hakim asked. An angry frown sat across his brow. 'You bring me shame when you behave in such a manner.'

Sarah's voice failed her for about thirty seconds. 'I bring you shame? Ah, now I understand.'

'Understand what?'

'Why you deserted me the very moment we entered the building. Please accept my apology for the shame my presence gives you. Now if you will excuse me I need to sleep so I can forget about tonight.' She turned her back to him.

The mattress dipped on his side of the bed. Hakim placed his hand on her shoulder. She shrugged it off.

'Please, don't. I've had enough of men and their filthy hands on me tonight.'

'Excuse me? Who dared touch you?'

'You didn't care earlier so don't pretend you care now. I obeyed your instruction about my problem. I dealt with it.'

When his arm reached around her, she ducked under it and tugged the covers over her.

'Sarah, you know I will not harm you.'

'Physically no, emotionally yes. The man tonight gave me the creeps, scared me, brought back flashbacks but you ignored my request for help. Tonight, I can't tolerate any physical contact. Please don't force me to sleep elsewhere because I will be too scared to close my eyes. Tonight I need you close to keep this intense fear at bay but being touched is not negotiable.'

'What did the man in Sydney do to you?'

'Stalked and tormented me for almost a year before he broke into my unit to torture me with mind games before he came within seconds of killing me. He tied a silk scarf around my neck... cut off my air supply... I was unconscious – not just once.' She flipped back over to face Hakim. 'Why are men so cruel?' She choked on the words and had to gasp to get her lungs to work. 'Why do they think they have the right to dominate and take what they want? Why can't they control themselves as we women manage to do? Why do they pick on nobodies like me? I never encourage such behaviour, am always quiet and discreet. The way I dress doesn't invite sexual advances; I don't even speak to these cranks. This sicko tonight came up to me with crude comments. He swapped his place name for one of the women. His comments were inappropriate, offensive and his creepy hands were worse. And to top it all off, my own husband does a big fat nothing when I ask to be moved away. He tells me to deal with it myself. I obeyed. Good night.' When she flipped back over, she wriggled to the very edge of the bed.

'I seem to spend my life apologising to you. I am sorry.'

'My problem, not yours. All I want is to close my eyes, picture pleasant scenes and try to sleep to numb my brain.'

'I will have the night guard stand at the end of the passage. I will sleep beside you. If you need me please wake me. I will do my best to abide by your wishes but it will test me when I am desperate to hold you in my arms to ease your pain. And, sweet Sarah, you can never be regarded as a nobody. You are a vibrant, intelligent and beautiful woman. I will have this man tracked down and dealt with.'

Twenty Eight

It wasn't a surprise when Sarah woke to find herself snuggled against Hakim. She recalled the moment she woke from a ghastly flashback dream and was too darn scared to go back to sleep. Instead she sought his nearness. Upon waking, poor man held his hands in the air to show it wasn't his fault they were cuddled together. She initiated the kiss, took the lead in a hot session of lovemaking. Now her world was centred again but not enough to take public transport to the library. Instead, she asked the groundsman to drive her. Suhail, she now knew his name, had to be the friendliest, kindest man on Hakim's staff. It was his job to drive anyone anywhere, he told her with a twinkle in his eye after he'd informed her he was also trained as a bodyguard should she ever need it. This final piece of information managed to ease her taut nerves on the drive to the library. Suhail's jokes gained a laugh which relaxed her and started off the day with brightness and a huge dose of positivity.

It took an effort to force her mind back to work. She reached for the book, trailed through the index and flicked through the pages, happy the formula she needed was right there at the top. Normally she would have recalled the simple formula but her brain seemed to have taken a holiday. Probably too scared to remember.

Whoosh.

She glanced up and froze.

'You owe me an apology.' The man from last night pulled out the chair opposite.

'For what?' Her fingers resembled the tremors of an earthquake when they searched for the cover of the book which she slammed shut, closed her notepad and tried to swallow the wodge of panic. Please don't let me have a panic attack. Not now, not here, she begged her brain.

'You ruined my night.'

'Appalling behaviour has consequences,' she managed to get out while her brain rambled with questions. How did he find her? Had he stalked her?

'Oh, come now, women like you enjoy the chase.'

Sarah peered down to see if her heart was visible, since it hammered against her ribs. 'I would appreciate it if you left me in peace.' It was the politest thing she could think of while packing her gear and pretended to put an item in her pocket so she could sneak out her mobile phone.

His laugh sounded like a sneer. 'One thousand.'

'Excuse me?'

'One thousand dirham for twenty-four hours.'

'What an insult.'

'Not enough? You must be good if the prince pays you more. Five thousand.'

'Take your obscene offer and shove it where the sun doesn't shine.'

It was impossible to control the tremor in her hand while she stashed her bits and pieces into her backpack. She eyed the front door; certain she wouldn't make the distance if she ran. There had to be another way out, and she was safer inside where there were staff and other patrons. To step through the front door would be a step into hell.

'Don't lie. I know you sleep in the prince's home.'

Her already stressed heart imitated a thousand kettle drums pelted with thunderclaps. He had to have stalked her. Not again, please, please, please, not again.

'Get your filthy mind out of the gutter.' She stood, shoved both arms in the straps of her pack and piled the library books into one bent arm. It was a struggle to ease from the bench seat. She wriggled and managed to get free although she still didn't have a clue how to escape. The books had to go on the trolley. When she eyed it an idea came. Ignoring the man, she strode to the librarian's desk and stood in front.

A quick glance to her left – the man had gone.

She snuck a peek over her shoulder. The creep stood outside, no doubt because he thought she would follow.

'Can I help you?'

Startled, she twisted her head back. 'I hope so. The man outside. Last night he assaulted me. Today he followed me. Is there another way out, a staff entrance?'

The young man nodded with a smile before he gave directions to the underground staff carpark.

'In case he watches, can I go up to the second floor on the escalator and down to the basement in the elevator?'

'Yes.'

'Thank you.' A quick glance over her shoulder. The cretin had turned away. Sarah placed the books on the trolley, made a rapid beeline for the escalator and strode up the moving steps with head-flicks over each shoulder. A fast power-walk across the room with a nervous wait for the elevator car to arrive accompanied by constant glances behind. While descending to the car park, she phoned for a ladies only taxi; asked to be picked up at the staff entrance. The very second the door opened she shot out but stuck to the wall to sidle towards the entry. No way would anyone be able to sneak up behind her.

Her entire supply of adrenalin spurted when a man appeared from the elevator. It took several seconds in the gloom before she recognised him as one of the library security guards.

'Miss, you must come back. Your husband insists.'

The shock ceased her sidle. 'My husband?'

'Yes, he says you had a disagreement.' He closed the gap and edged closer to the entry to prevent her escape.

'He is not my husband. I don't even know his name.' Still, she sidled along the wall, kept a safe distance between them.

When he held his hands up at the side of his shoulders as though in submission she didn't trust him.

'I can guarantee the man knows little about me.' She gave details while step by slow step, she edged towards the wide opening. Freedom was less than ten metres away.

'Ah, you found my wife.'

Sarah froze, twisted her head. 'I am not your wife. Why do you tell such lies?'

'Like all women, my wife lies to make you believe her story.' He was halfway across the carpark.

'Keep him away from me.' She sped towards the security man.

Heavy footsteps neared from the opposite side.

Sarah closed the gap but kept a couple of metres away while she swung her head backwards and forwards to keep an eye on both men. Harsh words came from both but Sarah was too scared to absorb them. Her nerves twitched to snap, she stumbled, reached out.

A hand grabbed her arm. Tugged.

Through her panic, the self-defence trainer's voice shoved its way through. '*Breathe.*'

She hauled in a breath.

'*Grab, twist and bend.*'

In one swift movement, she grabbed the wrist clamped onto her forearm, pressed her thumb as hard as she could into the inside of the wrist. Thank goodness it was hard enough to make him let go. At the same time she grabbed the same wrist with her other hand, bent at the waist, shoved out her backside and begging for strength, flipped her body around to the left and knocked her attacker off balance. The moment he began to fall, she twisted his arm around until he squealed in pain. Somehow, the hours of practise paid dividends. To make sure he learned his lesson she took pleasure in the hard stomp with her heel on his groin.

She grinned at the scream, released his arm and ran full pelt towards the entry. A gush of breath whistled through her teeth at the sight of the pink-topped taxi a few metres away. Too bad if it wasn't the one she ordered. She hurled herself into the back of the taxi, spouted off the address of Hakim's office. It was the only safe place she could think of since it was more than possible the creep could lay in wait near home. Too dangerous to go home.

The car wove through the public car park with her hunkered in the footwell, not game to slither back onto the seat until there was a flash of high-rise buildings through the window.

Money for the fare was in her hand before they pulled into the wide entry of the government building. Even though she had never been inside before, her brain remembered the address. For once she was thankful for the way her brain recalled words.

'Keep the change.' Sarah dropped the money and alighted. Door shut, she ran to the large glass door, yanked it open, stepped inside and paused to give her innards time to cease panicking. At the first step, her leg shook so hard she had to pause again.

Mahmoud appeared stunned at her sudden arrival. 'Miss Sarah, the prince did not say to expect you.'

She rattled off the last hour of her life. 'I didn't know where else to go.'

'You must wait in the prince's office while I find him.'

Even though she was now safe, her innards hadn't received the message. Every organ twitched on high alert while she followed Mahmoud into an enormous room furnished with what could only be the best of items. Despite piles of papers and files, the room was neat. Desperate to get off jellified legs, she plopped into a leather armchair, dropped her head into her hands and willed her heart and lungs to work as they should.

Drawn from the meeting by the urgency of Mahmoud's brief message about a visitor in his office, Hakim hurried along the corridor, pushed the door open with one hand and stilled. The shock robbed him of breath.

'Sarah, what... you cannot be here. You must leave. Now.'

Sarah shot to her feet, swayed but found her balance. 'Why?'

'It is inappropriate. I cannot be seen alone with you at my place of work.' She stared. It was such a rarity for her to remain eye-to-eye, he couldn't draw his eyes away. Her mouth gaped; her eyes slammed shut a split second before her head rocked back as though she had been punched.

'Unbelievable,' hissed from her mouth before she spun around and shot past him. She raced along the passage and

256

disappeared from sight before he had a chance to even blink.

'Sarah.' Mahmoud yelled before his head appeared at the end of the passage. 'What happened?' He jogged towards Hakim. 'Why did you send her away?'

'Sarah cannot come here.'

'Even when she is in such danger. I do not understand.'

'Danger, what danger? She did not...' A tonne of lead settled deep in his gut. 'Dear, Allah, what have I done?' One hand swept down his face. 'Tell me,' he ordered. While they returned to his office, Hakim's blood pressure increased with each detail.

'Why did she not tell me?' he asked but he knew. Again, he had let Sarah down. He had not given her a chance to explain and had not, as yet, had time to follow up on his promise to track the man down and warn him off. Furious with himself, he searched his pocket for his phone and issued orders. 'Get two men from the Sheikh's security force to track down Bader al Kayd. Threaten death if he so much as even thinks about Sarah again. If Sarah comes to any harm I will personally tear him apart.'

He scrolled through his numbers, jabbed a finger on Sarah's. Her phone rang out. He called again with lungs refusing to work. A click.

'Go to hell.' The phone went dead.

Where RU? He typed in.

Hiding.

Where?

What do you care? Came back after a long pause.

Of course I care. Tell me where UR. Will send Tariq.

The only thing U care about is your over-inflated ego and personal image.

I am sorry.

Hollow words. Actions tell the truth.

The last words sent an arrow into his heart because it was the hard truth. It became obvious Sarah had turned her phone off for there were no more responses to either his voice calls or messages. He paced the room in an attempt to force logic to a brain which had turned into fairy floss. There was a meeting to return to, men to send out in search of Sarah, an afternoon jammed with back-to-back meetings, an important event after work and a wife who was so angry it would be a surprise if she ever forgave him. Reaching a decision, he blew out his cheeks, phoned Mariam, asked her to inform him the very second Sarah returned home. He put Tariq in charge to search for a woman he doubted wanted to be found, and a man who deserved to be emasculated before he was served his fried testicles on a plate. Hakim returned to the meeting certain he would not be able to concentrate.

The only relief he received over the day was to know Sarah was home and Bader al Kayd had been found and interrogated. Desperate to get home, he cut short the evening, citing an emergency the very second the meal was over.

He entered a silent house with only one light on. Mariam would be gone, which was good for fireworks were about to explode. To find his bedroom empty sent his pulse pounding but constant messages had assured him Sarah hadn't left the grounds. It took ten minutes to find her, locked in her old room, adamant there would be no discussion tonight.

After a shower, he crawled into the bed in the room next to Sarah and left the door open.

Twenty Nine

The silence at the breakfast table was ominous. Sarah ate, said nothing, kept her eyes glued to the table. The silence began to scream at Hakim.

'Sarah.'

Her head lifted a fraction. 'Yes.'

'Suhail is now your designated driver and bodyguard to stay with you whenever you need him. You decide if and when you use him. He used to guard my father, so is well-trained. We granted him a less demanding job after an injury in a car crash which killed his wife. He may appear to be only a groundsman but he is also a second line of defence. I doubt al Kayd will approach you again and I am sorry.'

'For what?'

'I did not give you a chance to explain why you came to my office.'

'My fault.'

'Why is it your fault?'

'I believed I could trust your word, could come to you for protection. But again you proved me wrong. It won't happen again. From today I will be who you demand.' She stood, dropped into a curtsey. 'Your Highness, in the hours I am not at work I will be the tourist you demand. Now, if you will excuse me I must hurry.' She picked up her backpack and went into the kitchen.

Lost for words, he followed to see Sarah give Mariam a hug. How had the relationship changed with such haste?

'Thank you, I appreciate your help.' Sarah placed four tiny jars inside her bag, went to the freezer and removed a plastic bottle half-filled with ice. After topping it up with cold water, she eased it in next to the jars.

His eyes widened at the smile between the two. 'Where are you going?' he dared ask.

'On a tour since I am a tourist.' Eyes down, she zipped the bag and flung it on her back. 'Have a fabulous day, your Highness.' She dropped another curtsey, strode through the dining room and out through the front doorway.

He turned back to Mariam. 'Where is Sarah going?'

'A day in the desert with other tourists.'

Regret settled in his gut. He had promised to take her but still hadn't made the time. 'Why the jars?'

'She wants to collect soil samples to study under a microscope.'

'She doesn't have a microscope.'

'At the university there is one she can use.'

Hakim muttered under his breath. He had forgotten about her enrolment at the university, hadn't even thought about it. How many weeks ago had she asked? 'How come you two now get along so much better?'

'We spoke. I was wrong. Miss Sarah is not how I thought. Her tears yesterday when she arrived home told me much.'

'Tears?'

'Too many. She stayed by my side all afternoon because she was too afraid to be alone.'

'Why did no-one tell me this?' He incurred a serious glare: one of contempt. 'I will be home for the evening meal.' He was not going to be but now would.

'Miss Sarah is dining in the desert. One of those barbecues for the tourists.'

An idea hit. 'Do you know which one?'

A sly smile crept from Mariam's lips. She handed him a glossy brochure with a convenient circle around a picture and price.

'Please excuse me tonight. It might be a good day for you to take time off to visit your children.' He had his phone out before he reached the front door.

In the light from the sinking sun, Sarah's gold hair gleamed like rich amber. Hakim strode across the sand, his heart hammered at the sound of Sarah's laugh: a sound he hadn't heard for too long, apart from the night with the Australian men. It was impossible to believe he had only known this amazing woman for so short a time for it felt she had lived in his heart for much longer. It was difficult to see what she was doing with her head bent over. A local woman in Arabian costume sat opposite her, also intent on whatever it was they studied with such intensity.

'Your Highness,' several locals said when he passed but with his gaze honed on Sarah, he barely nodded at each voice. Sarah's head shot around. A fist squeezed his heart when her delightful smile turned to a drooped mouth and frown with such rapidity.

'Good evening ladies. As the minister for culture I have come to see what delights our companies give to our tourists.' Sarah's glance was one of contempt. She knew he lied. 'Ah, the tradition of Henna designs. Did you choose the motifs or has our young artist chosen for you?'

'I chose,' came from the artist. A scowl came from Sarah.

'You chose well. He smiled at the young lady before he turned his eyes to Sarah. 'The leaf means happiness. The key denotes liberation and freedom but it also unlocks hidden knowledge and wisdom.' He indicated the lotus central on the back of Sarah's hand. 'The lotus symbolises perseverance and the opening of your heart.' He quirked an eyebrow in question. 'It can also mean fertility.' He couldn't help but smile at the blush that bloomed across Sarah's cheeks. 'But the best is the joined butterflies to denote a happy marriage. Your artist friend wishes all of these for you, as do I.' Delighted with the shock in Sarah's eyes, he turned away to speak with other tourists and organisers to make out it was the reason he had come. Only Sarah knew the real reason.

This set-up was one of the smaller traditional outfits with low tables set in the middle of woven colourful carpets. Large gas cookers to one side sent up delicious aromas of roasted chicken and meat. There were kebabs as well as small pieces of meat turned over by kandourah clad men. Trestles held bain-maries of traditional vegetable dishes with a separate smaller table of sweet treats. The amount of food for the thirty customers gave plenty of choice and there wouldn't be one person who left hungry.

When they were called to fill their plates and find a seat, Hakim ensured he settled cross-legged next to Sarah.

'Why are you here?' hissed from the side of her mouth.

He laughed. 'To dine with my beautiful wife. Entwined butterflies – so appropriate but I pray the lotus bears fruit very soon. You do realise the stain remains for many days.'

'I know.'

'Have you enjoyed your day?'

'Brilliant. The best day since I arrived in this country.'

He wasn't sure he liked her answer for it held a double meaning but tonight he intended to do his utmost to seduce his wife and make peace. 'Again I am remiss for not bringing you when I promised. It is still on my list. How did you go on the camels?'

'Much better than some.'

Hakim laughed and leant closer to Sarah's ear. 'How is your backside? I can massage any pain away?'

'No need.' When she choked on the words a shiver of delight wound through his innards.

'Pity but I doubt you would tell me of your pain.' He forked savoury couscous into his mouth, chewed and swallowed. 'What other activities did you immerse yourself in?'

'The dune buggy rides and quad bikes were brilliant.'

'I am not sure I appreciate the danger you put yourself in but it tells me there must be more than one sore muscle in need of a massage. I might warn you, my sweet Sarah, you will not sleep alone locked in a separate room tonight.'

Sarah rolled up a torn piece of flatbread and popped it into her mouth. 'You don't get a say.'

'I have already had my say, *habibti*.' At Sarah's hiss of surprise, Hakim stood to speak with other guests but caught her watching him every time he glanced her way. If there was one thing he was certain of in their relationship, Sarah turned to soft putty in bed. There was no way she feigned her pleasure under the sheets, nor the pleasure she gave him.

After the servers had cleared away the dishes and food, he again settled next to Sarah to enjoy the entertainment. Even though the *tanour* dancer was breathtaking, it was more of an Egyptian custom, not from the Arabian Peninsula. A rush of warmth swept through him at Sarah's laugh while the *Haridi* dancer went through his comedic routine. The final act was three belly dancers.

'It defies logic as to why you accept these women who show so much bare skin when you insist your own women show almost none.' Sarah twisted her head his way.

'I must agree but I am not married to any of these women. My woman is far more beautiful, far sexier even when she shows little flesh. She is also far more intelligent and the only woman I desire. My shy, quiet woman turns into a sensuous hot bundle of need when in bed. She is also an exquisite and generous lover. A woman I can never get enough of. I will be waiting at home, *habibti.*'

Hakim dared one glance over his shoulder as he headed for his 4WD and the two bodyguards who emerged from the dark when he got closer. He caught Sarah with her eyes trained on him. What delighted him was the need in her expressive face. He wondered if she knew what *habibti* meant.

A split second after Sarah stepped inside the house, Hakim swung one arm around her shoulder, drew her into his arms and planted his mouth over hers. He kissed her until her body sank against his and her arms crept up around his neck. It was difficult to get her still wearing the backpack, into his arms but he managed. He didn't bother to stop until he dropped her feet in front of the shower stall. The pleasure was all his while he peeled each item from her body but he ensured the pleasure was all Sarah's from then on.

Thirty

Thoughts scrambled while Sarah paced around the table set for four. Karim and Faria were due any minute. None of Hakim's brothers had come before, nor his parents. Nerves about to ping apart, she drew out a chair and sat. The table was set for a traditional meal with placemats waiting for dishes of food to share. Serving spoons sat by each empty placemat and forks by the personal settings. Use your right hand, she chided in her mind. Ornate glasses she'd never seen before waited to be filled with traditional cold drinks.

At the brush of footsteps, Sarah shot from the seat, pushed the chair in. 'Am I dressed all right?' she asked the second Hakim appeared garbed in fresh traditional robes. He'd said what she usually wore would be fine. Now she was unsure for he usually wore loose slacks and shirts when at home.

His smile didn't ease her angst. 'You look fine. It's only a casual family meal. Give me a minute to check with Mariam.'

The doorbell chimed as Hakim disappeared. Unsure what to do, Sarah glanced at the kitchen, the front door and back at the kitchen. The doorbell chimed again. Even though she didn't want to be the one to open the door, logic sent her feet on a frantic rush towards it. A third chime: she paused, heaved in a breath and twisted the catch. The air caught in her throat at the sight of Karim dressed in an ornate robe and his wife draped in gold and jewels over a sleeveless silk gown that had to be two sizes too small. Bare flesh oozed over the low neckline.

'We must be too early,' Fariah said to Karim. 'Sarah isn't dressed yet.'

The bubble of air landed in her gut like a lump of lead. Shocked at the rudeness, Sarah, fought to find the right words, 'Please come in. Hakim will be here in a second.' she hoped when she stepped back.

Shoes left at the door, both moved inside and stood with eyes glued to her. Never having entertained guests in this house before, Sarah didn't have a clue about what she was supposed to do.

'Where is your houseboy?' asked Faria.

'What houseboy?'

Faria's laugh wasn't of the humorous kind. 'The boy who opens the door and fetches things for you.'

'Karim, Faria, come in, come in.' Sarah had never been so glad to hear her husband's voice.

She turned towards him. He frowned. 'What is it, Sarah?'

'It seems the outfit you recommended I wear isn't appropriate. Excuse me while I speak with Mariam.' Embarrassed, Sarah raced away, desperate to rid herself of the lump of hurt in her gut and to replace it with a large dose of courage. Houseboy? She flew into the kitchen, raced to the sink, filled a glass with water and gulped it down.

'Miss Sarah, what is it?'

Sarah spun around at Mariam's voice. 'Need a moment to catch my breath.'

'What happened?'

'What's wrong with my clothes?'

Mariam frowned. 'You look fine, why?'

'Never mind. Any hints on what to do?'

Mariam smiled. 'Just be yourself. That one,' she nodded towards the dining room, 'needs to be spanked until she learns manners.'

'Oh, so it's not just me?'

Mariam laughed and shoved Sarah towards the door. 'No, you are much better. Go. I will serve straight away so she goes home sooner.'

Relieved, Sarah returned to the living room but paused at the entry when she heard her name. 'Why does Sarah not wear the jewels you buy for her?' asked Fariah. 'She looks so dowdy.'

Fire lit her belly. Sarah stepped into the room. 'I'd rather look dowdy than be weighted down with a mishmash of gawdy chains.' She held up both hands. 'I do wear the jewels my husband gave me.' Hakim sent her a warning glare. She shrugged. 'I'm not into bling.'

'But your earrings.' Fariah indicated with an open hand. 'The diamonds are so small. Surely your wife deserves better, Hakim.'

Hakim's mouth hung open then twisted into a grimace. Poor man didn't deserve this. 'My earrings were a gift from my grandmother when I turned twenty-one. She passed away two weeks later. To me, they are more precious than everything else I own.' She turned to Hakim. 'Mariam says food is about to be served.' Too angry to stay, she strode to the dining room, pulled out her chair and plonked into it, not giving a damn about the ritual of handwashing. Too bad if they thought her to be uncouth. It would add to the *dowdy* and *not yet dressed.*

Determined to be civil, Sarah obeyed all Arab dining etiquette. She waited until the guests had filled their plates, then Hakim, before she served herself. She waited for the guests to begin eating before she forked small morsels into her mouth – with her right hand. She sipped her drink, ate slowly and ate little. The brothers were jovial in their chatter, Faria interrupted in Arabic, while Sarah said little since no-one asked her many questions. The entire two hours were torture. The relief was bliss when the table was cleared and coffee and tea replaced food dishes.

In the sudden silence, Sarah dared a glance at Hakim. The way he leant back in his chair with his eyes centred on Karim sent her a loud peal of alarm bells.

'Why did you hire Bader Al Kayd to seduce my wife?'

The silence deepened into doom.

'You what?' asked Sarah at the same time Karim shot up from his seat.

'I never... how dare you?' Karim yelled. 'Why would I... I... how could you even think I would do something so... so... so obscene?'

'Al Kayd was grilled by palace security. He was adamant you gave orders to seduce my wife, although he was not informed of our marriage. You ordered him to take Sarah to his bed.' Hakim reached over and gripped Sarah's wrist to prevent her from leaving.

Karim sat. The shock on his face couldn't be fake. 'I gave no such order. I have never personally met the man although I do know who he is. I swear.'

'He had proof.' Hakim seemed too relaxed although the grip on Sarah's hand was tight.

'What proof?' asked Karim.

'Two direct debit payments to his account. The first for $100,000 US dollars as a down payment, the second for a further $150,000 US dollars yesterday as final payment after he successfully slept with my wife.'

Of its own accord, Sarah's bottom jaw dropped and wouldn't move.

'They certainly didn't come from my account.' Karim thumped a fist on the table so hard, his tea spilled over the top of his cup and puddled in the saucer.

Hakim leant forwards. 'No, but they did come from your wife's personal account.'

This time it was Sarah who shot up. 'Why? Why would you be so nasty?' Hakim stood next to Sarah, put his arm around her waist and gripped tight while Karim stared at his wife, also with a jaw that didn't seem to work.

Fariah sneered. 'To prove you are a liar, a cheat, a Christian prostitute, who sleeps with many men.'

269

Too shocked to keep upright, Sarah plopped back into her chair. 'Wow, such venom. Until tonight, you have never spoken to me so can't possibly know anything about me.'

'I know everything. You lie to Hakim so he will marry you. To get a rich man to think he is the father of your child.'

Sarah laughed, too shocked to do anything else until a shaft of logic hit. 'You are right.' She sure enjoyed the gloat on Faria's face. 'Hakim is not the father of any child of mine.' She paused long enough to see the gloat turn to a smug grin. 'How can he be when I don't have any children?'

'The child you carry.'

This time the laughter came from Hakim as he dragged his chair close to Sarah and sat. They caught each other's eye and grinned. Hakim nodded to her.

'What makes you think I'm pregnant?' Sarah asked.

'You said, at the family dinner, when you were ill.'

'No. I never said those words. Why would I when it wasn't true?'

'Sarah's illness was not because she is with child,' said Hakim. 'It was…'

Sarah nudged him. 'It is none of their business.'

'True.' He turned back to Faria. 'Sarah is not with child. But this still does not explain why you paid a man a quarter of a million dollars to harm her.'

'She is a Christian whore…'

'Sarah is not Christian and knows every word of the Qur'an,' Hakim butted in with a squeeze on Sarah's hand.

'I don't believe you,' Fariah spat.

'Maybe you will believe the imam who tested her. And it seems she follows the rules of Islam better than you for she accepts all people for who they are with no racial or religious bias. Unlike what you have demonstrated tonight.'

A loud hiss came from Fariah - a gulp and angry frown from Karim.

Sarah jabbed Hakim in the ribs. 'Please tell us how you came to these conclusions.' She leant back with a squeeze on Hakim's thigh.

'I have proof, a lot of proof.' Fariah stared at Hakim. 'She slept with Bader. Spent twenty four hours with him. I have proof. He sent me the photos I demanded before I paid the final amount.'

'This I have to see,' said Sarah. 'Show me. Prove it.' She turned to Hakim. 'You need to remind me what night I didn't sleep in this house since the day we married. It seems to have slipped my mind.'

'You lie,' Fariah screeched before she set her eyes back onto her phone and tapped and swiped.

'Sarah never lies,' said Hakim. 'There has not been a single night when Sarah has not slept in this house and she certainly never spent an entire day with another man.'

'There. Proof.' Fariah shoved the phone across the table.

Hakim picked it up, stared and held it out for Sarah. There was a photo of a naked woman spread out on a bed. Headless. Hakim laughed. 'This is not Sarah.'

'Of course it is. You just say that to cover for her.'

'You think I do not know what my own wife looks like? This is an Arab woman. Look at the colour of the skin. It is dark against the white sheets. Sarah's skin is much paler, especially in the areas not touched by the sun. Look at

271

Sarah's hair. There is not a strand of black – anywhere on her body.'

'Hakim,' Sarah squeaked with a tight grip on his thigh.

He smiled. 'You tell me, brother. Is this photo of Sarah or an Arab woman?' He passed the phone over the table.

'The missing head says a lot. Definitely a woman of local heritage. You have been foolish, Fariah. Very foolish.'

'What about the social media pages, they do not lie? Her social media is full of disgusting pictures.'

Sarah laughed. 'Go on.' She leant over to whisper in Hakim's ear. 'I don't have a profile on any social media. Could never see the sense and never had the time.'

'I know.'

'You do? How?'

Instead of answering, Hakim turned back to Faria. 'I also searched all social media sites for background on Sarah before we married. I found none whereas there are numerous articles and photos about me.'

Fariah grabbed her phone from Karim. Her fingers were frantic in search for the sites. 'There.' She jerked the phone under Hakim's nose. 'Filthy pictures and messages with so many men.'

When Sarah leant over to peek, shock caused heat to rise in a rush up her neck and face. The pure porn photos were confronting. It took a few seconds before she could find the nous to seek out the name on the site. It took three deep breaths before she had calmed enough to confront Faria. 'You claim to know everything about me yet you can't even spell my name. Both the first and last name on this profile are spelt different to my name. This is a Sara, not Sarah and the country indicated is England.'

272

'You are English,' Fariah shrieked.

'I've never even visited the British Isles and I have never set up my profile on any social media websites.'

'Sarah comes from Australia, and...' Hakim gripped Sarah's hand. 'I can guarantee my wife has never been with another man. I was her first and since she has spent every night with me, I am her only.'

'I do not believe you.' Fariah glared but she had gone pale.

'I don't much care what you believe,' said Sarah. 'I'm only too glad Karim is not the crown prince.'

'Why?' Karim folded his arms but Sarah noticed he had moved away from Faria.

'What little I know of your parents I know they are kind and well respected. Your mother is a lovely woman. It would be a disservice to this country to have a leader whose wife could be so nasty and vindictive to any person she took a dislike to the way Fariah has been with me. I apologise if my truth is uncomfortable for you but the pain Fariah has inflicted on me is indescribable. Please excuse me.' Sarah fled.

Hakim stood. 'My brother, you are welcome at my door any time but I beg you never bring Fariah with you. My need now, is to find my wife although I have no doubt she will be in tears. I also doubt she will sleep because she will be too afraid to close her eyes as she was after her first encounter with al Kayd. For your information, Fariah, two hundred people saw Sarah tip a plate of food in al Kayd's lap and heard her accuse him of sexual misconduct while they watched her flee the room – alone. While al Kayd disappeared into the bathroom, to clean himself, my security guard saw her get in a taxi – alone and rang home to ensure she arrived safely where she was guarded until I could get home. The next morning she insisted a guard drive her to the library because of her fear. Two hours later she arrived at my place of work, terrified because al Kayd accosted her again in the library.' Hakim paused when a thought niggled.

He leant across the table in front of Fariah. 'How did he know where Sarah would be?'

Fariah shrugged but guilt swept across her face.

'You will tell me the truth or I will ensure you are put in a prison cell for treason.'

'Treason?' Fariah spat the words out but her fear became more obvious.

'Yes, treason, for you hired and paid a hit man to bring harm to a royal princess. Treason. The truth. How did he know? How did you know, for her attendance at the dinner was a last minute inclusion and was not publicised?'

'Hafiz,' she whispered.

'Hafiz? You paid Hafiz as well?' Hakim roared so loud both Fariah and Karim jumped. He spun around and swore. His own guard betrayed him.

Furious, he fronted his brother. 'I ask you to show yourselves out so I can beg forgiveness from my wife.' He pointed a finger to Fariah. 'Never do I want to see you again. You are not worthy of your status.' Even though he would love to wring the woman's neck, he turned away and raced towards his rooms.

'Hakim!' His brother called.

Hakim paused, turned and glared. 'Yes?'

'Please apologise to Sarah on my behalf. I am sorry. I swear I never knew about this.'

'I doubt Sarah will accept your apology for you are not the one at fault. She has an intrinsic belief that it is up to the perpetrator to beg forgiveness.' He turned and hurried.

Sarah sat on a lounge in the courtyard. Her chin rested on bent knees with arms gripped around them. His heart twisted at how vulnerable she looked. He squatted in front of her, reached out, touched her hand. She shuddered.

'You are troubled.'

Sarah shrugged but lifted her head a fraction. There were no tears but there had been. 'This isn't going to work is it?' she whispered.

'What do you mean?'

'Us, you and me, this marriage.' A tear escaped.

'Why would you think this?' He swept the tear away with his thumb.

'I have caused disharmony in your family.'

'No.' He gripped both of her hands. 'You have done nothing wrong. It is Fariah who has caused the disharmony with her acrimony. She has changed. It has been difficult for many months for Karim to find love in his heart for his wife.'

'What do you mean?'

'She has grown selfish, more demanding over the past year. Most days she spends time with other women at the shops, buying expensive fripperies for the sake of owning them. They have two young ones but she leaves the care of them to a nursemaid. She goes days without any contact with her own children. Karim has often told me about his concern. It is possible this appalling behaviour will cause him to seek a divorce. I hope he does.' He wriggled next to Sarah, drew her against him. Her sigh turned his innards into mush.

'There is another matter I need to tell you. You were right to be concerned about Hafiz. You read him well for he was the one who told Fariah where you would be. She paid him for the information.'

'Hafiz? Why would he?'

'Greed. He will no longer work for me for he has betrayed my trust. I can no longer depend on him for our safety. I am sorry. I should have heeded your instincts for they were acute and right.'

'If I wasn't here, none of this would have happened.'

His innards hollowed out then turned to lead. He knelt on the ground by her side, gripped her hands.

'Sarah, I beg you to listen to my words. The worst moment of each day for me is when I walk out the front doorway every morning. When I leave you. All day you live in my heart and my thoughts. All day I yearn for the day to end so I can return home – to you. I know it has been difficult for you until now with my over-full schedule of appointments I have begun to detest. It will ease off soon.'

He reached up, pecked her cheek. 'The best part of my day is when I enter the house in the evening. My heart jumps when I see you. Even better is when I touch you.' He ran a hand along her leg. 'Better still is when our lips meet.' He smiled, leant up higher, brushed his mouth against hers. 'This is when my heart melts but the best is when you allow me access to your body and we join in the most intimate of ways. If you weren't here... I cannot even think about it.'

He stood, scooped her into his arms and carried her to bed where he showed her exactly what she meant to him.

Thirty One

Even though utter loneliness etched at her innards, Sarah filled each day to the brim with activities. The two days at university were the best, for young student voices pushed the loneliness to the background while laughter and genial chatter lifted her spirits. In between university days, she went on excursions from the list Saeed's children had suggested and others she had found on various sites.

In the old town, the middle eastern food and culture walk with tastings had been brilliant and she now understood the different spices better, although some still overpowered her tastebuds. She followed the tour with a journey across the river in an old wooden water taxi to the gold and spice souks, where she indulged in delicious street food which seemed to taste better with the rich spice aromas in the air.

To fill in more time while Hakim wasn't home, she sought out the children's centre the charity had raised money for and offered assistance. She also visited with Aisha twice a week but only during the day when Tariq wasn't there. Not once did Hakim ask how she filled the hours. He still didn't have a clue she had memorised where he would be each day and the times he would be home.

Today he might find out. Standing in line outside the racecourse gates, she glanced down at her new purchase. It screamed defiance but her outfit was no different to those worn by any other female tourist. The short, smart summer dress showed off uncovered arms and legs. By the end of the day she might regret the dressy sandals but a blister or two would be worth the surprise on Hakim's face. Tough. He was here with his entire family in the *Royal Enclosure* but again she hadn't been invited to be a part of the family.

On-ground betting didn't occur due to cultural reasons but she could bet on-line. Only once a year did she indulge in a betting fling on the Melbourne Cup back home. But today, defiance, tinged with bravado, meant she was determined to bet on every race. She had studied the form guide, made calculations and chosen two horses in each race. Today she gloried in how her stupid brain worked. It had rarely got it wrong with the Melbourne Cup so here was a super opportunity to earn a few dirhams.

An excited energy thrummed when she found a seat out of the sun. Horses for the first race paraded past by handlers adorned in the same uniform. She studied each animal, searched for hints of a limp or awkward gait, rippling muscles, alert eyes and flared nostrils to show the horse's readiness to get out there and win. Jockey's silks gave brightness to the parade. Echoing voices through many speakers detailed each horse and rider as they passed. Happy with her choice, Sarah used her phone to lay bets for the first race before she went in search of a booth to buy a bottle of water. If she won she would indulge in a glass of bubbly at the bar for westerners.

Adrenalin spurted while handlers coerced the final two horses into their barrier gates. Handlers scampered away. A silent pause for about five seconds.

The barriers shot open.

Everyone rose on a murmur of anticipation. The atmosphere became electric. Crowd noise heightened. People joggled up and down as if they were the riders urging their mounts to go faster and faster. 'Come on, come on,' came from most, including Sarah when one of her numbers passed two others to take the lead. Her other horse was on the outside but had gained speed. The cheer from the winning punters was much louder than the groans from the losers as spectators either jumped in delight or sank back into their seats. Sarah smiled. First and second, along with the quinella.

'Yes,' she whispered to herself on the way to the bar where she bought a glass of Champagne.

Between races, Sarah either sat quietly or wandered with an occasional glance at the royal party. At one stage she thought Hakim caught her eye but wasn't sure. So far neither he nor his men had come near, not that Hakim would lower himself to talk to her in public. Now she accepted it, thought it laughable but it didn't prevent the stabs into her innards.

When hunger pangs hit, she went inside to a large restaurant with one section for the wealthy where they ordered food from individual servers who delivered it to their table. She went to the self-serve section for the lower-class like her where she purchased packaged sandwiches and a plastic bowl of diced fruit. She found room to settle her backside at a small round table, opened her sandwiches and took a bite.

'What are you doing here?'

The food bolted down her gullet at Hakim's voice. 'Obeying your orders.'

'Excuse me? When did I order you to attend the races?'

'You told me to be a tourist.' She choked before she was able to catch her breath and swallow down the panic attack. Shouldn't have sat with her back to the door. 'So, like every other western tourist here, I watch horses and riders race each other around a track.' She took another bite.

'This is not a place for you.'

This time she turned. 'Why not?'

'I don't wish to see my wife at such a place, especially dressed in... in...'

'In what? The same as every other female tourist? My dress reveals a lot less than many of these others but allows me to fit in.' Oh, my, she sure enjoyed his wince. 'You wish for me to have the freedom to do what I want. This event has been advertised for weeks and besides, you are here, along with your parents, all of your brothers *and their wives,* and children. You'd better be careful; people might see you consorting with the riffraff.' She took out her phone. 'If you will excuse me, your Highness, I need to lay bets on the next race.' She flicked to the site.

'You gamble?' Hakim rasped.

'Of course. I've won on each race so far. It has boosted my savings account quite a bit. I suggest numbers three and five in the next race.'

Hakim rounded the table, pulled out a stool and plopped onto it. Impressed by her admission – he was not.

'How much have you won?'

'It's rude to ask about a person's finances.'

'But what if you lost?'

'I'm not an idiot. I came prepared to lose twenty-five dirham.' She punched in her numbers and the amount of her bet. 'In the first race I put five dirham each way on numbers two and ten plus five dirham on the quinella. If I lost, I wouldn't have placed another bet. But I won. I put aside my original twenty-five dirham and was able to double the amount to bet on numbers three and six in the second race. Again I won. So far, after four races, I have made more than enough to pay my entry fee, this dress, my refreshments with a tidy sum to go into my savings account.'

'How do you know which horses to bet on?'

'I studied the form guide, the weather, the track conditions, past rides and every other detail to indicate how each would ride today. I made calculations. Came up with the most logical winners. Easy.'

'Do you do this often?'

'Rarely but today I wanted a bit of fun since my husband wants nothing to do with me.'

'You know that is not true.'

'Do I? It's obvious I'm not a welcome member of your family.' She indicated the royal arena. 'While Faria still is. Message received. All that's required of me is to be a body in your bed for your sexual gratification.' Close to tears, she stood, gathered up her food and hurried away, fighting hard to not let the tears fall. Hakim didn't deserve her tears.

For the rest of the day she hid in a corner, laid her bets. A brief bout of disappointment hit when she got one wrong but was overjoyed when the meet ended with more in her bank account than she had when she arrived two months ago. Now she could afford to enjoy more of the tourist delights without worrying about finances. It had taken a bit of effort but she'd managed to lengthen her work visa for another eight weeks. With Hakim's refusal to publicly acknowledge their marriage, she couldn't apply to stay on spousal grounds. Who, in the relevant authority, would believe her claim she was married to Prince Hakim al Fasir? No-one.

Before the last race finished, she noticed Shahir headed towards her. Her final bet of the day was that Hakim had sent him to collect her to ride home in the car. It wouldn't happen. She snuck away via the ladies' rest rooms, came out in a group of women, hidden from Shahir who stood on the opposite wall. Two well-endowed ladies in flowing abayas, hid her well. The taxis outside were plentiful since she emerged before the crowds. A grin split her face while she rode home to a quiet solo dinner since Hakim was supposed to dine at the racetrack which meant she would have been locked in his car for hours.

Thirty Two

It had taken Hakim twenty-four hours to chew over
Sarah's words. He had wanted to discuss her
accusations last night but she was asleep when he got
in. Her words about sexual gratification had rankled for she
enjoyed their lovemaking as much as he did. Every day he
grew more intolerant of his position but with so many
appearances set in stone, months ago, it was almost
impossible to pull out. Like this morning, he had to present
athletic awards. Pre-Sarah he would have enjoyed the event
but now it was a painful chore. He tore off his keffiyeh the
moment he stepped inside and shut the front door to go in
search of his wife.

The frustration of the past twenty-four hours reared
again when he couldn't find her until Mariam mentioned
Sarah had been swimming in the pool. He opened the door
but paused at the sound of her voice. She must have a guest

but she had never brought anyone home before, which was a pity in one sense for she needed friends. But gossip would spread faster than the strongest desert winds if she did bring someone home.

'I miss you so darn much,' said Sarah. 'Say hi to everyone. I bought a dress with the money… Yes an actual real dress… Got to go. Love you heaps. Bye.'

Love? Steam bubbled and rose in an instant. Hakim stormed through the doorway, across the paving to Sarah who sat wrapped in a towel with her back to him. He reached over her shoulder, grabbed the phone and searched for the call she had made. The word, Pete, showed up.

'This Pete is a man?'

Defiance glared back when Sarah turned. 'Yes.'

'In Australia?'

'Yes.'

'How old is he?'

'Twenty-eight.'

Beyond furious, Hakim scrolled for other names. 'And this Danny? A man.'

'Yes.'

'How old?'

'Thirty.' Sarah shot from the chair and spun around: arms crossed.

'Sam, how old?'

'Twenty-one.'

Hakim undid the back of her phone, took out both battery and sim card, pocketed all three pieces.

Sarah fought to retrieve them. 'What are you doing?'

'You dare tell another man you love him when you cannot tell me, your husband.' He had to pause to contain his fury. 'You will speak to no other man but me. You can use the landline for local calls but you are not to ever speak to anyone back in Australia. I will know if you call for they will be listed on the bill.'

'You have no idea what you are doing?' The words were so quiet he barely made them out.

'You are my wife. No other man has the right to your words of love.'

She glared. 'Maybe Pete deserves my love.'

Hakim reeled around at the insult. A pain lanced through him. He paced from one end of the patio to the other and back again, desperate to regain control of his fury.

'I will be in my office until we leave tonight.'

'Leave? I thought you had the night free of commitments.'

'Which is why my parents invited us to share their evening meal. They also have a free night. Dress is semi-formal. Be ready at seven.' He turned on his heel and fled, too afraid to open his mouth again, too angry to stay.

The statue perched on the edge of the couch took Hakim's breath away. Ramrod straight back, hands gripped together in her lap, Sarah wore the long green skirt he'd seen before but this time a different top with a wide neckline which draped in three soft folds. Even though the top was discreet and plain, it was downright sexy, inviting a man to explore beneath the folds. A gold halo of hair was fuller than normal. Even though she still wore no make-up she was exquisite.

'Are you ready?' Hakim asked.

Sarah stood, nodded, turned towards the front door and was in the car before he pulled the door shut. It would be a long night unless he could break this tension.

Seated, he wrapped his fingers around her hand, surprised when she didn't tug it free. 'You are stunning.'

'Thank you.' Her eyes stared straight ahead.

He ran his thumb in circles on the back of her hand but there was no relaxation in her tense muscles. 'You are very quiet.'

The silence was profound. 'Why do you not answer me?' he finally asked to break the tension.

Her head turned a tad. 'You didn't ask a question for me to answer.'

Frustration hit. Hakim ran a hand down his face. 'Why are you so precise with such things?'

'It's the way my brain works. A question is a question which requires an answer but you gave a statement telling me I am quiet.'

'Is this attitude because you are angry with me?'

'No, not angry. Disappointed. Hurt.'

'As am I disappointed you speak to other men about love, but not to me. Because of this my heart is in pain.'

'I'm sorry but...'

'We have arrived. Can we put our differences aside while we dine with my parents? They wish to get to know you better.'

At last Sarah caught his eye. 'I do know how to behave in social situations even though I come from inferior breeding.'

Hakim reeled back. 'Sarah, never have I inferred or even thought of you as inferior.'

Sarah opened the door and alighted. 'Yet I'm not good enough to be seen with you in public or acknowledged as your wife.' She raced ahead but came to a stop at the front door.

Before he had a chance to say a word, the door opened. His father's chief aide ushered them inside. 'The Sheikh awaits you in the drawing room.'

Hakim placed one arm around Sarah's waist to guide her. The very second they reached the archway his mother stood with a welcome smile and approached with arms held out wide in welcome.

'My dear, at last we can spend time together.' She wrapped her arms around Sarah and kissed her cheek.

'Thank you for inviting me but I find myself in a difficult situation.'

Hakim's breath stalled.

'No-one has instructed me on correct protocol when I meet you and the Sheikh. Please accept my apologies.'

'No apologies are needed. My son is remiss, not you. I am your mother-in-law or *Hamah* while my husband is your *Hamw*. In private, you have no need to call us anything else. In public, you give a brief curtsey. I am addressed as Your Royal Highness Sheikha Arva while my husband is Your Royal Highness Sheikh Iqbal. For you, it is only required on the first meeting of the day. After that Sir or Ma'am is sufficient. Now, my dear, come and sit by me so we can chat.'

As he stood aside, Hakim closed his eyes, thankful Sarah had turned on her charm. Eyes open he noticed his mother's scowl when he drew a chair close to Sarah's side to be on hand.

'Why have you not joined us at our family functions?'

Hakim froze at the question from his father.

Sarah turned to his mother. '*Hamah,* now I have another problem. Please could you give my sincerest apologies to the Sheikh but I am not allowed to speak to him.'

Hakim winced at the audible hisses of shock from both parents.

'Why not?' asked his mother.

'My husband has ordered me to speak to no man but him.'

'Sarah, this is family,' he whispered.

'Your family, not mine. Your orders said no man but you.' Sarah did not whisper.

'Sarah has no family,' he said to his parents.

'Everyone has family.' Sarah sent him another glare. 'Both my mother and father have four siblings which gives me eight uncles and aunts. All eight are married, therefore another eight uncles and aunts by marriage. Each couple has an average of three children, giving me twenty-four first cousins. Most are older than me. Twenty of them are married. There are a further thirty two children from those twenty couples and I have three grandparents still alive which totals over a hundred family members. We are a very close-knit family.'

'But you said...'

Sarah's glare stopped any further words. 'Said what?'

'That you have been alone since you were fifteen.'

'No, I said I have been independent since I was fifteen. I boarded away from home to complete my education and held down a full time job so was financially independent as well.'

'Why did you never tell me about your family?'

'I did mention them. You never asked any questions.'

'This does not explain why you are not allowed to speak to me.'

At his father's voice, Hakim searched the ceiling for inspiration. 'This is neither the time nor place.'

'If my daughter-in-law is not permitted to speak with me, I have a right to know why,' said his father.

'*Hamah*, maybe you could tell the Sheikh, Hakim eavesdropped on a phone call to someone who is close to me.'

'Sarah told another man she loved him. It was inappropriate.'

290

'My love for Pete is purely platonic the same way you love your brothers.'

'My brothers are men, not from the opposite sex.'

'Your mother is female. Don't you love her?'

'Of course but she is my mother. You may speak with my father.'

'You will give me back my phone?'

'No.'

'Then I obey your orders.'

A bark of laughter came from across the room. 'You have chosen well for your wife, my son. She both obeys and disobeys you at the same time. Very clever. I have learnt much about young Sarah in this brief time. She is smart, beautiful and perfect for you. Sarah is not afraid to stand up for herself, has excellent manners and shows utmost respect. She is quietly spoken, unfazed by our status and most important - takes no nonsense from you. Sarah, my dear, while we dine, you may speak to me through my wife but since what you say will be heard by me I am going to enjoy this evening. I no longer have any doubts about your suitability to be the wife of my son. Now, it is time to eat.'

Stunned, Hakim wrapped one arm around Sarah's waist and guided her as they followed his parents into the small family dining room.

The meal was torturous despite Sarah being the perfect guest. She laughed, chatted and obliged his father with quips fielded via his mother. There was nothing about her manner or behaviour he could fault unless he listed her stubbornness about not speaking to any man but it was of his own making: which he now regretted but would not change. He recognised the serious sense of jealousy for what it was but he would not allow his wife to speak such words to another man.

Thirty Three

At the sudden silence, Hakim peered over the balcony. His breath caught. Every eye turned to the stunning woman who had just entered the theatre foyer. The vivid peacock-purple silk gown shimmered but was simple and modest. It also screamed sexiness and it was his wife wearing it.

'Bring Sarah to me,' he said to Ali while he kept his eyes on the siren who ignored everyone as she crossed the foyer to an usherette. She glanced at a piece of paper in her hand, nodded at what the young woman said and turned in the direction indicated. When Ali caught up with her she listened, glanced up. He couldn't drag his eyes away the entire time she mounted the steps with the grace of a prima ballerina. One hand lifted the front of the exquisite gown as she floated upwards. He wasn't the only one who watched. He didn't think there was a single eye turned away which was not only going to be awkward but also renewed the spurt of jealousy.

'Your Highness.' She dropped a small curtsy. 'You need to inform your men I can't speak to them.'

'Why are you here?'

There was a swift audible inhale through her nose along with a glare. 'For an intelligent man, you ask dumb questions. This is a theatre. As per your orders,' one finger pointed at his chest, 'I am a tourist. One who wishes to experience a live performance of *Les Miserables*.' She shot a glance over her shoulder at the sound of the warning bells. 'If you will excuse me, I must find my seat.'

'You will join me in the royal box.'

'Not likely.'

'You defy me again?'

'If you had wanted me here, you would have brought me. I now know my place in your life. It is obvious you are too ashamed of me to accompany you in public so I will sit where I belong, with the riffraff and common people. Your Highness.' Her curtsy sent a wave of something he couldn't describe, through him as he watched her scamper down the stairs. Regret simmered along with a tinge of anger but also admiration. Few would dare defy him. The gown was new, he was sure. Was this the dress bought with the money she spoke about on the phone? Money from the man she loved.

'Sir, they wait for you.'

Hakim jolted to awareness at Ali's words. 'Sorry, I am coming.'

Never before had the ritual of the audience standing for him, grated as it did now. While upright, he searched for Sarah but could not see a golden-haired goddess. 'Find where Sarah is seated,' he said to Ali and eased into his chair. Even though he kept his eyes glued to the stage, he absorbed little since his mind was stuck on the past few days.

There had been little change. Sarah had been quiet during the drive home from the palace but their lovemaking had been as hot and tempestuous as ever. Breakfast had been normal the past three mornings but what she had done each of those days, he had no idea. A growl rumbled from deep down. He should know but never thought to ask and was usually too exhausted to even think, let alone ask, by the time he got home each night. Was this why she likened herself to riffraff? From now on he would make a point of showing more interest.

'Sir, the princess sits in the far back corner beneath us.'

'Why would she sit so far back? Surely she cannot see well from there.'

'Miss Sarah always sits where she can see all the people near her. Always with her back to a wall.'

'You think she is still afraid?'

'She still startles at sudden movement near her.'

Regret slithered through Hakim's stomach. Why did he not know this? Why did he not notice? 'Thank you. When the show ends, make sure you collect Sarah and take her to the car.'

'Sir.' Ali sat in a seat two rows back.

For the remainder of the first session it was difficult to concentrate on the superb performance. Delight filled him when he went to the supper room at the intermission. Somehow he would convince Sarah to join him in the royal box for the second half. His breath stalled when she entered the room. She placed a couple of savouries on a small paper plate. Her eyes scanned the bar but she frowned, turned and settled her back against the wall near the entry doorway. While she nibbled her head hung low. A man confronted her, spoke but she turned away. When the man's face creased into anger, Hakim hurried across the room. The man was smart enough to step away.

'You do not have a drink,' Hakim said to Sarah.

'No.'

'Why?'

'There are only men serving.'

'*Habibti*, I did not mean you could not ask men for basic necessities.'

'You meant exactly what you said – shouted your order. Like a good Muslim wife, I obey.'

'Sarah, please, this has gone too far.'

'Will you give me back my phone?'

'I cannot.'

Sarah stacked her plate on top of his. 'Then I obey your orders.' She spun around and scarpered through the doorway. To go after her would create a stir he did not need, more for Sarah's sake than his. Nausea churned as he placed the uneaten food on the end of a table. He purchased a bottle of water, handed it to Ali. 'Please take this to Sarah. Make sure she keeps it but she will not speak to you.'

'Why not?'

'My fault, my regret.' Without stopping to chat to any of the people he should talk to, he returned to his seat, certain he would not enjoy another minute of the show.

When the last song began, Sarah sidled along the wall to the exit. With no-one else yet outside she took the taxi at the head of the line. At home, she hung the gorgeous dress on a hanger she pinched from Hakim's wardrobe, had a quick shower and curled under the blanket.

When Hakim stepped into the bedroom, it was a shock when he opened her single robe and drew out her dress.

'Where did this come from?'

Uncertainty shimmered through her innards as she sat with arms crossed. 'A shop at the mall.'

'Who paid for it?'

Her eyes screwed. 'I did.'

'You told your lover you bought a dress with the money.'

Sarah laughed - she couldn't help it. 'Money from my race winnings and I'm about fed up with your arrogance.'

'Excuse me?'

'Every night I put aside any disharmony. Never go to bed angry, my mother always told me. Every morning I begin the day with a positive frame of mind. Every day I do my best to fill and enjoy every minute despite the ache of loneliness. Every day you throw out arrogant comments about things you *think* are correct. You have mastered the skill of jumping to conclusions. *You* suggested I buy new clothes. I obeyed, bought two dresses but you create in your mind some fanciful story about an imaginary lover. You *know* I have never been with another man. Get this straight, Hakim. I don't have a lover, boyfriend, manfriend or any romantic interest in any other man. I do not accept money from any man, including you. I pay for my own purchases with *my* money.'

'Then what did you mean about buying a dress with the money?'

Sarah stood and laughed again but it came out cynical. 'When one is rude enough to eavesdrop they are only privy to one side of a conversation but if you must know, instead of giving me Christmas presents this year, my family banded together and deposited money into my bank account to buy myself a gift I would enjoy. I used the money to enjoy the one thing I most wanted to experience in this country - a day in the desert. There was enough to buy the dress I wore to the races.' She grabbed her robe, slung it on over her nightie and stalked to the door.

'Where are you going?'

'Tonight, I'm too churned up to put anger and pain aside. You have spoilt a fabulous night with your snide innuendos. I will sleep elsewhere.' She turned and ran.

'Sarah, wait.' Hakim grabbed her arm. 'Please can we talk.'

She paused but didn't turn. 'Talk.'

'Why did you leave the concert early?'

'To avoid the ignominy of being herded to your car and hidden away in shame while you spend half an hour socialising.'

'Sarah, no…'

'Yes. That is exactly what would have happened.' She spun around. 'Deny it but tell the truth. You were going to get Ali to take me to your car out of sight of the public. Yes, or no?'

Hakim sighed, glanced away. 'Yes but my wish is to protect you from gossip so you can have your freedom and are not under the same restrictions Muslim wives have in this country.'

'As I thought.' She tugged her arm free. 'Good night, sleep well.' To make sure Hakim didn't come after her, she ran to her original bedroom and locked the door.

Thirty Four

'Your Highness, how can I help you?' Shock spread across the face of the Dean of Science. He shot to his feet with one hand outstretched.

'I wish to speak with a student of yours, Miss Sarah Anderson.' Hakim shook the proffered hand.

'Not a name I know. Let me search.' Still upright, the man typed on the computer keyboard.

Hakim shifted from foot-to-foot, anxious to set things right with Sarah. So far, the day had been horrendous. It began with Sarah not at the breakfast table. Mariam's message that Sarah had taken a taxi to university had sent a shaft of anxiety through him which added to the lethargy from a sleepless night with Sarah not in his bed.

To find the two hours needed to come here now, he had upset several important people to cancel a meeting. Right now, he did not care. He glanced at the man bent at an awkward angle in an attempt to remain standing as a sign of respect yet read his monitor at the same time.

'Please, sit.' He gestured to the man's chair.

The dean sat with a frown. 'I'm sorry, your Highness, but we don't have a student with such a name.'

Hakim dragged a chair with his toe and sat. 'Are you sure? Australian woman with short gold hair.'

The dean grinned. 'Oh, you mean Sarah al Fasir. Remarkable woman. The students love her. Such an asset. Oh...' he stalled. 'Al Fasir, I was not aware she was married to a member of your family.'

It was a struggle to think of a response. 'Sarah wishes it to be kept quiet.' And damn him for lying but why did she use his name? Muslim women kept their maiden names upon marriage.

'Oh, I see. Sarah's session has almost ended. Laboratory two at the end of the passage on the left.'

Hakim shot up. 'Thank you.' He nodded and strode along the long passage. He pushed the door open, stepped inside to organised chaos as individual students behind Bunsen burners, beakers and test tubes chatted to each other while they fiddled with their apparatus. He searched the benches but could not see his prey.

'Ladies, we have a visitor. If the prince speaks with you, you are to address him as Your Highness.'

Hakim spun around to see Sarah behind the lecturer's desk. She's the lecturer? 'I find it interesting you speak with male students.'

'No, I speak only to the ladies. I have a female assistant to speak to the men. Why are you here?'

'To eat the midday meal with my wife since she was not home for breakfast.' The surprise on her face was a delight.

'Give me ten minutes.' She stepped away to move among the benches. 'Ladies, every item must be washed and put away. Any position not left perfect will incur a mark deduction for the person responsible. Write up the notes on the experiment and post them in my cubbyhole before Monday morning.'

It fascinated him to watch Sarah move through the group of twenty students. She passed comments to the females but ignored the men. A young woman trailed after Sarah to pass on messages to the men. With a nod of her head after she had inspected each work station, she released the students one-by-one.

When she joined him, her arms were filled with a pile of papers. They walked side-by-side to an office where she dropped the papers on the edge of a large desk.

'Why did you not tell me you were teaching?'

A long sigh escaped her pursed lips. 'I did.'

'When?'

'When I asked your permission to take classes two days a week. I said I needed your permission to *work* here.'

'I thought you had enrolled to attend lectures.'

'Big difference in attending lectures and actually taking the classes.' When she caught his eye, there was fear in hers. 'You're going to make me stop teaching aren't you?'

'No, why would you think it?' Even though she might shrink from him, he reached out and grasped her upper arms.

She shrugged but didn't answer.

'Do you have time to join me for lunch?'

'No, my next class starts in…' she glanced at her watch. 'Forty-five minutes.' Sarah opened a drawer, took out a wrapped sandwich which she opened out and passed him half.

With the fingers of his free hand under her chin, he drew her head up. Before she could pull away he settled his mouth over hers in a gentle kiss and swallowed her sigh when she relaxed and kissed him back. Still holding the sandwich, he wrapped his arms around her to draw her into his body. 'My only hunger right now is for you. I slept little last night without you in my arms. I missed you at breakfast and now have cancelled an important meeting because my need to be with you is far more important.'

Sarah wanted to believe him as he parted her lips, searched the inside of her mouth and began mating with her tongue. Her fingers grasped the robe at his chest, the need inside desperate for more. This need was too much, like an all-consuming fever. It was more than physical. It came from somewhere much deeper: so ingrained she had no hope of resisting. Why? She knew why. Despite his skewed views on what was best for her, she loved Hakim and would do her darndest to make him see her side.

His hand skated down her back to cup her backside and draw her closer still. Pleasure swept through her before she broke off the kiss and pulled away. 'We can't do this here. I have to set up for a lecture.'

He rubbed a hand down his face on a slow exhale. A wry grin spread across his face. 'You are right, but maybe now I can return to work with the knowledge the world has been reset onto its correct axis. But before I go, I am curious about two things. How did you manage to get Mariam to make these sandwiches?'

'I make my own lunch. And the second?'

'Surely a bachelor's degree is not an adequate qualification to be a lecturer at a university.'

The stab of pain seared her innards at his unfounded conclusion. 'Surely a bachelor's degree in commerce is not adequate qualification to be a government minister,' slipped out in retaliation before she had time to think.

Hakim's eyes widened in shock. 'How did you know?'

'I may not be qualified enough to instruct the students of your country, or good enough to walk by your side in public but I am damn good at research. At least I care enough about you to want to learn about the man I married and the internet has a great deal of information with many pictures of you with your host of female companions, including the one who had her hands all over you in public at the fundraiser. And you dare comment on my purely platonic relationship with a single male while you have an ex-girlfriend pawing you in public. Maybe I should ask exactly where you've been each time you come home? Maybe I should question which woman you've spent the hours with. As to my qualifications? The faculty dean was more than happy with my qualifications, my experience and the reference from my Sydney professor.' With renewed pain and anger threatening to bubble out, she snatched up her laptop and the thumb-drive she had prepared, spun around and ran.

While she set up for the lecture by testing all the electronics, Sarah wasn't sure if it was anger, frustration or a severe sense of inadequacy, which refused to go away. All three, she conceded after a series of long slow breaths with her eyes shut until a murmur of voices and scuffle of feet indicated the first of the students entered the lecture theatre. Sixty students. She needed to gain some semblance of peace to teach sixty first year science students on how to present their findings in both the written and spoken form. She sat with her back to the auditorium until the scuffles and murmurs ceased. At the sudden silence, she stood, turned, sent her eyes around to each student until they landed on the two men seated up the back near the door. Hakim with Tariq next to him. Damn.

It took a moment before she was able to remember the light-hearted banter she usually used to get the students laughing and at ease. Their laughter made her determined to show Mr High and Mighty Prince she was worthy of being employed. This would be the best lecture she had ever given. She tossed Hakim from her mind, clicked the button for the first diagram and forced her brain to concentrate on a lecture she had given many times before. Bachelor's degree my foot. Did he really think she was so dumb it would take so long to gain a single degree?

Even though she had the students in fits of laughter, she noticed when Hakim and Tariq left. The intense relief made the rest of the lecture a breeze. Back in her office, she used the landline to call Mariam to say she wouldn't be home for the evening meal. According to the schedule she had memorised, Hakim would be at *AFC*, whatever it was, until nine. It gave her a chance to spend an hour or two at the centre for which the auction had raised money. The children were a delight to work with, especially little Amira who had recently been orphaned. Even more, the children eased her acute loneliness.

Cheers from her team sounded alongside jeers from the opposition when Sarah managed to loop the basketball through the hoop. With a wide grin, she bowed and turned around but the grin vanished at the sight of Hakim who stood, arms folded, on the side of the court. The anger in his eyes said she was in deep manure.

'You cannot be here.' The words were ground under his breath but loud enough she stalled.

'Why not? I've been coming here for weeks. The staff welcome me as do the children but you...' Words defied her. Not game to say another word, she left the court, walked over to the group of youngsters who were completing the task she had set them. 'Sorry, my pets but I must go.' She knelt on the floor to be at their level.

'Why?' Amira asked in stilted English.

A knife stabbed her heart at the instant wash of tears in Amira's eyes. 'The prince says I cannot be here.'

'No!' Amira screamed and threw her tiny body at Sarah's chest.

'What is going on here?' Hakim demanded.

Furious, Sarah shot up and thrust Amira against his chest. He grappled to keep a hold of the girl. 'You caused this, so you can fix it. Explain to a little girl who has recently lost both parents in a car crash, why I can longer be her best friend.' She spun around, unhooked her backpack from the pegs and ran full pelt down the driveway until she reached the road. It took half a kilometre of powerwalking before she could hail a taxi. Thoughts tumbled as fast as adrenalin spurted for the entire fifteen minute drive.

On a super adrenalin high, she needed to run off her agitation so changed into workout clothes but veered into the kitchen on the way out. 'I'm going for a run.'

Mariam jerked around from the sink. 'Oh, Miss Sarah, you scared me.' Both hands covered her chest.

'Sorry, I'll be half an hour – one lap around the block.'

'Have you eaten?'

'No, but I can make a sandwich when I return.' Sarah turned away. Any form of food was the last thing she could manage. The food would shoot straight back up with a stomach so tense. After stepping off the front step, she ran, desperate to rid her body of her angst and a bucket full of adrenalin.

'Sir, a call from Mariam. She sounds anxious.'

Hakim stepped away from the boys he had been helping with homework to take the phone from Ali,.

'Mariam, is there a problem?'

'Sir, Miss Sarah. I am worried.'

His stomach clenched on a sucked in hiss. 'What happened, is she harmed?'

'I do not know. She went for a run. She always returns after thirty minutes but it is now an hour and a half. She is never late.'

Unaware Sarah even went for a run, Hakim glared at the phone. Why did he not know? The same way he had no idea Sarah had spent several hours a week at the centre or how the youngsters adored her? Nor did he know she'd been lecturing for almost four weeks. Why did she never inform him of her activities? He scrambled for ideas on what to ask so he didn't appear to be an utter fool? 'Do you know her route?'

'Always around the block either once or twice. Sometimes three times. Tonight she said one lap.'

'Ask Suhail to drive around the block, I am on my way.' With a hammer punching his ribs at a frantic pace he shut the phone down and ordered Ali to get the car. 'Have to go,' he remembered to tell the boys before he broke into a run. He yanked on the car door handle, dived into the back seat. 'Did you know Sarah went jogging?' he asked the men in the front.

'Yes, after dark on the nights you are not home.'

The hammer pounded harder. 'She runs alone? In the dark?'

Both guards eyed each other before Ahmed answered a hesitant yes, which sent Hakim's anger on a level to equal a volcanic eruption. 'Why did no-one tell me this? Why does no-one watch over her? Drive faster.' He brushed tense fingers through his hair, dislodging his head-dress. Furious, he scrunched it into a ball and hurled it onto the floor. 'Which block does she run?' There were several ways she could go from his house. Did she cross the road, go north, south?

'Out the gate, turn left. She loops the block, crosses no roads,' came from a subdued Ahmed. 'Usually two laps, sometimes three but if she needs to hurry, only one.'

Before he had a chance to let loose with a round of demands, Hakim's phone rang. He glanced at the name. A surge of adrenalin joined the hammer. He tapped the button. 'Suhail, please tell me you found her.'

'Yes, Sir.'

'Sarah is unharmed?'

'Yes, Sir but there is a problem.'

Hakim hissed with eyes closed and stomach clenched. 'What is the problem?'

'There is a young child asleep in her arms but Sarah will not speak to me.'

'Where is she?'

'On the side of the road behind your house. Northern end. Almost at the corner.'

'We will be there in five. Keep her safe.' After shutting down his phone he gave directions and leant forwards to peer through the windscreen. The hammer had eased off a tiny bit now he knew Sarah was safe but he still wanted to tear someone apart from limb to limb and crush all the body parts into the desert sands.

He was out of the car before it drew to a standstill and knelt by Sarah's side within a second. High-lighted by the street light, a young lad, wearing shorts and a grubby T-shirt, lay in her arms with his head nestled against her shoulder. 'Sarah, who is this child?'

'I don't know.'

'Why... what... how did you come by him?'

'He ran out onto the road, almost got hit by a car. I managed to grab him.'

'Dear Allah, you could have been killed.' A vision of the scene raced through his mind.

Her eyes shot darts when she glanced up at him. 'This child could have been killed.'

'Why did you not ring me?' The moment the words were out, he regretted them. It was his fault – again. 'Surely he comes from around here. One of these houses?'

'Which is why I am here. What else could I do? If his parents are nearby, they'll surely search these streets. I couldn't take him home: he is too heavy to carry and I could miss those who search for him.'

'Did you not ask him?'

Sarah snorted. 'He gabbles in Arabic but I think his name is Muhammad.'

'Like half the male population of the Arab world. Come, we will sit both of you in the car while Ali rings the police. It will be far more comfortable.' He lifted the child from her arms and passed him to Ahmed before assisting Sarah to her feet. There were two things he wanted to do to Sarah; kiss her senseless and berate her for daring to run alone at night. He would do neither but running alone was off the agenda. He could not handle the stress. Instead, he dared to wrap her in his arms to convince himself she was safe.

'*Habibti,*' he murmured before planting a kiss on her head. 'My heart still thunders from worry after Mariam rang me to say you were missing.' He was reluctant to let her go but the flashing lights of a police car forced them apart. He settled Sarah in the back seat of his car, his innards doing tumble-turns to see the way she swept her hand with such tenderness over the sleeping child. She will be an amazing mother – to his children.

It warmed his innards to see Sarah's reluctance to leave the child in the care of the police after thirty minutes of questions but at last they were home. While Sarah showered and ate the meal Mariam had kept warm, he didn't dare raise the issue of running alone after dark, nor question her about the children's centre, nor her outburst about qualifications or even compliment her on the way she had an entire auditorium of students leaning forward to absorb every word of her lecture. There was no doubt she was exhausted, for she said little and there was an aura of caution about her, which he wasn't game to ask about. He also doubted her introspective mood would allow their usual lovemaking. Instead, after slipping under the covers, he drew her body against his and spooned around her with a kiss on her cheek. 'Tomorrow, I have cleared my schedule so we can have the day together.'

'Thank you.' Sarah whispered, sighed and was asleep within seconds.

Thirty Five

All day it had been difficult to wipe the smile from her face. The weekend had been fabulous: two entire days of doing things together, much of it in bed. It was the longest time they had spent together since the day they met. It not only reinforced her love for Hakim but now she was sure he might like her as much. Soon he would be home.

She spooned the pale yellow flummery into individual dishes, topped each with a dribble of passionfruit sauce and a few small mint leaves. It looked pretty and the flavours yum, according to Mariam and Suhail, who had already eaten. Whoever was on guard duty would also get to sample one of her family's favourite meals although the men ate either in the kitchen or out on the patio, depending on the weather.

After putting the tray of desserts in the fridge, Sarah turned to the cook-top to check on the orange sauce with added spices to cater for Hakim's palate. When his footsteps echoed in the passage, her excitement level thrummed. Ten minutes to shower would give the crispy duck breasts a chance to rest before she sliced them and placed the pieces on top of the parsnip puree, which already waited to be spooned onto warm plates. Green beans, middle east style, were ready. Carrot fingers cooked to perfection in butter and spices – check.

Ali and Ahmed came in the back door, sniffed and grinned. 'Smells amazing.' Ali pulled out a chair at the table on the far side of the room. With a scrape of chair legs across the tiles, Ahmed joined him.

Sarah spread out the warmed plates, sliced the four duck breasts and grinned at the slightly pink flesh. A large scoop of puree went onto each plate, topped with angled pieces of meat. Next, she took care to arrange men-sized portions of beans and carrots to give the plates a professional appearance. As a final hurrah, she spooned plenty of yummy, spiced sauce over the top. Steam rose. The wafts of spices tickled her nasal passages and set gastric juices flowing in anticipation. The moment Hakim's footsteps entered the dining room, she served both men but said nothing at their words of appreciation.

Mariam must have heard Hakim for she came into the kitchen from the laundry. 'Looks good.'

Sarah lifted the last two plates from the table and headed towards the dining room where she placed Hakim's plate in front of him at the head of the table, dropped a kiss on his cheek and moved to her place at his right. She sat, put her plate down and swallowed down a lump of fear when she noted Hakim's face.

'What is this?' He swept one hand over the plate.

'Your evening meal.'

'Take it away.'

Disappointment tightened her stomach muscles. 'Why?'

'I cannot eat this.'

A cold icicle pierced her heart. 'What happened to it being bad manners to not eat what your host has prepared for you?'

'Mariam knows better than to serve such insipid food. This is fit only for pig swill.'

Determined to not show her pain, Sarah stood, picked up both plates and walked tall through the doorway. Without a word at the curious stares, she scraped Hakim's food into the slops bucket. She grabbed a knife and fork, carried her plate to the door and turned. 'I apologise, Mariam, but His Highness would like you to prepare him food which is not suitable only for pigs to eat.' Close to tears, she fled but didn't miss the loud gasps at the profound insult since Muslims regard pigs as filth. Determined to eat her favourite meal, she found a seat hidden in the garden, sat and shovelled the food in her mouth but it replicated the swill Hakim described.

Hakim lifted his head from the newspaper at the scrape of footsteps behind. A plate slammed in front of him. He glanced up to see Mariam's furious face glare at him. 'What is wrong? Where is Sarah?'

'Outside weeping an oasis of tears.'

Hakim frowned. 'Why, she was fine a few minutes ago.'

'That was before you insulted the meal she spent all day preparing for you because she wanted to please you. You don't deserve her as your wife.' Before he could drag his jaw together, Mariam stormed from the room. A door slammed.

Hakim followed. His men glared at him. They had cleaned their plates and were spooning a white, fluffy concoction into their mouths. 'Do not say a word,' he ordered.

'As always, Miss Sarah's cooking is out of this world delicious,' Ahmed dared as he stood and made a show of scraping every skerrick of white from the glass dish and licking the spoon. He opened the dishwasher, nestled in his dishes and sauntered out the back door. 'Got to get back on duty.'

Hakim eyed Ali. 'As always? Sarah has cooked for you before?'

'Yes, many times. She is a superb cook but now I understand why she refused to serve her food to you.'

'Where did she go?'

Ali indicated the back door with his chin. 'Out there.'

'Find her.'

'Sir, I doubt Miss Sarah wants to be found. I will do my best but it could take a while.' He joined the trail of bodies departing through the kitchen doorway.

Hakim grubbed fingers through his hair with his eyes shut and called himself all kinds of a fool. This aberration would be impossible to apologise for. Would he ever get anything right with Sarah?

After only two bites of the food Mariam had presented, he tipped it into the slops bucket, grimacing at what was already there. The amount of spice Mariam had used was a deliberate message. He had to grin at her audacity but the grin changed to a frown on his way outside to search for his angry wife. Ali met him at the door.

'Did you find Sarah?'

'There is a statue sitting in the arbour behind Suhail's cottage.'

Hakim lifted his shoulders on a long sigh. 'Thank you.'

There was no movement from the statue when he approached. With a wodge of fear lodged in his throat, he settled next to Sarah. 'I am deeply sorry for my words.'

'It is me who is sorry.'

'Why? I do not understand.' And her meekness worried him.

'Mistakes are for us to learn from. Tonight, I learned my lesson well.' She stood, collected a plate still with half of her congealing food. 'Never again will I make the mistake of offending your Royal taste buds with my inadequate culinary skills.' With her head high and back straight, she strode towards the house. 'The same as after this next week I will never inflict my inadequate qualifications on any more of your country's students.'

Hakim chased after her. 'Sarah, no…'

'Nor will I ever again ask to be a part of your social or public life since it is obvious you are too ashamed of me and my social skills and since I'm not good enough to be regarded as your wife in public nor am I good enough to be your wife in private. Now I would appreciate it if you left me alone.' She yanked the kitchen door open and shut it in his face.

Hakim paused, drew in a long breath and rubbed a hand down his face. 'Dear Allah, I am in need of your guidance,' he said aloud before opening the door to step inside. Sarah had a dishcloth in her hand, wiping down benches.

'What are you doing?'

'Cleaning up my mess.'

'This is Mariam's job.'

'My mess, my job. We have an agreement.'

'I do not want to ask,' he muttered before he dared step behind the woman who was taking her anger out on the kitchen furniture. There was nothing elegant about the way she swiped and rubbed but benches might need to be replaced.

'*Habibti*, you are an amazing teacher. I was awed at the way you had every single student enthralled in your lecture. I will never ask you to give up your work if it brings you joy. This is one of the reasons I have kept our marriage quiet so you are free to do such things. Nor do I think your social skills to be inadequate. Never have you done anything for me to be ashamed of. I have no idea how you came to such a conclusion. I was a fool to discredit your cooking for Ali and Ahmed informed me I have much to regret in missing out on, "food that is out of this world delicious," according to Ahmed.'

When he reached out to grasp her shoulders, she shook his hands off and moved towards the refrigerator where she stashed a couple of covered bowls. Two glass dishes of the white fluffy dessert caught his eye. Did he dare? He reached around her and managed to get his fingers around one bowl before Sarah snatched it away.

'Not in this lifetime. They are for the night guards.' Sarah shoved them out of his reach.

He doubted they were for had he not been such an idiot, he was certain both bowls would have graced his dinner table for them to have enjoyed together. 'What do you call this dessert?'

'Passionfruit swansdown.' Sarah slammed the fridge door, moved to the dishwasher where she clattered in the last couple of plates and cutlery and set it going, which gave him a huge clue she was familiar with the workings of this kitchen. He needed to have a talk with Mariam who, he now realised, had disappeared.

'Where is Mariam?'

'Probably in bed.'

'I cannot recall giving her the night off.'

'You didn't. She fled in fear.' Sarah spun around, folded her arms and leant against the sink. Her face was fierce but cute, her mouth set in such a straight line, it begged him to kiss it into softness.

'Is there any chance I might be forgiven for tonight's sins?'

'Nothing to forgive. You spoke your mind. My food is not to your liking even though you didn't have the good manners to sample it before insulting me. Such a hypocrite.'

'But you are angry with me.'

'Not angry but there has been a gouge slashed through my heart.'

'I am sorry.'

'No-where near as sorry as I am. Now if you will excuse me I am tired and wish to go to bed.'

She took the long way around to avoid contact. He followed. Concern mounted when she took a few clothing items from the robe and stacked them on the end of the bed. Fear lodged in his throat when she went into the bathroom and returned with a handful of toiletries. On the way past the bed, she snatched her nightwear from under the pillow. Hakim barred her way when she headed for the bedroom door.

'Where do you think you are going?'

'Anywhere but here.' There was a crack in her voice.

Hakim swallowed the lump of wood in his throat as his heart stilled. He should have learnt by now that when Sarah said something, her stubborn pride ensured she carried out her threat. 'You will sleep in my bed.' It came out as a plea.

Sarah skewed her head to one side. 'Still *your* bed but never *ours*. Your words confirm my thoughts on my status in your life. It appears my belief on what a marriage means is much different to yours. Where I come from the way you treat me would deem me to be a sex slave, useful only at night.' She ducked under his arm and raced down the passage. 'Sleep well,' she called over her shoulder before she vanished.

Instinct and a serious sense of self-preservation told him to go after her would be both useless and insane. Since sleep would be impossible, he retired to his office, dropped into an armchair and searched his soul. He had got things so wrong by trying to give Sarah her freedom from Muslim restrictions. All he had managed was to alienate her and put a huge rift in their marriage. He had always believed every problem has a solution and by morning he would have a solution. While he searched for the solution he scoured the next few weeks of the still overfull schedule, stabbed a finger on the date he had promised Sarah they would dine alone in the restaurant of her choice. 'Perfect.'

The following Saturday he was to appear at a family function: the ideal place to present his wife to the public.

Thirty Six

Tariq stood in the dining room doorway with raised eyebrows and a grin Hakim was sure he did not like. A glance at his watch told him it was changeover time.

'If I ever insulted Aisha's cooking I would have to fend for myself for a month and probably sleep alone for as long.'

'What happened to the privacy terms of your contract?' Hakim growled back.

'I was warned to be wary, I needed to know why and how wary.' The grin hadn't moved but Tariq's eyes moved over Hakim's shoulder and the eyebrows lifted even higher followed by a laugh. 'It appears even your status does not make you immune from the wrath of a scorned wife,' he dared to whisper.

Hakim turned to see Sarah arrive from the single women's quarters which made it obvious where she had spent the night. She paused and dropped her head before she brushed past both men and took her seat at the table. Black crescent moons had taken residence under her eyes, matching those on his own face but hers were fiercer against her much paler skin.

'Do not say a word,' Hakim said to Tariq who sashayed to the front door, outside of which he would wait.

'Nothing needs to be said,' Tariq said over his shoulder, followed by another mocking laugh.

Hakim turned back to the dining room, paused, hefted his shoulders on a long sigh. Sometimes he wished the man wasn't such a close friend. A split second after he sat, Mariam placed a single plate of food before him. He eyed the flat bread, hummus, sliced tomato, boiled egg and a spoonful of spiced beans. Today there were no separate dishes from which he could make his choices. He was still studying the plate when Mariam returned with two more dishes which she placed in front of Sarah.

'You are an angel, Mariam. Thank you.' Sarah sprang from her seat and wrapped her arms around Mariam.

Hakim studied the two women who now seemed to be the best of friends then turned his eyes to Sarah's food. A bowl of diced fresh fruit with a dollop of yoghurt and a drizzle of honey was definitely far more appetising than what was on his plate. Next to it was a plate with a piece of English style toast covered in mashed avocado and a fried egg. Where did the sliced bread come from? They never ate western bread.

'What is going on?' He swept a hand towards Sarah's food.

'This is Miss Sarah's favourite breakfast.' Mariam scuttled away.

Hakim so much wanted to say something but clamped his lips together. He was in enough strife already. Instead, he tore off a piece of flat bread, spread hummus on and shoved it in his mouth. The beginnings of a grin turned up the corners of Sarah's mouth before she spooned fruit into her mouth and rolled her eyes in pleasure.

'We have a dinner date on Thursday,' said Hakim.

Sarah held her spoon in mid-air and glanced at him. 'Yes.'

'Instead of sitting opposite each other, we will sit together.'

The spoon dropped. Sarah's eyes and mouth widened in surprise.

'It will indicate to those present that there is a closeness between us.'

A choking sound came from Sarah. He glanced at her and realised a mouthful of food had caught in her throat. Her eyes watered, she gulped, swallowed and sucked in a breath.

'Are you serious?'

'Yes. I was wrong. But it will mean no more running alone at night and...' He paused at the glare.

'Why?'

'It is not safe.'

Her eyes closed and chin dropped. 'It's a lot safer to run around the block in this up-market suburb, in the dark where nobody can see me than it is to sit in your public library where I was accosted, sexually compromised and physically attacked.'

'Attacked? You never mentioned...'

'You never bothered to ask what happened in the library.'

'Tell me.'

'My problem, I dealt with it, as per your orders.'

Hakim winced at his own words flung back to him. Words he will always regret.

'It is safer to run in the dark here than it is to sit at a function less than twenty metres from you and both your

321

guards where all three ignored my pleas after I had been both sexually compromised and abused.'

Sarah stood. 'Excuse me for one minute.' She raced from the room but was back before he had a chance to chase after her. A pad and pen landed on the table by his side. She leant over and wrote in capital letters: THINGS SARAH IS ALLOWED TO DO.

Puzzled, Hakim glanced at the page then back at Sarah. 'What is this?'

'I need, in your writing, the things I am allowed to do because you tell me I am free to do what I want but you continually dictate new things I can't do.'

'I do not understand, you can do anything you like. This is why I gave you your freedom.'

Sarah snorted, grabbed the pad, tore off a second sheet and slammed the pad back down next to him. 'I will write the things I am *not* allowed to do.'

While writing she spoke the words. 'Sarah can't run to regain her fitness after an ankle injury. Sarah can't, under any circumstances, show her face at the high and mighty prince's place of work. Sarah is never to approach, speak to or get anywhere near the prince when in public for he is ashamed of her. In the mighty prince's eyes, Sarah isn't qualified enough to teach his country's students nor is she allowed to donate a few hours of her time to help out disadvantaged children at the children's welfare centre.' She stopped writing and stood. 'Do the things regular western visitors do, you tell me so I spend a day in the desert but the mighty prince turns up to check I am not carousing with an imaginary lover.'

'Not true, I wanted to spend time with you.'

'I go to the races along with half the population of the city and wear a dress to fit in with the other western women but the mighty prince disapproves of my attendance, my dress and my little bit of fun betting on the horses – like every other westerner does. Buy some clothes, he orders me so I buy an evening gown to attend the theatre but the mighty prince has to demean the only dress I have ever felt pretty in by inferring it was paid for by the same imaginary lover.'

'You were not pretty.'

Sarah's jaw dropped. He noticed tears sweep across her eye before she screwed them shut to prevent them falling but her face filled with pain.

'You were the most beautiful woman there and I asked you to sit with me.'

'If you had wanted me there you would have taken me. But you didn't. I got the message.'

'Sarah...'

She held up her hand to stop him. 'Thanks to your petty jealousy and over-heightened arrogance I am not allowed to speak to a single male apart from you. Nor am I permitted to make a phone call to anyone in Australia which means I am not allowed to speak to my mum, dad, brothers, sister, grandparents, aunts, uncles, cousins or life-time friends.' The tears leaked and spilled over. She fisted them away. 'Some freedom. The only two people I can talk to are you and Mariam and you are hardly ever here.'

She grabbed a tiny purse from her pocket. 'I presume I am permitted to go to the pharmacy all by my little old self to purchase personal toiletry items.'

'Of course but can we speak about this family I had no idea about?'

Sarah spun around with her hands held against her ears. A loud groan erupted. 'Only because you never actually listen to what I tell you because you get these fanciful ideas in your head and because you *think* it, your arrogance tells you it must be true despite anything I say.' Her glare was fierce. 'More than once, I have mentioned my family. And now, just so you are sure my non-existent lover isn't buying me things…' she emptied the purse and counted out the notes and coins. 'I have thirty seven dirham and a couple of coins from the amount I take from the bank each week: *my* money, earned from hard work. Enough to buy what I need.' She scooped the money back into her purse, turned and stalked to the archway. 'Enjoy your day.'

'Sarah, wait.'

'No, if I stay I will get really angry and it is something I don't enjoy.'

Stunned, Hakim followed her to the door to see her run down the driveway. 'Suhail will drive you,' he called after her.

Sarah paused, turned and laughed. 'Sure thing. How is he supposed to know where I want to go if I can't speak to him due to your orders to speak to no man but you and since I don't have a phone I can't ring him to tell him when and where I am ready for him to pick me up. All thanks to your insufferable arrogance.'

'You want some advice, my friend?'

Hakim spun around to see Tariq seated on the bench under the veranda. 'No. Maybe. What a mess.' He scrubbed his hands through his hair. 'Did you know she had family?'

'Of course. Two brothers and a sister.'

'How do you know?'

'She told Aisha about them.'

'Aisha, when?'

'Every time she visits Aisha she talks of her family and her life back home.'

'Every… she visits? Why do I not know this?'

'Good question. Sarah is your wife. Surely you discuss these personal things with her. Sarah adores her brothers, especially Pete.'

'Pete is her brother?' Hakim plonked onto the bench next to Tariq. 'Dear Allah, I have made such a mess of things. Never have I seen her this angry.'

'No, anger is not something Sarah usually allows. Always she is positive. Always she brushes off negativity but today it appears she can find nothing to be positive about. Never does she allow anyone to see her tears but there was a stream down her cheeks just now. You, my friend, are in a pile of trouble. Can I ask why Sarah is not allowed to speak to any of us?'

'No. My mistake but when I told her it didn't include you she insisted she take me at my original words.'

'One of many mistakes.'

'I do not need you to tell me this.'

'No but maybe you need some advice on how you can fix this disaster before Sarah decides she needs to come to me as her legal guardian and ask my help to gain her a divorce.'

A sledge hammer pounded against Hakim's chest. 'Divorce? Never. I cannot lose her.'

'Maybe you can think about this on the way to work. Already we are thirty minutes late.'

'Make my excuses. I need another thirty minutes. There is something I need to do.'

Inside, Hakim put Sarah's phone together and set it on charge. While he waited for enough battery strength, he wrote her a letter instead of the list she demanded and placed it on her computer. After a search of her phone he found the numbers he needed, wrote them down to ring once he was at work. It would take him a while to figure out what to say and how to mend this chasm with Sarah. Today he would make everything right.

Thirty Seven

'What now?' Hakim watched the man go through the rigmarole of security checks at the entrance. The day so far had been torturous but incredibly revealing with his second in command left to deal with all of Hakim's meetings. It wasn't new to the man for with the number of times Hakim was called away on urgent business and family duties, his poor deputy was used to filling in. Hakim searched his grey matter for any legal problems he might have while his lawyer collected the briefcase and mobile phone from the end of the x-ray belt.

'Muhammad.' He held his right hand out in greeting. 'Do I have a legal problem?'

'No.'

'Then why are you here?'

'I need you to tell me something about the Australian woman you had me check over her contract.'

'Sarah? Why?' Hakim led the way to his office and ushered the man ahead of him at the door.

'I have been asked to represent Miss Anderson. I need to know more about her.'

'There will be no divorce,' Hakim shouted with his heart flying to his throat and his stomach going in the opposite direction where it bounced up and down before it turned into a tight ball of dread.

'Divorce? What are you talking about?' Muhammad dropped his briefcase onto a chair before he turned to face Hakim. Shock creased his features even deeper than age. 'Miss Anderson has been arrested.'

'Excuse me? Arrested? For what?'

'A list of serious charges. Fraud, stealing, false pretences and assault.'

Hakim dropped into his seat, sending up a *poof* of leather-scented air. 'No way would Sarah commit any of those crimes. She is the most honest person I have ever met, even when honesty is to her detriment.'

'Are you sure? How well do you know her?'

'Far better than you realise since she is my wife but not well enough after the revelations earlier this morning.'

'Your wife?' The briefcase disappeared and landed with a thump on the floor at the same time Muhammad plonked into the chair. His face changed from shock to a light-turning-on moment. 'Ah, divorce. She wants a divorce.'

'Sarah has not mentioned it but we had words. I am in the process of fixing things for she means the world to me. Where is she?'

'Central police station. A female officer rang me. Apparently your wife won't speak to any of the men…'

'I understand.' Hakim stood, pocketed his phone and called for Tariq to get the car. 'You can either come with me or I will meet you there but I can assure you, Sarah is not guilty of any of these crimes.' Deep worry gnawed at his innards as he rushed to the door.

'I will meet you there.' Muhammad trailed behind but went ahead when Hakim paused to speak with his personal assistant, to give another list of instructions for the man who had filled in for him all day and would not get home to his family for several more hours.

At the police station he swept through the glass doors and raced towards the front desk where Muhammad was speaking to an attendant.

'Where is Sarah?' He paused at his own harsh words. 'Sorry but I am anxious for her welfare.'

Muhammad turned to him. 'Sarah will be brought to interview room three, over here.' He took Hakim's elbow and spun him left. Tariq trailed behind.

Fear had him follow without comment about being manhandled. Two officers sat behind a long table. Both men's jaws dropped before they glanced at each other, back at Hakim then sprang from their chairs.

'Your Highness,' they both said at the same time. 'Why...' said one. 'What...' said the other in unison.

Hakim held his hand up to shush Muhammad. 'I wish to sit in on the interview.' He paused at a scuffle from behind, turned and choked at the sight of a barefooted Sarah in handcuffs. There was no colour in her face, her hair replicated a messy bird's nest and her clothes were limp, torn and dirty.

'Get those cuffs off her now.' He turned back to the officers.

'She is dangerous, assaulted a security officer at the mall.'

'He grabbed me from behind, put his arms around my neck, squeezed. I...' Sarah swayed. 'Flashback... pani....' She folded like a concertina.

Tariq flew past Hakim, grabbed Sarah around the waist and rolled to the floor with Sarah on top of him to prevent her being hurt. Before Hakim collected his wits, Tariq had Sarah in the recovery position.

'Get these cuffs off her,' Tariq repeated. 'Sarah suffers from post-traumatic stress disorder. If she was grabbed around the neck she would have suffered a flashback from an attack which almost took her life a few months back.'

'How did you know?' Hakim asked.

'She told Aisha.'

'Only today I learned more about the terror Sarah went through.' Hakim turned back to the officers. 'She was stalked for almost a year with photographs of her taken at a host of everyday activities, sent to her home along with ever-increasing lewd and threatening comments. It came to a head when the man broke into her unit while she slept. He used cable ties to bind her hands and feet before he wound a silk scarf around her neck, which he tightened until she could no longer breathe. He loosened it off long enough for her to catch her breath, then repeated this several times and only stopped when Sarah's flatmate came home unexpectedly to find Sarah unconscious. The man managed to escape. Her father took two weeks off work to accompany Sarah to university so she could complete the requirements for her degree. Her brother accompanied her to daily sessions of self-defence classes for a month before Sarah came to our country. If she threw her attacker to the ground, she acted in self-defence.' A shudder wound through him at the visions Sarah's father had described over the phone earlier.

Hakim glanced down at Sarah where Tariq rubbed her chafed wrists after the removal of the cuffs. He placed the back of his hand against her forehead to check for fever.

'Clammy cold.' Tariq eyed Hakim. 'I need something soft under her head. I am certain she fainted.' As Tariq spoke he held her wrist to test her pulse. 'Her pulse rate has levelled out but I fear her blood pressure is way too low.'

Hakim tore off his long keffiyeh, bundled it up and knelt by Sarah's side. His hands shook as he lifted her head and shoved the fabric underneath. Her grey pallor scared him. 'How long has she been here?' He glanced towards the officers.

'Since eleven this morning.'

Anger raged through him. 'Why did you not contact me?' He stood, leant over the table and glared at the men. Five hours and he had no clue of her suffering.

'She wouldn't talk to us. Refused to open her mouth.'

Hakim grubbed his hands through his hair in frustration. Damn stupid woman, he thought but this was his fault. 'What is she accused of?' It was a struggle to keep his voice under control.

'Apart from the assault, she stole a pair of shoes and…'

'No, I paid for them.'

Hakim spun around at the soft wavery voice. Sarah was trying to sit up but her entire body shook. 'Sarah.' He squatted next to her, reached out and held her by the shoulders. 'Tell me what happened.'

'The sole of my sandal split in two when I went to the pharmacy. It wasn't repairable.' One shaky hand rubbed at her brow. 'The assistant told me where I could find a good shoe store.' She wobbled again so he tightened his hold. 'I tried on three pairs of sandals. Paid for the ones which fitted well. You know how much cash I had so I had to use a credit card. The assistant took them out the back to check they were a matching pair. She took ages. An arm whipped around my neck and… and… and… I was dragged against this man's body. I thought… it was… he had found me

331

again. Hakim, I was so scared. I must have blacked out because I woke up handcuffed as I was bundled into a police car.'

'Why did you not tell them who you were?' Hakim helped her into a chair, dragged another closer with his foot and sat close enough he could support her with one arm around her shoulders.

Sarah glared at him.

'Your phone is on charge, next to your computer.' He kept his voice low so no-one else heard.

Her eyes popped wide. 'Really?'

'I promise and I am sorry for this entire mess.'

'I did not steal the shoes.' Sarah turned a fierce face towards the officers.

'But you paid for them with a stolen credit card.' The officer's voice tapered off with every word. A glorious shade of red rushed up his neck.

It didn't take genius status for Hakim to figure out whose credit card Sarah had used. 'My credit card? If you had bothered to contact me I would have assured you my wife is entitled to spend as much as she wants on my credit card. She could have spent a million dirham if she needed to.'

The blood rushed from both officer's faces. 'Your wife?' one gulped out.

'Yes, but I have not yet made my marriage public and if news gets out before I do make a public announcement I know where the news came from.' Even though to point was the height of rudeness, he pointed to both men in turn. 'I believe there is also a charge of false pretences. Can you detail the charge for me?' He grinned at the embarrassed glances for he had already figured Sarah had made claim to being his wife. He turned to her.

'I was told you never spoke to these men so how did they come to the conclusion you were pretending to be my wife?'

'Writing is not speaking but they brought me a female officer to speak with.'

Hakim laughed; he couldn't help it. '*Habibti*, you are an amazing woman. Where are the sandals you bought?'

Sarah shrugged. 'The same place as the bracelet and wedding ring you gave me and my ear studs. I said we were married and gave all of your contact numbers as well as Tariq's but they just laughed.'

Hakim frowned as he picked up Sarah's hands in turn to find them bare except for streaks of grime and angry red marks around her wrists. He turned to the officers. 'I thought everyone was innocent until proven to be guilty but you have presumed guilt without a single attempt to find out the truth. Sarah always tells the truth but regardless of who Sarah is, you have not treated a visitor to our country with care and respect. He stood and leant over the men. 'You did not phone me to inform me about my credit card? Why?'

'No time.' One man dared to stutter while the other paled.

'Five hours?' Hakim thumped a fist on the desk. Everything rattled and shook. Both men's eyes widened in fear. 'One simple phone call five hours ago would have solved this. Instead, my wife has been handcuffed and held in a filthy underground cell for five hours. I know where you imprisoned her. I *will* ask her how her clothes became so torn and covered in filth. If I discover she has been unfairly treated or there has been even a hint of physical abuse, you can be sure I will report to the Sheikh for this is not the way we handle investigations. There is *no* excuse for you to not phone me. Now please, Sarah's belongings. I wish to take her home.' He stood, held out his hand and

333

helped Sarah up, but had to catch her when she wobbled. 'Have you eaten today? You look fragile.'

'All they gave me was a small bottle of water.'

'Another item to report to the sheik,' Hakim said to the officers before he placed an arm around Sarah's shoulder to assist her to the reception desk where a plastic tray was placed in front of them. It contained Sarah's belongings. Hakim pocketed the lot, signed the form.

'Your credit card isn't there,' Sarah whispered. 'Nor any of my shoes, even the old ones.'

He raised his eyebrows at the officer who shrank back under the glare.

'They were placed in evidence bags.' The poor man looked as though he wanted to vanish in an instant.

'Why was I not phoned?'

'I... I obeyed orders.' The man shifted from foot-to-foot but glanced towards the interview room they had been in.

'You *will* have my card and the sandals delivered to my residence within the hour and *I* will demand an explanation and apology.'

He wished he dared carry Sarah in his arms as they made their way to the car. When she stumbled a couple of times he figured she was close to exhaustion both mentally and physically. Not caring about social conventions, he kept one arm around her shoulders for support until they reached the hot pavement when he found an excuse to lift her into his arms to avoid her feet from getting scorched. He placed her on the car seat, waited until she wiggled over, shut the door and joined her from the other side, ensuring he brushed up against her.

'Excuse me a moment, I need to make a brief phone call.' He spoke in Arabic to Mariam, shut the phone and turned back to Sarah.

When the car pulled away from the kerb, he grasped her chin to bring her head around to face him. 'I have great sorrow weighing down my heart for the ordeal I have put you through. I did order a card with your name but it has not yet arrived. Tomorrow I will chase it up. All day, I have worked to put in place major changes to my life in order to right the wrongs I have inflicted on you.' He dared a peck to her mouth and both stunned eyes. 'I have much to tell you when we arrive home. But first…' He wriggled one hand into the pocket of his robes and drew everything out. A paper bag with her pharmacy purchase fell to the floor. When he scooped it up the contents fell out. He picked up the small but long box, read the heading and paused, unable to believe his eyes.

'Does this mean what I think it means?' He spun his head to Sarah. 'Are you with child?'

Sarah lurched over his lap to grab the box but he held it out of her reach. 'I'm not sure.' She sounded terrified.

'But to buy a pregnancy test must mean you have a suspicion?' A flood of heat and joy thundered through his veins.

'Yes.'

'Allah has answered my prayers.' He pocketed the box but kept the jewellery in his hand while his other arm wrapped around Sarah's shoulders to draw her closer.

'You want a child?'

'Of course but only with you as its mother. Every morning in my prayers I ask Allah to soon gift us with a child. I am overjoyed. Maybe this is what caused you to faint and why your face is so pale.' He wrapped the bracelet around her wrist. 'You have never taken this off.'

'No.'

'May I ask why?'

'You bought it for me.'

A grin he had no hope of holding back, swept out. 'I can only assume my gift means something to you.'

The flush of colour on her cheeks delighted him.

'It would give me a great deal of pleasure to buy you many gifts but somehow I doubt you would appreciate being swamped with beautiful jewels. But I do have a special gift arriving soon which I am sure you will be delighted with. Now…' He grasped her left hand, eased her ring back where it belonged and kissed both ring and finger before settling his mouth over hers. His kiss was cut short when the car drew to a halt in front of his home. He handed her the ear studs. 'I will leave you to put these in for my fingers will fumble with such tiny objects. Come, my sweet. You need to eat and shower before I tell you what I have done today to rectify my appalling behaviour as a husband.' He grinned at her baffled glance and supported her as they walked inside where he called for Mariam.

Thirty Eight

A raft of emotions tangled with each other, all wanting to explode while Sarah walked beside Hakim. Exhaustion was prominent, playing with her confused mind. She so wanted to believe him but experience told her otherwise. And what did he have to tell her? What could have changed so dramatically in so short a time? Maybe he figured she was too needy and wanted to end this marriage. A rush of tears flooded her eyes but she willed them back. Why was she so darn emotional?

In the kitchen Hakim spoke in Arabic to Mariam, which further increased Sarah's anxiety. An itch of premonition settled in her chest. Never did he speak in Arabic when she was with him. What didn't he want her to know?

Nerves notched up to snapping point when he led her back into the sitting room but instead of turning down any of the passages, they mounted the steps to the second storey, somewhere she had never dared venture.

'Why are we going up here?' She coughed to hide the crack in her voice.

'There is a hot tub in the master suite. I rang ahead to have it filled.'

'A hot tub?' A sudden heat prickled the backs of her eyes and her throat clogged with emotion. It sounded so darn good. All day, a creeping sensation of filth had settled on her skin. To scrub it off would be amazing.

'Mariam is preparing a tray of food. I will bring it up while you soak in the tub. You need nourishment. Then we will talk.'

Fear replaced the spurt of joy. They passed a series of shut doors until they reached the last door on the right. Hakim opened it to reveal a beautiful large bedroom cum sitting room where no expense had been spared but like the rest of this house, it was understated luxury with nothing gaudy. Hakim's arm didn't ease from around her shoulders while they crossed the cool tiled floor. He opened a glossy white door into a massive bathroom, a huge shower area the main feature but in the corner sat a bubbling hot tub. After Hakim settled her on a small stool, he tested the temperature and emptied a small bottle into the swirling water. A spicy aroma erupted as bubbles foamed.

Hakim turned to her, smiled and held out one hand. 'Come, *habibti*.' After helping her up he cradled the sides of her face, studied her for a minute then settled his mouth over hers. His warm, hard kiss zapped her body with electricity as it always did. It was something she was never able to resist.

After releasing her, he slowly eased her top over her head and steadied her when she swayed. He tossed the garment in the corner, hooked his fingers into the elastic of her long cotton pants and shimmied the fabric down her legs, taking her underwear with it.

'So beautiful,' he murmured as he rose, sending a shot of hope to her confused brain. Her bra joined the pile. Hakim held her hand while she stepped over the edge and eased down. A sigh escaped at the bliss of hot water as it slid over her skin and the scent of perfumed bubbles erupted. This was so, so good.

'I'll be back in a minute. Sit back and relax.' Hakim disappeared and Sarah did exactly as instructed, relaxed back against the padded edge until her head rested on a cushion. A long sigh escaped at the ecstasy of the gentle warmth. Her eyes closed but Hakim's footsteps scraped across the tiles when he returned; the stool screeched when he dragged it over the marble, the tray rattled as he settled it on top, liquid glugged as he poured it into glasses, then silence.

She forced languid eyelids apart to see Hakim drop his own clothes on the mounting pile.

'Sit forward.' He climbed in behind her and tugged her back against his chest.

'You must eat.' He picked up a fresh date and brushed it against her lips. She chewed and swallowed the sweet flesh. A soft cloth dribbled warm water down her shoulders. A trail of foam swept over her breasts.

'Do you trust me enough to know I would never physically harm you?' The words brushed against one ear before Hakim landed a peck on the lobe.

She shivered in response. 'Yes, of course.'

'I am going to kiss you, only once, on your neck.' Without giving her a chance to move away or say a word, he settled his mouth on her nape for a brief kiss.

'I...'

'Every day I will kiss you on your neck until you lose your fear. Now, do you know what *habibti* means?'

'I was told it is an Arabic endearment.'

Hakim chuckled. 'It is but the true translation is, my love, and you are the woman I love, the woman I can never let go because you mean the world to me.' A soft kiss landed on the top of her head. 'I have never said the word to any other woman because I have never loved before.

The itch in her eyes turned to salty moisture. 'You never said.'

'I know and am sorry but we married in such haste when we barely knew each other. I wanted to give you time to learn to love me the same without putting any pressure on you. Do you recall the night of the fountain?' He scooped a dollop of dip onto a torn piece of flat bread and held it in front of her lips.

'Yes, of course.' She took the food into her mouth, wrapped her tongue around it and chewed.

'It was while I watched you absorbed in the beauty of the dancing water when I realised I was in love with you.' A long sigh hissed out. 'I regret not saying what was in my heart for it seems all I have managed is to turn you against me. I have tried hard to cut my engagements short but some are impossible to change at short notice. I honestly believed by keeping our marriage quiet to give you freedom, I was doing the right thing by you. I was wrong - so very wrong and I am sorry from the depths of my soul.'

She had no hope of controlling the stream of moisture that poured down her cheeks but Hakim couldn't see it so she didn't fight the tears away. Instead she took in the chunk of tomato he held out.

'I need to tell you about Lissa.'

'Who's Lissa?'

'The woman you saw with her hands on me. It is possible she will turn up again. She is a pest. If you had watched longer that night, you would have seen my men usher her outside and bar her entry.'

340

'Is she an old flame?'

'No, there has never been anything between us. Quite the opposite. I was introduced to her about three years ago as a possible bride. Our first meeting was in her home with her family as chaperones. Lissa was quiet, well-spoken and showed impeccable manners. The second meeting was in a café where we spoke over coffee. Her brother sat with us but the questions they both asked were odd.'

'Odd? How?' She drank from the glass of apple juice he held out for her.

'They were keen to know how many rooms of the palace I had as my own, hinted at my wealth, what cars I owned, along those lines. I knew where it was leading. It wasn't the first time a woman and her family were more interested in my position and wealth than they were in me. Good manners kept me in the café. The brother left us alone to visit the bathroom. As soon as he was out of sight, Lissa left her seat, sat next to me and began to paw me. The brother returned at the same time my men dragged her off. The next day, the father arrived and demanded I offer marriage for compromising his daughter. It was a good job Tariq was on duty both times and spelt out the way I was set up. Lissa now has a bad habit of turning up at various functions where I am in attendance and does what she did that night you saw her. This is despite legal proceedings where she has been ordered to keep her distance. Please forgive me for not telling you of this before. I would never dishonour you by having any form of a relationship with another woman. This I promise.'

'As I would never dishonour you, but you don't trust me enough to believe me.'

'Jealousy over-rode my common sense. I have learned my lesson for this jealousy has almost driven you away. I have never loved the way I love you. A love so deep and

341

strong, it overwhelms me at times. This is the reason why today, I resigned from my position.'

Water splashed over the sides as she twisted around onto his knees. 'Why? You love your job.'

'No, I love you. My job is merely a position I took to better the life for my people. Since I am a member of the ruling family I have no choice but to work for my country and my people. I did it to the best of my ability, took on more public appearances to fill the void in a lonely life. It is possible Allah knew I needed to change so he sent you to me and now you, my sweet Sarah, are the most important thing in my life.'

'You really love me?' A wodge of emotion and disbelief made her words come out all funny.

Hakim smiled. 'Of course. Don't I show you every night with my body?' He pecked her mouth. 'It is the reason, the only reason I married you even though I used other excuses as a means of getting you to agree for at the time we barely knew each other. Your time in my country was so short and I couldn't bear to let you leave.' His two thumbs swept the moisture from her cheeks. 'Your tears scare me for until now you have never shared them with me.'

'Happy tears.' She sniffed then dropped her head onto his shoulder where the tears flowed freely before she regained control and sniffed them back. His arms swept around her, tugged her close until she sat in his lap with her legs wrapped around his rib cage.

'I can only hope maybe this means you might love me the same way.' He lifted her head with the crook of one thumb and searched her eyes.

'I think I knew I loved you about the same time. I would never have agreed to marriage if I wasn't sure my heart belonged to you.'

'Dear Allah, thank you,' Hakim whispered before he covered her face in soft kisses then settled his mouth over hers in a kiss so gentle yet it held so much meaning.

He pulled away. 'There is more to tell you. Al Kayd is to spend six months in prison for what he did to you. I have viewed the library security footage. I am impressed by your self-defence capabilities. I pray you never have need to practise on me.' Hakim smiled with a raised eyebrow. 'Al Kayd will then be exiled back to his own country. The money he was paid has been forfeited and will go to the children's centre. Never will he be allowed to return. After discussions with my father, Karim has divorced his wife. My father was horrified with her behaviour. She has been sent back to her parents in disgrace with the remnants of her *Mehr*, which isn't a lot for her careless spending habits have drained her account. There will be no further financial settlement to her because of her treasonous behaviour. She is lucky she will not spend time in prison. The children are to stay with Karim since Faria had so little to do with them.'

'Surely they need their mother.'

'She gave birth to them but since that moment she has left them in care of a nursemaid who will remain their carer. She never even took either to her breast for nourishment. Karim has spent far more time with them and is the far better parent. To take them away from those they are familiar with would be cruel and unjust. If Faria had been any sort of a mother she would have had equal access.'

'I can't understand a mother not loving her own children. To me it is inconceivable.'

'You, my sweet, have the softest of hearts. I've seen the way you treat children. You will be the best of mothers. Now, today I have done little work except to instruct my deputy to stand in for me. He will take over my role as Minister and the poor man will stand in for me for all those scheduled business appointments. Most of the day I have been on the phone to fix all the errors I have made. My family owns two private jets. One is, at this very moment, on its way to Sydney. When it returns it will bring your family for a visit.'

Water sloshed as Sarah jerked back. 'My family but how...'

His grin was wicked. 'I have a confession. I searched your phone for numbers and spoke at length with both of your parents and your brothers, one of whom has the name of Pete.' He raised his eyebrows. 'Your words about loving him the same as I love my brothers now make sense but you could have been a lot more explicit. Your sister, Sam, short for Samantha, was unavailable. Today I learned much. So many things now make sense, *Doctor Anderson*, who has recently gained her PhD after she began university when she was only fifteen because she has a photographic memory and is so intelligent she is a member of Mensa.' He cradled her cheeks to bring her head back up. 'But you hide your intelligence as though embarrassed, which is a great pity. But on the other hand, you have such humility so I understand.'

'I was tormented as a kid and even at university, where fellow students befriended me because they wanted to use me. When they got what they wanted, they turned their back on me. Many made fun of me, said nasty things.'

'So I understand from what Pete said. What exactly is a photographic memory? I only ask because I want to understand you better.'

'According to the specialists there is no such thing for a photograph shows every minute detail whereas a human misses some of those details. And it's not the same for everyone who has a so-called photographic memory. Some are able to recognise a person in a crowd from a mere glance at a photograph. Many have the ability to compute complicated mathematical problems with ease. There is a famous young man who drew the outline of London in minute detail after a ten minute study. I don't recall such detail. My brain seems to recall written words. I stare at a page for about three seconds. Given a cue, I can relate every word on that page. It's more a hyper-ability to recall.'

'This is why you could quote the Qur'an passages.'

'Yes, your imam cued me in by reciting lines. My brain found the passage and I could recall every detail. It's more of a hindrance than a blessing.'

'How so?'

'It's really hard to find true friends. You wouldn't believe the hurtful slurs thrown at me all through my school years. Sure, it helped me with my studies but that doesn't compensate for the downsides. I was at university at fifteen, still a child in an adult world. I wasn't old enough to drive a car, drink alcohol or vote yet was smarter than those in my year who were three years older. Socially I was inept. It was a lonely life. None of the guys would be caught dead with a fifteen year old kid.'

'I am sorry you had to go through such bad times. I also learned how your special gift causes you to be a literal thinker, which explains why many of the things I have said have been taken so literally. I will learn to speak clearer in the future. Your brother also explained how hard it has been for you to learn the social skills needed to operate in normal society and how Pete was instrumental in teaching you to use eye contact when it scares the pants off you. Those were Pete's words. At one stage they classed you as autistic until the professionals figured out your brain is wired a little different to theirs.

'Now let me see what else they told me. *Sarah will never impart any personal details unless asked a specific question, will always tell the truth and has no time for royalty or the class system.* I might add it took a while for me to convince your family that you are now a real princess. The laughter was very unbecoming. An insult in fact.'

'Oh, my gosh. I'm sorry but I… oh, gosh, how do I explain?'

'No need for your father told me of your views on people with wealth and how it is unfair. But you never told your family of our marriage.'

'They never asked.'

Hakim laughed. 'According to your father it was not a question they expected to ask while you were away but they understand and are delighted you have found a man who loves you the way you deserve to be loved.' A kiss landed on her nose. 'I wondered why you chose a date so far into the future for our dinner date but now I know the significance of this Thursday. Even though birthdays are not something Muslims celebrate, we will make your twenty-third birthday special. An excuse for me to buy you another gift, *habibti.*'

'You don't have to. I'm not into material items I don't need.'

'I know, yet you wear the bracelet I gave you all the time, even to bed and I want to give you something you can enjoy. I now understand your reluctance to use my money because of an innate need to be independent but you will get used to it. You are my wife and I will support you in every way. Especially if the test kit you bought today shows you are with child.' He placed his large hand across her abdomen. 'I pray it does but we will make an appointment to visit a physician to be sure.

'Already, today, I have opened an investment account in your name, in which I deposited the *Mehr* you refused on our wedding day. It is for you to do with as you wish. You are blessed with a unique gift and I believe such a gift is given to be shared with others. I will support you in any endeavour you undertake whether it be in furthering your research or if you want a career in teaching or any other career.'

'Thank you.' Sarah sniffed, fighting back another bout of stupid tears.

'Your family will be here for a week. When they return home, we will go with them.'

Sarah's heart pounded as a hot sting of adrenalin spurted. 'Really? But I can't... it's not safe.'

'Yes, really. I was told your attacker is now in jail. He was caught by using a sting. A female police officer impersonated you, as though you were again home. Your attacker had been watching your home. He foolishly tried to abduct you, was caught and is in prison awaiting trial at which you are required to attend. I will leave it to your father to give you the details. It appears the man was obsessed with you, which I understand for I might also have this same obsession with a deep need to keep you as my life-time partner.'

A leaden mantle lifted from her shoulders. The relief was indescribable. She dropped her head against Hakim's chest.

Hakim drew her head up with the fingers of one hand. 'Another of my long phone calls today was with my father. He understands my need to resign to spend time building our marriage to make it strong. He is very fond of you; thinks you are the perfect woman for me. I must agree with him.' He smiled, glanced at her mouth then settled his mouth over hers, easing her angst even more.

'You have spent these past months doing your utmost to fit in with my life so I will take two months sabbatical to fit in with your life back in Sydney before I take up a new position.' He snorted. 'I cannot remember when I last took time off for a holiday.' He brushed his mouth over hers again before he pulled away on a long groan.

'My father has suggested a way we can get the best of both worlds. One of our overseas ambassadors is soon to retire due to ill health. My new position will be as an ambassador for my country but I will be based in Canberra - only a short flight from Sydney.'

Unable to believe him, Sarah flung herself against Hakim's chest. 'I don't believe this but you don't have to do this for me. I'll go anywhere with you, even stay here. All I wanted was more time with you, to be a part of your family, to…'

His arms swept around her. 'I know, my sweet. But to me, this new position is a blessing. Since the day I was born, I have never had the freedom you enjoy. I think this may be why I was determined you would not be stifled by our strict customs. The very minute I walk outside my front door, I can never be myself or be by myself. Always I must perform to the standards my birth dictates. Always, I must have bodyguards with me. I can never go out alone to escape, to be free. Not even a drive in the desert can I be alone. Everybody knows my face. In your country, I will be able to walk alone in the crowds and no-one will know who I am, especially if I wear western clothes. You have no idea how much I look forward to the freedom.'

'This is why you wanted to keep our marriage quiet.'

'Yes, I didn't want you to have the same restrictions but I was wrong. My logic was skewed and I never asked you what you wanted.'

Sarah dropped her head onto his shoulder. 'You, I want you, to be your partner in every aspect.'

Hakim cupped his big hands around her head. 'I understand. Your family will arrive in time to be present at an important event where the entire Royal family must appear. I will use the event to present you to the public as my wife but there is one thing you must understand.'

A stab of fear replaced elation as Sarah sank back. 'What?'

'You will still be free to do whatever you want but when in this country you will have your own security detail at all times whenever you leave the house. This is the Middle East where there are nearby neighbours who don't enjoy the same stability my country does. There is always a chance someone will make threats to those in power. Having a guard is not an option but they will be discreet.'

'I'm okay with that. I see how you are with your men.'

'There is one more thing I would like to discuss.' The smile on his face sent a shiver of unease down her spine.

'Have I done something wrong?'

'No, my sweet. While I spoke with your mother, a thought came to me.' He grasped both of her hands. 'Will you marry me?'

'Huh, we are already married – aren't we?'

He smiled. 'Yes, but I thought we could have a another ceremony, in Sydney. One where you can go on a shopping spree with your mother to buy the best ever wedding gown. Where your father walks you down the aisle, where your sister can stand by your side and...'

Sarah plastered her body against Hakim. 'Are you serious?'

'Yes. This pleases you?'

'You have no idea.'

'At last, I have found a way to give you happiness.'

She grinned, wrapped her arms around his neck, rubbed her lower body against him and whispered in his ear, 'You make me happy every night. I've never made love in a bath before.'

He laughed. 'You are the most amazing woman. Allah knew what he was doing when he dropped you in front of my car. I love you so much, my sweet.' He thrust his hips upwards. Water sloshed over the top. 'This could get messy.'

'But worth it,' Sarah managed to get out before her mouth was covered.

Everything was right in her world now. Perfect, in fact.

www.ingramcontent.com/pod-product-compliance
Lightning Source LLC
Chambersburg PA
CBHW070048120726
47909CB00002B/322